PICNICS AND PROMISES AT STRAWBERRY FIELDS

VICTORIA WALTERS

Boldwood

First published in Great Britain in 2026 by Boldwood Books Ltd.

Cover Design by Alexandra Allden

Cover Images: Shutterstock

Chapter Image: Shutterstock

Every effort has been made to obtain the necessary permissions with reference to copyright material, both illustrative and quoted. We apologise for any omissions in this respect and will be pleased to make the appropriate acknowledgements in any future edition.

A CIP catalogue record for this book is available from the British Library.

Paperback ISBN 978-1-80557-094-3

Large Print ISBN 978-1-80557-093-6

Hardback ISBN 978-1-80557-092-9

Ebook ISBN 978-1-80557-095-0

Kindle ISBN 978-1-80557-096-7

Audio CD ISBN 978-1-80557-087-5

MP3 CD ISBN 978-1-80557-088-2

Digital audio download ISBN 978-1-80557-089-9

This book is printed on certified sustainable paper. Boldwood Books is dedicated to putting sustainability at the heart of our business. For more information please visit https://www.boldwoodbooks.com/about-us/sustainability/

Boldwood Books Ltd, 23 Bowerdean Street, London, SW6 3TN

www.boldwoodbooks.com

To Kiley Dunbar and Mary Jayne Baker for always being there for me.

the only way is up

1

I stood outside Birchbrook Café wearing a wedding dress, my heart pounding. The whole journey here, my pulse was racing and I was trying to take deep breaths to warn off the panic that threatened to overwhelm me. I had become an expert at pushing it to one side but today, it was proving harder than usual to beat.

Sucking in one more deep breath, I walked inside the café, all conversations ceasing instantly as I had feared they would. Even the staff behind the counter froze to take a look. I longed to shout out, *Have you never seen a woman in a wedding dress, trainers and her hair in pin curls before?!* but I settled instead on looking around at the staring faces for the one I had come in to find.

'Daisy!' The woman I wanted to see jumped up and hurried over to where I hovered by the door. 'Your text freaked me out; I was about to leave to come to your wedding. Are you okay?'

'The wedding is off,' I said, conscious that everyone was still staring and blatantly listening to our conversation. 'Maybe we could...' I gestured outside.

'Oh yeah, of course, come on,' she said, grabbing my arm and steering me out of the cute café with her into the High Street, which was currently bathed in late-May sunshine. We walked out of sight of the large window and my cousin, Willow, pulled me in for a tight hug. I leaned against her, the adrenaline of the last two hours draining out of me. 'What happened? Are you okay?'

I half-fell against her, my heart still thumping. 'Not really, but I hope I will be.'

Willow leaned back to look at me. My bridal make-up made me look most unlike myself, I knew. She frowned with concern.

We hadn't seen each other for five years but she looked just the same to me. Her glossy brunette hair was in its usual messy bun, her dark brown eyes pretty and large, and her frame was still petite. But unusually for her, she wore a dress ready for my 'big day'. It was midi-length and floaty floral, and I felt guilty seeing how lovely she looked in it, knowing she wouldn't need to keep it on now.

'Have you really run out on your wedding?'

I winced at the words even though they were true. I stepped out of her embrace and nodded. 'Yeah, I have. I didn't know where else to go.'

'You did the right thing in coming to Birchbrook. Come on, let's go to the farm and you can tell me what happened. Plus, you probably want to get out of your wedding dress.' Her lips twitched and despite the situation not being at all funny, she let out a giggle. And just like that, the panic slipped out of me and I laughed along with her. I knew, in that moment, I had done the right thing in coming to see Willow.

'How did you get here?' Willow asked me as we started to walk to where her car was parked.

'I jumped into a taxi that had brought a guest to my wedding,' I said, the irony not lost on me. I had sent a message to Willow as I approached the town to make sure she hadn't left yet for my wedding, and she told me she was in the local café picking up a coffee so I'd headed straight there to see her.

'Alone?' she asked me gently.

'Yeah.' I looked away. Willow had been the only guest coming to the wedding just for me. Everyone else had been invited by my groom-to-be's parents. I tried not to feel the sting of Willow being my only family or friend invited but it was impossible not to. Right now, I felt alone. And that was something I had been desperate to avoid for five years.

'It must have been so hard to leave on your own,' she said, her eyes full of empathy. I knew she understood. To a point. She lost her mother five years ago. I didn't have either of my parents, though.

'It was,' I whispered, unable to fully comprehend that I had left Henry.

She slung an arm around my shoulders. 'Don't worry. You're not on your own now. It's really good to see you again. It's been too long.'

I nodded, grateful that she was being so kind to me. 'I know. I'm sorry.' It had been mostly my fault. The last time I had been to Willow's home, Birch Tree Farm, was the day of Willow's mum's funeral. The wake had taken place there, and the farm, which had given me such joy growing up, felt forever changed. That day had brought up so many painful memories of my parents' tragic car accident two years before that I left feeling like I needed to get away from it all. I'd decided to move to the city, a few hours away from Birchbrook, and we had grown apart.

Five years later though, I was running away from the new life I had made there.

We reached Willow's car then and as she opened it, she glanced over and said, 'Let's go home.'

My heart swelled with gratitude for my cousin. Willow could

have turned me away but that wasn't my her style, thank goodness. My wedding venue, a stunning countryside stately home, was only an hour away from Birchbrook so I had managed to get here before she left to come to the wedding.

We climbed into the car and set off towards the farm. 'I know that I never met Henry,' Willow said as she drove, 'but your wedding invite was beautiful and that venue is gorgeous. It sounded like it was going to be a fairy tale. What went wrong?'

I sighed. 'It's a long story.'

'I bet. You don't have to explain. You can relax at the farm first.'

'That sounds good. I felt like such a fraud today. I didn't feel at all like me. I want to feel like me again.'

Willow glanced across at me. 'You do look very different. Gorgeous, Daisy, as always but...' she trailed off uncertainly.

I glanced out of the window, catching a glimpse of my reflection. And I saw myself through Willow's eyes. I was only a couple of years older than her but I looked more than that today.

My light-brown hair had been highlighted into a honey-blonde colour. I had on bright-red lipstick. The sweetheart neckline of my lace wedding dress, which had been designed to fit to the curves of my body perfectly, had such a full skirt, I rolled it up to get into the car. Still on my finger was the huge diamond ring I'd been wearing for six months. It was so expensive, I was terrified of it being stolen or lost. But at least I'd had time to swap the designer stilettos I was nervous to walk down the aisle in for my trainers before diving into the taxi.

And underneath all the make-up and shiny hair, there were dark circles under my green eyes and my skin was pale from the lack of sleep and anxiety I had wrestled with ahead of the wedding.

It was supposed to be the happiest day of your life but it had felt like the exact opposite.

'I didn't get to choose any of this,' I told Willow, gesturing to my bridal look.

'Why not?' she asked, her eyebrows raised.

'As soon as I said yes and Henry's grandmother's ring was on my finger,' I said, waving my hand so she could see the huge rock that sat there, 'I was swept up in this event that his family had paid for and were creating supposedly on our behalf. But it didn't feel like my wedding. None of it felt like me. Including my fiancé. They didn't ask me to choose anything. They didn't... let me.' I whispered the last two words.

'Let you?' she repeated in disbelief that I needed anyone to let me do anything.

That realisation was what had finally woken me up. 'I spent the past five years going along with everything that they wanted and the wedding was more of the same. But then this morning, I stood in the room I was getting ready in and I looked around and realised my wedding was completely different to how I had ever pictured it would be. There was no one in that room who meant something to me. I had a hairdresser, a make-up artist, Henry's mother and his little cousin who was going to be my bridesmaid, but that was it. I realised that all my friends were partners of Henry's friends. I couldn't confide in them. I had no family there.'

Willow shook her head. 'I'm sorry I couldn't come earlier; the farm is so busy right now. Dad wanted to come but he would have found the day too hard; his arthritis is worse. And my boyfriend needed to look after things while I was gone,' she said.

'I'm not blaming you. It was just a fact.' I looked across at her. 'I thought about you coming then. You would have walked in and thought everything was perfect. And that's what it seemed like: perfect. But I knew none of it was real. I panicked then. What if the rest of my life was just the same? Looking perfect on the outside, but a complete lie on the inside?' I exhaled shakily. 'Then Henry's mum started talking about the future. God, Willow. What she said... I couldn't believe it. What if I spent my whole life with Henry going along with what he and his parents wanted for me, and not choosing anything for myself?' My breaths came out faster and shallower then as I thought about how I'd almost given up everything I wanted.

And I knew why.

I was scared to be alone.

But even worse, I was scared to love.

2

'You have to choose the life that you want,' Willow said, nodding furiously. 'Life is too short; we know that more than most people. And you deserve to be happy, Daisy.'

I shook my head as I wasn't so sure about that but then I looked out of the window, catching sight of the wooden sign that declared we were turning into Birch Tree Farm. Thoughts of my wedding faded as I saw the farm again for the first time in five years.

Willow turned into the drive that was lined by beautiful birch trees, in full green bloom, swaying in the gentle, early-summer breeze as if they were directing me to somewhere safe.

'You don't think I'm a real bitch, do you?' I asked Willow as she drove towards the quaint, red-bricked farmhouse ahead of us. 'For leaving Henry pretty much at the altar?'

'How do you feel now you've left?' she asked.

'Relieved. Like I am finally... free,' I admitted.

'Then you did what you had to do,' Willow said firmly. 'Come on, we need tea and cake, and... did you bring anything with you?'

'No,' I said. 'I just... ran.'

'Okay, don't worry. I can lend you clothes so you can change out of that dress.'

I let out a snort. 'That would be great, thanks.'

Willow parked her car outside the farmhouse as the door to it swung open.

Out stepped Willow's dad and her border collie dog, followed by a handsome man I hadn't seen before. I braced myself. I had been so nervous to come back to the farm in case it had lost all its warmth and comfort, and now I had to face all its inhabitants and their questions as to why I was a runaway bride. I tried to keep my nerves at bay but it was proving to be very difficult.

'Are you sure about me coming in?' I asked Willow uncertainly before she could climb out of her car. 'You really don't mind me turning up like this after so long?' I bit my lip.

Willow shook her head. 'Of course not. Daisy – we're family. We have always loved you being here. We've got you. It will all be okay.'

Her words were the reassurance I desperately needed. I broke into a relieved smile. 'Thank you, Willow.'

'Come on.' She jumped out and I watched as she beamed at the sight of the three people – and animal – who were clearly her favourite in the world. I realised then just how badly I had needed to hear that things would be okay.

Before I followed her, I felt my phone buzz in the pocket of my wedding dress – which had been sewn just so I could have my phone in there. Henry's family liked me to have my phone with me at all times. I pulled it out. There were fifty-plus notifications. I gulped and opened the glove compartment, chucked my phone in, shut it up and climbed out after Willow, deciding that I couldn't face any of what was on it just yet.

'Welcome back, Daisy,' my Uncle Adam said, giving me a tight hug. I guessed, by the lack of shock on his face, that Willow had warned him I was on the way. Adam had been my dad's elder brother and it was always a shock to the system to see the similarities between them. He looked much older than he had five years ago. An age my father would sadly never reach. My uncle was now completely salt-and-pepper grey and there were lines on his face that hadn't been there the last time I'd seen him. I knew he suffered with arthritis, and his movements were a little stiff as he pulled back from me, but his smile was warm and welcoming just as it had been when I was growing up.

'This is my boyfriend, Dylan,' Willow said then.

Dylan smiled and held out a hand for me to shake. 'I've heard a lot about you.' He was tall with almost-black hair and bright-blue eyes. He had a posh accent too.

'I would ask if it was all good but under the circumstances...' I gestured to the white elephant in the room – my dress – with a grimace.

'Oh, well, it definitely was,' Dylan said, clearing his throat uncomfortably.

Willow nudged me. 'You should style it out – act like it's the new latest fashion trend for spring/summer.'

I chuckled – she had always been good at diffusing any awkwardness. 'Yeah...' I trailed off at the sound of a car on the driveway behind me. For a moment, I was worried it was Henry chasing me from the wedding. But when I turned around, I soon realised with relief that I didn't recognise the car.

'Shit, I forgot that Blake was coming now,' Dylan said then.

'Oh, that's right,' Willow said, giving me an apologetic smile. 'One of Dylan's old friends – he's coming to stay for a couple of weeks in one of our Airbnb cottages.'

My heart sank a little bit. It was hard enough to be back at the farm again, let alone meeting new people. I'd had to deal with meeting Willow's boyfriend and now I had to face one of his friends too. In my current frame of mind, and dress, I wasn't at my most social. I tried to push my shoulders back and stay confident but I was on the verge of crumbling.

Out of the car climbed a man who did a half-handshake, half-hug with Dylan, who had headed over to greet him. Willow and Uncle Adam also approached, while I hung back self-consciously.

'You must be Blake,' Willow said, smiling and holding her hand out.

'This is my girlfriend, Willow Connor, and this is Blake Daniels,' Dylan introduced them and Willow and Blake shook hands. Then Blake moved to greet my uncle. 'Her dad, Adam.'

'It's nice to meet you all,' Blake said.

Dylan looked behind to where I stood, feeling out of place. 'And this is Willow's cousin, Daisy.'

Blake turned to look at me and his eyes widened as his gaze looked me up and down, taking in what I was wearing.

'Rocking this season's "it" dress,' Willow joked as I looked back at Blake.

He was so tall, I had to lift my face up slightly. He must have been six foot five. He had light-brown hair that was short and tidy and a line of stubble around his chin. He wore chinos and canvas shoes with a white shirt – kind of preppy-looking, the opposite of Dylan in his beat-up farm clothes. I started to smile but his gaze flicked over me, looking at my dress, his hazel eyes cold when our gazes met. 'Is this some kind of sick joke?' he spat out, his deep voice suddenly sounding bitter.

There were a couple of seconds of shocked silence.

'Um... no...' Dylan said awkwardly. 'Daisy is...' he trailed off, stumped.

'Wearing a wedding dress,' I supplied, hating that I was making everyone so uncomfortable. 'This was supposed to be my wedding day but I couldn't go through with it.'

'You left your fiancé at the altar?!' Blake said incredulously. He stepped back a few steps like I might be contagious.

I narrowed my eyes. This man didn't know anything about me but disapproval oozed out of him and it made me feel even worse than I already did. 'Not that it's any of your business but yes, I did.'

'Look, why don't we get you settled into the cottage?' Dylan said hurriedly, putting a hand on Blake's arm. 'Willow can get Daisy settled in the farmhouse,' he added, clearly desperate to separate me and Blake.

'Sounds good to me!' Blake said, abruptly turning around so I got his back view. 'Let's go.'

I raised an eyebrow as he started walking, clearly desperate to get away from me. Dylan threw me and Willow an apologetic smile and then followed him. This guy was really rude. 'Not sure about your boyfriend's taste in friends,' I said to Willow, loud enough that Blake hopefully heard me as he left.

'Sorry, yeah, that was awkward,' Willow said. She shrugged. 'I haven't met him before. He actually lives in the city too. Said he needed to get away so Dylan let him have a cottage. He's going to renovate them this summer but he wanted to make room for a friend in need. Come on, let's go inside. You won't have to see him much, I'm sure.'

I didn't want to cause any more drama so I threw on a tight smile. 'Yeah. Maybe I could get out of this dress to stop any more awkward questions, though?'

She gave a tense laugh. 'Definitely. Let's go upstairs.'

'I'll put the kettle on,' my uncle said, walking in slowly.

'Perfect,' Willow told him as we followed. 'We're trying to fix up the place as it has fallen into a bit of disrepair the past few years,' she said, gesturing around as we stepped inside the farm-house. It looked just how it had done five years ago although I could smell fresh paint in the hall, which they had brightened up. It had a low ceiling with beams and the floors were polished wood but with comfortable rugs making the place cosy. They still had family photographs dotted around. I could see one of me and Willow one summer out in the crop fields having a picnic. Carefree days that I had loved and missed.

'You'll want to stay tonight, right?' Willow asked me.

I hesitated, wondering how that would feel, as I followed her upstairs. But really, I had nowhere else to go. I lived with Henry at his parents' house on the edge of the city. I didn't want to face them today. I needed some space to take stock of the decision I had just made. 'If you're sure that would be okay?'

'You don't even have to ask,' Willow reassured me. 'This is your home too for as long as you need it.'

It felt too much. 'Even though I haven't come back for five years?'

Willow stepped into the spare room that I had always stayed in when my parents and I had spent time on the farm in the school holidays. 'Listen, it was so hard for all of us...' she broke off, her voice failing her.

I touched her arm. 'I should have been there for you both more like you were for me.'

'We all coped the best we could,' she said, seemingly no hard feelings about me not coming back to see her and my uncle. Her grief at losing her mum had brought mine back and I hadn't coped. I'd moved to the city where I took a job working for Henry's dad as his PA. And soon after, I'd met Henry and we'd started dating. I'd slipped into this new life as Henry's girlfriend and it had been easier to stay away from Birch Tree Farm.

Guilt washed over me as I looked around the pretty room. There was the same floral bedspread, the same fireplace with a vase of lavender on top, the same mirror on the far wall and the window that displayed the farm in all its glory. The sloping roof made the room feel cosy. I used to love sleeping in here. I had been scared it would make me feel sad to return to it but something about the room soothed me instead.

I smiled, this time without the need to force it. 'God, it's good to be back.' Yes, it was sad that Willow's mum wasn't here. I could feel the place and the people had changed but Willow wasn't broken, nor was my uncle, and I'd feared they would be changed forever – like I had been when my parents died.

'It's good to have you back. And it kind of feels perfect. The past few months, we've really tried to pick this place back up. And it's working. Things feel so much brighter. And they will for you soon too, I know it. Hang on...' She left the room and I perched on the edge of the bed, my body sinking into its softness. I suddenly felt exhausted.

'Okay. Here are some of my clothes,' Willow said, coming back. 'Have a shower if you want, change, refresh yourself... then we can have tea and cake down in the kitchen when you're ready? And you can stay tonight, and for as long as you like. This room is yours.'

'I don't know how to thank you,' I said, swallowing the lump that had appeared in my throat. It had been such a crazy day; I needed a moment to myself, and Willow was giving me that. 'I left in such a hurry. All my things are at home with Henry and his parents. I work for Henry's dad. My whole life is there, I don't know what I'll do next...' My eyes were definitely watering now.

'Listen, just take it one step at a time,' Willow said gently. 'Take that dress off. Have a cup of tea. We'll sort the rest of it out soon. Okay?'

I nodded. 'Okay,' I managed to choke out.

She left me then and I let a tear roll down my cheek. I had blown up my life running away from my wedding. I felt relieved but terrified. I was exhausted but I saw a glimmer of hope on the horizon. I looked around the room. It was safe. It was familiar. It was comforting.

I didn't know much right now but I knew one thing: I had made the right decision coming to Birchbrook.

And that was enough for now.

3

I looked into Willow's bedroom mirror and for the first time in a long time, I seemed more like myself.

I had washed out the pin curls and now my hair hung loose and damp over my shoulders. I'd scrubbed all the heavy bridal make-up off my face and after my shower, I'd changed into the clothes Willow had given me: a pair of denim shorts, frayed at the hem, and a basic white tee. Right now, I looked older than my twenty-eight years with my green eyes dull and my skin in need of sunshine. I also wanted to sleep, but first I was desperate for the tea and cake Willow had mentioned so I hurried downstairs.

In the inviting farmhouse kitchen, Willow, her father and dog waited at the pine table for me. I was relieved that Dylan and Blake were nowhere in sight.

'Better?' Willow asked. She had changed as well, putting on similar shorts and a T-shirt to the ones she'd given me.

Her dog, Maple hurried over with her tail wagging and I leaned down to pat her, smiling at the sweet greeting.

'Much,' I said.

'Come and sit down. We have tea and Dad made sandwiches plus we have the cake from the café I was in earlier,' Willow said with a warm smile.

My stomach rumbled. I realised I'd only had champagne all day so far. I sat down eagerly.

'How was your old room?' my uncle asked me.

'Just like I remembered.' My parents' car accident had happened while I was at university and I had spent the summer break afterwards with Uncle Adam, his wife and Willow. I had stayed on the farm all that summer and it had helped a little bit. But when my aunt died just a couple of years after my parents, I'd backed away from them. It brought all that grief and pain back. It hurt so much, I wasn't sure I could take losing anyone else I loved ever again.

It had been easier to stay away and not take the risk of hurting again.

I had been living by that rule for five years.

'You can stay for as long as you need,' Uncle Adam said.

'I told her that,' Willow said. 'It might be chaotic as we enter our busy season, though,' she added with a laugh. 'And Dylan is going to renovate the cottages this summer so we can grow our Airbnb business. We'd put that on hold as usually, we have summer staff staying in them to help when we open for pick-your-own, but our usual help have other plans this year.' She frowned. 'I'm not sure what we're going to do but it means we can get started on the renovations sooner than expected, I guess.'

'You sound like you have a lot on your plate,' I said, worried that my arrival was the last thing they needed 'And you have Blake staying as well. Won't it be too much for us both to be here if it's the busy season too?' I asked her.

'The more the merrier,' Willow said with a shrug. 'You need some time to think about what to do, right? You said you didn't want to go home just yet. And I get that. Living with Henry and his parents, that can't have been easy and now especially...' she trailed off.

'Yeah. I have no idea what happens next,' I admitted. I lived and worked with them. What would I do?

'Don't worry about that now,' my uncle said. 'Come on, tuck in.' He poured me a cup of tea and handed me a huge plate of sandwiches, from which I took a couple of triangles. He instantly encouraged me to take more so I took another two. The sandwiches were made with crusty homemade bread. I took a big bite. They tasted so good after years of supermarket sandwiches eaten hastily on lunch breaks at work. We all tucked in for a bit, then I saw Willow and my uncle exchange a couple of glances.

'We can talk about it,' I said, knowing they must have a lot of questions for me. I wasn't sure if I'd be able to answer them all, though. I still felt discombobulated.

'You said that Henry's mum made you panic that you couldn't marry him?' Willow asked me gently.

'Should I let you two talk...' my uncle said, offering to leave.

'It's fine, Uncle Adam,' I reassured him.

'Feel free to drop the uncle now you're an adult, Daisy,' he said with a grin.

'I'll try.' I smiled back. The name was a polite habit which I wasn't sure I'd be able to completely break. 'Stay, please,' I told him. 'I've just turned up here with barely any notice; you both deserve to know what's gone on.' I took another bite of food and a gulp of tea. 'I told Willow that Henry and his family had planned the wedding. His mum had taken control over the whole thing. I'd gone along with what they wanted. I thought I didn't mind that I hadn't much of a say. That they saw it as an opportunity to grow Henry's father's business. They run an investment firm. I'm his PA... Anyway, they invited all sorts of contacts: people they wanted to network with, clients, and people at the country club they belong to. But I didn't have anyone I loved coming – only Willow.' I dropped her a grateful smile. 'I've been really stressed in the lead-up to it. But Henry didn't notice, didn't think I minded any of it. I haven't been sleeping. I've felt so worried, so anxious about it all and then today...' I paused to take a breath. 'I stood in the room feeling lost and lonely as I got ready. And then Henry's mum started talking about what would happen after the wedding. "Of course you want to try for a family straight away so Henry and my husband think it's best you stop working after the honeymoon," she was saying...'

'God, that's a bit old-fashioned,' Willow said. 'But if that's what you wanted...' she added quickly in case.

I shook my head. 'No. We'd never discussed that. I asked her if Henry had really said that. She said he had told his parents that and basically, it had all been agreed. His father had even started to recruit for my job! Without me knowing anything about it!'

'Bloody hell,' Willow said.

'That's not right,' Adam said more mildly.

'I freaked out. Was I signing away my whole future? Did I really want a life where everything was decided for me? The past five years just suddenly snapped into focus like I'd been dreaming my way through it all. I realised this was what it had been like since I'd started dating Henry. And I had gone along with it because I'd finally had what I thought I'd wanted: a partner, a family, a life where I didn't have to worry or be scared...' I trailed off, hating to admit how much I had wanted some kind of safety and security after losing so many people I loved.

'Oh, Daisy,' Willow said with sympathy. 'But do you love Henry?'

I hated to admit this the most. I shook my head. 'No. But I thought that didn't matter. Or maybe that was even better.'

'How could that be better?' my uncle asked with a frown.

'Then it wouldn't hurt that much if I lost him,' I whispered.

Willow nodded. 'I understand that. You were scared of loving again. Of losing people you love. But that's no way to live.'

I sucked in a breath to continue. 'I went to see Henry. I told him what his mum had told me. I asked him why he hadn't said anything to me. Why he hadn't asked me what I wanted for our future. And he said that I always wanted the same things as he did, so he had assumed that I would want this too. He seemed confused why I was upset. Why I didn't want us to start a family. Why I wouldn't want to give up work...' I trailed off, remembering the shocked look on his face. Wondering why suddenly, I wasn't going along with what he wanted. 'I realised that I had tried so hard to mould myself into the perfect woman for him that he didn't know the real me at all.'

'Because you wanted stability?' Willow asked me.

I nodded. 'I met Henry soon after I started as his dad's PA. Everything happened so fast. Henry pursued me immediately and I was flattered. The boss's son. He's handsome, and rich, and they're a big, close family and I... didn't have that. I wanted it so badly,' I said, my chest hurting from thinking about my parents and the family I had lost. 'I clung to what Henry was offering and made sure he would choose me. I wanted him to fall for me and I suppose I did my best to make that happen. But when I stood in front of him in my wedding dress, I knew I'd done such a good job that he hadn't fallen in love with *me*. But with his ideal girlfriend. And he had assumed I'd be the ideal wife too. We'd have a perfect wedding then a perfect family; it was all planned in his mind. My future was mapped out for me. But I couldn't go through with it. How could I marry someone who didn't know the real me? Who didn't love the real me? And who I didn't love either?' I slumped in my chair, exhausted from telling the truth to Willow and my uncle. It hurt to admit what had happened but I also felt better for finally telling someone. But I was worried that I'd ruined Henry's life. 'Am I a terrible person?'

'Of course not.' My uncle gave my hand a quick squeeze. 'You've been through so much, Daisy. You tried to make a new life, to try to move on from all the pain, and you realised before it was too late that it's not the life you want.'

'Or deserve,' Willow added. 'You deserve to love, and be loved. For you. For who you really are.'

I wasn't sure that was at all possible so I said nothing.

'How did Henry react?' Willow asked after a moment. 'What happened when you told him he didn't know the real you?'

'He tried to argue that he does know me, and that he loves me. That he didn't realise I wasn't happy with the wedding. That we could sort things out. Then he said I owed it to him and his parents to go through with it.'

'No way!' Willow said indignantly.

I nodded. 'He said it would be really embarrassing for them if I stopped the wedding, and they had spent a fortune on it all plus there were important people there...'

'I'm glad you didn't listen,' my uncle cut in fiercely.

I sighed. 'Yeah. I knew I couldn't go through with it just to save face. It wasn't right for either of us. Before he could stop me, I took off. I ran and kept on running until I got here.' I exhaled shakily. He had looked so stunned when I'd left. It had all been so horrible. 'I feel like a coward for not being able to face Henry's parents, or to talk to him any more, but I thought he might persuade me to go through it. I just had to get out of there.'

Having blurted out all of my sorry story, I braced myself for their disapproval.

4

'He should have listened to you,' Willow said. 'I get why you took off. You went with your gut.'

Adam nodded. 'You couldn't marry him just because of what people would think about you stopping the wedding. You can't spend your life with someone you don't love.' I remembered how much in love Willow's parents had always seemed. It was so sad that they hadn't got their forever. 'You both would have been miserable.'

'I think we would have,' I agreed, but I wasn't sure Henry would ever see that. I took another bite of a sandwich for more fuel. 'I should have said something sooner, though. His parents must have spent a fortune. And maybe if I had said I wanted more of a say in the wedding or in our life, they might have listened...'

'It sounds like they didn't give you a chance. That they didn't ask you what you wanted. That seems quite...' Willow searched for the right word. 'Controlling?'

'Maybe,' I agreed, thinking that Henry's father did seem to control a lot of our lives. 'But I went along with it all. I made a lot of mistakes trying to find a way to be happy.' It hadn't worked, though. I hadn't been at all happy. What if I couldn't ever be? What if I could never let love in again? I was so scared of feeling that pain of loss again.

'I think they will understand in time,' my uncle said kindly. 'And they will realise it was for the best.'

'God, I hope so.' I lapsed into silence, wondering what Henry and his parents had done after I'd left the wedding venue, and what they thought of me now. I wasn't sure when I'd be able to face the messages on my phone stored in Willow's car. I just wanted to hide out here for as long as possible. Although part of me knew it couldn't last long.

'How about some cake?' Adam started to get up then, but Willow told him to stay seated and she jumped up and brought over a delicious-looking lemon drizzle cake.

Adam cut the three of us a big slice each and passed them over.

'I've been too stressed to eat,' I said, tucking in. 'This is all so good. Henry and I just eat out or get takeaways. I've forgotten what home cooking is like.'

'I'll make us a delicious dinner,' Adam promised instantly.

Willow chuckled. 'Dad loves to feed people so you've come to the right place,' she said, looking at him fondly.

I smiled. They hadn't lost their good humour and were as close as ever, it seemed. I was so relieved. And the farmhouse was cosy and there was still the old warmth to it despite all the tough times it had witnessed. It was so lovely to see. I hadn't realised how much I had needed to be back with my cousin and uncle, and in their home again.

We finished up the lunch and then Willow reluctantly said she'd better get back to work. 'Why don't you have a rest upstairs? Then we can all have dinner together at the end of the day.'

'Are you sure?' I felt bad that she was so busy but was sending me for a lie-down.

'Daisy, today was supposed to be your wedding day. Take a minute to chill.' Willow whistled for her dog, Maple, and they headed out of the farmhouse. I refused to go straight upstairs, though and helped my uncle clear away our tea things although he told me not to.

'Willow seems so happy,' I commented as he washed up the plates and cups and I dried them. I thought about how devastated she had been five years ago at her mum's funeral. It was nice to see the spark back in her eyes.

Adam smiled. 'She is. Last year, we thought we might have to give up the farm but she fought for this place. And I was so proud to see it. I can't do as much now with my health but Willow has been amazing. And Dylan and her make such a good team. She's so pleased you came here.'

'Really?' I felt even worse for not keeping in touch more than I already did. 'I don't want to get in the way.'

'She won't let you. She runs a tight ship, that one.' He winked.

I let out a laugh. 'Well, maybe I can help out with some of the farm chores while I'm here, like I did when I was younger.' I had no idea how long I could stay on the farm but I was in no hurry to go back to Henry's family home, that was for sure.

'Willow was right, though – for now, you should take it easy, okay?'

Seeing there was no point in arguing any more, I finished helping my uncle then I went back upstairs to the spare room, closing the door. I went over to the window and looked out at the farm. It stretched out for over three hundred acres. Behind the farmhouse were fields of different fruit and vegetable crops and to the side of the house were polytunnels where they grew more crops. I also saw where they kept chickens and where Willow was currently walking with Maple, carrying wood from the barn. Then I looked over at the Airbnb cottages and saw Dylan talking with Blake outside, reminding me of how critical he had seemed of me walking out on my wedding. I was worried about seeing him again. He was clearly judgemental and I didn't need that right now.

Turning away, I went to lie down on top of the bed. I sank into the comfortable covers with a contended sigh.

Outside, I could hear Maple let out a bark. I could hear the chickens in the distance. The sun streamed in through the window. The life of the farm somehow was the balm I needed. I closed my eyes and knowing that I wasn't alone any more, I slipped into a deep sleep.

* * *

When I woke, it was close to dinner time. The long summer days were starting so the sun hadn't set yet when I went back downstairs.

Willow, Uncle Adam and Dylan were bustling in the kitchen getting everything ready. Maple was eating her dinner in a bowl near to the Aga on the tiled floor. It all seemed so cosy and inviting that I forgot for a moment the reason I was here, and I smiled at the scene. I walked in but paused when I saw Blake was sat at the pine table. I couldn't forget the reason then.

'Daisy, did you have a good nap?' Willow called out and all eyes turned to me. Reluctantly, I glanced at Blake, who shook his head and turned away from me again. This guy really had taken a dislike to me.

Rolling my eyes, I asked Willow if I could help but she told me to sit down as it was all ready. I sat at the opposite end of the table to Blake – petty but necessary. I looked out at the birch trees in the drive, stretching up to the endless sky.

Everyone came over with dishes for the table, declaring they were starving. I remembered that because the farm day started early, dinner here was usually at 6 p.m. I had got used to working late and grabbing a hasty dinner with Henry at 8 or 9 p.m., but more often, I ended up eating alone as he'd been stuck at the office with his dad or out with a client or his friends at the country club they all belonged to, and which I had tried to avoid going along to as much as possible. I hated trying to make small talk with people I had nothing in common with there. Henry's parents had seemed to live separate lives and were rarely home with us during the week. So it was a novelty to be at the table with so many, eating an early and homemade meal.

Uncle Adam had made honey and mustard chicken with new potatoes, along with a huge bowl of salad and crusty homemade bread. Also on the table were bottles of wine, water and lemonade. I loaded my plate and poured out a large glass of wine. My appetite had suddenly come back and I wasn't going to argue with it.

'I still can't believe you live on a farm; you used to be scared of our horses,' Blake said to Dylan once we all started to tuck in.

I raised an eyebrow. He really seemed judgemental to me.

Dylan chuckled good-naturedly, however. 'As soon as I came here, I had this feeling like I was home,' Dylan said with a smile across at Willow, who sat opposite him. 'Which seemed crazy to think but that feeling just never left me.' He looked back at Blake. 'I guess you don't see your horses much now? His family run a riding school,' he added to explain to the rest of us. 'You must miss your old home living in the city?'

Blake sighed. 'More than I thought, I've realised today being here,' he admitted quietly then quickly took a gulp of wine like he hadn't planned on saying that.

'Dylan said your hometown isn't far away from here,' Willow said. 'Are you planning to visit your family?'

'Um, maybe...' Blake said, avoiding her eyes.

I couldn't help but wonder what the story was there. If his family lived nearby, why was he staying here and not with them?

'Well, like I said, mate, the cottage is all yours. We can start work on the others first. You can even stay longer than the two weeks you've booked for, if you need to.'

My eyes widened at the idea, and Blake noticed my reaction. 'Two weeks will be fine, I'm sure, thank you,' he said shortly.

I hoped it wouldn't be this awkward every time I saw Blake while I was here. I distracted myself by eating more of Uncle Adam's tasty food.

Willow looked over at me. 'More chicken?' She quickly put more on my plate. I looked down and realised I'd already eaten my first portion. 'Did you not eat at your fiancé's house or something?' she asked with a laugh.

'Not like this,' I said. 'It's delicious, Uncle Adam. I've had way too many takeaways or dinners out lately. I've missed home cooking like this. Henry and his family rarely ate together unless it was an occasion we went out for.'

'We love eating together,' Adam replied, looking surprised that other people didn't feel the same way.

'We've been the same lately,' Blake piped up suddenly. 'Me and Sarah, I mean. We've put everything into our business; we just had takeaways or ready meals.' He shook his head. 'Maybe that's why things have gone so wrong,' he added quietly. His voice was tinged with bitterness.

I wondered if this Sarah explained his bad mood. His girl-friend, I assumed as he didn't wear a wedding ring.

'You both wanted the business to succeed,' Dylan said. 'It was natural you focused on that.'

'It can be hard working and living together sometimes,' Willow agreed.

Maybe Blake and his girlfriend had recently broken up. Maybe that had caused some of his earlier hostility towards me. Still, it was an overreaction to a stranger. It's not like it was my fault if she had left him. And I couldn't say I blamed her.

'Hey,' Dylan teased Willow.

She grinned. 'You know what I mean; we have to make sure we keep time just for each other, right?'

'Definitely,' he replied, again exchanging that smile with Willow that made my heart ache. I got the sense that even though they worked and lived on the farm together, their rela-tionship wasn't just surviving as mine had been; it was thriving.

'Sometimes, all Henry and I talked about was his family's business,' I mused, thinking that should have been a warning sign for us both that we didn't have much in common apart from that.

'God, I was guilty of that too,' Blake muttered, staring at his plate.

'Don't blame yourself, mate,' Dylan said.

'It wasn't your fault what happened,' Willow added softly.

Curiosity got the better of me then. 'What happened?' I blurted out before I could stop myself.

'My girlfriend didn't wait for quite the worst moment to break my heart like you did to your fiancé, but it was almost just as bad,' Blake said darkly, lifting his eyes to meet mine. There was that open hostility again.

My blood boiled at his assumption I was just like his girlfriend even though I didn't know their story, but he was clearly angry and broken-hearted. I didn't understand why he had to take that out on me, though. If he treated his girlfriend like this too, I was on her side. 'You don't know anything about me,' I told him coldly. 'Thank goodness, I might add.'

'Um, now, how about dessert?' Willow said loudly.

'No, it's okay, thanks; I'm full,' Blake said, standing abruptly, causing his chair to scrape against the kitchen tiles. 'It was a long journey here; I should get an early night.'

I leaned back in my chair with relief that he was going. I knew I hadn't handled things well today but the last thing I needed was a stranger making me feel even more like crap.

'Let me walk over with you,' Dylan said hastily, getting up too. They left and Willow went to get dessert so I looked over at my uncle, the two of us left at the table.

'Things always look better in the morning,' Adam said with a reassuring smile.

I sighed. 'I hope so, I really do.'

'So, Dad, tell Daisy all about your girlfriend...' Willow said with a teasing smile when she came back. She was clearly trying to shift the mood in the room.

'Willow, don't call her that, at our age... Taylor and me... we're just good friends,' he said, but there was a twinkle in his eyes.

'Well, whatever you like to call her, Dad and Birchbrook's mayor have been spending more and more time together,' Willow told me.

'That's great, Uncle Adam,' I said sincerely. I knew he'd never get over losing his wife but it was nice to think he wasn't alone any more. 'You deserve to be happy.'

'You do,' Willow agreed.

'Oh, stop it, you two,' he said, waving his hand as he ducked his head, his eyes definitely turning misty.

'What about you and Dylan?' I asked Willow, enjoying speaking about their love lives instead of my disastrous one. We had messaged and called each other sporadically since we last saw each other but there was nothing like being together face to face. I watched as she talked about her boyfriend and I could tell she was head over heels in love.

Willow had lost like I had, but her heart was open.

I wished mine was too.

5

Alone in bed later, I felt restless. My room was dark and the farmhouse was quiet. Willow, Dylan, her dad and Maple were all fast asleep after the long day. But maybe my nap earlier was keeping me awake, or maybe it was just my jumbled thoughts. Either way, sleep seemed very far away.

I rolled over and looked for my phone. Then I remembered, I'd hidden it in Willow's car earlier. I dreaded what notifications were waiting for me but was also compelled to go and have a look. My mind was running over and over what I'd said to Henry and what he had said to me. What was he thinking now? I had spent most of the past five years lying next to him in bed. It felt strange to be without him tonight even though I'd made the decision to walk away.

Deciding that there was no point tossing and turning any more, I jumped out of the bed in Willow's spare room. I quickly pulled back on shorts and a T-shirt, tying my hair up into a ponytail before slipping on my trainers and creeping downstairs past the kitchen, hoping Maple wouldn't bark. She stayed quiet thankfully as I slipped out of the front door and headed for Willow's car. She said she never bothered locking it out here so I knew I'd be able to get into the glove compartment.

A light caught my eye from the cottages. Clearly, Blake was also unable to sleep tonight. I hoped he was berating himself for how he'd spoken to me, but I doubted it. He probably was only thinking about himself.

I was unused to such quiet at night. There was no city noise here on the farm, and it was completely dark so I had to rely on the light from the silvery moon to find her car.

As I walked outside, I tripped a bit in the semi-darkness, letting out a loud, 'Ow!', which echoed around the silent farm. 'For God's sake,' I added as I gingerly went the rest of the way to Willow's car, wincing a bit. I opened it up and leaned in to reach for the glove compartment.

'Hey, what are you doing?' a sharp voice cried out from behind me as my fingers found my phone.

I started in surprise and hit my head on the car roof. 'Ow!' I said again, and scooted back across the seat, stepping back onto the ground. I switched on the torch on my phone and shone it into the equally surprised face of Blake. He stood next to my car wearing joggers, a hoodie and trainers. 'You scared the crap out of me!' I told him, annoyed. 'Why are you sneaking up on me in the dark?'

'Hey, you were the one who scared the crap out of me,' Blake accused, holding his hand up. 'I thought someone was trying to steal this car!'

'Surprised you didn't offer to help them,' I replied grumpily. I rubbed my head then leaned down to rub my ankle, both of them sore now. Awesome.

'You really think I'd do that?' Blake questioned then, sounding offended.

'How am I meant to know?' I flung back. 'You've been hostile to me since you arrived.'

He sighed. 'I'm sorry but I was worried someone was trying to steal this car,' he repeated.

I put my hands on my hips. 'Out here?' I asked, eyebrows raised, looking around at the dark, peaceful farm. 'We're not in the city now.'

Blake squinted at the torch on my phone, holding up his hand and wincing. 'Okay, fine, I guess it was an overaction. But why are you out here at this time of night?'

'You first,' I returned as I shut the car door. I lowered my torch so it wasn't shining directly into his eyes but so I could still see him.

'I couldn't sleep so thought I'd go for a run. I often do it when I can't sleep,' he replied with a shrug.

'It's not as safe out here with no street or car lights.'

'I grew up with this, though,' Blake reminded me. 'Let me see you back to the farmhouse, make sure you don't injure yourself more.' He smiled then, and I think it might have been the first time he had properly smiled at me since we met earlier. I couldn't help but notice that he had a dimple in each of his cheeks, making his smile very cute: a surprising development.

'I don't trust you being nice,' I warned him, unsure whether to agree but on the other hand, I didn't want to trip again.

'Shit, we really have got off on the wrong foot, haven't we?' He stared at me for a moment then he cleared his throat. 'Please let me.'

'Okay, fine,' I replied but I wasn't sure if we could salvage our bad first impression of one another, or if I even wanted us to.

We fell into step to walk back up to the house together.

I dared to look at my phone then and I let out a sigh, causing Blake to glance at it too. I let him see the screen, which now had over a hundred notifications on it. My pulse picked up at the thought of reading all the messages and listening to voicemails from Henry and his parents, and whoever else wanted to tell me I was crazy and/or a bitch for running out on Henry like I had.

'Bloody hell, who's trying to contact you that much?' Blake cried, shaking his head. 'Oh, sorry, that was nosy...'

We reached the farmhouse door then and both paused, hovering as we faced one another, just able to see in the moonlight.

'Who do you think?' I replied. 'I know you judge me for what I did today but you don't know the full story,' I snapped, suddenly weary right down to my bones.

Blake shifted uncomfortably. 'I'm sure. Look, I think we both have a lot going on right now. Maybe we could start over again?' He held out a hand in the darkness. 'I'm Blake Daniels.'

I hesitated but I knew it was better if we could co-exist peacefully on the farm while we were both here. I held out my hand and shook his. His handshake was firm and warm. 'Daisy Connor.'

'Nice to meet you,' he said, looking down at my hand and the diamond ring still on my wedding finger. I hadn't thought about taking it off; everything had happened so fast. He dropped my hand. 'I am sorry for being so... cold towards you. It was just the wedding dress. And this ring. They remind me of what's going on in my own life. It was a shock. Like the universe was punishing me or something.'

He seemed to feel bad and I didn't like holding grudges so I nodded. 'I really do feel terrible about leaving my wedding. Your reaction just made me feel even worse about myself but I know that most people would have probably reacted the same way. It's not like I ever planned to be a runaway bride. I'm judging myself so you don't need to.'

'I'm not judging you,' he said quickly. 'As you said, I don't know what went on.'

'I know I left it too late but I haven't been on my own for a long time and I was... scared to call it off,' I admitted to this almost-stranger in the darkness, glad he could hardly see the shame on my face. 'I don't expect you to understand, though...'

There was a beat of silence. 'My reaction was mostly about me. I found out my girlfriend – well, my ex now, I should call her – was cheating on me. Actually, I walked in and found him in our apartment...' He coughed uncomfortably. 'I thought we were in love, the real thing. That she was... Never mind. Let's just say seeing you in a wedding dress reminded me that I'm alone now too.'

'Shit, Blake. I'm sorry she did that to you.' I didn't exactly forgive what he'd said to me earlier but I did understand his hostility towards me now. I knew if someone I loved had cheated on me, I would hate the whole male population for a very long time. 'Now we know why we're not at our best right now.'

'Hopefully, being on the farm might help us both. Do you know how long you're staying for?'

I shook my head. I knew Willow and my uncle had said the spare room was mine for as long as I needed it but I had no idea how long I might want it for. 'But we can stay out of each other's way while we try to decide what to do next, right?'

'That might be difficult but I'm glad we cleared the air,' Blake replied. 'We should try to get some sleep. Things always look better in the morning, don't they?'

'So people tell me,' I said dryly. I opened up the farmhouse door. 'Night, Blake.' I walked inside and closed the door, surprised that we'd opened up to each other. But at least we both now knew why our first meeting had been so fraught.

I went back upstairs and sat cross-legged on the bed and took a deep breath before opening up the notifications on my phone. There were so many calls and messages from Henry along with his parents. Plus a few from my colleagues at their family business, along with a couple from Henry's friend's partners. I knew my leaving would be prime gossip at their country club. A couple did sound genuinely concerned about me but I was too worried they would report back anything I said to Henry so I didn't reply. I hadn't got close with anyone in my city life.

Now I was back with my family, it felt surreal that I'd kept away from them for so long. But at the time, I had run from pain and grief and fear. That had made me keep everyone at a distance in the city. Even my own fiancé.

Nervously, I began to scroll through the messages he had sent me since I left.

Darling Daisy, you misunderstood what I told you, come back and we can talk about this, please? You can't seriously have left me?

Darling, you're being unreasonable and irrational. We are so good together. Why are you throwing that away?

Everyone is asking what is going on, come back so we can talk!

My father said come back now and we can sort it out. You can't walk away from all of this, Daisy. All that we've done for you!

I can't believe you're ignoring me. How could you have left like that? My parents have spent a fortune on this wedding.

You are humiliating us. Why?

This is crazy. I'm your fiancé. You want to be my wife. I know you do. Where are you?

Are you sleeping with someone else? Is that it?

I closed down Henry's furious messages at that point, and listened to one of the voicemails he'd left me.

'I've just told my parents you've gone. They are as shocked as I am. We have no idea why you've done this, Daisy. Darling, I know you love me. You are happy with me and my family. This wedding is a dream for any woman. You have everything you ever wanted. Why are you throwing it all away like this? Come back and talk to me.'

I put my phone down and sighed. Henry still sounded certain that I loved him and wanted a life with him. He hadn't listened to me when I'd said that the future he and his parents had decided for us wasn't what I wanted. I'm not sure he had ever really listened to me the whole time we were together. He liked to call the shots, and expected me to go along with what he wanted. He expected me to come back.

Henry thought I loved him. And that he loved me.

But how could he when I had kept him at arm's length? When I hadn't told him all my fears because of the past? Or my hopes for the future?

And could he really love me when he hadn't asked about them?

Then a message came through from him. I jumped as my phone vibrated. He must have seen that I was online. Clearly, he couldn't sleep either. My heart beat faster as I picked my phone back up to read his message.

Just please let me know you are safe at least.

My chest sagged when I read that. It was a sharp reminder that we had been together for five years. I thought back to my first day working as his dad's PA. Henry came into the office looking handsome and suave and charmed the pants off me. He was clear quickly that he wanted me and that had been flattering. His parents seemed to think we made a good match too. They made no secret of the fact they wanted him to settle down. And I liked the security that he, and them, were offering me.

But I had kept my heart from him.

I felt bad about that. Although he hadn't done much to try to break down my walls. He was happy with our relationship as it was. Working together, living together, attending functions together, having sex once a week and then rolling over to opposite sides of the bed. I hadn't reached for him for affection or emotional support. I hadn't ever asked that of him. Because I was scared that would open up my heart. And he hadn't asked me for it either. Which felt sad for both of us.

The message he sent though sounded like he did care about me. And I did care about him too.

I also felt incredibly guilty for leaving him on our wedding day. For the expense spent by his parents. I felt like I owed him something.

Taking a deep breath, I hit reply.

> I am safe, Henry. I'm staying with my cousin. I really am sorry about today. I hope you'll be able to forgive me.

He responded instantly.

> We need to talk. You can't end everything in one conversation. We almost got married today! Please, Daisy.

I hesitated. I didn't know what to do. But I knew I wasn't ready to talk to him just yet.

> I need some time alone, okay? Some space
> while I sort my head out. I'll be in touch soon.

I sent the message then turned off my phone so I wouldn't see any more notifications, and put it on the table by the bed. Then I curled up into a ball and finally I was able to drift off to sleep.

6

When I finally woke up the following morning, the farmhouse was empty. Coffee had been left in the pot for me and there was homemade bread by the Aga with butter and jam plus a fruit bowl so I had a quick breakfast, showered and pulled on the same outfit as yesterday. Then I went in search of my cousin, needing to take my mind off of the fact that my life suddenly was completely different today.

Willow was leaving the barn with faithful Maple, carrying a bucket. She wore denim shorts too but with wellies and a long cardigan slung over her T-shirt. And her hair was in a messy bun. She waved me over when she spotted me. 'How did you sleep?'

'Actually, I slept well in the end. I looked at the messages on my phone from Henry and his parents,' I said as I fell into step with her, giving Maple a pat as she wagged her tail excitedly. 'He asked if I was safe so I said I was here and needed some time and space. I suppose I didn't really think what would happen after I left yesterday. Like, what do I do next?'

I looked around the farm. The hazy morning light made it

look even prettier. Birds sang from the birch trees. There was no city noise out here. It was peaceful. Usually, I woke up feeling jittery for the day ahead. My mind started listing a hundred things I needed to do. I never felt rested.

But this morning, I didn't feel tired. I didn't have a to-do list. It was disconcerting. I was confused and unsure about what lay ahead for me. But there was also a part of me that was glad to be out of my routine. That wanted to embrace this change.

'I get that must be scary. But maybe it's also a bit exciting too?' Willow asked as if she could read my thoughts. 'I find nothing helps me make decisions or come up with ideas more than being out here. Keeping busy doing manual things has always soothed my mind.'

'Is this your way of saying I should make myself useful?' I joked with her.

She smiled but then a frown took over as we reached the chickens. 'I woke up early a bit worried about the summer season. Our usual staff can't come this year – a mixture of finishing studies, going travelling, taking other jobs – but it means there is a lot for us to do to get things ready to open for the pick-your-own season. It's usually our busiest time although last autumn, we had a big influx of visitors to our pumpkin patch.'

I smiled. 'You sent me a photo of that, didn't you? It looked so cute. Did you have help for that?'

'Well, a lot of the town ended up helping out. But I had Dylan and Dad working with me. I don't want to put pressure on my dad to help too much this summer, though. And Dylan will have to split his time between the farm and the cottage renovations.' She slipped inside the chicken enclosure and scattered their feed from the bucket.

'Has Uncle Adam's arthritis got worse?' I asked as I followed her inside. 'Can I do anything?'

'Can you collect any eggs, please?' She pointed out a basket that I picked up and I ducked inside the pen to hunt for eggs. 'Yeah, he signed the farm over to me, actually.'

'Wow. That's what you've always wanted,' I said as I crouched down to find the eggs in the hay, something I didn't think would have been in my plans for today. I was supposed to be waking up in a room at our wedding venue next to my husband and then off to our honeymoon later in the Maldives.

Willow came over and smiled. 'It is. He did it because he is struggling to do manual labour now. And we were in trouble last year, to be honest. I was worried we'd lose the farm. But the pumpkin patch allowed us to clear our debts and carry us through the quiet winter.' Her smiled faded and she frowned again. 'We need to make sure that success carries on this summer, though, just in case. We are due to open in June for people to pick fruit and vegetables and I had big plans to make it more of an event like the pumpkin patch but now I might have to scale it back. I need to move the pumpkins I've sowed indoors outside so they can grow ready for autumn and this year's pumpkin patch. But with less help, I don't know if I can do all that I had planned.' She bit her lip and I could see she was unsure what to do.

'You can't put the renovation of the cottages on hold?' I asked as I carried the basket of eggs out.

'It's all booked in. I'd feel too bad taking work away from local traders. But I want Dad to start his retirement soon like we all planned.' She sighed. 'Sorry, is this too much farm talk for you?'

'Of course not. You've listened to my problems!' I brought the eggs over. 'So, what do you do next?'

'Let's go out to the crop fields and check everything is being watered properly and nothing has been damaged overnight. I usually do a lap around everything in the morning,' Willow said. 'If you're sure you want to come? I was only joking about helping out.'

'I'm happy to,' I assured her. 'It'll take my mind off of worrying about the future. Plus, I can earn my keep.'

We laughed and dropped off the eggs into the farmhouse. We passed the cottages and I saw Dylan and Blake talking with a builder. They both waved and I thought back to bumping into Blake last night. I found myself telling Willow all about it.

She chuckled. 'He thought there was a carjacker out here?'

I smiled. 'Yeah. I'm glad we cleared the air a bit. Sounds like he's pretty cut up about his ex. I hope Henry isn't feeling just as bad.'

'He's going to have wounds to lick, I'm sure,' Willow said. 'But hopefully, he will see that it was the right thing for you both in the end?'

I nodded. 'That would be good. I hate hurting anyone. He probably hates me right now.' That felt strange. Although I wasn't sure Henry had real feelings thanks to the wall I kept up to keep him out, I also didn't want him to think badly of me. We had spent almost five years together. I did want him to be okay.

'I think you need to remember why you left. You said he didn't let you have any say in the wedding, and planned your future without you... He has to realise that was wrong,' Willow said as we walked around the farmhouse out to the crop fields, beginning with the sunflowers that were curled up to face the morning sun.

I wasn't sure Henry had ever admitted he was wrong but I didn't say anything. It was nice that Willow was on my side but it didn't stop me feeling terrible for telling Henry how I felt so late.

'So, what did you want to do differently for this pick-your-own season?'

'I wanted to make it more of a day out so people don't just come and pick the one or two things they want, but can spend a few hours here, like they did at the pumpkin patch,' she said, excitement creeping into her voice. 'We could have photo opportunities, food and drink, a picnic spot maybe... I don't know, I have so many ideas but Dylan said maybe it will be too much work to do it all myself before we open in June. I thought I'd have my usual summer staff to help or I would have started earlier. But I was so focused on getting the crops in the best shape possible. And they are but will that be enough to bring more people to the farm?' She shook her head. 'Dylan is really good at business plans while I'm the one with the big ideas.'

'It sounds like you make a good team,' I commented. I couldn't help but envy her a little bit.

'We do. But I need to be able to put my ideas into action, don't I?' Willow went over to check the sprinkler that was currently watering the sunflowers.

'I forgot how big and beautiful this place is.' I looked around at the rolling fields of crops, the polytunnels that covered anything that needed protection from the elements, and the chickens off to the side, enjoying the sunshine too. It was idyllic out here. I took a deep breath, filling my lungs with fresh air. I had spent so long hunched over my desk, it felt really good.

We left the sunflowers and went over to the polytunnels and she showed me the pumpkins she had sown. 'I need to plant them out in that field there,' she said, pointing. 'I sold pumpkins I had bought in last year but this will be even more special selling ones I've grown myself. If they flourish like I hope they will. And we'll make more profit this way too, of course.' She then took me past the rest of the fruit and vegetable crops before we reached the final two fields. 'These are the strawberry fields, always the most popular part of our pick-your-own selection.' She bent down to check some of the plants as I looked out at the ripening fruit stretching as far as my eyes could see.

'It's beautiful,' I told her. 'I bet they will taste delicious. I remember us sneaking out here when we were younger to eat as many as we could,' I said with a smile as I thought back to those times.

'That was so fun, although my mum told us to leave some for our customers,' Willow said, shaking her head as she picked off a strawberry. 'Almost ready,' she said, holding it up so I could see. 'What's wrong?' she asked when she saw my face fall.

'I just feel really bad that I stayed away for so long. That I didn't keep in touch as well as I should have done. That you guys were in trouble and I wasn't there for you. I really am sorry, Willow.'

She nodded. 'I know. We missed you. But I understood. It's been a difficult few years for us all. And I get why you wanted a fresh start in the city... I buried my head in the sand about the farm being in trouble for a while. I avoided the truth. It's not easy to face tough things.'

'That's for sure.' I had done the same thing about my relationship with Henry. 'But the farm is doing better now, right? And you have your ideas for the summer?'

'Yeah. Things are better. I just don't want to rest on any laurels. I saw this being the big finale out here,' Willow said, gesturing to the growing strawberries around us. 'But can I make that happen now?'

* * *

For the rest of the morning, I followed Willow around and tried to help with her farm chores. She then said she needed to fix the door on one of the barns as it wasn't closing properly. My uncle said he was meeting Taylor in Birchbrook for lunch, and Dylan and Blake were still with the builder so I went into the farmhouse and made Willow and I sandwiches. Then we took them onto the grass outside and sat down to eat.

'I rarely eat lunch,' I said as we tucked into the chunky sandwiches. 'Or if I do, it's at my desk in a hurry. This is much better.' I smiled as the sun kissed my bare arms and I drank in the silence out here.

'Working in an office would probably be my worst nightmare, I have to be honest,' Willow said with a wry smile. 'Dylan did that but once he came to the farm, he didn't want to do it any more. Don't get me wrong, he still loves inputting numbers on his laptop but nothing beats being outside all day.'

'You look much healthier than me,' I had to admit. 'So, you convinced Dylan to leave the office behind?'

'Dylan worked for his brother's property company. That's why he turned up here. They wanted to buy the farm.' She saw my wide eyes. 'Yeah, it was a big turnaround, wasn't it? But he fell in love with this place.'

'And with you,' I said.

She grinned. 'That too. I don't often stop for a picnic lunch, though; there's too much to do. We loved doing it as kids, didn't we? My friend Sabrina would come over too and my mum would pack us up a basket to take out into the fields.'

'That was so fun,' I agreed. 'I remember Sabrina loved horses, didn't she? We kept begging your parents to buy a pony and offer pony rides. Your mum thought it would be popular but your dad said it would be too much work, didn't he?'

'Oh God, yeah,' Willow said. 'We all argued about it over breakfast almost every morning one summer.'

'And I was freaked out by the scarecrows you guys had over there,' I said, pointing to the crop fields, the memories flooding back to me.

Willow smiled. 'Oh yeah, the old owners had them even though they didn't actually do much to deter birds. Dad took them down years ago. But I used some in my autumn display last year.'

'I don't know if I'd ever want to see them again,' I said with a shudder.

'They have cute faces,' she said with a laugh.

'It has been really nice today. Thank you, Willow. I didn't realise how much I had missed it here. And you and my uncle.'

'There's no rush to leave again. We love having you here. And if you don't know what to do next, you might as well hang out with us until you do?'

'That would be great,' I admitted. 'I guess if it's completely over with Henry then I have to find a new job, and a place to live...' I trailed off worriedly. I knew that when I stood in front of Henry in my wedding dress, I had realised that we shouldn't get married. But I hadn't thought any further ahead than that. The summer was now suddenly stretching out uncertainly.

'It's all still so raw; you need some time to think about what you want, right?'

'I haven't thought about what I want in a long time,' I confessed.

'You can do that here.'

'If I can,' I said, wondering what I even wanted to happen next. I had lost so much already and now I'd also lost the future I had thought I was going to have. Even though that had been my choice, it still left me unsure. So much had been decided for me for five years; now I needed to make decisions for myself. And that was scary.

'Of course you can. You just need to remember the girl you were when you were here. And get her back,' Willow replied firmly.

She made it sound so simple. I hoped she was right, but that girl had been through so much since those carefree childhood days here on the farm.

What if she had disappeared forever?

7

In the afternoon, Willow wanted to clear an area next to the strawberry fields and I offered to help. Being outside and keeping busy was doing wonders for my state of mind. I seemed to feel less worried about what was going on in my life when I focused on farm work. So, we set about clearing some of the wildflowers and weeds that had sprung up.

'Sometimes, we've hired an ice cream van near to the farmhouse but I thought it would make more sense to have something out here, almost like a grand finale to the pick-your-own fields. The café you found me in when you arrived came to the pumpkin patch to serve food and drinks, and they are up for doing the same for summer. If I can convince them there will be enough visitors to make it worth their while like it was in autumn,' Willow explained as she carried some of what we'd cleared over to her wheelbarrow and dumped it in.

'What else did you have at your pumpkin patch then?' I asked as I wiped my brow. The May afternoon sun was warm and this was hard work.

Willow told me all about it, and it did sound like a really fun place to visit. 'I'm just not sure how to do it for summer as the patch was under polytunnels and I created a trail for people to walk around so they saw everything. Often, people just come out to the crop they want to pick then go home. Even if we do offer food and drink, will they stay? Maybe it will be too much work to make this into more of an experience.' She looked downcast at the thought of abandoning her idea, though.

I paused and turned around to look back at the crop fields and the farmhouse behind them. I squinted against the sun. 'You know, it's kind of a large circle from the farmhouse, isn't it? So, you could create a trail to get visitors to walk all around the fields like you did in autumn.'

Willow came over to stand beside me and look. 'Hmm. If people parked out by the driveway then they could walk around it all and then go back this way,' she pointed, 'to arrive back where they started. Plus, that's where we usually have a table and till set up to take payment for what has been picked. But maybe creating a trail would be too much work in such a short space of time.'

'I can help. You could mark it with, I don't know, pretty stones maybe? And signpost it all? You mentioned photo opportunities...'

'Well, I was thinking of having props or summer scenes people would take photos with. Like what we did in autumn...' She pulled her phone out of her pocket to show me. 'Would you stay this week? Maybe we could do it together then. I mean, I hate to beg but I would love the help. And your idea is really great.'

I smiled, pleased that I had come up with something to help after feeling so guilty about not being there for her in the past.

And the fact that she'd opened up her house to me, no questions asked.

'Unless you feel you should go and see Henry?' Willow asked when she saw me hesitate.

'No,' I said quickly. 'I've turned my phone off. I told him that I need space. And I need to think. I have enjoyed today. Being with you, being outside, it's helping me calm down. I could stay,' I said, my heart lifting at the thought of being in this sanctuary for a few more days. I'd be able to really think about what I wanted to happen next.

Willow beamed at me. 'I think it would be fun but more importantly, it would be a huge weight off of my shoulders. I didn't know what to do without my summer staff and making sure Dad doesn't take on too much, and with Dylan focusing on his project—'

'Willow,' I cut in. 'You're worrying about everyone but yourself.'

She shrugged. 'I can't help it. We came so close to losing the farm, I want to come up with things that make certain that won't happen again, you know?'

That settled it. I had left Willow and her dad alone for the past five years, but they were my only family. I had to help them now. And selfishly, everything I'd left behind in the city was such a mess that I was happy to leave it all for as long as possible. 'I can stay and help you this week,' I said. 'I want to help.'

Willow rushed over and pulled me in for a hug. 'Plus, Birch Tree Farm has never failed to help someone in need,' she said as she pulled back to smile at me.

I raised an eyebrow. 'You think I'm in need?'

'Well, yeah, Daisy – you seem so different. So lost. There was a reason you came back to the farm now. I can feel it. You need the farm as much as it needs you.'

'It isn't a person,' I said with a laugh. I didn't want to admit it out loud but it was nice to have someone truly care about me again.

'But only if it's what you want. I don't want to decide anything for you,' she added quickly.

'I know,' I assured her. Willow was nothing like Henry or his parents. I could see how worried she was about me. And everything she loved in her life. It felt good to be included in that despite pulling away from her. I realised that even though I'd been gone for five years, I cared about Willow and her uncle and this farm as much as I ever had. I was so scared of losing people and things I loved. I had tried so hard for five years to keep up a wall around me.

But Willow wasn't about to let that stick. Being back on the farm, it already felt like that wall was crumbling. Because I did love my family, and this place, and I would be devastated if I lost any of them. So, I needed to do my best to make sure that didn't happen.

'I want this, Willow,' I told her then. 'I shouldn't have stayed away for so long. You're right, I have been lost. But I don't know. I already feel a bit better about things. Maybe you're right – this place will be good for me.'

'It will,' she promised.

I had walked away from the prospect of a half-life.

Now I wanted to find a life I would love.

* * *

After dinner, Willow declared we needed to go out for a drink. It had been a long day and we'd tucked in to a hearty dinner made by Uncle Adam and once we were all cleared up, Willow suggested heading to the local pub.

'I could do with a glass of wine,' I admitted. I ached in muscles I'd forgotten all about and a relaxing drink sounded great.

'I'm in,' Dylan said. 'Coming?' he asked Blake.

Blake had been quiet during dinner but any open hostility had passed, thank goodness, since we'd bumped into each other outside late last night.

Blake looked at me. 'I do fancy a beer, if that would be okay?'

I was sure we would never be friends after our shaky start but I wasn't against being in a pub with him so I shrugged. 'Sure.'

Blake merely nodded.

I turned back to Willow. 'Should we change?' I asked, looking down at what I'd been wearing all day.

'No way. We'll sit outside; the evening is still so nice. Everyone in Birchbrook will be dressed like us,' Willow said. 'Come on, let's walk over before a chore comes up that I forgot about.'

I was surprised she didn't think we should change but it was a relief to not have to make a big effort like I was used to doing. If I'd been going out with Henry for drinks at his club, I would have needed to be wearing a dress with my hair all done and make-up polished, and we'd have planned it at least a week in advance. This felt spontaneous and casual, and far more relaxed. Even with Blake involved.

The four of us walked to the Birchbrook Arms. It was a picturesque walk from the farm slightly downhill towards the pretty High Street of Willow's small countryside town. Even the local pub was quaint and cosy with wooden beams across the ceiling and a thatched roof outside.

Willow and I headed into the beer garden while Dylan and Blake bought a round of drinks. Outside were picnic-style benches on grass and each table had a LED lantern ready for when the sun finally dipped in the sky. It was busy and lively thanks to the lovely evening. Beyond the pub, I could see rolling hills and the sun beaming down on them. It was a lovely view and again, I felt some more of the tension roll off my shoulders.

'At least we're old enough to drink now,' Willow said as we sat down at a free table.

'I can only imagine the mischief we would have got into if we had been able to when we were younger. Do you remember when we took a Victoria sponge your mum had made out into the fields and ate the whole thing? She had been saving it for when the vicar came round.'

Willow shook her head. 'My mum rarely got angry but she was furious with us. We had to walk to Birchwood Café and beg Pat, short for Patricia, to bake one to serve instead.'

'Your mum made such good cake,' I remembered aloud. 'God, I wish mine was around right now. I thought about her so much when I woke up on my wedding day, wishing she was there. I never would have got into such a mess if she had been.'

I knew, though, part of the reason I had almost walked down the aisle to Henry was because I had lost her. I thought marrying someone I didn't love would save me from pain. And maybe it might have done. But I knew it also meant I'd lost joy from my life. I was already having more fun this evening than I'd had for a long time.

'I think that all the time,' Willow said softly. 'But mistakes are part of the journey, right? Like, in autumn, I stuck my head in the sand about our farm being in trouble but if it hadn't been such a desperate time, I might not have come up with the pumpkin-patch idea.' She glanced behind me and smiled. 'Or met Dylan.'

I couldn't help but hope that my mistake might turn out just as good.

Dylan and Blake returned then with our drinks.

'Let's have a toast!' Willow cried as she passed me a glass of wine then picked up a glass for herself.

Dylan and Blake sat down at the table – Dylan beside Willow and Blake next to me – with their pints of beer.

'To old friends, to family, and to the best summer yet on Birch Tree Farm!' Willow's good mood was infectious and despite ourselves, Blake and I smiled and joined in with the cheers, clinking our drinks with Willow and Dylan. I took a long sip of wine; it was cold and refreshing and felt so good after our busy day.

'How long have you been friends?' I asked Dylan and Blake. If I was going to stay on the farm for a few more days, I knew I needed to help us try to put our awkward first meeting behind us.

'We went to the same school,' Dylan said. 'And hung out in the holidays. I guess we lost a bit of touch when we both went away to university...'

'Then I moved to the city a year ago,' Blake picked up. 'We met up a few times before Dylan moved to Birchbrook. He was the first person I thought of when I wanted to get away from the city and... everything,' he said, mumbling the final word. Perhaps he had been about to mention his ex again.

'I'm glad you did,' Dylan told him.

Blake asked him how he met Willow then. Dylan and Willow launched into the story of how he'd turned up at the farm wanting to buy it and she was having none of it. We listened and laughed, and I saw how they looked at each other. I was sure Henry had never looked at me like that. And I hadn't looked at him that way either. I had been certain I didn't want to find true love. The heartache that could come with it wasn't worth the pain after all I had been through. But they seemed so happy. I couldn't help but feel a little envious. And wondered if I might ever find something like that.

But even if I did, I had no idea if I'd be able to let it in, or whether I'd run and hide from it.

8

'Let's get the next round,' Willow said to Dylan then, shaking me from my melancholy thoughts.

I looked down at my glass, surprised to find that it was empty. The evening was going by quickly. I had spent a lot of nights with Henry and his friends feeling awkward and out of place, longing to just go home. But this evening, I didn't feel that way. Willow and Dylan were fun. And Blake seemed less intimidating with a beer in his hand. Although when they left us alone to buy more drinks, I wondered if I would feel awkward again.

A phone started ringing then. Blake pulled his out of his pocket and stared at the screen in shock. 'It's Sarah. My ex,' he said, looking at me in horror.

'You can take it if you want,' I said.

He seemed to be debating internally. Then he said, 'Um... excuse me,' and got up from the table, walking away. I tried not to look but couldn't help notice that his face was tight with anger as he spoke to her.

Dylan and Willow returned with the drinks.

'Blake looks tense,' Willow said when she saw him.

'It's Sarah on the phone.'

'Oh. Did you ever meet her?' Willow asked Dylan.

'No, but I saw his sister a few weeks ago and she said the family hadn't seen him since he moved in with her a year ago and she thought...' Dylan abruptly stopped talking as Blake returned to the table so I didn't get to hear what Blake's sister had thought about his ex-girlfriend but it didn't sound like it was going to be good.

'You okay?' Dylan asked him gently.

'That was Sarah. Said I can't just end things like this. That we need to talk about our business. Which I guess we do. She wants to come to the farm. I said I'd think about it.'

'It'll be hard to see her,' Willow said sympathetically.

'Yeah. But we do work together; I didn't really think about that when I left. I just had to get out of there and away from her.' Blake looked at me suddenly. 'Have you heard from your ex?'

I shifted uncomfortably at him calling Henry my ex. I mean, I guessed he was now I'd ditched our wedding but we hadn't actually said that to each other. Yet. Plus, his grandmother's engagement ring was still on my finger. 'He's left voicemails and sent lots of texts. I replied last night to say I'm safe and staying with Willow, and that I need time before I can talk to him properly. Then I turned my phone off,' I admitted.

'Daisy is going to stay for a few days, aren't you?' Willow asked me.

'That would be good. But I know I can't hide out here forever. Even if I wish I could.'

'I know that feeling,' Blake muttered as he picked up his drink and took a long gulp from it.

'Neither of you need to do anything you don't want to,' Willow said firmly. 'They can both wait until you're ready to see them.'

'Let's change the subject. Please,' Blake pleaded.

'Daisy came up with a great idea to make a trail for summer like we did in autumn,' Willow said, and started to talk about her plans for the pick-your-own opening. We all made suggestions and drank our second drinks talking about the farm and not our personal lives, which seemed to suit all of us.

Once we'd finished, we headed back to the farm. Dylan and Willow strode on ahead, more used to the slightly uphill walk, while Blake and I trailed behind. The sun had set now but the night was still warm. I looked up to see the stars. There was nothing to hide them out here, and they were beautiful.

'The sky feels like it stretches on forever,' I said. 'I remember staying on the farm when I was young; Willow and I camped out in one of the fields. We spent most of the night looking up at the stars. Imagine doing that as an adult.'

'Maybe they would have some answers for us,' Blake said. 'Maybe we should try it one night while we're here.' He smiled at the idea. I knew that would never happen.

'Are you okay after... earlier?' I asked, not wanting to bring up Sarah by name.

'I guess I knew I couldn't just end things for good when I walked out that day. When I realised she had a man in our bedroom, I just packed a bag and took off. But we live and work together. God, why does everything have to be complicated?' He sighed. 'You're right; I wish I could go back to being young and looking up at the stars without a care in the world.'

I nodded. 'I feel like that a lot. Especially lately. I think that's why my first thought when I left my wedding was to come and see my cousin. I'd stayed away because I was worried the farm wouldn't feel the same as I did when I was a child. But it does. I'm glad I came back.'

'When I left the city, I thought about going to my family's

home but I wanted space to think and I thought they would just say they told me so about Sarah.'

I remembered Dylan indicating Blake's sister had thoughts about his ex. 'They didn't approve?'

'I took Sarah home once to meet my family, and it didn't go great. My sister made it clear she thought I was making a mistake moving away with her. My dad said I had to make my own decisions but he wasn't happy either.' Blake sighed. 'I thought that coming to stay with Dylan would be better for clearing my head. I do feel bad not going home, though.'

Sometimes, I missed my parents so much, it physically hurt. It was hard to understand wanting to avoid them like Blake was doing. 'I'm sure they'd want to see you,' I said, trying not to have another go at him. 'Maybe you should see them when you know what you're going to do. They'd understand about Sarah, and support you, surely.'

Blake was quiet so I didn't push it.

'I'm sorry she cheated on you; it must be rough going through that.'

'And not just that...' He looked quickly across at me, scuffing his feet on the path as we wound our way towards the farm. I could see lights ahead from the farmhouse, ready to welcome us back.

'What is it?' I prompted as he hesitated to finish his sentence.

'I had just been about to propose to her,' he blurted out, shaking his head. 'What a fool.'

'God, Blake.'

We were silent for a moment.

Blake looked across at me. 'I bought a ring and I'd been thinking about how to propose, and what our wedding would look like. Sarah standing beside me at the altar in a white dress...'

'Oh,' I said, understanding our first meeting more now. 'So, when you saw me in a wedding dress...' I thought about him thinking he might get married soon then bumping in to me running from my own wedding. And despite the fact it was a bad situation all round, I let out a laugh.

Blake looked across at me in surprise and I clamped my hand over my mouth but I couldn't stop myself from giggling. 'Sorry, it's so not funny but I just thought – no wonder you were so shocked.' Was I hysterical? Possibly after the recent events. Plus the wine might have gone to my head. But our first meeting suddenly seemed absurdly funny to me.

Blake stared at me. And then suddenly, his shoulders dropped and he smiled, flashing those dimples again. 'It was like I had seen a ghost,' he agreed with a chuckle.

'Wow, I'm sorry. No wonder you hated the sight of me.'

'No,' he said quickly. 'I was just shocked, and I guess I did take my anger at Sarah out on you. I thought the universe was playing a sick joke on me. Rubbing salt in my wound. And that you were just like Sarah: jilting your man.' He dropped his voice. 'But I know I don't know anything about you, or your fiancé. I am sorry I was so hostile to you. I'm not usually like that. It's been a rough few days, I guess.'

'It has,' I agreed. I didn't want him thinking badly of me. But I felt badly of myself. 'I should have said something sooner, and stopped it all before I got to my wedding day. But I thought it was what I wanted. And then my fiancé's mother started talking about their plans for me after the wedding and it was like I woke up from a dream... I didn't want the future they had all planned out for me.'

'They planned your future?' He sounded confused, just as Willow had done. Seeing their faces made me realise how much I had ignored in my five years with Henry and his family, how much I let the fear of being alone blind me to how unhappy I was becoming.

'They planned everything. I had to leave. I need to find the life that I want. I let myself get swept up because I wanted the security they were offering me, I think.'

Blake was quiet then he sighed. 'I let myself get swept up too. Sarah wanted us to move to the city and work together. And I went along with it because I thought we were in love. I thought we would be happy. But I don't think we were. So, maybe I understand more than most. I feel a bit like I've woken up from a dream too.'

We looked at each other, our situations feeling more similar than we'd realised when we first met. Almost as if we were both meant to be seeking sanctuary in Birchbrook together.

'But now I am alone,' I said, my voice so soft, it blended with the summer breeze.

Blake heard me, though. 'I'm sure you're not. What about Willow? You have her. She wants you to stay.'

'Yeah.' I smiled as we walked through the gates of Birch Tree Farm.

Willow and Dylan had their arms around each other in front of us, talking quietly, proving love didn't always have to be difficult.

'That means a lot after I stayed away for five years. A long story,' I added, because I wasn't quite ready to talk about my parents with him. It was nice that he had confided in me about proposing to Sarah, though. I wasn't sure he'd ever get past the fact I'd run out on my wedding but it felt like we had come to a truce that would make being on the farm for the next few days together much easier.

'Can I ask why you are still wearing his ring?' Blake asked me gently.

'I don't know. Maybe it's the same as you and Sarah. It feels like we haven't had... closure.' I looked at him. 'By the way, what is your business together?'

'You won't believe this...' Blake trailed off with a grimace. 'We had started up a dating app.'

That was it. I burst out laughing again.

This time, Dylan and Willow stopped and turned around to see what was going on.

'Yeah, ironic or what?' Blake said, chuckling along with me.

'What's so funny?' Willow called back to us.

'My misery, apparently,' Blake called back, making me giggle even harder.

9

There was something about the air on the farm. I thought I'd be overthinking about Henry and everything but I slept like a log, and woke up to my room flooded with sunlight.

Then I heard Maple barking. And voices outside through the window I'd left open when I went to bed.

Groaning, rolling over and stretching, I climbed out of bed and pulled on the dressing gown Willow had lent me. Heading downstairs, I saw the front door was open so I walked out to see what all the commotion was about.

'There you are!' Willow cried when she turned around to see me in the doorway. I pulled my dressing gown tighter. Everyone else was dressed. 'Come and see what just arrived!'

Sheepish at being in bed so much later than the rest of the farm, I reluctantly walked out of the door and joined the group gathered in the driveway, blinking at the bright sunshine outside.

Dylan and Blake were there with Willow and her dad with Maple sat by them, letting out a small growl. There were two men I hadn't seen before and when I stepped closer, I realised then that they were each holding something that was causing all the drama.

'Willow,' I said, shaking my head with a smile when I saw that each man was holding a lead attached to a Shetland pony – one was a lovely reddish-brown colour with a cream mane and tail, the other was mostly the same reddish-brown but with white patches.

'What have you done?' Adam added with a sigh at his daughter. He turned to me. 'Is this your doing, Daisy?'

I swallowed down a giggle as my uncle looked very unimpressed. 'I might have reminded Willow of that time we and Sabrina kept asking you and my aunt to buy ponies...'

My uncle shook his head. 'Oh dear, I remember that...'

'How did you find them so quickly?' I asked my cousin, marvelling that two ponies were already here.

'I was talking to Dylan while we were buying drinks in the pub yesterday and Craig here heard and called me first thing this morning,' she said, gesturing to one of the men. 'Said they have been trying to sell their two ponies for a while. And I was thinking that the tractor rides we offered at the pumpkin patch were really popular so for summer, why not offer pony rides? And Blossom and Jasmine are just too cute. Plus, we love flower and tree names around here,' Willow said, beaming at the ponies as she went over to stroke them. Maple followed cautiously. 'You will all be great friends,' she promised her dubious dog.

'We've never kept ponies or horses. It's too much work; that's what I told your mother all those years ago,' Adam said. 'You two really are like peas in a pod sometimes,' he added under his breath. I got the impression usually he saw that as a good thing but sometimes, like now, he definitely did not.

'They will be so easy to look after, won't they?' Willow addressed the men she had clearly bought the ponies from.

They quickly nodded.

'See?' She gave a triumphant look at her boyfriend and dad.

'You're thinking of offering kids rides on them? Who will manage that, though?' Dylan asked her. 'And where will they live at night?' he asked, with so much patience, I assumed this was often the dynamic around here: Willow coming up with ideas while the other two debated things more rationally.

'They can live in the small barn; I'm sure it was used for horses before we came to the farm,' Willow said, only answering one of his questions.

'I could help you get them settled in,' Blake said out of nowhere. 'I have a horse, after all. Well, my sister currently looks after her at my family home. She runs a riding school there.' He moved towards the ponies. 'I'd love to help,' he said, his face relaxing into a smile. There were those cute dimples again. I wish I hadn't noticed them. Again. Surely, my brain had more important things to be thinking about right now?

'Oh, that's right,' Willow beamed at him, then faced her boyfriend. 'See? Blake can help us!'

'What about when he leaves in two weeks?' Dylan countered.

So, Willow turned to her dad instead. 'Don't you think visitors will love them?'

'It's your farm now, love,' Adam replied but he shook his head. 'I just hope you're not taking on more than you can handle. Maybe I can do more...'

Willow shot me a pleading look. I knew she was worried about her dad's health and wanting him to move into retirement, not take on extra things on the farm.

'Don't worry,' I assured them all, 'I'm staying for a while; I'll help too. The ponies will be really popular, I bet. And they can be part of the new pick-your-own experience we're going to create.'

'You really want to stay and help?' Willow asked me again. I could tell she wasn't sure whether to fully believe that I was going to stick around after being away for so long. But I wanted to. Being here just felt... right.

'I really do. For as long as you need me,' I promised. Immediately, I felt better too. Like some of the weight on my shoulders had lifted a little bit. I wasn't so lost now; I had a plan. I was going to do some good while I decided what I wanted for my life. Free to make my own decisions again.

Blake looked over at me and smiled, like he knew what a big deal this was for me.

'Yay! See, Dad, Dylan? We have enough help,' Willow said excitedly. 'I think this summer will be our best yet,' Willow said as one of the ponies leaned over to chew on the necklace around her neck. 'Oh, shit,' she yelped, stepping away. 'I better take my mum's necklace off around these guys,' she said.

'They can be a lively pair,' Craig, one of farmers, said with a chuckle. 'But they'll feel part of the family in no time.' He handed one of the leads to Blake and one to Willow as he and the other man stepped back and turned towards their truck to head off.

'Out of interest – why were you selling them?' Adam asked as Blake and Willow started to encourage the ponies to walk towards the fields behind the farmhouse. Maple hurried after them with a bark, clearly keen to help herd the ponies.

The men exchanged a look.

'They can be a bit... mischievous,' Craig said finally. He waved. 'Okay, bye!' Then they hastily climbed into their truck.

'Mischievous,' Adam repeated, then he turned to me and Dylan. 'Is it me who thinks that word sounds ominous?'

'Not just you,' Dylan agreed. 'Willow said she got them at a very good price. But Blake is great with horses so I'm sure they'll settle in quickly, right?'

Neither of us had an answer for him.

10

Once I had got dressed and drank a large cup of coffee, I wandered out to find Willow leaning against the fence in the small field she had put the ponies in. She wore matching shorts and T-shirt to what she had given me to wear – and I thought that maybe I needed to do something about the fact that I had none of my stuff here now that I was staying for a few days at least. Maple sat beside her still regarding the ponies with a look of deep distrust as they chewed on grass.

'I had been keeping this space to try growing some new fruit and veg for next year so it was free for the ponies. We'll need them closer to the pick-your-own area to offer the pony rides, though. Maybe we can build an enclosure over there? They seem to be settling in okay,' she said without preamble. 'Blake is making sure they have all they need in the barn. Thank God he's come to stay for a couple of weeks is all I can say.' She turned to me. 'I'm so happy you're staying for a bit. Have you turned your phone back on yet?'

I swallowed hard. 'No, I just need a bit more time before I speak to Henry. Think about what I want to happen next.' There was so much up in the air between us and I knew I couldn't avoid dealing with it for much longer but right now, the space felt like it was a good thing.

'You would have been on your honeymoon anyway, right? It's not like you've left them in the lurch at your work or anything?'

'We had a two-week break in the Maldives planned,' I said. 'I thought I would be back to work after that but they had planned for me to leave. Henry's mum said they'd already started recruiting for a new PA for his dad. I had no idea.'

'That's so shady of them,' Willow said.

'Yeah, but now I'll have lost my job anyway.'

'You think they would really sack you?'

'I do. Henry's dad likes to be in control of everything. Me leaving the wedding was completely out of his control. He will be furious.' I shook my head. 'I wouldn't want to go back to working for him now. I didn't really enjoy it. And it gave him so much say over my life. But what I will do instead, I really have no idea.'

'There's no hurry in working that out,' she said. 'I really am so grateful you are going to lend a hand with the farm.'

I bit my lip. 'I have no idea how good I'll be at all this, though.'

She shrugged. 'You're a Connor. You've spent a lot of time here. And you have always had a creative eye. Like your mother. You'll be fine.'

It had been so long since I'd been around anyone who knew my parents, her words sent a jolt through me. Yes, it was sad to remember them but it was nice to hear that she thought I was creative like my mum.

'You loved arts and crafts and making things pretty; remember that fort set-up we made in the house one Christmas?'

'That was so cosy,' I agreed, thinking about the fairy lights, cushions and bean bags we put inside the tent. It had been a long time since I created anything. For Henry's dad, it was all admin, admin and more admin. I hoped Willow was right and I'd be good at working on the farm.

'You're a lifesaver being here,' she added.

'I think it's the other way around,' I replied. Willow had offered me a life raft. She needed my help, sure, but this was giving me a much-needed moment to breathe.

Willow slung an arm around my shoulder. 'Well, these ponies are all your fault as you gave me the idea so, it's really the least you can do to help me look after them,' she joked as gave me a squeeze.

I chuckled. 'I think they might possibly be your best idea yet.'

'Oh, I have plenty more up my sleeve,' she replied with a twinkle in her eyes.

'Should I be worried?'

'Always.' She winked and we both giggled, reminding me of when we were younger and carefree, not devastated by grief or scared about what life had in store. Maybe for this summer, we could be those girls again.

'Well, I'm excited to hear them all,' I declared.

'And I need more from you too!'

'I'll do my best,' I replied with a smile.

Maple barked then and we turned to see what she was looking at. Dylan and Blake were striding towards the barn together carrying hay bales. Both had shorts and T-shirts on too and I couldn't help but notice the muscles in Blake's legs and arms as he lifted the hay.

Willow wolf-whistled, earning herself a wave from Dylan. Blake looked over and I ducked my head, not wanting him to see I'd been looking too.

'Blake told me he found out his girlfriend was cheating on him,' I said. 'It's so weird we're both here running from relationships.'

We turned back to the ponies, Maple running off to catch up with the men. Blossom and Jasmine wandered over to us, and we reached over the fence to pat them.

'Yeah, I must admit, it's a crazy coincidence,' Willow said. 'I don't know what went wrong between them but Blake sounded desperate for somewhere to stay when he phoned Dylan. Thankfully, we had the cottage free for a couple of weeks. Who knew the farm would become such a sanctuary for people?' Willow smiled and nudged me. 'I'm glad, though. It's so nice having you here. And Blake is already proving to be a great help too. I know there was a bit of awkwardness at the start but I'm glad that's gone.'

'Yeah, I think seeing me in a wedding dress gave him a bit of a fright,' I replied with a wry smile although I didn't want to share his secret that he had wanted to propose to Sarah. 'I can't blame him. He must be really crushed by what happened. I can't believe his girlfriend cheated on him.'

'God, yeah. If Dylan ever did anything like that...' She shuddered at the thought.

'He won't. You two seem so solid.'

'We made no sense on paper when he arrived at the farm but somehow, we fit,' she replied simply.

'You deserve it.'

'So do you,' she replied.

'I just feel really guilty about leaving the way I did. Even if I do think I was right to leave.'

'It sounds like Henry didn't give you many opportunities to tell him how you felt, though.'

'Yeah,' I agreed. 'I bet he's so pissed off at me, though...' I bit my lip. 'I'm nervous to speak to him again.' I used to feel so anxious back in the city. I was already feeling so much calmer out here. I didn't want to let the anxiety back in just yet.

Willow looked worriedly at me. 'You don't need to yet. At least give yourself the rest of today? I can keep you busy if you want,' she added with a twinkle in her eyes.

'Yes, please,' I said eagerly.

Willow stepped back from the ponies. 'Shall we brainstorm how we're going to create this summer trail?'

'I'm in,' I said readily.

Before I could follow, Blossom leaned in and nuzzled my chin before chewing on a strand of my hair.

'That's not for you,' I said, yanking it away from her. 'God, these ponies like to eat whatever they can get their hands on,' I said, hurrying after Willow with a shake of my head.

I hoped they weren't going to be too much of a handful for us.

* * *

Willow called Blake and Dylan over to join us at the start of the crop fields behind the farmhouse. The sun was hidden by fluffy clouds now, casting a hazy brightness over the farm. Maple ran ahead of us, wagging her tail as we followed. Willow led us all to the first field that visitors would be able to pick things from: the sunflower field. They had grown tall already, reaching up to the sky with their smile-like faces almost ready to be taken home and put into vases on windowsills that would bring summer joy.

'They always look so happy,' I said, reaching out to touch the petals of one near me.

'How can a flower look happy?' Blake asked as Willow nodded in agreement with me.

'They just look like they are smiling,' I told him. 'My mum named me Daisy after her favourite flowers; she said they always looked friendly. And sunflowers have happy faces.' I always felt a pang when I talked about her but she had loved flowers, and this had always been her favourite part of Birch Tree Farm. That was nice to remember.

'That's why I planted them in the first field,' Willow said. 'It's like they're greeting visitors.' She walked on with Dylan; Blake and I followed behind them.

'Where is your mum?' Blake asked me.

I glanced across at him. 'She passed away when I was at university. And my dad,' I said, hating having to tell people this. 'They died in a car accident. It was raining and late at night, and a lorry swerved into them on a bridge...' I trailed off, wishing I could forever erase the knock at my door, the police arriving on campus to tell me I was now an orphan.

'God, Daisy, that's so awful. I'm really sorry.' He reached out and gave my arm a gentle, quick touch.

'Thanks.'

'I never would have asked if I had known,' he added, clearly feeling terrible.

'Don't worry. I guess it must have seemed strange that my parents weren't around for my wedding and why I came here.' I sighed. 'I am so grateful for Willow. It's nice to think about how my mum loved the sunflowers here, actually. She was a florist,' I explained to him.

'Now calling you Daisy makes perfect sense,' Blake replied with a smile that showed his dimples and made me feel that weird sense of connection with him again.

Willow stopped and started talking, oblivious to our conversation. 'So, my best friend Sabrina made cool wooden signs for our pumpkin patch. I was thinking when she gets back from her holiday, I can ask her to make sign for the start of the sunflower fields. That could mark the beginning of the summer trail you suggested, Daisy, then we can end it in the strawberry fields – that'll be our big finale. We can create a path that leads everyone here...' She gestured to the section of the farm where she was growing vegetables – cucumbers, lettuce, carrots, courgettes, onions – and then onto the vast amount of tomatoes and potatoes they had. After that, we walked to where she was growing raspberries and then the last two fields were the strawberry ones. Beyond that, she said would be the pumpkins as we moved into autumn but they wouldn't be part of the summer trail.

'If everyone is going to end up in the strawberry fields, I thought we could offer pony rides over there. People can park to the side of the farmhouse as usual and then follow the trail to finish right here,' Willow said as we looked out at the strawberries. 'I'm also going to see if Birchbrook Café wants to set up their food van like they did in autumn. I'll try to persuade Paul to sell ice creams.' Willow turned to me. 'But only if you can help me come up with ideas for the finale here,' she added.

I looked out at the strawberry fields, my mind whirring. 'I looked at your pumpkin-patch photos and we can definitely set up some cute places for people to have pictures, and stay for a picnic too.'

Willow looked at Blake. 'How would you suggest we organise the pony rides?'

'Well...' He turned to the side of the strawberry fields where there was a patch of grass that Willow had said the food van could use. 'We could build a small enclosure over there and have the two ponies inside. Then get kids to line up and someone could take one on each pony for a couple of laps around. You could offer them just in the afternoon so the ponies won't get too tired maybe?'

'That would work, great. I know you're here for a break but do you think you could help us get it set up?' she asked pleadingly.

He grinned. 'Sure, I said I would help. I love the ponies. And honestly, I hate not doing anything. I'd rather keep busy.' Blake glanced at me and I smiled because I felt exactly the same way.

'I wish you'd still be here to run them. Dylan, that might fall to you, babe.' She gave him a wink as he threw Blake a panicked look.

'Maybe we could find a white bench,' I mused as I tried to picture a set-up in my mind. Thinking about my mum made me want to use lots of pretty flowers. 'Like something out of *Bridgerton*. Maybe I could set up a flower arch around it; that would be so lovely.'

'Could you really do that?' Willow asked me.

I thought about how many times I had watched my mum work with flowers in her shop. I loved helping her when I was younger. 'I think it would be fun.' It felt like the perfect thing to focus on right now.

'And I'll get started on all the publicity we need to bring people out here,' Dylan said. 'And sort out the budget you can have to make this trail happen,' he added, giving Willow a stern look.

She sighed. 'Yeah, yeah, I know, I can't overspend. Hopefully, together, we can pull this off. We only have a couple of weeks and I don't want Dad doing too much; I think he might be hiding how rough he's feeling at the moment.'

'We can do it,' I assured her, desperate to make up for not being there for them by making sure this worked. And the thought of anything happening to my uncle was too much to bear.

'I can mark out the trail but I might have to focus on the

pumpkins for a while so knowing that you two are in charge of the strawberry fields is such a weight off my mind!' she said, smiling at me and Blake.

'Um...' I started to say but Willow was already walking towards one of the barns.

'We need wood for the pony enclosure and stones to mark out the trail...' Her voice faded as she walked and Dylan hurried to catch up with her as they started to talk passionately about their budget, something I could tell Dylan was a stickler for making Willow stay within.

Blake and I looked at each other.

'Your cousin is, like, impossible to say no to, isn't she?' he said, seemingly dazed by what had just happened.

'Oh, definitely,' I agreed. 'So...' I shifted my feet. 'Can we do this? Work together for the next few days?'

'Of course,' Blake said easily. 'I shouldn't have judged you when I met you. And if you don't judge me either then we can work together, and be mates, right?'

I liked that idea but I thought about what he had said, and frowned. 'Why would I judge you?'

He looked away but I saw a flash of pain in his eyes. 'I can't have been a great boyfriend if Sarah felt she had to cheat.' He walked off before I could reassure him. Cheating surely had more to do with other person than the one they cheated on? But I supposed I didn't really know Blake at all, and I didn't know his ex, so I couldn't comment. I appreciated him not judging me and was glad the air was clear and we could work together to support Willow.

I had made a shit ton of mistakes and had no idea if I could fix the mess that was currently my life. But I knew I wanted to. And being here and helping my family out was the first step.

11

The following day, I joined Willow on a trip to a town an hour or so away from Birchbrook to pick up supplies to turn our summer ideas into reality. There were still grey clouds in the sky holding back the sun so we both wore jeans and thin cardigans over T-shirts, plus the obligatory trainers on our feet.

'Thank you so much for lending me things over the last couple of days,' I said to Willow. 'But as I'm staying longer, maybe I can find some clothes and toiletries where we're going?'

'Sounds like a good idea.'

'Wearing your clothes has made me feel like I want to switch up my style; I've forgotten how good it feels to wear comfortable things,' I said as I looked out of the window at the rolling green countryside, feeling a million miles away from the city I had lived in for five years. My outfits there had been either work wear – trouser suits with heels – outfits for the country club, which were smart dresses also with heels, or silky nightdresses for bedtime. Henry and his family didn't really do casual. That's why jeans felt kind of freeing right now. But Willow's style didn't feel quite like me either. 'Not that I know what I want to switch it to exactly.'

Willow grinned as we passed a field full of wildflowers, bursting with colour and natural beauty. 'That's part of the fun. Trying out a few things. There's a big clothing shop next to the homeware place and garden centre so we can hit all three and get what we need.'

'Great. I haven't been out shopping in ages. I always ended up ordering online as I worked such long hours, and I guess I haven't had any real girlfriends to go out with in the city.'

'Real girlfriends?'

'I used to hang out with Henry and his friends with their partners but we never got close. I guess I kept a distance from people. Put up a barrier to not let anyone in. Even Henry.' Sighing, I looked at my cousin. 'That's why I stayed away from you. You make me open up.'

Willow gave a wry laugh. 'I just know you well, and know how you used to be... I don't like seeing you so worried about things. And I don't want to upset you, but your parents wouldn't like seeing it either.'

'I'm just so scared of losing someone else that I love,' I blurted out in a rush.

'I get that: wanting to protect your heart. But doing that means you also miss out on so much.' She reached over and gave my hand a quick squeeze. 'We've been through a lot since we were kids, haven't we? But we've got each other.'

'Even though I've been a rubbish cousin the past few years?'

'Life got in the way a bit, for both of us, but we're family.' Willow pulled into a car park. 'It's like we've never been apart, isn't it?' she added with a shrug.

It was weird, but she was right. We had slipped right back into the easy familiarity of our childhood.

'Right, let's shop,' Willow said eagerly as she parked and switched off the engine. We jumped out and hit the shops. For the farm, we picked up some wood as Willow didn't have quite enough to build a pony enclosure plus she needed some for Sabrina to make trail signposts. Then we found small, pretty, pink stones to create a path that would guide the way around the farm for visitors. We then found a pretty, white, iron bench. Willow said she already had a metal archway that I could drape flowers around. The bench could go in the middle with a *Strawberry Fields* sign behind it for photographs. We also picked up a couple of white baskets that I thought I would fill with flowers and put on the floor by the bench. Willow had organised to hire benches for the picnic area. She borrowed some from the local school in autumn but they'd be needed for sports day so it was an expense Dylan had agreed to. I could see how pretty I could make it all look and we left the shops excited to get started.

We had a brief coffee before going into the huge clothing shop. I had saved pretty much the majority of my salary while working for Henry's dad and I still had the money my parents had left me. I hadn't had to pay anything for rent while I lived in Henry's family home. I didn't want to spend too much, though.

Henry telling me that I should have gone through with the wedding because of what his parents had spent on it was weighing heavily on my mind. I felt so guilty about it. I wondered if I had enough money saved to pay them back. It was another thing to sort out. In the back of my mind, I knew I couldn't hide for much longer without facing Henry again. I was just scared to do it.

For now, I'd let myself spend a little bit of money so I had enough things with me at the farm. And maybe new clothes might help me to get some of my old spark back. I wanted to feel like myself again but also like the woman I wanted to be. To break away from who I'd been for the past five years, I supposed.

I took a big pile of clothes into the changing rooms and ended up buying a few pairs of shorts, but instead of Willow's frayed denim, I chose comfy linen in a few colours including some striped ones. They all had matching linen shirts, making them cute co-ord sets. I also bought a couple of pairs of trainers but also a couple of pairs of comfy sandals. Then I picked up several sundresses, all in floral patterns, which seemed perfect for the farm, as well as a couple of pastel cardigans for cooler days or evenings. I found two pairs of pyjama short sets, which I added to my bag, so I didn't need to keep borrowing night things from Willow. A straw hat, some white-framed sunglasses and a bow for my hair completed my big purchases.

After grabbing some toiletries on the way to the till, I was done. I couldn't wait to wear it all back on the farm.

As we headed back to the car, though, a hairdresser's caught my eye. I touched my highlighted hair. Soon after I met Henry, his mum took us to her hairdresser and encouraged me to lighten up my hair to a similar colour to hers. I also had been growing it for five years and it now trailed down my back. Suddenly, I wanted it gone.

'Do we have time to go inside?' I asked Willow, who grabbed my arm excitedly and practically dragged me over.

An hour later, we were on our way back to the farm.

As we drove, I pulled down the passenger mirror and looked at myself. My long, honey-blonde hair had been cut into a long, layered bob that framed my face and was an easy style that I could just wash and leave. Then the stylist had darkened it to be closer to my natural colour of light brown again. It somehow made me look younger and made my eyes look greener. And thanks to a couple of days spent out in the fresh air, along with some good nights' sleep, my skin was already looking healthier, plus my eyes looked less dark and tired. I put on the new coral lip gloss I had bought and I smiled. 'I feel... better,' I announced.

'You seem so much brighter,' Willow agreed. 'I love the new look and it's nice to see you smiling again. Put your clip in.'

I chuckled. Willow had found a daisy hair clip that she said I had to have. I slid it into one side of my hair. 'It is cute,' I admitted, looking at myself again. It was playful, something I hadn't been around Henry and his family. They were always kind of serious. Willow was definitely helping to bring back the side of me she had known when I was younger. God, I missed that young, carefree, playful girl. Could I get her back this summer? I knew I'd never be quite the same after losing my parents but Willow was right that they would have hated to see me to be anything other than happy.

Willow turned off the road to drive through the gates to the farm. We were singing along to the radio loudly, giggling at the songs we were playing from our youth, when we both noticed a fancy car in the drive. We stopped singing as Willow drove up to park beside it. It was bright red and polished in a way that no cars in Birchbrook were. A glamorous brunette was climbing out of the driver's door.

'Hi there, can I help?' Willow asked, walking towards the woman. 'I own the farm.'

I followed behind, taking in the woman as we approached. She was wearing a pencil skirt and blouse, her glossy hair in waves and sunglasses on her face. She had four-inch heels on. Her whole look screamed money. She was pretty and polished in a way I recognised from Henry's country club. Henry had encouraged me to look just like her. I had no idea what he'd say if he could see me now in my shorts and trainers, and my new hair and minimal make-up.

'Oh yes, I'm looking for someone,' she said in a cut-glass tone, smiling at Willow. 'I'm trying to find Blake Daniels. I'm his girlfriend, Sarah.'

I stared at her, stunned, while Willow's smile faded.

Before Willow could respond, I heard another car behind us coming up the drive. I spun around, wondering who else had suddenly turned up to the farm.

Then my stomach dropped. Everything seemed to go into slow motion. The farm became smudgy around the edges as I recognised the blue sports car. The roof of the car was down, the man driving it wearing his usual designer shades. He pulled up at a fast pace beside Sarah and parked his car.

'Who is that now?' Willow asked, clearly as dumbstruck as me at these two unexpected new arrivals.

My heart started to thump as I watched him start to get out of his car.

I swallowed hard before I could answer Willow.

'It's Henry.'

12

'I'll find Blake,' I suddenly said before Henry could get fully out of his car. 'Back in a min!' I hurried off before Willow could stop me. I knew it was shitty to leave her to deal with both Sarah and Henry but I needed a minute to get my thoughts together.

Henry was on the farm! He'd tracked me down.

I was annoyed at myself for telling him I was staying with my cousin. I had mentioned the farm a few times while we were together, and he must have remembered that and looked it up. Now he'd driven out here. I had no idea if he was ready to have a go at me or try to talk me into going back with him but either way, I was in no hurry to find out. I wasn't sure when I'd become such a chicken but after running out of our wedding, I was now doing it again. This time, just across to Willow's cottages as my pulse raced.

I banged on the door where Blake was staying and called out his name.

The door opened and Blake stood there wearing a surprised frown. 'What's up, Daisy?' he asked, taking in my harassed appearance. 'You changed your hair.'

'Oh.' My turn to be surprised as I touched it. 'Yeah, I did.'

'It really suits you.'

That flummoxed me for a moment. 'Thanks. We have a problem, though... Sarah and Henry have just turned up at the same time on the farm.'

Blake stared at me.

'Your ex, Sarah, is here! And so is the man I left at the altar!' I repeated, hoping he'd cotton on fast as they were both waiting for us with poor Willow. 'What do we do?!'

Blake's eyes widened. 'I told her I'd think about meeting her. She's just turned up?'

'They both have,' I repeated.

'I wished I hadn't told her where I was now.' He looked as agitated as I felt.

'My phone is still off. I told Henry I was here but I didn't think he'd even remember where it was! I feel bad – I left Willow with them. We can't hide or run, I guess...' I trailed off, wondering whether we could actually try to do that.

Blake sighed and came out of the cottage, closing the door behind him. 'No, I guess we can't. Shall we face them together?' he asked, understanding floating between us. We both didn't want to do this, for different reasons.

I felt a bit better that I wasn't alone in this. I nodded. 'Okay.' I took a deep breath and together, we set off walking back towards the farmhouse.

As we drew nearer, I saw Willow and her dad were outside now with Sarah and Henry. It looked like a stilted conversation was being had. Maple saw us and came bounding over with a bark, clearly excited by all the people on the farm.

'Hey, girl,' I said, giving her a pat as she came over, weaving in between us. Blake had to move over to avoid walking into her and then I didn't see my shoelaces were undone so I tripped a little bit.

'You okay?' Blake grabbed my arm to steady me as Maple ran back towards Willow at her whistle. 'Your laces,' he said, gesturing as we stopped. He kept a hand on my shoulder as I bent down to tie them back up. When I stood up, we were suddenly really close together. He caught my gaze and smiled reassuringly, rewarding me with a flash of his dimples again. 'It'll be okay,' he promised in a low voice.

I smiled back gratefully. 'You too.'

Blake let go of me and we set off again, walking towards the group, who were watching us closely. Henry and Sarah walked away from Willow and my uncle towards us. Willow and Adam stared at us all like they couldn't believe what was happening.

Neither could I.

I reluctantly met Henry's piercing gaze when we stopped in front of them.

But it was Sarah who spoke first. She put her hands on her hips as she glared at Blake. 'So, you thought you'd get your own back and find someone else?' she asked, gesturing angrily towards me.

I glanced at Blake in surprise. I realised we were standing close together after he'd stopped me from tripping, and he'd waited with me while I re-tied my shoes. Blake looked down at me, also shocked.

'I suppose I asked for that, but seriously, Blake? After all we've been through! You could have let me explain everything before you jumped into bed with *her*!' Sarah continued furiously, not waiting for a response.

Both Blake and I flinched. Before I could defend myself, Henry stepped forward, giving me an incredulous look, his face turning red. 'You can't seriously have left me for this man? I won't believe it! I know that you love me. We belong together. You don't belong here, with this man, it's madness, Daisy! You need to come with me now so we can discuss this. Right now.'

I stared at him, my stomach plummeting at that tone I recognised all too well. It was the one he used when arguing in business meetings like his word was fact and the rest of the world was wrong if they didn't agree with him. He had jumped, right along with Sarah, to the conclusion that something was going on with me and Blake.

'I said come on,' Henry reiterated.

'How dare you speak to her like that!' A low growl came out of Blake, causing all three of us to stare at him in surprise. 'She's not your property to command,' Blake continued calmly but coldly, staring down at Henry with disgust, their height difference appearing even bigger now that Blake was angry.

'What has it got to do with you? You two can't be together?' Henry looked between us both, shocked and disbelieving that I would choose to consider any man but him.

I spluttered but couldn't get any words out.

'Did you meet her in the few days we've been apart?' Sarah demanded of Blake then. 'It's ridiculous; she can't mean anything to you.'

Henry glanced at her. 'They're not together; Daisy took weeks to say yes to having dinner with me.'

'We're old friends,' Blake blurted out. This time, I stared at him. He turned to me. His eyes were wide, his expression apologetic. He lifted his hands in the air then put them back down. 'Aren't we?' he asked, his tone uncertain. I didn't know what to say.

'That's right.' Willow stepped over to us then. 'They're old friends. They went to school with my boyfriend, and are staying on my farm, for as long as they want.'

I felt like this was all getting out of my control but I didn't know how to stop it. Henry was furious, Blake was glaring at him and Willow was looking at me anxiously. I was so confused.

'Well, Daisy? Is this true?' Henry said to me.

Taking a deep breath, I knew that if I said Blake and Willow had made that up, Henry would be proved right that Blake and I were just strangers, and he would assume that I would go home with him. I panicked that I would have to leave when I was starting to feel better here so I went along with the pretence. 'Yes, we are old friends...'

'Is he an ex?' Henry demanded. 'Is this why you never mentioned him?'

'Not an ex, but we have reconnected here, yes,' I blurted out, my back up at his condescending tone.

'So, I was right – you're seeing each other?' Sarah demanded of us.

'I don't believe this,' Henry repeated, shaking his head.

A gust of wind blew across the farm then, and Sarah cried out as she clutched her hair. 'I need to go inside,' she exclaimed. 'Please, Blakey. You can't just end it like this!'

'Good idea,' Henry said quickly. 'You two go and talk somewhere. Daisy, let's go for a walk. I want to talk to you alone.'

'Don't speak to her like that,' Blake told him again, glaring.

'Maybe we should all calm down...' Willow said worriedly. It did seem like Blake and Henry could easily come to blows if this carried on.

Sarah grabbed Blake's arm. 'Please, Blakey. Can we talk alone inside? I know you've done this to punish me. I get it. But she can't mean as much to you as I do. And what about our business together?' She stared up at him with glistening eyes.

I watched as Blake's chest sagged. He was clearly torn. I felt bad for him. He'd stuck up for me and lied to Henry to help me and now he felt terrible for lying. Pushing aside my nerves, I did what I needed to do to help him in return. 'It's okay,' I said, looking at Blake. 'Go and speak to Sarah in your cottage. Henry, let's go for a walk.' I glanced at Willow. 'It'll be fine,' I promised her although I wasn't at all sure it would be.

'I don't want to leave you,' Blake said. All eyes were on us but for a second, I didn't notice them as I met his earnest gaze.

'It will be okay,' I said softly.

Henry let out a loud puff of air. 'Can we go, please?' he said impatiently, starting to walk away. I remembered then all the times he had walked on ahead of me like he couldn't bring himself to match my slower pace.

'Finally,' Sarah said, starting to move towards Blake's cottage.

Blake kept his eyes on me. 'Well, I guess, I better...'

Somehow, I found myself reaching out to give his arm a gentle squeeze. 'I'll see you later,' I said.

'You will,' he promised me. It made me feel a tiny bit better.

'Daisy,' Willow said as I started to follow Henry. 'Make sure you do what you want to do, yeah? I'm here if you need me.'

I nodded, grateful that people cared about me here. 'Thanks, Willow.'

It felt way too soon to face Henry but I had no choice. Like he always did, he'd bulldozed in, giving me no chance to work out how I felt by turning up here. And now I'd fallen into a lie that Blake and I weren't strangers but old friends that were reconnecting. Sarah thought we were seeing each other and neither of us had denied it.

Everything felt like it was swimming out of my control. I didn't like being sucked back to feeling like I wasn't in charge of my own life. I'd had five years of it. And was just starting to think about what I wanted again.

But now, Henry was here and I was scared that I'd go back to who I was before our wedding. So, I needed to go along with the pretence that I was dating Blake. And hope that would make Henry give me the time and space I needed.

13

Henry and I walked out towards the crop fields. The breeze was strong but I liked the coolness of it. It helped to keep my head clear.

'This feels like the last place you belong,' Henry said once we were alone.

It was the opposite to how I'd been feeling. It made me stumble a little in my step. Was he right?

'And you changed your hair,' he continued, giving me an appraising look. 'Why?'

I glanced across at him. Henry was handsome. I couldn't deny that. He was polished to perfection with dark hair, clean-shaven, smelling incredible thanks to the expensive aftershave he wore; he even had manicured hands. His outfit was expensive as well as his sunglasses. He was trim but he was only a bit taller than me, something that I knew bugged the hell out of him. I'd never pick a man based on height but sometimes, his hang-up about it had made me worry. He was quite judgemental about other people's appearances and I thought maybe it was to cover his own insecurities, but sometimes, he could be mean.

'Yeah, it was kind of an impulsive decision but I really like it,' I said, touching my new hair. I knew I never would have had the nerve to do it with him around. He always said he liked women with long hair. 'Henry, I said I came here for space. Why did you follow me?'

'Are you serious?' He looked out at the crop fields and shook his head. 'We really are in the back of beyond. Daisy, I came so we could talk. You ran away from our wedding. Out of nowhere! You never said you were unhappy before then. Suddenly, you're telling me the wedding is off. I've been going out of my mind,' he cried, with more passion that I thought him capable of, to be honest.

'I'm sorry that I left it so late to say anything.'

'Why did you?'

We walked past the sunflowers. I glanced at Henry, who was watching me intently. 'It had all been getting out of my control. I'd had no say in my own wedding! And you didn't seem to notice. And then your mum started talking about what was going to happen after the wedding...' I said. 'That I would give up my job and have babies immediately. We'd never even discussed that, Henry. You were all planning your future without me having any say in it! That's not what I want from a life partner.'

'You're right.' Henry paused and I stopped too, shocked at his statement. We faced each other. He took off his sunglasses, his dark eyes meeting mine. 'My parents took over; I can see that now. I should have seen it, and put a stop to it. I was just so busy with work and I thought you were fine with it. But I really regret it. I should have asked how you were feeling more. And what you wanted. I just thought we were on the same page. You usually agreed with me about everything. I thought we were both happy and excited. You really shocked me when you said you couldn't go through with it,' he said, and he did look genuinely upset about that.

'I feel really guilty for calling it off on the day. And I know your parents went to a lot of trouble and expense, but it's worrying that you thought I was fine about everything. When I really wasn't. I know that's partly my fault. And that's why I knew I couldn't marry you. It wasn't fair to either of us.'

'What do you mean?'

'I never let you in!' I cried. 'You don't know the real me. I was so scared to be alone that I became your perfect girlfriend. I did what you wanted. I grasped at the security and family you were offering me, Henry. I hadn't had either for so long. But I couldn't let you see the real me. I couldn't lower my walls. I couldn't open up to you. Because I am so scared to lose people I love. And you didn't notice. That's why I don't think what we had was real... at all,' I confessed in a rush, finally being honest with him. I hadn't wanted to be alone but I realised now that I'd been lonely with Henry.

'No,' Henry said, stopping. He turned to me and grabbed hold of my hand, forcing me to stop and face him. 'That's not true. Daisy, you're mine. You belong with me. We belong together. And we will get married. We'll just do it right next time – we'll plan it, not my parents. And then everything will be okay,' he said firmly.

I raised my eyebrow. He wasn't listening to me. How could I argue with this man? So, I clutched at a straw. 'What about Blake? We're here together; we might have something,' I said. 'Why would you still want to be with me if that's the case?'

'You and Blake?' he scoffed. 'Have you slept with him?' he demanded.

That would have been one lie too far. I shook my head once.

'Good. I don't see the two of you together. I don't see this.' He let go of my hand to gesture around the farm. 'None of this is you. You are my fiancée.' He pointed to my hand. 'You still wear my ring, darling. You don't have really feelings for that man.'

I stared at the sparkling diamond ring. Why hadn't I taken it off yet? I was scared of facing the future alone, I knew that. But I also didn't want to be with someone and still feel lonely. I shivered at the thought.

'You're cold. That Sarah was right; the wind out here is freezing. Let's walk back and get you into the warm,' Henry said, taking off again without waiting for my reply.

I trailed after him. I had been enjoying the fresh air. I liked being outside. It was freeing. But once again, he'd decided for me.

'I know you're confused right now,' Henry continued. 'But you love me. You love our life together. We live in an amazing house, you have everything you want, *we* have everything we want. I'm sorry about the wedding stuff. My parents got carried away. I should have said something; that's on me. I apologise. Daisy, darling, we can work this out, can't we? Don't throw away five years because of one day.'

I hesitated, feeling trapped. Then Willow came out of the farmhouse and waved us over. 'Who's hungry? My dad has made loads of food. Want to join us?'

I clung to the idea of a group situation instantly. 'I'm starving,' I said, quickly throwing her a grateful smile. She had saved me from having to answer Henry, thank God.

'Can we talk more afterwards?' Henry asked me.

'Sure,' I mumbled, hurrying after Willow into the safety of the farmhouse. Henry sighed but he followed me. I was relieved Willow had bought me some time. I walked into the kitchen and paused to see Blake and Sarah already at the table with Dylan and my uncle.

'Oh, great,' Sarah said, loud enough for everyone to hear.

Blake gave me an apologetic smile. They were seated next to each other. It felt wrong to sit down with Henry but I did it anyway. I longed to know what had happened with Blake and Sarah once they were alone. Had it been as difficult as talking to Henry was for me?

'It's been a long day all round,' Willow as she joined us at the table. 'Some food and drink is just what we need,' she added, her cheerfulness for once sounding forced.

I wondered if there had ever been a more awkward foursome in history than this.

I seriously doubted it.

14

My uncle and Willow had laid out a summer spread of chicken and vegetable pasta bake, salad and crusty bread. Dylan was pouring out wine, I was relieved to see.

'It feels like we need to go around and say our names and what we want to achieve in five years' time,' Dylan joked as I sat down opposite him.

I rolled my eyes. 'That gives me flashbacks to a team-building event I had to go on in my first office job,' I said with a shudder.

'They are terrible, aren't they?' Blake agreed.

'My father runs great team-building events for our company; it's all about setting the right objective before you start and then everyone will have a productive day,' Henry said.

There was a brief silence.

'Sounds horrific,' Willow commented.

'I'm glad I'm out of the office world,' Dylan agreed.

Henry glowered but didn't respond.

Adam started serving the food and we all piled up our plates and began eating.

'That's why we set up our own business, wasn't it?' Sarah said, turning to Blake with a flirtatious smile. 'We wanted to be our own bosses.' He just nodded.

'I couldn't imagine having a boss,' Willow admitted.

'You wouldn't cope well with one,' I told her with a grin.

'I'm amazed it suited you,' she said, smiling back. 'You always did what anyone told you not to.'

I chuckled. 'Yeah, I wasn't good with authority when I was younger. When I started at school, I was told off on the first day for wearing a skirt half an inch shorter than the requirements and for talking in assembly. But I had to ask the girl in front of me where she had got her moon necklace from.'

Willow and my uncle laughed and so did Blake, but Henry was looking at me aghast and Sarah was sipping her wine like I hadn't spoken.

'Thank God you've changed now,' Henry said. 'You wouldn't have lasted five minutes working for my father otherwise.'

'What's your father like?' Willow asked him.

'A sharp businessman. We run an investment company and we're growing rapidly each year. I learn a lot from him. He went through a fair few assistants until Daisy came along. She charmed him like she charmed us all,' Henry said, in the proud way he always spoke about his dad. He smiled across at me. 'He told me she's been his best assistant ever.'

'And yet he wanted to sack me,' I couldn't help but say. It wasn't that I didn't like Henry's father exactly. He was great at his job and although demanding, he always respected how organised and capable I was, and after a while spoke to me as an equal. But outside the office, he was just as demanding and his word was law in Henry's family home. I felt like he controlled every aspect of my life, just like he did with Henry and Henry's mum too.

'They just thought you'd want to focus on being a wife and mother, like my mum did after they got married,' Henry said. 'And so did I,' he added, reaching to touch my hand. He looked over at Blake to make sure he saw the move. I started eating again so he had to let go.

'That's really old-fashioned,' Sarah spoke up then. I was amazed she was on my side on this. 'I'm so focused on my career. We've set up a dating app and I think it's going to be really successful. Right, Blake?'

'Well, we need to talk about that,' he mumbled, glancing over at me.

Sarah saw and narrowed her eyes. 'You can't just walk away when we've only just begun.'

'I thought that's what you wanted,' Blake replied, raising an eyebrow. He looked confused by her words. I supposed if you found out your partner was cheating, you'd assume they didn't want the life you had together any more. But here she was talking about their business still.

'I just told you – he had nothing to do with us, or our life. Just like this hasn't,' she said, waving a dismissive hand in my direction.

'Exactly what I said,' Henry said, giving Sarah a nod of approval.

I stared at him. He was so arrogant. What if I really had started to date Blake? Henry was acting like there was no way I could even consider another man. It appeared Sarah was being equally dismissive about us too. It kind of made me want to dig my heels in further. But Blake might feel the opposite way, I had no idea.

'I'd love to hear about your dating app,' Dylan said then, smoothly moving the subject away from our personal drama, thank God.

'Our app uses AI to find matches for you and start conversations with them if you're stuck for what to say: how to flirt and ask for a date, things like that,' Sarah said. 'Basically, it will help people who are hopeless at using dating apps to get that first date so they can impress in person when they wouldn't when communicating solely online. Like Blakey, for example.' She shook her head. 'We matched on a dating app but he was so dry when messaging and took ages to actually ask me out. I almost gave up on him.'

I glanced at Blake. He had blushed and was taking a sip of his wine. It felt uncomfortable to hear her dismissing their early interactions.

'But isn't that giving a false impression?' I couldn't help but ask.

'What do you mean?' she snapped.

'Well, it's all a lie. You're chatting to AI and not a potential partner. It means you don't really know what they are like so, you could form an impression that will turn out to be completely wrong when you meet.'

'When I met Blakey, he was so different to how he was online, I was pleasantly surprised. Our app means you won't dismiss having a date with someone because of how they've communicated with you.'

'But it will also work the other way,' Dylan pointed out.

Sarah arched an eyebrow. 'What do you mean?'

'You could end up on a date with someone who is completely different to what you thought, and then you've wasted your time going on a date with them.'

'You don't understand,' she said dismissively. 'This will help so many people. Won't it, Blakey?'

I wondered if Blake enjoyed her calling him that or not.

He shifted in his seat. 'I do think there are lots of people who need help with how to navigate dating apps, but we are discussing how we can make sure there is transparency, and people are as honest as possible so that real connections can be made,' Blake said diplomatically.

'That sounds good, mate,' Dylan said.

'What work did you both do before?' Willow asked them as she helped herself to more food. I did the same. Adam was such a good cook. I didn't want another takeaway ever again.

'I worked for a tech company so I always knew I wanted to create my own app one day,' Sarah said. 'And Blakey worked with his father in his shop.' She said that sentence with an audibly snobby edge.

'Oh, I loved your shop,' Dylan said enthusiastically. 'The antiques were so cool. My mum bought quite a bit from there when I was growing up, didn't she? Willow, we should take a trip there one day; you'd get happily lost in it.'

'Sounds great,' she agreed.

'It's not that far from here, is it?' Dylan asked Blake.

'It's about a forty-five-minute drive away,' Blake confirmed. He seemed a bit sad when he said that; maybe he was thinking he should visit his father's shop.

'I'd love to see it too,' I told him, earning myself a small smile.

'I've already been there of course,' Sarah said, throwing me daggers. 'The town is really small and quiet. Blake wanted to do more with his life. Didn't you?'

There was another beat of silence as awkwardness washed over us all.

'I think I need some air.' Blake pushed his chair back and got up. 'I'll be back in a minute.'

I watched him hurry out and I knew that claustrophobic

feeling well. Like you just had to make a break for freedom. I wasn't sure why I did it exactly, but I pushed my own chair back.

'I'll check on him,' I said, and then rushed out after Blake before anyone could say anything to stop me.

15

'Are you okay?' I asked when I walked out behind Blake.

He was pacing outside while I stood and watched, wondering why I was worried about a complete stranger. Maybe it was because his situation was so similar to my own. And now that we had lied to Sarah and Henry, we were in this together.

'I don't know. It's all so confusing. Everything moved so fast with me and Sarah. We only met a year ago and now we live and work together, and I bought a ring... and then I walked in and found her with another man in our apartment. And now she's here saying it didn't mean anything and I should take her back.'

'Only a year?' My eyes widened as that sank in. 'You really changed your whole life so quickly for her? You must have been head over heels,' I couldn't help but say.

Blake stopped pacing and looked at me. 'I did fall head over heels but everything happened so fast, I didn't have a second to think about what I really wanted. That's why I came to stay here: to think. But now Sarah has followed me and I'm feeling that same feeling all over again – like I'm on a rollercoaster that I'm not sure how to slow down.' He shook his head. 'I'm sorry I blurted out that we knew each other but I didn't like how Henry was talking to you. And your face... I wondered if you also felt like you were on a rollercoaster. I never lie. I feel terrible about lying. But then Willow confirmed it, and I couldn't take it back.'

'It's okay. I know you, and Willow, just wanted to help me. But I don't think it's worked. Henry seems unable to believe I'd consider another man. I don't think he buys that anything is going on between us.' I realised then that I wanted him to believe it. That maybe it would stop me from going back to him.

'Sarah believes it, but she thinks I'm only doing it to punish her for her betrayal, that it doesn't mean anything in the same way she says that her fling with *that man* doesn't.' He said the words 'that man' with bitterness.

'She thinks we're... dating?'

'I'm sorry,' Blake said, thinking that annoyed me.

'No, maybe she can persuade Henry that we really are,' I said hopefully.

The farmhouse door opened and Sarah walked out, closely followed by Henry.

'I can't believe you two are sneaking off like this,' Sarah said. 'Blakey, I told you I made a mistake. Why won't you let me fix this? Are you really choosing her over me?'

'I don't know,' Blake said, looking from her back to me, sounding as confused as I felt. 'I asked for space, time to think, but you just showed up and now I don't know what to do.'

'You want space?' she repeated, confused.

'Yes,' Blake snapped. 'I want some space to think!'

'Fine. But whatever this is,' she glared at me, 'won't last five minutes. You're just a rebound. He belongs with me!' She turned to Blake. 'When you realise that, call me!' Then she flounced off towards her car.

Hope rose inside my chest that Henry might also leave.

But he turned to me and said, 'Daisy, can we finish our conversation, please?'

'You don't have to,' Blake said quickly.

'Daisy. I've come all this way. We almost got married. You owe me this, don't you?' he added to me.

'Daisy—'

'Seriously, can you leave us alone?' Henry interrupted whatever Blake was about to say to me. His face was turning red again. I didn't want things to escalate any further.

'It's okay,' I told Blake. 'Henry, let's go up to my room and we can talk,' I added. Although I was nervous to, I did feel like I owed him a conversation.

I hesitated before I followed Henry back inside. I glanced at Blake. He gave me a reassuring nod. It made me feel a tiny bit better. I nodded back. More understanding floated between us. We were connected now.

Inside, I led the way upstairs, Henry following close behind me. It felt so strange to have him on the farm. He seemed completely out of place. When I walked into my room, I could see him looking around and judging it. It was very different to our bedroom back at his parents' house; that was grand and plush and modern. And far less cosy.

Henry closed the door behind him. I went to sit in the armchair so Henry had to perch on the bed.

'God, Daisy, I can't believe you want to be here on this farm when you could come home with me to a mansion.' He didn't even say it in a snobbish way, just still matter-of-factly confident that my life with him was what every woman would want.

I now really was angry at his inability to listen to me and what I wanted. Was it any wonder I had snapped at the last minute on our wedding day? I took a breath and tried to be calm but firm. 'I can stay on this farm. And I will. Because right now, that's what I want to do. You need to open your eyes and ears and hear that I'm not happy in our life together. Why would I have left our wedding otherwise? I'm sorry but I don't think we're right together. I don't think we should get married. Not now. Or... ever.' I said the last word softly. I didn't want to hurt him. But once the word was out of my mouth, I felt relieved. He had turned up expecting that our wedding day had been just a blip. But I knew deep down, it wasn't.

Henry stared at me for a long minute. I think finally, he had heard me. He looked stunned. More so even than when I'd told him in my wedding dress that I had to get out of there. He had been expecting to be able to talk me around, like he was able to do with pretty much everyone and everything in his entitled life. Then he stood up and came to stand in front of me. 'Daisy, I have spent five years loving you. I can't, I won't, just stop. You need time, I get that now. But when you're ready, I know you'll realise you love me too, and our life is what you want.'

'Henry—' I began, sure he couldn't love me because he didn't know me. I had made sure he didn't.

'I'm sorry I let the wedding get away from us,' he talked over me. 'That won't happen again. You are my future. And I'm yours. What will you do without me? Can you picture not working with me and living with me? Our home, our life: it's everything. You will be completely alone if you don't come home with me. I know you want security and safety, a partner and a family; I can give you all that.'

He'd taken what I said about not wanting to be alone as a positive thing. I knew it had kept me with him when I didn't love him. I knew it had meant I let him dictate everything. But he saw it as offering me security and safety. And wanted to know what I was going to do without any of that. What would happen if that safety was taken away from me?

Could I decide my future without him?

Panic swept over me.

I had no idea what to do next.

The future looked blurry, like a polaroid picture before you shook it into existence. What if I couldn't shake the future I wanted into existence? What if I stayed forever stuck and uncertain, and... all alone?

I sucked in air desperately but now, I was struggling to breathe.

The room spun.

I felt light-headed and like I might pass out.

Yet somehow, I couldn't take a proper breath.

This was something I'd been worried would happen ever since I fled our wedding. I had been keeping the panic at bay but now I couldn't.

'Daisy, what's going on?' Henry was on the floor then, crouching in front of me. His hands touched mine gently. 'Breathe, Daisy. Breathe with me.'

Confused, I met his eyes and did what he instructed. He sucked in deep, calming breaths and I copied him. For a few seconds, the only sound in the room was us breathing in unison.

Henry squeezed my hands. 'That's it. You'll be okay.'

'Will I?' I asked him – and the universe – feeling light-headed and dizzy. My pulse and heart rate were still rapid but I could take in air now.

'Yes, I promise.' Henry leaned in and kissed me once gently on the lips. 'I'm not leaving you. Not now. You need me even if you can't see it yet. Look at what's just happened. The thought of leaving me made you panic.'

I felt confused. Did it?

'I knew there was nothing serious going on between you and Blake. He can't look after you like I can. He can't help you like I can. You're mine to take care of. You don't want me to leave today, do you? You don't want me to go home yet, do you?'

The thought of an unknown future was what made me panic but if I stayed with Henry, it would be known. That was suddenly appealing in this moment. I might sometimes feel lonely, but I wouldn't be alone. Maybe that was enough. I felt myself shake my head.

Henry beamed. 'That's the right decision, Daisy. I'll find somewhere in Birchbrook to stay for a couple of days. We can talk about things more, then you can come back home with me. Everything will be okay now I'm here with you. We belong together. I'll be patient until you realise it too.'

I looked into his eyes. I was shaky and scared, but knowing I had someone who wanted to look after me helped. That's what Henry had done from the start. He'd taken away the ache of loneliness in my heart that had been there since my parents had passed away. Panic that I would be alone forever. That life would always seem dark.

Fear washed over me at the thought of letting that anchor go. I would be adrift if I did. Like a boat lost at sea. I had been lost for so long. What if I never found my way home?

'You need me,' Henry said, firmly then.

And in that weak moment, despite the fact I hated myself for it, I agreed with him. 'Okay,' I said. Because it was easier to let him stay. To keep him close. To not finish things between us. I took the coward's way out again. I couldn't tell him to leave me for good. Even though there was that whisper again deep down in my heart that told me I would be ultimately happier if I did.

I pushed the whisper away.

Henry smiled. 'That's my Daisy.'

What had I done?

16

Blake found me later that evening as I was walking Maple around the farm. Once Henry had left to book into the Birchbrook Arms, I'd asked Willow to let me take her dog out with me, wanting the company and needing the fresh evening air to help revive me. I felt strange after the panic I'd experienced in my room, like my body had been put through the wringer. I was tired but also wired. I hoped the walk would calm me down enough so I'd be able to sleep but I kept replaying what had happened over and over, the beautiful farm scenery not able to banish my turbulent thoughts.

'Mind if I come along? I could use the company,' Blake said as he fell into step with me.

'I don't think I'll be very good company, but sure,' I replied. I watched as Maple tore across the farm, looking joyful in a way that I wish humans could.

'I'm all talked out from earlier, so same,' Blake replied.

We walked for a couple of minutes in silence. We headed towards the strawberry fields without discussing it. I thought about all the props I'd bought earlier with Willow – that felt like such a long time ago. We hadn't even got them out of her car before Henry and Sarah turned up and the whole day turned into something completely different to how it had begun.

'Henry is staying in town,' I said, finally able to say something. I looked up at the sky, which was turning a dusty pink as the sun slipped down below the horizon. Out here, it felt like the sky went on forever. I couldn't see an end to it. It made me feel small. A tiny piece in the universe. Somehow, that made me feel a bit better, though. Problems seemed so large sometimes but really they, and we, were all so small. 'I couldn't tell him to go,' I admitted as I looked across at Blake, his face lit up by the golden hour in a way that made him look even more handsome. 'I'm scared to let go. Is that pathetic?'

'No, Daisy. It's hard. Sarah cheated on me but we have the app together; I feel like I can't just tell her to go away for good. But at least she's given me some breathing space now.'

'I don't know what happened with Henry. I'm confused. He didn't even want to entertain the idea of us,' I said, pointing between me and Blake.

'Sarah thought I was with you to punish her. Maybe that's why I told the lie. To get her back for what she did? I don't know.' Blake sighed. 'Shall I tell her the truth? I mean, if you want to get back with Henry then we can't keep pretending we're seeing each other, can we?'

'I don't want to get back with him,' I said quickly. 'I'm just finding it hard to think about what the future looks like without him.' I hated what I was saying. What if I ended up spending my life with someone just to avoid being alone? I'd never feel that kind of love that my mum had talked about having with my dad. Or that Willow seemed to have with Dylan. Or what my uncle had had with my aunt. 'Am I weak, Blake?' I blurted out. 'The thought of Henry going, of being alone, made me panic and I just...' I gulped in the fresh air quickly, scared of what happened earlier happening again.

Blake stopped walking so I did too. He faced me and touched my shoulder just once. 'I don't know you well, Daisy. At all even. But someone who walks away from something that wasn't making them happy isn't weak, okay? You are strong. I can see that. Everything is up in the air for you right now. For both of us. But you can follow your heart, and it will lead you right. I believe that.'

'And you?' I asked him softly. 'Will yours lead you right too?'

'I hope so. I want to stay for the two weeks I planned to here. And then I'll see how I feel.'

'That's a good plan. I need a plan.'

'Maybe if you can't let him go, Henry is your future.' Blake avoided my eyes and said Henry's name tightly.

'You think that would be a mistake, though?'

'I didn't like the way he talked to you, or acted with you, no,' Blake said carefully. 'I just hope that whatever decisions you make, they are your choices, Daisy.'

'Me too,' I whispered.

Maple barked, looking back at us like we were ruining her vibe. We continued to walk after her.

'If I do leave Sarah, I have no idea what we'd do with our business. And you work with Henry's dad, you said?' Blake asked after a minute.

'Yes, I'm his PA. I never planned to have an office job, or to be someone's assistant,' I confided as we passed the strawberry crops rapidly springing up, the fruit growing and ripening before our very eyes. It was amazing to think Willow had planted all this as seeds and soon people would be picking them and taking them home to have with yogurt or whipped cream.

'What did you want to be when you were younger?' Blake asked.

I smiled as I remembered. 'A florist. My mum was a florist. She had a flower shop in the village we lived in. It wasn't a million miles from here. That's why I spent so much time with Willow growing up. God, Mum loved flowers. She knew the history, and the meaning of them all. Hence my name.' My smile faded. 'She wanted us to work together one day. I thought that's what would happen. But when she died, the shop was sold and I never could bring myself to do it without her.'

'Do you enjoy the office work?'

The question took me off guard. Neither Henry nor his father, nor anyone actually, over the past five years had asked me that. I shook my head. 'No, not really. I'm good at it but I don't enjoy it. It's just work.' I shrugged, wondering how many people really enjoyed their jobs. I knew Willow did but the farm was a vocation, a way of life, for her. It was different.

'That's a shame. I know how you feel, though. I never quite got into my stride working with Sarah. Maybe I will; it's early days. I mean, if we carry on. But I always thought I'd work with my father.'

'In the antiques shop?' I asked, wondering if he realised that his eyes had lit up from just mentioning it.

Blake nodded. 'My dad is so passionate about it, it rubbed off on me and I liked helping him out when I was younger and then after university, I sort of looked for other jobs but I enjoyed working with him too much to pursue them. He was upset when I left to work with Sarah, although he tried not to show it. My sister, on the other hand, was furious with me.'

'She doesn't work there too?'

'No. She and her husband run a riding school, hence why they have my horse right now. They have two kids so they are super busy. They still live in my family home with my dad, though, so they help him when he needs it. I feel far away from them even though geographically here on the farm, I'm really not.'

'You didn't want to stay with them after what happened with Sarah?'

'I upset them so much a year ago when I left them to be with Sarah. I'm not sure they want to see me. We speak on the phone sometimes but it hasn't been the same since. I don't know what to do.'

'They are your family, you don't want to lose them; believe me, I know,' I said softly.

'I'm sorry, Daisy; that must sound terrible when you have lost so much.'

'Families are tricky, I get that, but just don't do something you might regret one day.'

'You must miss your parents so much,' Blake said.

'I'll never be the same,' I said simply.

He nodded. 'Of course not.'

'Don't be too proud to go home, Blake. Yes, maybe it was a mistake with Sarah – you're not sure yet about that – but either way, you need them. And they need you.' He had no idea how lucky he was that they were out there for him to go home to if he wanted. I could never go home again. I was so grateful to my uncle and cousin right now but this had never been my home. I had no idea where I belonged any more.

'You're right. I'm being a coward avoiding them. I have been for the past year. It's been easier not to go home, especially as Sarah was never keen on visiting them after that first time.' He sighed. 'What if they were right about us? I have been careful and cautious my whole life; for once, I took a chance with my heart. Now I feel like I shouldn't take chances ever again.'

'Well, you can't think that way,' I said. 'If this doesn't end up working out then at least you tried, you went for it and followed your heart. You shouldn't feel bad about that at all. So many people don't take any chances in life and regret it. I wish I was more like you. I used to be but I don't think I can be now.' I once was fearless; now I tried to play it safe. To avoid what had happened to my parents happening to me maybe. They'd lived life to the full. But their lives had been cut short. Maybe I thought living smaller would mean living longer.

'Are you happy with the woman you are now?'

Blake's question hung between us for a long time as we turned back towards the farmhouse. The sun had faded fully now and the sky was turning darker by the minute. I could see the stars starting to show up. I found the North star, glowing brighter than the others, and remembered something my dad had told me once.

See that star, Daisy? That one used to guide people home. We've forgotten to let the stars guide us nowadays. But it can still give you hope in dark times. If you find that star in the sky, you will know that you can find your way back home.

I willed it to guide me home.

'No, Blake, I'm not. But I'm not sure how to change who I am.'

'Maybe it's not about changing who you are. But accepting it. And knowing that even if you are different to who you used to be, you still love yourself.' He sighed. 'I'm working on that too.'

We paused as we reached the path that would lead Blake into his cottage, and me onward to the farmhouse. Maple was already heading towards the door, eager for her bed.

'Maybe we can work on that together,' I suggested.

'Maybe. Goodnight, Daisy.'

I lifted my hand in a wave then followed Maple inside, feeling just a tiny bit less alone in the universe now.

17

The following morning, I joined Willow, Blake and Dylan out in the pick-your-own fields to start work on making the area ready for visitors. Henry had sent me a message to tell me he'd checked into the Birchbrook Arms and wanted us to have dinner once the work day was over. As he wasn't on our honeymoon as planned, his dad had given him work to do remotely and I had told him I'd promised to give Willow a hand so thankfully, it suited us both to stay apart for the day.

In the warming late-May sunshine, my panic last night with Henry seemed very far away and I was hoping I could push it all out of my mind and focus on helping on the farm. While Willow took charge marking out the trail we wanted visitors to walk along, and Blake and Dylan started to build an enclosure for the ponies near to the strawberries using the wood Willow had gathered, I set out to create the main photo opportunity in the strawberry fields. This would be the finale of the trail and we wanted it to look as good as possible.

Willow had really liked my idea of using the white bench we

bought and then creating a floral arch behind it. She had made a metal arch for her pumpkin patch tying autumn leaves and lights around it, so she had dug that out and I positioned it behind the bench. I set about cleaning them both as I looked around to see what everyone else was doing.

Willow was pushing a wheelbarrow with the pink stones she had bought for the trail over to lay them out. My uncle was trying to take the wheelbarrow to help but she was telling him to let go. I smiled as they argued about it. I looked over to where Dylan and Blake were building an enclosure for the two ponies. Blake had taken off his T-shirt. That made me pause in my cleaning. His chest was toned and tanned.

'I see you,' Willow said, making me jump. She had walked away from her dad as he raked out the stones she had put down, the wheelbarrow empty as she headed towards the barn to collect more stones, having won the argument.

'What?' I said, feeling my cheeks brighten even more than they already had from my work and the sun.

'It's okay to look; you are dating, after all,' Willow said with a teasing smile.

I shook my head. 'I can't believe we're in this situation.' I wasn't sure who was to blame – Blake, Willow or me – for Henry and Sarah thinking we were old friends reconnecting on the farm, and now dating, but it had sent Sarah away and done the opposite with Henry; he seemed determined to prove it was nothing. And I was confused as hell about what to do about any of it. 'I wish Henry had taken it as seriously as Sarah did.'

Maybe if he had done, I wouldn't have wobbled about leaving him like I had. Maybe he would no longer be in Birchbrook and I could do what Blake was doing: think for myself about what I wanted. But I had been too weak to force him to leave.

I was wrong; it felt like my mess. And I had no idea how to clear it up.

'He still might if you carry on eyeing Blake up like that,' Willow teased.

'I was not!' I replied indignantly, but I knew that wasn't convincing either of us.

'All I'm saying is, there are worst men in the world to pretend you're dating. I bet Henry is jealous. Blake is every woman's type, surely.'

'I'll tell Dylan that, shall I?' I teased her right back.

'I'm the exception, obviously,' she said. 'It won't do any harm if Henry has to change his ways if he wants to keep you, Daisy. You deserve to be treated like a princess, okay?' I heard the sincerity in her voice. And I thought about the look on her face yesterday when I told her Henry was staying on in Birchbrook. She didn't think I should go back with him, that was clear. And deep down, I knew she was right. I just wished I could tell the little voice of fear trying to persuade me otherwise to go away.

'You have to say that, you're family,' I joked as I didn't know what else to say. Then I let my smile slip. 'I don't know what I'm going to do.'

'It will work out how it's supposed to,' Willow promised. 'Birch Tree Farm can help anyone and anything, so let it do its magic.'

'I'm enjoying taking my mind off it all by doing this,' I said. I looked at the arch set up behind the bench, both clean and looking good. 'Now, we need the flowers. Can I borrow your car and go and find some? Where would be good to try?'

'The florist in town stocks faux flowers; the owner told me that so many people now want them, she'd rather they go there than one of the homeware shops outside of town.' Willow hesitated then lowered her voice. 'Are you sure about going in there, though?'

'Of course,' I replied breezily, although I had to admit, walking into flower shops always gave me a moment's pause, even all these years later. Memories of my mother always came flooding through.

'Willow, we need paint!' Blake yelled over then. He started to walk towards us. 'I think we should paint the pony enclosure white to match Daisy's bench,' he added, gesturing to my set-up.

Willow beamed at him. 'That's such a good idea.'

'Dylan thought of it,' Blake said. 'I had to supervise building the enclosure but he knows what looks good,' he added with a shrug.

Willow chuckled. 'What can I say? I fell in love with a man who's obsessed with his laptop, but he now has had to embrace farm work. I just have to keep whipping him into shape.' She dropped me a wink before taking her keys out of her pocket and tossing them over to me. 'Why don't you both go into town? You can look for flowers, Daisy, and Blake – you could get white paint from the DIY shop as we don't have any here. Kill two birds with one stone.' She strode off before either of us had a chance to disagree.

I looked at Blake. 'I suppose that is a good idea?' I asked, wondering how it would be between us if we went into town. We didn't know each other well but were connected by our relationship drama. I'd been more honest with him than I had with Henry, which made no sense, but also hadn't felt weird. Blake was easy to be around. To be *myself* around.

Blake smiled. 'Yeah, works for me. Can we get a coffee too? I'll be needing a strong one to get this enclosure finished.'

'An iced coffee would go down a treat,' I agreed and we fell into step to walk back towards Willow's four-by-four, which was parked outside the farmhouse. 'Have you heard from Sarah since she left?'

'No, nothing,' Blake said, sounding relieved. 'What about Henry?' he asked as we climbed into the car.

'We're planning to have dinner together. He's working all day too. I don't know how I feel about seeing him later, to be honest.' I started the engine and we set off for Birchbrook town.

'Want to talk about it?'

'Not really. You?' I said, glancing at him before we left the farm.

'Nope.' He smiled at me. 'Okay, let's talk about something else. How's your photo set-up coming along?'

'I think it'll work well. I just need to find the right flowers for it. Unfortunately, it doesn't make sense to get real ones with them being outside in the heat of the day, so I need to find faux ones that look good. It means going to the florist in town, which always brings back memories of my mum.'

'What was her flower shop like?'

'I haven't thought about it in so long.' I could remember it perfectly, though. 'It was right in the heart of where we lived. It had a green and gold sign outside. There was a bell on the door. And a sign shaped like a daisy that said *Open* or *Closed*. Mum had it made especially. The shop was crammed with flowers. The smell hit you even before you opened the door. She kept them outside too. Any space possible. And in the middle of the shop was her counter with the till, and she had a cuckoo clock on the wall that struck every hour. I used to go in every day once school had finished. She always had the radio on and would sing along while she made up bouquets for people. I know she had to get up early for the flower market – running a small business was hard even back then, let alone nowadays – but she seemed to be so passionate about it, you know?'

Blake nodded 'My dad is the same. He lives and breathes that shop. It has this distinct smell. Old but clean. Like it has all these secrets and memories. I enter and I just relax instantly. I guess it's the nostalgia of spending so much of my childhood in there. I loved hearing the stories behind everything he sells too.'

I nodded. 'Mum would tell me why someone had ordered a bouquet and why she had included the flowers she had chosen for them.'

'Do you know why she called you Daisy?'

'Each flower has a few meanings but Mum said the one that struck her with daisy was "new beginnings". She and my dad tried for a long time to have a baby so when they had me, they saw it as a new beginning, plus she bought her flower shop while she was pregnant. So, she felt like it was a new beginning both personally and professionally.' I sighed. 'The irony, right? I'm named after new beginnings, but I'm struggling with change and the future... Anyway, what about you? Does Blake have any significance?'

'My dad liked William Blake's poems. He used to read them to my mum when she was pregnant.'

'You don't mention your mother much,' I observed as I found a parking space on the High Street close to the café.

Blake sighed as I stopped the car. 'I don't really see her now. My parents got divorced when I was young and she lives up north. My sister and I stayed with my dad. Some people thought that was unusual at the time. But we were closer to him and settled there. I suppose sometimes, we did wonder why she was happy to move so far away from us.' He looked startled then. 'I don't think I've told anyone that before.'

'I've spilled enough of my dark secrets to you,' I said, taking my seatbelt off. I couldn't help but feel pleased that he wanted to confide in me like I was doing with him. It felt so easy between us somehow.

'Your secrets aren't dark, Daisy. You've had a lot happen to you, yes. But you, yourself, could never be dark,' Blake said, his eyes steady on mine.

18

Blake's words echoed around my mind.

You could never be dark.

We hardly knew each other but he said those words with confidence regardless.

'Thank you,' I whispered. There was definitely something calming, something reassuring, about this man. I smiled. 'Shall we?' I was feeling more than a little unnerved at how he saw me. I wondered how long it had been since I felt like someone really did see me.

Jumping out of the car, I forced myself to focus on my surroundings and not Blake. I'd been in such frantic state when I first came back here, I hadn't taken much in.

Birchbrook High Street was as quaint and pretty as it had been when I used to visit in my childhood. Each shop and business had a hanging basket from a hook to the side of it bursting full of colourful flowers. Birchbrook Café also had pots of pretty flowers outside the shop. Hanging across the High Street, tied to the lampposts, was triangle bunting in pastel colours, the sky a perfect blue above it.

'It's so pretty here, I forgot,' I said half to myself.

'I can see why Dylan wanted to move here. My hometown is like this too. I do miss it being in the city now.'

I nodded. 'Me too. I grew up not far from Birchbrook, and spent a lot of time here then. Henry and his family live on the edge of the city; it's so different.' My eyes fell on the florist. 'Shall we meet back at the café when we've got what we came for? Say in an hour?'

'Perfect,' Blake agreed, lifting his hand in a wave as he headed off towards the hardware shop to find paint. I turned to go to the flower shop, steeling myself for the inevitable memories it would stir up. I had told Blake what my mother's shop had been like. I don't think I'd ever told Henry that. He hadn't asked me, though.

I realised then that he hadn't asked much about my life before him. It hadn't really bothered me as my past was such that it was often easier to try not to even think about it. But strangely, talking about my mum's shop just now with Blake hadn't wrecked me. It had almost been nice to think about it again. The trouble was grief and sadness had made me forget some of the happy times. And I really didn't want that to be the case.

Birchbrook Flowers was a haven for all pink lovers. The sign was dusky pink and cream, and the window was bordered with pink stencilling and white flowers. Outside was a pink bike covered with flowers bursting out of the basket.

Pushing open the door, the bell sounded just like it would have done if I had been walking into my mother's old place. It was also a small shop with buckets of flowers on all sides, the owner behind the counter tying a pink ribbon around a posy of daisies. I did a double take. I wasn't a massive believer in signs really. But that felt like one.

'Good afternoon,' the woman greeted from behind the

counter, looking up from the flowers she was arranging with a warm smile. She had shoulder-length, grey hair and black-rimmed glasses, and I immediately warmed to her.

'Your shop is so pretty,' I said, looking around, the scent of roses and lilies mixed with lavender and gardenia filling my nostrils. 'I'm helping out at Birch Tree Farm and I need flowers for an arch we're putting up for the pick-your-own season. A photo opportunity. I'd prefer not to use fake ones but they won't stay fresh for long in the heat. Willow said you might have some faux flowers or know where I could get some really good ones?'

She smiled. 'I went to Willow's Pumpkin Hollow last year and it was lots of fun. I knew she'd up her game this summer season.' She stepped out from behind the counter. 'I carry faux flowers and can easily get more for you at my wholesaler. Come out back with me.' She gestured to the room behind the counter. 'I'll give you business rates as I do for all the local businesses here. We have to support each other.' Then she peered more closely at me. 'You look familiar, but you don't live here?'

Willow always said everyone in Birchbrook knew each other and could spot a newcomer a mile away. I smiled. 'I spent some time here growing up, Willow is my cousin. I'm Daisy Connor.'

'I knew your mother!' She clapped her hands in delight. 'I knew I recognised you; you look so much like she did.' Her smile faded. 'Sorry, maybe I shouldn't have...'

'No, no, it's fine, it's nice,' I assured her. 'How did you know my mother?' I asked, eager to hear about her suddenly.

'I've run this shop for almost all my adult life, and I got friendly with Willow's mother and father when they moved here. So, when your mother came to stay, I would see her. Your mother wanted to run her own flower shop so she used to grill me about this place a lot,' she added with a fond smile. 'One time, she showed up pregnant with you and asked if she could help out for free as she'd put in an offer for a shop and was nervous about it. She thought if she spent a couple of weeks here not doing anything, she'd freak out, as she put it. So, she came to help a couple of hours every day. A lovely woman.'

I nodded. 'She was. She loved that shop she bought. It was sold after...' I trailed off and turned to look at some roses to swallow the lump that had risen in my throat.

'That's a shame. Well, now, let's see about these flowers,' she said, gesturing for me to follow her, sensing I was getting emotional. 'I'm Mary, by the way.'

'Daisy,' I said.

'New beginnings.'

'That's right,' I said, impressed she knew the meaning, especially the one that had meant so much to my mum.

Mary looked over at me, and seemed to be a bit misty-eyed herself. 'We talked about what she might name her daughter. I've always loved the meaning of flowers, and your mum did too, so we discussed it a lot. I'm glad she went with Daisy. You suit it, dear.'

I smiled, pleased she thought so.

Mary led me then into the other room where there were pots of faux flowers stems. 'I never thought I'd sell faux flowers but I kept being asked for them. I make arrangements in vases for home décor and also sell stems for people who want to create their own displays. It does brilliantly at Christmas and in spring. Less in summer so I have a fair few in stock. Did you have a colour scheme in mind for the arch?'

'Pink, purple and white with greenery mixed in,' I said as I picked up one. It was really good quality for a faux stem. Some of them you'd be hard pressed to clock as being fake apart from the fact they didn't have a fragrance. The eucalyptus was particularly convincing.

'That will work perfectly on the farm. You could also have a couple of yellow in there maybe; that would look pretty...' She bustled around, showing me various stems, and I stood for a moment, watching her. The resemblance to my mother was uncanny. My mother had obviously learned a lot from Mary. The thought popped into my head that maybe I could learn from her too.

But that made no sense.

I didn't need to learn anything about flowers, or a flower shop. I was just helping out Willow for a bit before going back to my office work life.

* * *

An hour later, I had to leave the shop to meet Blake. It had been so fun choosing flowers but also listening to Mary talking about the shop and the town and sharing memories of my mother too. Mary helped me load everything I had bought into Willow's car and told me to call her if I needed any more and she'd go to her wholesaler for me. I had pretty much cleared her out of faux flowers.

Mary also told me to come into the shop again while I was still in town, and I already knew I would go back. After she left me, I felt lighter.

When Blake joined me at the car, the afternoon sunshine was dazzling us.

'Got the paint. How did you get on?' he asked, gesturing to the tins of paint he held in each hand. I unlocked the car so he could put it in the boot.

'Actually, it was nice. Mary met my mum years ago, she even worked in the shop for a bit, and she said we looked alike. That was nice to hear.'

'You'll have to show me a photo of your mum,' he said, closing the boot. 'Ready for coffee?'

'Definitely.'

We walked over and Blake held the café door open for me to step inside. It was still the quaint café it had been when I used to visit Birchbrook. There were round tables with baby-blue gingham cloths on and a small vase of pretty flowers on each. Like the High Street outside, colourful bunting was strung across the wall behind the counter where three people stood. In front of them was an array of yummy-looking treats that instantly made my mouth water and stomach rumble.

'Hi, Pat,' Blake greeted the woman behind the counter, who smiled as we approached.

I raised an eyebrow. 'You just arrived and you already know everyone?'

'I chat to people,' he replied with a shrug.

'Hi again,' I added to Pat, short for Patricia, who owned the café with her husband, who was also called Pat, short for Patrick. It was a bit confusing.

'Daisy, we heard you were back in town,' female Pat said to me.

'Plus Daisy was in here the other day in her wedding dress,' a dry voice said behind her. I glanced at the man who looked around our age with a scruffy beard and hair, making a coffee at the machine. I recognised him to be their son.

Pat turned around. 'Yes, okay, Paul, I was trying not to refer to that, actually,' she said crossly. 'Sons, who would have them? Anyway, you're both staying at Birch Tree Farm for a bit, I hear?'

I nodded, glad she had moved away from the topic of my wedding dress at least. I could feel a few curious eyes in the café on me, though. 'Yes, I'm helping Willow out with the pick-your-own season.'

'Oh, how lovely. I think we'll have our café van there like we did for the pumpkin patch. Paul is looking forward to it, aren't you?'

He just rolled his eyes.

'Anyway, what can I get you both?' she asked us brightly, as if Paul had given her an excited reply.

Blake ordered a latte and I asked for an iced one. 'Now, Pat,' Blake continued, 'all your food looks so good; what shall we try?'

I watched him talking with her and thought about Sarah telling him his conversation on dating apps had been rubbish. He seemed confident and friendly here. He ordered a piece of lavender-flavoured shortbread and a slice of strawberry cheese-cake and refused to let me pay for anything. 'Why don't we sit in and have these? We deserve a break,' he suggested.

'Okay, sure.' I was happy to sit down for a bit. Working outside on the farm was using muscles I hadn't used for anything other than in a yoga class that Henry's mum had dragged me to. We found a table by the window where the sun was shining in and when I took a sip of my iced latte and tried a bite of the treats, I remembered instantly why everyone loved this place so much.

'Good, right?' he said. 'I stopped in on my way to the farm, and I've popped in every day since so far.' He smiled at the expression on my face. 'I'll put on a stone while I'm here at this rate.'

'I doubt it; you're so tall, you can probably eat anything and be fine.'

'When I was young, my dad said I'd eat him out of house and home; I haven't changed much since.' He shrugged.

'You got yourself a fan back there,' I added softly, nodding back towards female Pat, who was telling her husband they needed to order more coffee beans, but was definitely keeping an eye on Blake.

'I have?' Blake looked confused.

I chuckled. 'You are a bit clueless when it comes to women, aren't you?' I couldn't resist teasing him. I thought about how Willow said he would be every woman's type; Blake hadn't got that memo. Which was a relief. It meant he wasn't at all arrogant. It was kind of sweet, actually.

Blake took a sip of coffee to hide the blush on his cheeks but I clocked it. 'Well, maybe, yeah. I have always been a bit shy around women. At school, Dylan told me once that I could never tell if a girl was flirting with me. I think maybe that's still the case.'

'Is that what Sarah meant when you matched with her on a dating app?' I thought the two of them seemed to be a very unlikely pair but somehow, they had come together so there must be more than I was seeing.

Blake sighed. 'Yeah. She said my messages were dry and asked if I was actually interested in her. I thought I had been flirting! I guess talking online has never been easy for me. I didn't want to try dating apps at all, but my sister made me do it, and filled the profile out for me. I've always been better face to face, but it's so hard to meet people now. Sarah used so many emojis, I had trouble deciphering what she was saying, to be honest,' he said with wide eyes. 'I told her I was interested and when we met up, it was easier. She was so talkative, I didn't have to worry too much about the conversation and she told me she liked that I was quiet.'

It was on the tip of my tongue to tell him she probably liked anyone who didn't disagree with her, but I kept that opinion to myself. 'You're not quiet with me. But I guess that's because we're only fake dating, right?' I said with a laugh.

'You don't make me nervous,' he replied softly. 'You're easy to talk to,' Blake said then, which stopped me laughing.

It was nice to hear. 'But if we were dating for real, you would be nervous?'

'I don't know. Not now that I know you. I don't know what would have happened if we'd also met on an app. Were you nervous when you started seeing Henry?'

Considering his question for a second, I shook my head. 'No. Maybe because I wasn't sure if I was interested in dating him. He asked me out and I took a while to say yes, and then...' I hesitated. 'Maybe I kind of went along with who he thought I was, and didn't let him see who I really am. So, I wasn't nervous because I didn't put my heart on the line.'

'You were scared to,' Blake said, no needing to phrase it as a question.

'Yes,' I whispered. I exhaled. Things with Blake always seemed to get deep quickly. 'Maybe we should move on from our complicated love lives,' I said lightly then. It felt dangerous to be revealing this much suddenly.

Dangerous for my heart.

'Sure,' he readily agreed. 'When we get back, I'll start painting the pony enclosure. Then we can move the ponies in and do some practice rides with them. I don't think Dylan is looking forward to me leaving, when he'll have to take that over. He's never been a horsey person. But when Willow puts her mind to something, she seems to see it through to the end, right? Dylan admires that about her too, I can tell.'

I nodded. 'She was like that even when we were kids. I envy that about her now. I find it hard to make decisions. To trust myself, I guess, to actually make them.'

'You recently made a huge decision, though,' he observed.

'Hmm. Yeah, but look what I've done since... Henry is here

and I didn't ask him to leave. I haven't got the time and space I'd wanted when I left our wedding.'

'I meant what I said about being here for you, Daisy. If you ever want to talk or anything. I like talking to you.'

I smiled. 'Me too.' I couldn't help but reach over and put my hand over his.

Blake's fingers entwined with mine. We both looked down at our hands. They felt comfortable being linked together.

'Oh my God,' Blake said under his breath then as he looked out of the window behind me.

I turned to follow his gaze and saw Sarah and Henry standing outside the café watching us with matching angry expressions on their faces.

19

'Why is she here?' Blake asked as we quickly moved our hands away from each other while Henry and Sarah came inside.

'This is very cosy,' Sarah said as she marched up to the table, throwing a glare at me then at Blake. 'Henry said I was wrong about the two of you!'

'I thought you'd gone back to the city,' Blake said, confused.

'I was about to but I stopped for a matcha latte, which they don't do, can you believe?! And then Henry came in and said he was staying because *she* said there was nothing going on between you two. And I thought then I would try again with us. So I booked into the pub to stay too,' Sarah said in an angry rush.

'No, I didn't say nothing was going on... I'm confused,' I said, hating that Blake looked so frantic to see Sarah was still here too. Bloody Henry. He had clearly fired her up to stay in town.

'I'm confused as well,' Blake said. 'I thought we agreed to have some time apart?'

'Well, I'm not going anywhere now.' Sarah crossed her arms.

'If you think I'm letting her have *my* man, you have another thing coming!'

'And you belong with me,' Henry added to me.

I looked across at Blake. He seemed just as lost as me. They were clearly not planning on giving either of us space or time. 'God, we just came into town for paint and flowers,' I said, frustrated. 'Maybe we could all chill out a bit? People are staring,' I added, feeling the two Pats and Paul giving us curious glances.

Henry looked down at me. 'Why are you getting flowers?' he asked.

'I told you, I'm helping my cousin on her farm,' I told him.

'You're working on a farm?!' He scoffed at the very idea.

'I'm helping my family out on the farm, yes,' I snapped. Why did he seem so surprised? 'You know, I grew up around here, I helped on the farm when I was younger, and flowers are kind of my thing, aren't they?'

'You always love the roses I buy you,' he replied with a satisfied smile.

'Her mum was a florist,' Blake said as he glared at Henry.

I looked at him in surprise. There was that blush again.

Henry turned too, eyebrow raised. 'What does that have to do with anything?'

Wow, did Henry really not remember anything I had told him about my mum?

'Blakey, I've had a breakthrough with our app,' Sarah butted in, clearly not wanting to be left out. 'We need to talk about it, okay? Work is different to what's going with us, right?'

'I guess,' Blake muttered, seeming as tired as I suddenly felt.

'Let's talk about it while you walk me back to the pub then you can go back to the farm if you need to, I guess. But we can spend the evening together, can't we?' Sarah asked him.

'We're having dinner,' Henry said quickly, giving me a look that dared me to disagree.

'Yes, I know,' I replied, irritated.

'Come on, Blakey,' Sarah said, before flouncing off. She muttered under her breath about needing a matcha latte.

Blake sighed but got up. He glanced at me. 'I'll see you back at the farm later?'

I nodded and watched him follow Sarah out, wondering why that felt so wrong to me.

I didn't want Henry to get comfy so I jumped up before he could think about ordering and sitting down. 'I need to go back now. Willow is waiting for me.'

'I'll pick you up for dinner then?' Henry asked, trailing after me as I headed for the door. I wanted to get away from Sarah and Blake. I wanted to get back out into the fresh air and sunshine, and back on the farm where I could breathe properly and think clearly. 'I'll take you somewhere. I don't want to eat with your family or those two,' he said after we left the café. 'I just want to be with you alone. We have a lot to talk about still.'

It was the opposite of what I wanted but I was aware that he was staying here to be with me. I couldn't really refuse after I hadn't asked him to go home so I nodded. 'Sure, come at seven; I'll be ready.'

'You really look so different with your hair like that,' he said as I reached Willow's car, opened the driver's door and climbed in. 'See you later.'

He waved and set off, not going back into the café but walking back towards the pub.

I glanced at my reflection in the rear-view mirror. I touched my hair. I looked different. That wasn't a compliment, was it? Henry clearly wasn't a fan of the cut but I liked it. I realised then how Mary had recognised me so easily. My mum had had her hair this length and style when she had been pregnant with me. I looked much more like her now. That made me feel a whole lot better.

* * *

'Wow, Daisy,' Willow said as twilight hit. I stepped back from the archway as she looked at what I had done so far. 'It's so pretty already!'

'Mary helped me pick the perfect flowers,' I said, looking at what I had draped across the archway so far. It was almost half-done. Once I'd returned to the farm, I'd set to work immediately and it was a wrench to have to leave it for the day but I knew I needed to get ready to eat with Henry. 'I still can't believe my mum helped out in her shop years ago. I felt closer to her today than I have been for years.' I glanced at Willow. 'I've been scared of the memories here. But now, I wish I'd come back to Birchbrook ages ago.'

Willow smiled. 'Me too but I understood why you stayed away. I love the fact I walk every day the same steps my mum walked. Yes, it can be painful when things happen that I know she would have enjoyed, like the pumpkin patch or me getting the ponies,' she said with a mischievous grin. 'Or the fact she'll never meet Dylan. But being here in our home still means so much to me. She loved the farm and I know she would have been proud and happy to see me still here.'

I sighed. 'I wish my mum would have been proud of me too, but I can't see it.'

'You need to give yourself some grace. She would be proud to see you back here on the farm helping us out. And how beautiful this flower arch will be. Your mum would definitely be proud of that.' She touched my shoulder before walking off. I looked at my work and I did let myself smile. I think my mum would have liked it too. But I was still unsure if she would be proud. I felt incredibly lost. The future seemed so uncertain.

I walked back to the farmhouse and had a shower, after which I pulled on one of the floral summer dresses I had bought with Willow. I thought about Blake asking if I had been nervous about dating Henry. I had protected myself from the start and that meant I hadn't felt nervous or had butterflies. I had just become the woman Henry wanted me to be. I hadn't had to wonder if he loved who I was; I had hidden that from him. I hadn't wanted an epic love story. It had been enough to feel safe and secure.

But as I got ready now, it didn't feel right not to have butterflies, or be excited to see him. It felt wrong that when I heard his car on the driveway and left the farmhouse to go out to him, I didn't feel anything at all.

I climbed into his car. He wore a blue shirt and dark trousers combo I'd seen many times before, his aftershave as familiar as my own perfume.

'Where are we headed?'

'Well, there is a distinct lack of French restaurants around here,' Henry said as he pulled back out of the driveway. I looked over at the cottages but there was no sign of Blake. I wondered whether he was eating with Sarah and if he felt butterflies before going out with her. 'But I found an Italian that has pretty decent reviews about half an hour away. At least we can get a better bottle of wine there than in the Birchbrook Arms.' He shook his head at what he thought was a poor wine list, clearly. 'You're lucky I love you, Daisy; that's all I can say.' He grinned across at me but I couldn't bring myself to return it. I wasn't at all sure how he could believe he was in love with me.

On the journey to the restaurant, Henry talked about work.

His father had already employed a new assistant, clearly lined up prior to our wedding to cover my honeymoon, but I assumed they'd all planned to keep her on after that as I was meant to want to give up my job for married life. 'Mum had a good idea for you, though,' he said as I started to zone out. I looked over at him with trepidation. 'You could start a charity together,' Henry said excitedly. 'So, you could organise parties and dinners, all sorts of fundraisers. That would give you something to do alongside starting our family, right?'

Startled, I eyed him. 'But I told you that was the reason I called off the wedding: you all deciding my future for me.'

'I don't know why you're being so difficult,' he replied. 'Any woman would give their right arm to be part of our family. You could have everything you want. You could still work on the charity and have a family: the best of both worlds, right?'

I thought about all the charity dinners I'd gone with him to. Fancy black-tie events where it was all about being seen, nothing to do with what the charity actually was raising money for, and my heart sank that he thought that was something I'd enjoy doing. It was like he couldn't understand why I wouldn't want to be like everyone else he knew. I ignored the work thing and focused on the family. 'I don't know if I want to have children,' I said. I wasn't sure I could handle the anxiety that would come with it. The fear of losing someone so close to me again. That was the reason I'd protected my heart from Henry. I couldn't do that with a baby. It all felt too much right now to cope with.

'Daisy, you don't really mean that...' Henry trailed off as we both saw something up ahead.

On the side of the road, a car was on the verge, the bonnet open and a figure ducked under it.

'Shall we pull over?' I asked.

Henry tutted, clearly not wanting to.

'Henry, we can't just drive by.'

'Fine, fine.' He pulled in behind the car and we both climbed out.

'Need some help?' Henry called over as I realised I recognised the car.

Blake ducked out from under the bonnet and glanced at me then Henry then me again. 'Oh, hi.'

'Jesus,' Henry muttered, shooting me a glare.

'What's happened?' I asked Blake, ignoring Henry.

'Dylan warned me my car might be useless on these country roads. He won't give his up but rarely drives it any more, he said. Look at that mud...' He gestured to the mud we hadn't yet reached. 'I swerved to miss it and then bumped against this hedge, and everything spluttered and stopped. There may have been some smoke too...' He grimaced. 'I have no signal to call anyone out here.'

'Bloody countryside,' Henry said, looking at me with a *what have you got me into* expression.

I pulled my phone out. 'No signal for me either.' I looked at Henry, who put his hands in his pockets, not bothering to check his phone. 'We can drive you back to the farm and then you can call someone to get your car from there,' I suggested, ignoring Henry, my heart undeniably lifting at the thought of having to change our plans to help Blake.

Blake raised an eyebrow. 'Aren't you going out?' His eyes flicked over my dress briefly.

'Yes, we are,' Henry said, taking hold of my arm. 'Let's go before we lose our reservation.'

'We can't just leave Blake here. There's no other option. Let's all head back to the farm,' I said. 'My uncle always makes loads of food so we can just all eat there together.'

'For fuck's sake,' Henry said, turning around and stalking back to his car.

'Are you sure about this?' Blake asked under his breath.

'I'm not going to just leave you here. Where were you heading anyway?'

'Sarah wanted me to get us some food so we can carry on talking about the app but I'll tell her to meet us at the farm too then. I appreciate this, Daisy. You saved me,' he said as we followed Henry back to his car.

'I think you might have saved me instead,' I muttered.

He looked across at me in surprise and I couldn't meet his gaze. But my lack of belief in signs was starting to wobble. I had felt stuck in that car with Henry as he planned our life out for us, and the universe had found a way for me to avoid it all, and I was so relieved.

Climbing into the passenger seat, Henry avoiding my gaze, I leaned back in the seat and let out a long exhale. Blake jumped in too and we turned around and went back to Birch Tree Farm.

* * *

'This time last year, it was just you and me rolling around this place on our own,' Uncle Adam joked as he passed Willow the jug of homemade lemonade.

Once we got back, Blake arranged for a local garage to tow his car and fix it. My uncle had made plenty of food as I'd predicated so once Sarah arrived from the pub, we all sat down together: Willow, Dylan and my uncle, Henry, Sarah, Blake and me. Maple was curled up in her bed in the corner keeping an eye on us. Adam had made a delicious chicken and courgette lemon pasta, and there was plenty for us all. He was smiling, happy to have a houseful even if not everyone around the table was enjoying the impromptu meal like he was.

'Now we're full to the brim,' Willow said, shaking her head. 'Is what happened to Blake making you think twice about keeping your car?' she joked to Dylan.

'I have to admit, I use it less and less,' he said. 'But the thought of giving it up...'

'You're not going anywhere though, right?' she asked, tilting her head.

Dylan reached for her arm and stroked it. 'You're stuck with me, baby.'

'Oh, what a shame.'

I looked away from them and at Henry who was opposite me and definitely sulking. He picked at his pasta like he couldn't bring himself to enjoy it even though it was delicious. I shifted my gaze from him onto Sarah, who was also sulking because she wasn't eating alone with Blake. She too picked at the pasta as if carbs were her enemy.

When I turned back the other way, Blake caught my eye, like he also had been looking at Henry and Sarah. His mouth twitched like he was trying not to laugh and I hid my smirk by scooping up another mouthful of food.

'Well, I'm grateful Daisy and Henry were around to rescue me,' Blake said. 'I was about to attempt the walk back to the farm. It would have taken at least an hour.'

'We need to harden you city folk up,' Willow said, accentuating her accent for effect. 'An hour's walk is nothing. I do that every morning around the farm.' She rolled her eyes. 'You're all too delicate.'

Blake and I laughed. 'Fair point,' he replied affably.

'It was very convenient for you to be at the side of the road we were driving along,' Henry suddenly said. 'Anyone would think you two had planned it,' he added, looking at me and Blake.

That caught Sarah's attention. 'What do you mean?'

'You promised me a dinner together to talk about repairing our relationship but there is your "old friend" waiting to ambush us.' Henry ignored her, doing cringey air quotes.

'It definitely wasn't planned,' I said. 'I was as surprised as you were to see Blake. It was an accident. And we helped him out, which I would have suggested we do for anyone.'

'But this is the man you claim to be dating,' Henry pointed out.

'I'm sorry but are the two of you dating or not?' Sarah said then. 'He's right. We were meant to eat together too,' she said, pointing to Blake. 'So maybe you two did cook it all up so we'd get stuck here all together again.'

'Charming,' Willow muttered. 'They make a much better couple than they did with you two,' she added, louder.

'Willow...' I began, uncomfortable with all the lying and anger around the table.

'Sarah, I know we have to talk about work but I asked for time about us. You were with someone else,' Blake said. 'You cheated on me. I left. You can't be pissed off with me.' His calmness was cracking now. And I didn't blame him.

'He didn't mean anything!' she cried. 'I keep telling you that.'

Blake shook his head. 'How can I trust that?'

'I'd never cheat on you,' Henry cut in smoothly to me. 'You know you can trust me.'

'Can I say something here?' my uncle saved me from responding. He spoke with calm authority and we all turned to him. 'There seems to be a lot of hurt feelings and no one is at their best right now. I suggest you all park this now. And both Blake and Daisy seem to be asking for space. It would be respectful to give them that, wouldn't it?' he said gently to Sarah and Henry.

'But they will be here together,' Sarah said.

'Maybe that's what they need right now,' Adam suggested.

'This is bullshit.' Henry stood up abruptly. He looked down at me. 'You said we'd spend time together tonight and you've gone back on that. I won't listen to them any more,' he added, gesturing dismissively at the rest of the table. 'Please see me out at the very least?'

'Daisy, you don't have to,' Willow said quickly.

Guilt settled on me, though. I had said we'd eat together. And Henry had been part of my life for five years. I stood up. 'It's okay, let's go.' I followed him outside.

'I feel really confused, Henry,' I said before he could say anything more. 'I know I asked you to stay. It was wrong of me when I don't know what to do.'

He sighed. 'I just want us to go back to how we were.'

'But we can't. I keep telling you that we want different things. And I never let myself love you. Or let you love the real me.' I honestly didn't know if I could have loved Henry if I had been open to it. The way he was behaving right now made that seem unlikely. I was seeing more sides to him that I didn't appreciate. 'How about this? My uncle is right that we're going round in circles. Give me some space; how about you give me tomorrow to think and then I'll meet you the day after, okay?'

Henry sighed. 'I suppose my dad does want me to have a meeting tomorrow. If I don't see you tomorrow, you promise me we can be alone afterwards, properly, and sort this out once and for all?'

He still seemed confident I would choose him. I nodded, relieved I'd be able to sort my head out. 'I promise.'

'I'll convince you that the right thing is to be with me.' He leaned in to kiss me but I turned my head so he had to kiss my cheek. 'I'll wait then. I just want you back, Daisy. I have to be persistent. I always am.'

I had the feeling that he just didn't want to lose like he never wanted to lose. It didn't feel like this was about me. But about him. I nodded, though. I was too tired now. 'I promise.'

Sarah came out of the farmhouse then. 'Can I have a lift back to the pub, please?' she asked Henry, avoiding my gaze.

'Sure, come on.'

I watched them walk off together and my chest sagged with relief. I never thought when I called off our wedding that things would become even more complicated and confusing, but they really were.

Heading back inside, I returned to the table. 'Thank you,' I said to my uncle. 'That was so tense.'

'I don't like to see any of you unhappy,' Adam said. 'I hope you all follow your hearts. You know how you feel. Don't let anyone make you feel differently out of obligation or fear or guilt.'

Blake and I looked at one another.

The rest of the meal was far more peaceful. Willow chatted about the farm with Dylan and my uncle while Blake and I were quiet. It felt like it had been the longest day.

Blake rubbed his shoulder. 'I ache everywhere.'

'You work muscles you didn't know existed being on a farm,' Willow told him.

'Who needs a fancy gym membership?' Blake tried to smile but it didn't fully work.

'I haven't been to a gym since I moved in here,' Dylan said down the table to him. 'Farm work is the best workout you can have.'

'Maybe not the best workout,' Willow said in a low voice.

'I'll pretend I didn't hear that,' Uncle Adam spluttered.

Willow and Dylan giggled like teenagers and it helped; I smiled and so did Blake, and some of our tension faded.

Willow sighed then. 'Crap, I forgot to put the ponies into the barn for the night. It's meant to rain so I don't want to leave them outside.'

'I can do it,' Blake said readily.

'I'll come too,' I said. 'I better cover the flower arch if it's going to rain a lot,' I added. 'There's spare tarpaulin in the barn, right?' I asked Willow.

'Yep, use whatever you like.'

Blake and I headed out to the barn together.

'Did I ruin your evening with my car issues?' Blake asked me as I hunted for the tarpaulin to cover the archway up.

'I was relieved to get out of the dinner with Henry. Is that bad?'

'No. I'm glad that Adam seems to have convinced Sarah to give me some space. Maybe I've let her have hope about us getting back together but it's hard. She was my life for a year. And you and Henry had five years.'

'Yeah. My uncle said follow your heart but that is really terrifying.'

Blake met my gaze. 'Tell me about it.'

I went to pick up the tarpaulin but Blake got there first. 'Thanks.'

'Come on, let's go to the field.'

We left the barn and Blake seemed to be considering what I had said. 'When we first got together, I wanted to spend all my time with Sarah; I loved it when it was just us. Now, I don't want to be alone with her. When I am, all I can do is think about her with that man I saw in our apartment.'

'I get that. Do you think you can ever forgive her?'

'Maybe it's more that I'm not sure I want to. What about you and Henry?'

'Before we spotted you on the side of the road, Henry was still talking about the future he sees for us. He hasn't listened to anything I've been saying to him since our wedding day! He still hasn't asked me what I want.'

We headed around the farmhouse out towards the strawberry fields. 'What do you want, Daisy?' Blake asked me then.

I let that question sink in as we reached the archway. Blake dropped the tarpaulin and together, we covered up the arch. I thought about my mum and how much she had loved being a mother, how much she'd loved my dad, their pretty house in the village, and how much she had loved her flower shop...

I turned to Blake with fire in my eyes. 'I want someone who makes me feel certain. I want to be excited for the future, not scared by it. I want to love and feel loved. I don't want to be alone. But I don't want to be with someone just because I'm lonely. I want to feel passionate about my life. I want to make my parents proud of me. I don't want to feel anxious or to panic. I want to be able to breathe. I want to be happy. I want to just be...' I said, all in a rush, my chest heaving. I sucked in a breath as I looked at Blake, who was watching me like there was nothing else that was more important to look at right now. 'I want to just be me.'

'Daisy...' he said huskily, stepping closer to me. He touched my cheek gently with his fingertips, his eyes searching mine for something. 'I want that too. All of it. I have felt so lost. I thought it was ever since I walked in and found Sarah with *him*, but I think it's been since I left my hometown and my dad and his shop and my sister for this life that I'm not sure I want. But weirdly, standing here right now with you, I don't feel as lost any more.'

My heart soared inside my chest. I looked up at him and smiled as realisation hit me. 'I don't feel as lost right now either.'

Blake leaned down so slowly, so cautiously, his eyes fixed on mine like he was waiting for me to pull back, to stop him, to look away, to do anything, but I didn't want to move or speak or hide from his gaze. I wanted him to see me. I wanted to see him. I wanted this moment, whatever it was.

When his face was finally close enough, he brushed his lips against mine. Just once. So soft. So gentle. So delicate. And yet I felt it...

Everywhere.

20

Blake pulled back to look at me. 'Was that okay?' he asked anxiously.

'No,' I said.

'Shit, I'm—'

'I need more,' I interrupted before he could spiral and step away from me.

Blake's lips curved into a small smile. His eyes shone in the golden-hour light round us. 'More, huh? I think I can oblige...' He leaned back down and touched my lips again. His kiss was still soft and careful but it sent a sweet heat through my body. He wrapped his arms around my waist and I stood on tiptoes so I could put mine around his broad shoulders as I kissed him back, enjoying his lips like they were sweet, juicy strawberries. And they tasted just as delicious. Blake was tall and he felt strong but he touched me so gently, I felt weirdly like I could cry. Which would have been really embarrassing.

Blake leaned back again and reached out to touch my hair. 'I thought when I first saw you in that wedding dress, you had been sent by the universe to torture me,' he said in that same gruff voice he had said my name in. It sent another thrilling shiver through my body.

'Torture you how?' I asked, unable to hold back a smile after that great kiss. My body hummed with the feel-good energy from it. I felt lighter on my feet suddenly. And brighter too. Like somehow, things might actually be okay if you could have a kiss like that.

'You looked... perfect. Like the woman I'd always dreamed of marrying. In a freaking wedding dress. And I felt so broken, it didn't feel fair. I assumed you were someone else's and that pissed me off in an irrational way considering I didn't even know you.'

I reached up instantly and pressed my lips against his, earning a surprised smile from him. 'How can you say you don't know how to talk to women after telling me that?!' I cried, grinning giddily at his words.

Blake looked sheepish. 'I don't know. It's just easy to talk to you. I like telling you things. I like being honest with you. Even when it's embarrassing.'

'That was not embarrassing,' I said, shaking my head. 'It was beautiful. I thought you were judging me. I know now, I was judging myself. But I also wanted you to approve of me in a way I hadn't really felt about a stranger before. And earlier today, when I saw you over there with your shirt off...' I bit my lip as my cheeks flushed. Blake was grinning now too, his dimples on full show, making him look young and carefree. 'I thought I'd picked a damn good guy to fake date.'

'You think this is fake?' Blake reached down and pulled me into his chest again. This time, his kiss wasn't gentle. He kissed me with hunger like now he'd had a taste, he wanted the whole thing. And I was right there with him. I clung tightly to Blake as his tongue caressed mine and I murmured contently as he cupped the back of my head, his fingertips tangling with my hair. His hands were on my waist then he moved them to my back. I slipped mine down to his shoulders. The world around us faded as I lost myself in Blake's kiss. My body was full of heat. I thought about how easy it would be to pull his shirt up over his head. How much I wanted him to slip his fingers under my top. How I needed his touch. I murmured against his mouth and was about to suggest that we did all those things when Blake abruptly pulled away from me, leaving me breathless.

Blake's breathing was as rapid as my own. 'I'm sorry, I'm getting carried away,' he said, reaching out to touch my cheek. 'But there's nothing fake about our kisses, Daisy.'

I nodded. 'I feel it too.' My heart was hammering inside my chest now, desperate to escape and jump right into Blake's heart.

'What's going on? Our exes are still here, wanting us back. We were pretending to date but this is feeling real.'

'Even though Henry doesn't believe it,' I said lightly.

'I think Sarah can see there is something between us, and we were pretending to begin with, but she's right, isn't she?'

'Yes,' I whispered. 'I'm still wearing Henry's ring, though.' I stepped fully out of his embrace. 'What do we do?'

'See what this space away from them does. Decide what our hearts are saying.'

The problem wasn't knowing what my heart was saying; it was having the courage to listen to it. I nodded, though. 'Okay.'

He sighed, running a hand through his hair as I sucked in a calming breath. 'So, want to take the ponies in?'

'That would be good.' I knew if we stayed here, we'd kiss again. And we might not stop. But neither of us were ready for that.

We left my flower arch and walked past the enclosure Blake had put up today and was going to paint tomorrow, and went to where the ponies currently were. They stood by the gate as if waiting for us to get them. It seemed crazy to believe it was due to rain overnight. The sun was dipping down low in the clear, blue sky and there was a dreamy haze to the light around the farm. It was the kind of light you pictured having your first kiss in while wearing a pretty dress, and I couldn't believe I'd done exactly that with Blake. I kept my eyes off his, my cheeks still flushed, as we took a pony each by a lead and walked them out of the enclosure and into the barn to shelter for the night.

They both tried searching our pockets for food, making us chuckle, and we gave them a treat and water, and then made sure the barn was clean and they had enough hay.

Blake locked them up for the night and looked up at the sky. 'It's still so clear. All the stars are coming out.' The sky was now turning inky blue but the clouds hadn't rolled in yet. I looked up and saw the North star twinkling down on the farm. 'Come on.' Blake beckoned me to follow. I didn't think twice. I didn't want to part from him yet even if I was tired and achy from a day's work on the farm. I could wait for sleep.

We walked behind the barn where the sunflowers were. They curved their faces up to the setting sun as if they were saying goodnight to it. There was a gentle breeze making it appear as if they were dancing in a uniformed line. Blake sat down on the edge of the sunflowers on a patch of grass so I climbed down too.

'Lie down,' he said.

'Excuse me?' I raised an eyebrow.

Blake shook his head. 'Not like that. Let's look at the stars. Like you said you and Willow did when you were young.'

'You remember that?' I watched him lie on his back, laying his arms across his stomach. I thought about what I'd said to him. 'You thought they might have some answers for us as adults and that we should try it one day.'

'Lie down then and we can see if they do,' he said with an encouraging smile.

I shook my head. 'You're crazy.' But I did what he asked and lay back on the grass, also putting my hands on my stomach as I tilted my head up to see the stars above us.

21

We stayed in silence for a few minutes. I felt tiny and insignificant as I gazed up at the stars and that made me feel better. Like everything that was up in chaos in my life was so small in comparison to the universe around me. So, surely that meant that my problems could be solved? That I could solve them?

Finally, I turned my head and looked at Blake, who was still staring at the sky. 'I've enjoyed working with Willow more than I have for Henry's dad already. I like being back here and being outside. I feel like I can breathe better. I feel less anxious, less panicked, less claustrophobic. But when I think about leaving the life I've had for five years, of following my heart and doing what I really want, that anxiety, that panic...' I took a deep breath before I could finish my sentence. 'It comes back. Why?'

Blake turned his head and met my gaze. 'Change is scary. That's okay. It's okay to be scared of it. When I saw Sarah with that guy, I was scared because it meant that the decision I made last year, the one that at the time I was so unsure of, had been the wrong one. And now I don't know what my future looks like.'

I nodded. 'The future is so uncertain. I have clung to something that was certain. But I don't think it's right. When I lost my parents,' I swallowed the lump that appeared in my throat whenever I mentioned them, 'I didn't think my life would ever be certain again. That it would ever make sense again. So, when I found something that offered me security, I clung to it. And I ignored that same feeling you had. That it wasn't right.'

Blake reached out and entwined his fingers with mine, giving them a reassuring squeeze. 'Is this okay?'

'Yes,' I whispered, needing his touch.

'How do we know when something is right?' he whispered back.

'I hope we will just know.' Kissing Blake had felt much more right than kissing Henry had, which was crazy and terrifying and like it might blow my whole life up, which I was so not ready for. So, I didn't tell him that's what it had felt like. He didn't either so I had no idea if he had the same feeling or not, and there was no way I was going to ask. 'What do we do now?'

'You know what I want to do?' he asked.

I nodded and waited.

'I want to go and see my family. I want to see my dad and his shop, my sister, and my horse. But...' This time, he trailed off as his eyes searched mine. 'I don't want Sarah to come. I want you with me.'

'You do?' I whispered, my heart picking up pace at him wanting me to join him.

'I feel like you'll understand,' he replied simply.

I thought about my mum's flower shop and how I had felt going into the Birchbrook florist's today. I did understand. 'I'd love to see your father's shop and meet them. We could go tomorrow?'

'Really?' Blake asked.

'I asked Henry to give me tomorrow.'

'And Sarah said she'd let me think,' Blake said.

'So, let's do something with the space they are giving us.'

He smiled, flashing me his dimples again. 'With you by my side, I think maybe I could do anything.'

My heart soared. I turned back to look at the stars and felt Blake do the same, but our hands stayed locked together.

'Me too,' I said after a moment.

* * *

The next day, I got up early to finish the flower arch before I went with Blake to see his family. Willow continued making her trail while Blake finished painting the pony enclosure.

Dylan was at the cottages clearing the two that were empty ready for the renovation to begin. He had ordered a few shrubs to plant around the cottages to spruce up the outside of them so when he mentioned they needed picking up outside of town over breakfast, Blake suggested that we could collect them for him after we dropped by his family home.

As lunchtime approached, we finished up our work. Willow said Blake could drive her car as his was being repaired, plus it had plenty of space for the shrubs. Her eyes seemed to twinkle knowingly as Blake and I left the farm together. I hadn't told her about our kiss yet. It felt too new. I wanted it to be our secret for a bit longer. And until we knew what we were going to do.

But I was sure that she could see we were growing closer.

The sky was the colour of corn flowers as Blake drove us out of Birch Tree Farm. The sun cast a warm, golden light down on us as we passed through the farm gate and out into the countryside around Birchbrook. Blake's family lived in a small town about a forty-five-minute drive away. The plan was to go to the High Street and surprise his dad at the antiques shop first then head over to see his sister at the family home, which doubled up as her riding school. Blake could see his horse too. And then we'd stop off at the garden centre on the way home to pick up Dylan's shrubs and be back to Birch Tree Farm for the evening. It was a relief to not worry about Henry for the day. I had to see him tomorrow but I pushed that to the back of my mind.

'Tell me about your dad and sister,' I said as I settled back in the seat and watched green fields pass by the car window.

'My dad is the most reliable man I've ever known. I always knew he was there for me and my sister, no questions ever. But also for the community. He's the person you go to in an emergency or crisis. He can fix anything and everything. He loves the past. He reads history books, spends any free time finding things for the shop, and he loves watching old movies. My sister once said he was like a cosy slipper that you can't bear to part from.' Blake smiled as he spoke, his fondness for the man clear and bright. 'I like things from the past too. Especially music. My sister loves to take the piss out of me and my love for seventies music. I don't know anyone modern. Sarah bans me from playing music when she's around.' He shrugged like it didn't bother him. 'I guess that's why I'm not great with technology either. Or dating apps.' He glanced at me with a smile.

'Better that than someone who can write the perfect message but when you meet face to face, has zero conversation. I went on a few internet dates and the best messagers turned out to be the worst dates.' I shuddered, remembering some of the ones I'd been on before I met Henry. I decided I would never use apps again and I would be sticking to that, whatever happened next. 'What about your sister?'

I liked hearing Blake talk. His voice was deep and calm and

he really thought about what he was saying. I hadn't known him long but somehow, being with him was relaxing.

Blake shook his head. 'Bronte is a live wire. If you describe me and my dad as quiet and sensible, she is the opposite. She's fun and feisty and lives life to the beat of her own drum,' he said, smiling but still with the same fondness with which he spoke about his father. 'She always tells you exactly what she thinks. Not in a mean way, although she can be brutal if you need to hear it.' Then his smile faded. 'I guess things haven't been quite the same between us this last year. Since I moved away to be with Sarah. Bronte thought I was making a huge mistake.' He shifted in the car seat. 'She made it clear to Sarah too. So, I haven't seen her since the day I introduced them to one another. It didn't go well. I've spoken to both my dad and Bronte on the phone but I haven't been home for a year.'

'I'm sorry you guys fell out like that. I'm glad you're going to see her today. Family is important.'

'God, I'm sorry, Daisy. I shouldn't be laying any family drama on you when...' He trailed off, unsure how to finish his sentence.

'It's okay. I know it must be difficult. I just think that you'll regret it if you don't make things up with them. They sound important to you, so don't let, I don't know... pride maybe... stop you seeing them. Even if you do see what happened with Sarah as a mistake, it's still okay that you didn't listen to Bronte's advice. We have to make our own mistakes in life. I'm sure she's made some too. When you're in love, you don't always see things clearly.'

There was a pause as Blake absorbed what I said. 'Do you think you and Henry might turn out to have been a mistake?'

'I made a lot of mistakes, I'm realising,' I admitted. 'I shouldn't have gone along with what he wanted, hid who I was really was, put up walls to protect my heart and let myself sink into this life that I never decided I wanted. And I regret waiting so long to call off the wedding. But his mother planning my future for me was the wake-up call. I knew then it was a mistake. Because I didn't want what they were planning for me.'

'It's understandable that Henry gave you safety and security, that you wanted that after all you've been through,' he replied gently.

'I'm scared of not having that any more,' I said. 'But I know that's not a reason to stay with Henry.'

'There was a moment – when I realised Sarah had another man in our apartment – where I thought about leaving and pretending I hadn't walked in... pretending I didn't know she'd cheated on me. Isn't that pathetic?'

We drove down a long, winding lane framed by trees that swayed above us on the summer breeze. Sunlight poured through the gap in the leaves, creating shadows on the car. It was a beautiful place. I couldn't believe how I'd forgotten how lovely the landscape was around here. How much I had enjoyed living in the countryside while I was growing up. The city felt very far away right now. And I was glad of it.

'No, not pathetic,' I said. 'You knew if you acknowledged she had cheated on you, everything would be different and so you had an instinctive reaction to keep things as they were. But you didn't, right?'

'I paused for a second and then I banged the door shut, so she could hear it. She came running out of the bedroom in shock. I had been supposed to be out all day looking at potential office spaces while she worked on the app but the last one cancelled on me so I came home early. I asked who he was. He had been her "friends with benefits" she said before she met me. Said he didn't mean anything to her. I walked out and when I came back, he'd gone and she begged me to stay. But I packed my things and rang Dylan. And now she's followed me. She seems to think I'm overacting. That what we have is love, and he's just someone she calls for fun sometimes. That's not what I want in a relationship.' Blake sighed. 'But you're right; it's not that easy to let go of something. Something you thought was going to be... everything.'

'It isn't easy at all,' I agreed.

22

We reached the outskirts of Blake's hometown then. It was pretty like Birchbrook with a pedestrianised cobbled High Street dotted with rose bushes that were bursting with colour. Blake parked in the small car park behind it and we walked together towards the shops. I glanced at him. He'd gone quiet and seemed nervous. I remembered the nerves I had seeing the farm after five years. I hoped he would feel better once he saw his family again, like I had done.

Halfway down the street was his father's antiques shop. It had a red sign with the name in cream – *Daniels' Antiques.* There was a black chalkboard outside with, *We buy and sell antiques at fair prices* written on it in white chalk, and a smiley face for good measure. The High Street was quiet despite the good weather and when we walked in, I could see the shop was empty of any customers.

The bell rang out merrily on the door and Blake held it open for me. Inside, the shop was long and narrow and bursting at the seams with treasures. Everywhere I looked, there was an object. Furniture, paintings, trinkets, mirrors, clocks, jewellery; everywhere there was space, something had been placed in it. I thought you could spend a whole day looking around but still miss half of what was in the shop. At one end was a counter and a till behind which a man stood replacing a battery in a watch. The radio behind him played softly. He looked up at our entrance and did a double take.

'Hi, Dad,' Blake said as we walked towards him.

Blake's father was an older version of his son – the same height and build with greying hair but similar dark eyes – and the slow smile that spread across his face, showing dimples, made him almost identical. He wore glasses and trousers instead of the shorts Blake had on but they were very much alike.

'Blake?' He phrased it as a question as if he couldn't quite believe it.

'Yeah. This is Daisy. We're staying together at Birch Tree Farm with my old friend Dylan and her cousin,' he said, gesturing to me. 'How are you?'

'How am I?' Blake's dad hurried out from behind the counter and pulled Blake into a warm hug. 'It's been too long, son. I thought you'd never... Anyway, it's so good to see you.' He glanced at me behind Blake's back. 'And nice to meet you, Daisy. You kept this quiet, Blake. What about...? Never mind.' He pulled back and grinned at his son. Then he held out his hand to me.

'It's nice to meet you too, Mr Daniels.'

He snorted. 'That makes me feel ancient, and I don't need more help with that, Daisy. Call me Bill, please. Let's close up and go and see Bronte.'

'We can wait until your lunch break,' Blake said.

'I'll take it now. It's quiet, as you can see. She'll be over the moon you're back.'

'Will she?' Blake asked with a frown.

Bill sighed. 'Of course she will. We've both missed you. And she'll want to meet Daisy. Come on, you two.' He grabbed his keys and was walking out of the shop before we could argue any further. I looked at Blake, who shrugged with a wry smile so, with a laugh, I followed them. Neither of us had stopped Blake's dad from assuming we were together but I knew we'd have to say something at some point. My family knew the truth; it would feel wrong to lie to Blake's family.

Bill hopped into Blake's car, which drove us out of the High Street, a few minutes outside town, and then down a bumpy lane to a pretty house with a lot of land around it. It was painted white and had rose bushes outside it like back in town. Behind the house, I could see a field and a barn with a sign outside saying, *Daniels' Riding School*. There were four horses grazing in the field. I assumed one of them belonged to Blake.

It was an idyllic place, not unlike Willow's farm, and the contrast between it and Blake's current city life felt stark. I wondered which one he felt he belonged in. I was beginning to see that I'd never fit in the city, not like I did around here.

The door opened and out walked a tall, slim woman with the same light-brown hair as Blake. She stopped to watch the car pull onto the gravel driveway. She looked as stunned as her dad when Blake parked and climbed out of the car.

'Blake?'

'Hey, sis.'

She let out a shriek, bounded over and jumped into his arms.

I watched Blake's face. He looked shocked then happy as he grinned and hugged his sister tightly. I saw their dad duck his head and wipe at his eyes. And I had to swallow a lump in my throat as I turned away with a relieved smile.

* * *

Being in the Daniels' house was similar to how I had felt in my childhood home, and how it felt being on Birch Tree Farm: warm, familiar and comfortable. Bronte and her father lived there along with Bronte's husband and their two kids, the four horses and three Labrador dogs. It was a large home and filled with things like in their antiques shop: cosy corners with armchairs, lots of books, soft rugs, lamps of all shapes and sizes, and a grandfather clock which they informed me was always exactly one hour and seven minutes slow no matter how many times they tried to fix it.

When we arrived, Bronte's kids were at school and her husband was out buying supplies for their business so we sat down to lunch as a foursome, choosing to go outside as it was so warm. The garden made me gasp when I stepped out from the French doors in the lounge. It stretched out into the field where the horses were and behind it were hills that appeared to touch the sky.

But it was the flowers in the garden that took my breath away. Hanging baskets with pink and red flowers hung along the side of the house. There was a decking area with a table and chairs. Above it, was a gazebo covered in climbing flowers that formed a pretty arch. Bordering the garden were roses of all different varieties that looked stunning and smelled amazing.

'My mother would have loved to see this,' I said as I took it all in. It was clearly carefully kept but also looked wild, as if the flowers had just sprung up in perfect bloom like they had always meant to be there. 'It's gorgeous.'

Blake was watching me. He smiled. 'Bronte's pride and joy.'

'Any chance I get, I'm out here,' she said from behind us as she carried out a jug of lemonade.

'I don't blame you.'

'Your mother is a gardener too?' she asked as she gestured for us to sit down at the table.

'She was a florist; she had her own flower shop. But she loved the small garden we had at home too. I think about that garden sometimes,' I replied wistfully.

Bronte frowned at me in concern.

'I lost my parents a few years ago.'

'I'm so sorry,' she said sincerely. 'Do you have a garden you can plant flowers in? You seem to love them so much.'

Her simple question stunned me. Why hadn't I made any use out of Henry's family's garden? I barely went into it, let alone planted anything or enjoyed the flowers there. But then again, they had a gardener and it didn't have the same feeling as this garden did.

'Daisy is making a lovely arch for the farm we're staying at with Dylan,' Blake said when he saw I wasn't sure how to answer. He pulled his phone out, to my surprise, and showed his sister and dad a picture he'd taken of my flower arch, telling them all about Dylan and Willow as well as the plans Willow had for the trail and strawberry fields. He then showed them the pony enclosure he had built.

'The arch is so pretty,' Bronte said, smiling. She was looking at us with curiosity. 'I'm glad you've reconnected with Dylan, Blake. You two used to be so close. You're staying on the farm for a couple of weeks?'

'Yeah, I just needed a change of scenery,' Blake said. 'I know I could have stayed here but...' He trailed off and coughed uncomfortably. 'I know you're all so busy,' he finished lamely.

'I need to point out the elephant in the room,' Bronte said then. 'You're here with Daisy, which is lovely, so does that mean you're not with Sarah any more?' I didn't miss the hope in her voice and I knew Blake must have heard it too.

'Well,' Blake began, 'kind of, I don't know, it's complicated. We did break up but we have the business and everything,' he mumbled awkwardly.

'But...' Bronte looked between me and Blake, confused.

'We're just friends,' I added quickly, earning a raised eyebrow from him. I tried not to think about our kisses, which was pretty damn difficult.

'You don't need to explain, son,' his dad said hurriedly, shooting a warning glance at Bronte. I could guess his thoughts; he didn't want her to make Blake not want to visit again. 'Leave him alone, Bronte. Let's talk about something else.'

'Okay, okay,' she said. 'I promise I'll be on my best behaviour, okay, big brother?' She smiled with mischief.

Blake relaxed into a smile too. 'Are you ever on your best behaviour, little sister?'

'They are always like this,' their father said to me with a chuckle. He looked relieved Blake was taking it with good humour.

I smiled back. 'I'm an only child so it's nice to see siblings banter. Although I guess Willow, who is my cousin, used to feel like my sister. It's nice to be staying with her for the summer. And helping out. Making the arch was fun.' I looked out at the garden again, enjoying the view.

'Tuck in, guys,' Bronte instructed. 'So, do you live on the farm with your cousin?' She was trying hard not to be too curious but I could tell she longed to know what was going on between us.

'She's just here staying in Birchbrook for a break too,' Blake said quietly, giving his sister a warning look.

'Right,' Bronte said, but I wondered how long it would be until she found out everything. She passed me a bowl of salad and I added some to my plate along with spicy chicken wings, a jacket potato and coleslaw. There was also quiche, crusty bread and a bowl of cold vegetable rice. Bronte definitely took after my Uncle Adam when it came to providing lots of fresh and tasty food for guests.

'It's okay,' I assured her. 'I wanted to stay with family as things are complicated with my fiancé,' I said, thinking she might have clocked my engagement ring.

'A lot of complicated relationships on this farm,' Bronte observed lightly. 'Well, I hope you work it out, guys.'

'If Sarah and Henry let us,' I said without thinking.

'You've met Sarah?' Bronte pounced on my words.

'She's in Birchbrook too,' Blake admitted while I shot him an apologetic look. 'And so is Daisy's fiancé. One big happy family,' he added with bitterness.

'Okay, sorry, but you can't just tell us that. What's going on?' Bronte said. 'I know you've stayed away because I told you it was a mistake to move in with Sarah and set up this dating app with her. All your calls home this past year have been small talk but you're here in our home now. Without Sarah. With another woman.' Bronte smiled at me. 'Who seems very nice.' She looked back at Blake. 'What's going on, big brother?'

'Blake will tell us when he's ready,' his dad interjected. 'Daisy, why don't you tell us more about Birch Tree Farm?' Bill asked. 'It sounds so idyllic.'

I glanced at Blake, who was staring down at his plate, and his sister, who was glowering at her father. To keep the peace, I did as Bill asked and launched into a speech about Willow and her dad, about how I'd grown up visiting the farm, and then how I hadn't been back for a few years. How Willow had created the pumpkin patch to save them from having to sell the farm. And how much I was enjoying helping them out for the summer. It was actually a relief not to be talking or thinking about Henry or Sarah, or even what had happened between me and Blake for a while. 'They've just got two Shetland ponies that Blake is helping them with. They're going to offer pony rides.'

Bronte turned to Blake then. 'I thought you'd given up horses,' she said shortly.

'The black horse is Blake's,' Bill said quietly to me. I looked over. The horse's coat shone in the sunshine.

'Midnight,' Blake said, also turning to look. 'I've had her for eight years. The other three belong to my sister and her husband for the riding school. Midnight stayed here when I left for the city.' He looked at Bronte. 'I'd like to see her.'

'Go ahead,' she said. 'She's missed you.'

'We all have,' their dad quickly added.

'I still can't believe you chose the city over all this,' Bronte added then with a shake of her head. 'Over *us*.' She spoke angrily but I could see the hurt in her eyes. She had missed her brother too.

'It wasn't that I chose the city over you all,' Blake said defensively. 'I fell in love with Sarah and wanted to make a life with her. There was so much to do – finding a place to live then trying to set up our company – and it's a long way and... I wanted to come and see you but I knew how angry you both were that I'd left. I suppose I thought that I wouldn't be welcome,' Blake finished in a quiet voice, looking down at his plate again.

Bronte tutted. 'As if you wouldn't be welcome. You know I thought it was a mistake to leave and be with *her*, but this will always be your home. You know that, right?'

'Yeah,' Blake said, but I could tell her words meant a lot to him. He took a deep breath and looked up. 'Things aren't great between us but I'd rather not hear an "I told you so".'

'I won't say that but you should have come home. Instead, you ran away,' Bronte said, her voice rising with passion. Her cheeks flushed. 'Just like our mother.'

23

There was a sharp silence after that.

Blake stood up suddenly, pushing his chair back angrily. 'And you wonder why I stayed away,' he said, striding off without a backward glance.

'You couldn't let us have a nice day together,' Bill said with a sigh.

Bronte lifted her shoulders. 'Sorry, Dad, but it's true. He acted just like her!'

'Maybe I should...' I gestured to where Blake was walking towards their horses.

'Yes, Daisy, maybe you can ask him to come back and finish lunch. Bronte won't say another word, will you?' Bill said firmly.

She sighed. 'Sure,' she mumbled, reaching for her lemonade and taking a long gulp.

'Okay,' I said, and followed Blake. I walked out to the riding school into the field where the family's four horses were enjoying the sunshine. Blake opened the gate and walked on through but I stopped outside and leaned on the fence to watch. Blake approached his horse, who lifted her head and walked over when he clucked his tongue. She sniffed him as he patted her and then she nuzzled into his neck, making him laugh. Watching him greet his horses sent a bolt of affection for him through me.

'I missed her more than I realised,' Blake said after a moment. I hadn't known if he had seen me follow or not. He turned to look at me. 'It's probably why I started running in the city: to try to recreate the feeling I have when I'm riding her. It didn't work, though.'

I nodded. 'I've been trying for years to feel the same way I did when I stayed at Birch Tree Farm one summer when I was young. Before my parents... before life took so much from me... but it's never worked.'

'No, because life can never go back to that point. But you can find that joy again. I know it, Daisy.' He stroked Midnight. 'I'm sorry, girl. I shouldn't have left you for so long.'

'Did you not consider moving her to the city with you?'

Blake walked over to the fence and leaned on the opposite side to me. Midnight followed and he produced an apple from his pocket to give to her. I hadn't seen him take it from lunch. 'Sarah doesn't like horses. That was a factor. As was how much time it would take to look after Midnight, plus she's only ever lived out here. I didn't think she'd like the city.' He sighed as she ate the apple. 'Bronte thinks I'm like our mother.'

'She's just hurt. She's missed you. She doesn't understand why you left and didn't come back.'

'Do you?' He looked at me over the fence.

'I couldn't go back to Birchbrook for a long time. I think maybe I was scared to be happy. When I stayed there after my parents died, every time I laughed with Willow, I felt guilty. The pain washed over me again. I thought if I stayed away, I wouldn't get sad but I also wouldn't feel guilty if I wasn't sad. The past five years, I wonder if I've only been living a half-life. Stopping myself from being really happy as well as stopping myself from being really sad. God, does that even makes sense?'

'It does,' Blake said reassuringly. 'But you deserve so much more than a half-life, Daisy.'

'So do you,' I reminded him.

'I think I'm scared of facing the fact that I failed. Maybe Bronte is right. Maybe I started to wonder why I stayed here in my safe hometown, in the family business, and didn't dream bigger. Like our mother did. Maybe I thought she was happier wherever she is. That maybe I would be too. Maybe I was worried I was like her so I left to almost prove myself right. Maybe I did fall in love with Sarah or maybe I just wanted to be loved so much, I let her talk me into this new life when there was nothing wrong with the one I was leading. That maybe I want a safe, small life. Sarah will think I'm crazy though if I tell her that.'

'So what?' I snapped.

Blake turned around to face me over the fence. 'So what?' He allowed himself a small smile at my question.

'Sarah might never understand this,' I explained, gesturing around us. 'She doesn't understand wanting to stay where you grew up. Being close to your family. Helping out your dad. Yeah, she probably will think you're crazy to leave the city and come back here. But just because you have different dreams to her doesn't mean one of you is right and the other is wrong. It just means you're not meant to be together. And frankly, the fact she could cheat on you should tell you that too. If I loved someone, I would be loyal to them. I would support their dreams. I would want to build a life together that we both wanted.'

Blake stared at me. 'That's what I want too. For us both.'

'You only fail if you don't try,' I murmured, remembering my mum telling me that once. She was nervous about opening her flower shop. But she did it anyway. I knew then what she would say about me being scared to cut ties with Henry once and for all.

'God, Daisy, I really want to kiss you again,' he admitted then.

My breath hitched. 'I want to kiss you again too,' I whispered back. My lips remembered the feel of his and my body remembered how good his arms felt around me. But my mind was still confused. And my heart. I had no idea what it wanted. No. That was a lie. But what it wanted was too terrifying to speak aloud.

'What do we do?' he asked, leaning on the fence that separated us. If he leaned forward though, he would be able to touch my lips. I both ached for him to do it and wished he wouldn't. Talk about confusing.

'I'm sorry,' I said then.

Blake shook his head. 'No, don't apologise. It's not like either of us expected to meet each other on the farm. And you're still unsure about what you feel for Henry. I get that. And it's not like I'm free either really. Not properly. Sarah is right there with us. And I have no idea what to do about it.'

'Bronte is confused about me being here.'

'Yeah. I suppose I should tell her what happened with Sarah. What's going on. I hate her thinking I'm like our mother. I don't want to be like her.'

'You know what? I think Bronte reminds me of my mum,' I said with a small smile. 'She always said things how they were, and had the best advice. Why don't we go back so you can talk to her? Sort things out so you can leave knowing you're both okay. You came all this way and after all this time. You should fix it. I mean, if that's what you want.'

Midnight gave Blake a nudge then and he chuckled. 'You're both giving me the same advice, so I better take it, right?' He reached out and tucked a stray hair of mine behind my ear. My body hummed from the chaste touch. Our eyes connected and they seemed to say a million things that we couldn't speak aloud. After a moment, Blake briefly brushed his fingertips over mine. 'Why didn't I meet you first?' he asked.

Then he stepped off the fence and turned to give Midnight a goodbye pat before heading for the gate.

His words echoed through me as we walked back to the garden. I couldn't help but wonder what path my life would have taken if five years ago, I had met Blake instead of Henry.

* * *

After lunch, I helped Bill tidy up the kitchen while Blake and Bronte stayed outside talking at the table in the garden.

'Thank you for bringing him here,' Bill said as he handed me a washed bowl to dry.

'It was Blake's idea,' I assured him.

'Maybe, but he didn't come home for the year he was with Sarah. Now he's met you... he's here. You know, you're only the second woman he has brought home to meet us.'

'Really?'

'Family has always meant a lot to him. I think he didn't want to bring anyone here who wasn't meaningful or special, you know? We were surprised, I'm not going to lie, that he chose Sarah.' Bill stopped then. 'I shouldn't be saying all this, should I? It's just you seem to fit right in.'

'I do?' That really shocked me. I had tried to mould myself for Henry and his family, but here, I was just being myself. And that was enough for Bill. 'That... that means a lot to me,' I choked out.

Bill gave me a kind smile. 'I can see it does. Sometimes, we worry too much about what we want, what the future is going to look like, that we forget to enjoy the moment we're in, to be happy right here, right now. So, we don't recognise what we should be hanging onto. The things that could become that future we want.' Bill grinned then. 'My kids are always telling me I think I'm a poet or a philosopher, so feel free to ignore anything I say or advice I give.'

'I like it,' I replied with a smile. I think we both knew I was really saying that I liked Bill. He reminded me of my uncle, and my father too. Blake was lucky to have him. I looked out of the kitchen window at Blake and Bronte. 'I'm glad they're reconnecting.'

'You know how important family is.'

'Yeah. I do,' I replied with a sigh. I thought about Henry and his parents. They could be my family. But they didn't care what I wanted, only what they did. I'd been so desperate to replace the family I had lost, I'd ignored the niggling doubts I'd had all along. I didn't really belong with them. Bill saying that it felt like I belonged here was comforting. It did feel that way. Which was crazy, wasn't it? I turned to Bill. 'Do you wish Blake would come home?'

Bill was putting the plates back in the cupboard, his back to me and the door. His back sagged a little at my question. 'Is that selfish of me? Yes, I do. The shop could be doing better. I maybe lost some of my drive and passion for it the past year. I always saw it as a family business. Bronte and her husband try to help but they have the riding school and their two boys to look after.' A beat passed. 'I guess I thought Blake loved the shop as much as I do.'

'I do.'

We both jumped and spun around as Blake and Bronte walked into the kitchen.

'I do love it, Dad,' Blake repeated. 'I think I believed I should be dreaming bigger. No... maybe Sarah made me think that I should. I feel crap about that. I was worried I'd made a mistake as soon as I moved to the city. But I didn't want to admit it. I didn't want to fail. I didn't want to have made a mistake.' Blake glanced at me. 'But I know you only fail if you don't try. I needed to try, I think. To get it out of my system. To decide what I want out of life. What I want for my future. Can you give me some more time? I'll come back soon.'

'Of course, son,' Bill said warmly. 'I only want my kids to be happy. That's all I've ever wanted. I understood why you had to go. And I'd understand if you still want to be there. But if you want to come back, this is and always will be your home.'

A sob rose up in my throat. Horrified, I took off, hurrying out of the room and out the front door into the driveway. It was all too much hearing Blake's dad tell him this would always be his home. It's what I desperately wanted but just couldn't seem to find.

A tiny voice deep down asked me if maybe one day, this could really be where I belonged. But that idea just seemed too outlandish to even entertain.

Blake followed me and placed a hand on my shoulder. 'It's okay, Daisy, it will be okay.'

I sucked in some quick breaths, trying not to panic or cry. I looked at him. 'Promise?'

'Daisy, you are the strongest woman I've ever met. You can do anything you want. You can have anything you want. I promise you.'

I found myself stepping towards him, and Blake opened up his arms. I leaned into his chest as he held me tightly, reassuringly. I hadn't felt strong for a long time but I knew I had been once. And my mum sure as hell had been.

I wanted to be strong again.

I would be.

'Let's go back to the farm,' Blake said softly into my hair. I nodded against him and sniffed. When we parted, it felt like something in the universe had permanently shifted.

24

Blake and I were quiet on the drive back to Birch Tree Farm. I knew we were both thinking over the visit to his family. We stopped off to pick up the shrubs Dylan had ordered from the garden centre and while we were there, I spotted white watering cans that looked pretty. After messaging to see what Willow thought, I bought five to dot around the picnic area we were making that I'd fill with flowers. I would need to go back to see Mary at her florist's in town and that thought excited me.

When we passed the sign welcoming us to Birchbrook, the sun was dipping in the sky, calling an end to what had been a long and emotional day.

'Are you okay?' Blake asked as we drove towards the farm.

'For the first time in a while, I think maybe I will be,' I replied. 'You?'

'I feel the same. We're both seeing Sarah and Henry tomorrow, though...'

'Things can't stay like they are,' I said, already dreading spending time alone with Henry. We drove through the gate and Blake parked outside the farmhouse. 'I think I might go and work on my arch for a bit,' I said, not really wanting to chit-chat with Willow, Adam and Dylan just yet. Plus, the more time I spent with Blake, the more the charged tension between us became almost unbearable. We both wanted to kiss but both knew we shouldn't. I wanted to get away from the temptation. I needed some alone time. 'I'll see you tomorrow.' I jumped out of the car and walked out to the strawberry fields.

I went to the barn and picked up the remaining flowers I had left there and carried them and the watering cans out to the fields. I had to make two trips but I didn't mind the walking after so long sat in the car. I lifted off the tarpaulin covering my arch and then carried on wrapping faux flowers around it.

I had forgotten how healing it was to work with my hands and be outside. My mind started to clear as I focused on what I was doing. I weaved flowers through the metal arch and tried not to think about what had happened since I'd come to Birch Tree Farm. Instead, I wanted to just enjoy this task. Maybe my mum had used her work with flowers to clear her mind too. I wished I could ask her but it was enough that I felt her presence with me out here.

The light began to fade then so I paused and looked at what I'd done. I stepped back to look at the finished arc. The colourful flowers mixed with eucalyptus draped around the frame gave me a burst of pride.

I heard footsteps behind me but I kept on staring at the arch. I hadn't had such a sense of satisfaction with anything that I had done for a long time. This felt like a big moment somehow.

'Hi, I'm just taking Maple on her last walk of the day,' Willow called out as they approached. 'Blake said you were out here. It's almost dark; you going to stop now?'

'It's done.'

'What? Oh my God!' Willow hurried to stand beside me and

wrapped her arm through mine. 'It's so pretty, Daisy. Thank you. God, I didn't think we'd get to spend this summer together or that you would help me with all this. I feel really lucky. You saved me!'

I laid my head on her shoulder. 'I'm the lucky one; you've saved me.' I took a deep breath. My mind hadn't been this clear for a very long time. I turned to my cousin. 'I want to stay here for the rest of the summer. Would that be okay?'

Willow smiled. 'Well, of course it would! Hell, you can stay forever if you want. We've missed you. It's so nice to have you back. And I was panicking about not having my usual summer help around and making sure I keep building on the success of the pumpkin patch, plus stop my dad from doing too much... You arriving was perfect.'

'That's how I feel too. I am loving being here. I feel more like myself. I'm not so scared about the future either. I want to do what my uncle said: follow my heart.'

'What's it saying?' she asked me.

'That I should stay for the summer so I can help you get it ready for the opening then I can watch people enjoy this farm as much as I do. I want to eat strawberries and have a picnic and keep watching the stars. And I'd like to spend time with Mary in her flower shop,' I said, smiling as I thought of things I wanted to do. Then my smile faded. 'I don't want to go back with Henry. I just don't know how to tell him so he will listen. And I'm still scared about walking away from him and his family into the... unknown.'

'But is the unknown scarier than living the life he wants for you both? The one you don't want?'

She knew. Willow knew me so well, she could see I didn't want what Henry was offering me.

'You're right,' I replied softly.

'Then you'll tell him. You'll find the right words. And he will listen because he will realise this is what you want.'

'How do you and Blake have so much faith in me?' I burst out, wondering why they both thought I could do this when I was so unsure.

Willow put her arm over my shoulders and gave me a squeeze. 'I remember after my mum's funeral, we both came out of the farmhouse, leaving the wake for a bit. We walked over there,' she said, pointing to where the strawberries started. 'We sat down and I asked you how I would ever be able to manage life without my mum. And I asked how you'd been managing without your parents.'

I thought back, remembering that night. The pain in her eyes. The way her voice had caught in sadness. The way we looked at one another, grief washing over us both. The loss we both felt for ourselves, and for each other.

'You told me that my mum would want me to live. That all she wanted was for me to be happy. And we could both be sad that we didn't have the people we loved the most in our lives any more but we couldn't let that sadness stop us from living. It was the last thing they would ever want. You were so inspiring. You believed in what you told me. And even though you've struggled to do that... we both have... you were right that night. My mum, your parents, they would want us to *live*.'

'But then I walked away and left you.'

'We had to deal with it all in our own ways. It took me a long time to start living again fully. It was when my dad handed me a letter from Dylan's brother's business offering to buy this farm. That shook me out of not living. And it took standing in front of a mirror in your wedding dress to shake you out of it. But it worked. You came back. This summer, you start living.'

'I kissed Blake,' I confessed then. 'I have no idea what it means. It made me feel alive, though.'

She smiled. 'Keep doing things that make you feel alive. That's what both our parents would want. Deal, cousin?'

I nodded through my watering eyes. 'Deal.'

* * *

The following morning, I nervously got ready to see Henry. It was one thing to tell Willow what I wanted, another to tell Henry what was in my heart.

Henry had messaged me to wear something smart so I assumed we were going somewhere fancy. I put on one of my new floral dresses with a cardigan over my shoulders, sandals and my new daisy hair clip pulling back one side of my bob, then I went outside to wait for Henry to drive onto the farm.

Blake came over wearing city shorts and a polo shirt, his hair tousled and still damp from his morning shower. 'I saw the flower arch after I bought the ponies out of the barn,' he said. 'It's perfect, Daisy.' Then he smiled, giving me the full dimple treatment. 'Also, you look lovely. Is that okay to say?'

'Thank you,' I said, a faint blush appearing on my cheeks. Then my smile faded. 'I'm really nervous.'

'Yeah?'

I longed to tell him that I didn't want Henry. But what if I chickened out again? 'Are you going to see Sarah?' I asked, wishing we could spend another day together instead.

'I said I'd go and see her at the pub. I guess we both need to make some decisions, huh?'

Then a car pulled into the farm but it wasn't Henry. Willow came out of the farmhouse so Blake said he'd see me later and went back to his cottage. Willow and I watched as her best friend Sabrina parked in the driveway and jumped out.

'I have the signs for the trail!' she cried excitedly as she climbed out.

'Already? Amazing!' Willow called back.

We went over to her car. 'It's so great to see you again!' Sabrina gave me a warm smile and pulled me into her. Her blonde hair looked like it was dancing on the light breeze. She was still petite and pretty as she had been when we were kids. She was a teacher at the local school, married, with a little girl, and she looked completely happy with her life.

'You too. Wow, these are so good,' I said as I looked at the signs Willow began lifting out of Sabrina's car boot. She'd made wooden signs with *Strawberry Fields Trail* written on it in white with red strawberries painted around the border. She'd also made one in the shape of an arrow to show the way people should walk down the trail.

'Are they okay?' Sabrina asked as she lifted another one out.

'They are so cute!' Willow cried. 'Thank you. They might even top your pumpkin signs. We can put one by the front gate and the arrow at the start of the trail then this one at the strawberry fields' finale.'

'I can't wait to see what you've been doing while I was away for a few days,' Sabrina said. 'I've heard all about your flower arch, Daisy.'

'Come and see it,' Willow said. 'Daisy is off out but I've got time for a coffee?'

'Sounds good,' Sabrina said. She eyed the signs. 'You know, one day I'd love to make a Christmas one...' Her eyes twinkled.

'Don't give Willow any more ideas,' Dylan said from behind us.

We all jumped.

'We have so many things going on as it is!' His eyes were wide as he shook his head.

'Sorry, Dylan,' Sabrina said hastily.

'You wanted to take over the Airbnb business,' Willow reminded him. 'It's not just me who keeps coming up with more ideas. Something festive around here could be fun one day, though...' She seemed to go into a dreamlike trance.

'Let's go and look at what you've all been doing,' Sabrina said with a laugh.

'I'm off to meet with a supplier,' Dylan said, going to his car.

'Henry will be here in a minute,' I said, my nerves growing.

'Good luck,' Willow said as she and Sabrina both hugged me goodbye and then headed for the strawberry fields. Then I saw Henry turning into the farm.

He beeped the horn so I went over to his car and climbed in beside him.

'Hi,' I said, feeling no joy at seeing him again.

Henry leaned over to kiss my cheek and then his eyes lingered on my dress. 'Oh, I thought I said to dress smart for lunch,' he said.

I stared at him. When we used to go to his country club, I would wear clingy dresses that he loved but I hated. I thought back to how he would make comments about my appearance, and I would end up going to change until my outfit met with his approval. I don't know why I ever thought that I should do so. 'If you want me to come for lunch then this is how I will be coming,' I replied shortly.

Henry put his hands up. 'No need to get snippy. Let's go.'

I put my seatbelt on and watched the farm fade away, wishing I hadn't got into the car.

'I finished my flower arch,' I said, thinking that I should try to make conversation.

'What flower arch?' Henry said as he put the satnav on to direct us to the restaurant. 'Oh, God, you remember that client last year who...'

Henry was off then talking about work as he so often did, not at all interested in what I had been doing. This wasn't what I wanted from a partner. I'd ignored it for too long.

We got through the journey and pulled into the car park of a beautiful hotel nestled in the countryside.

'I have a surprise for you,' Henry said as he parked, a grin on his face.

My stomach instantly plummeted.

25

I climbed out of Henry's car and followed him inside the hotel. I was instantly and firmly back in Henry's world. The chandeliers on the ceiling, the plush, red carpet, the uniformed doorman tipping his hat to us and the sounds of champagne popping as we walked into the restaurant. I felt uncomfortable and anxious and regretted agreeing to this. I didn't want a romantic lunch with Henry. This felt like completely the wrong place for us to talk.

Henry spoke to the maître d', who led us out onto the terrace. Outside were white, bistro-style tables under umbrellas. As we got closer, I saw two familiar faces. My heart started to beat faster. They were the last two people I wanted to see right now.

Sitting at the table with the best view of the rolling landscaped hotel gardens were Henry's parents.

I stopped walking instantly. I'd known Henry's surprise wouldn't be anything I would want.

'What are they doing here?' I hissed. This was an ambush. No other word for it.

Henry had to walk back a bit as he hadn't noticed I had paused. 'What's wrong?'

'Today, we were supposed to be talking,' I said, starting to panic. 'Just the two of us.'

He sighed. 'They've come a long way to see you. To see us. I thought we could all talk about what's going on.'

I shook my head. This wasn't supposed to be a relationship of four.

His parents saw us then. His mum waved while his dad narrowed his eyes, evidently wondering why we were just standing here. 'Let's just go,' I said, knowing I couldn't turn and run, although I sure as hell wanted to.

I felt trapped as I followed Henry to their table. I didn't know how I was going to get away from this.

'Daisy, there you are,' Henry's dad said after he'd shaken hands with Henry like he was a business associate. He leaned in to kiss my cheek. He wore a crisp linen suit like his son. 'You look so different,' he added, catching sight of my hair. He glanced at Henry, who shrugged like it was nothing to do with him.

Lovely.

'She looks beautiful as always,' Henry's mum chastised them as she leaned in to kiss me too. She wore a linen skirt and blouse, a straw hat and Chanel No.5, plus her signature red lipstick.

'You both look well,' I returned politely as we all sat down at the table.

Henry called over a waiter and ordered a bottle of champagne.

'Isn't this for celebrating?' I asked him.

'We are celebrating.' He chuckled. 'Us being back together.'

I didn't know if he meant the four of us, or him and me – either one was presumptuous. He really hadn't been listening to me since our wedding day.

The waiter returned and poured us all a glass of fizz. The contrast to yesterday's simple lunch with Blake and his family was so strong, I almost felt like I was in a dream.

'To us,' Henry proposed as a toast and we all took a sip, although mine was more of a desperate gulp.

'Okay, Daisy, let's put our cards on the table...' Henry's dad said then. He leaned forward and gave me a serious look. The dread in my stomach grew even further. 'We've talked to Henry about everything. We recognise that the wedding we planned wasn't what you imagined it to be, and we hope we can all move on from it. It was embarrassing what happened but we have made allowances for the fact you have no family, Daisy; it was clearly an upsetting day for you. I'm sure next time, everything'll go smoothly.' He paused and gave me a formal nod.

I took another gulp of champagne, wondering how I'd ignored how patronising he could be. I was too stunned by his words to speak so he carried on.

'I think we should wait until next summer to let the scandal die down. In the meantime, I know that Henry has spoken to you about you working with my wife on doing things for charity,' he continued. 'We also recognise that us all living together might not be the best thing for newlyweds so we are going to purchase the two of you a flat in the city and then you can come home on the weekends. Once you have a family after the wedding, we can talk about building a separate property on our estate maybe.' He leaned back and took a proud sip of his drink, as if he had just delivered a keynote speech. Which he probably thought he had.

My head spun. I could feel the situation getting away from me. Like it had so many times with these four. I'd gone along with so many things, but this was the rest of my life.

'And our next wedding can be anything you want,' Henry said, turning to me while I tried to gather myself. 'Within reason, as we'll still need to invite key people, of course, but the wedding planner will report to you this time and you can choose the dress you want.'

My eyes widened. Surely every bride should get to choose her dress? Why had I ignored that the first time?

'I realise I took over a bit, dear,' Henry's mum said then, more gently than the other two had spoken. 'I'm sorry for that. You didn't seem to want to take charge and you know I love planning events. But we'll do it differently next time. And I think you'll find you enjoy not working in an office any more.' She smiled but I couldn't return it. Once again, none of them were actually asking *me* what it was I wanted.

Abruptly, I pushed back my chair. 'Excuse me, I need to use the powder room,' I said, making a swift exit. I rushed into the ladies and stood by the mirror to suck in a breath.

I was dangerously close to panicking again.

But this time, I knew Henry couldn't soothe me.

He was the cause of it. And if I thought back, he had been the cause of my freaking out at the farm too, showing up and demanding things of me. This had been the case for five years. I never felt relaxed in their presence.

But I had been relaxed yesterday with Blake and his family. I was relaxed with Willow and my uncle, Dylan and Maple. And the ponies. I was relaxed on the farm. In Birchbrook. I couldn't ignore the contrast.

I looked at my reflection. Despite the fact Henry and his parents clearly didn't approve of my new haircut, it was part of what was making me feel like I was slowly becoming the woman I wanted to be here. And I didn't want to go back to the woman I had been with them.

The door opened and Henry's mother swept in. 'You need to tell me what's going on, Daisy,' she said in the voice she used with people working for her at her events. I knew better than to ignore it.

'There was nothing in what you all just said out there that I want,' I said in a rush, tumbling over the words before I chickened out. I tried to say something else but my breath caught. I clutched my chest. 'I can't breathe in here.' My eyes widened in fear that panic was setting in again. I gulped but it felt like no oxygen was coming into my lungs.

'Come on.' She took my arm and gently led me out to the front of the hotel. 'Take some deep breaths, Daisy.' She kept her arm on me as she breathed deeply. I watched and copied her. 'That's it. Breathe.'

My breaths and racing pulse both started to slow down as I breathed along with her. When I felt calmer, I nodded. 'Thank you.'

'What's got you so worried? You might as well tell me now, dear.'

I had never come close to breaking down in front of her before but she was right; I had nothing to lose now. 'Henry just takes over. You all do. I feel like I can't be myself. That I can't think for myself. That I can't breathe. I left my wedding because you started talking about the future you had all planned for me. But I don't want it. I'm not sure I want a family after losing mine. And I want to keep on working. I don't know what I want to do yet but I haven't been happy in a long time. And that needs to change.' I inhaled and exhaled again. 'I'm sorry. I clung to Henry offering me security after I'd lost so much. I didn't want to be alone but that's not a reason to marry him.'

Then I let out a sob and put my hand over my mouth. I couldn't stop the tears though and they trailed down my face.

'Daisy.' She looked shocked and – for the first time in all the time I had known her – not calm and composed. She pulled me into her and gave me a tight squeeze. I let her hold me and a part of me wished it was my own mum that I was hugging. 'I need to ask you something and I want the truth,' she said. 'Promise me.'

I nodded once.

'Good. Do you love Henry?'

I shook my head against her.

She tensed up, then relaxed and patted my hair. 'Okay. I understand.' She leaned back and reached out to wipe a tear from my face. 'There's a lot I have regretted in my life,' she began, 'but I started out loving my husband,' she said softly. 'You don't love Henry so you don't want this life, Daisy. Sometimes, you can feel lonelier with someone than you do alone. Remember that, okay? You are never alone anyway. You always have yourself.'

I wiped the remainder of my tears away. 'Why are you being so nice to me?'

I was confused. She had always seemed so formidable, never what I'd describe as kind. And I was about to leave her son, and family, for good.

'Because I'm lonely, Daisy. I made my bed a long time ago. I'm sorry I didn't see you were feeling the same. Maybe it was because, despite what you might think, I wanted you to marry Henry and be part of the family. I thought having a daughter-in-law and grandchildren might make me happy. That wasn't fair to you, though. I should have been thinking about your happiness. Well, I am now. Before it's too late. Let me tell my husband and son.'

'No,' I said, surprising us both. 'I need to do it. I want to do it.' I had to finish what I had started on our wedding day. I had been second-guessing myself, worried I'd made another mistake, worried about the future, and worried about being alone but Henry's mum was right; I didn't want to live a life that didn't make me happy. Even if I didn't know what I was walking towards yet, I knew I had to walk away from this first. Then maybe I would find what I was looking for.

She smiled. 'You can do it. And Daisy, I want you to know you can always call me. Promise me you will if you ever need to?'

'I promise,' I whispered.

Together, we walked back to the table.

Henry turned to me. 'You two have been gone forever.'

His mum sat back down but I remained standing. She gave me a nod of encouragement so I took another breath and told Henry what I should have said when he first followed me to Birch Tree Farm.

'Henry, I'm sorry but I've thought about what you, all three of you, have said today and I can't do it. Any of it. When I left our wedding, it was because I wasn't happy. I wasn't in love with you. I have been scared of walking away from our life, from your family, from you, but I know I have to do it. I can't be happy if I stay.' My voice had started out shaky but it got stronger as I told him the truth that was in my heart. My shoulders relaxed in relief as I got the words out. 'I'm so grateful for everything you have all done for me. And I want to pay you back for the wedding. I'm so sorry that it hasn't worked out. But it would be a mistake for all of us if I came back with you. I'm going to stay in Birchbrook for a while until I decide what I want to do.'

'You can't be serious,' Henry said, his eyes narrowing.

'I am.' I slipped my engagement ring off my finger and placed it on the table beside him.

'I can't believe this,' Henry's dad said, glowering at me. 'After all we've done for you.'

'This is because of Blake,' Henry said then. 'She's back with her ex. I found them on that farm together! They reconnected

and started seeing each other. And she's chosen him over me!'
Henry whined to his parents.

'You didn't tell me that,' Henry's mum said to me.

'No,' I said firmly. 'It's not true. Blake lied when he said we
knew each other. We only just met when we both came to the
farm. Blake's ex jumped to the assumption we were seeing each
other. Blake didn't like the way you were talking to me so he
went along with it, and so did I, hoping it would get you to give
me some space,' I continued. 'You said you didn't believe it so
why are you saying it's the reason I'm ending things?'

'I said I didn't believe it to put a spanner in the works!' Henry
cried, turning red with anger again. 'To make you feel like there
was nothing between you two, and you belonged with me! I'm
not blind. I saw the way you two looked at each other and when
you were holding hands in the café, you seemed so happy...'

'I did?' I asked, amazed that Henry had noticed all of that. I
had thought he didn't see me but maybe it took almost losing me
to finally open his eyes.

'You lied when you said you hadn't slept with him,' Henry
continued.

'Henry!' his mother cried. 'Don't be so crass and disrespect-
ful,' she said, shocked.

'I didn't lie. We haven't slept together. And we didn't know
each other. But we have connected, yes. He's been a good friend
and a good listener,' I said.

Henry scoffed loudly.

'I do like him, Henry. I don't know if anything will happen in
the future or not. But it doesn't have any bearing on us. I promise
you,' I added sincerely. Henry wasn't the man for me. Whatever
might or might not happen with Blake, I knew I couldn't go back
to Henry. His mum was right. I would be happier alone than
doing that. 'I really am sorry.'

'I wasted almost five years on you,' he spat out then.

'And all that money we wasted on the wedding!' his dad added.

'That's enough now,' his mum snapped. She turned to me. 'I'll have all your things sent to the farm. And don't even think about paying us back for the wedding, for any of it. It's our fault we spent what we did.' She turned back to her son and husband before they could speak. 'That is my final say on that.'

Henry scraped his chair back and jumped up. 'Don't come crawling back to me when he breaks your heart. Because he will. He's head over heels for Sarah. He told her so.'

I tried not to let his words affect me. 'This isn't about them; it's about us.'

'Whatever, Daisy. You can call him to come and get you; I'm not driving you back there. I'm going to the bar.' At that, he stormed off without a second glance.

'I'm so disappointed in you,' his father said then, his voice stone cold.

'Daisy...' his mum began but I gave her a smile.

'It's okay. Thank you for everything.'

It was weird. I'd wanted to keep them all happy for so long that now I'd finally told them how I felt, I was relieved. They had never wanted me to be myself. They didn't really love me, or even know me. And they didn't want to either. I walked off the opposite way to Henry, knowing that would be the last time I saw them. It was sad to close the chapter on the last five years of my life. But I knew in my heart, it had been the right thing to do.

I looked down at my finger, no diamond ring on it any more.

My fear finally faded away. I was free.

I pulled my phone out of my bag and called Willow. 'Willow, can you please come and pick me up?'

26

'How do you feel?' Willow asked me when we passed the Birchbrook sign. The drive so far had been quiet, Willow letting me think over the end of the chapter I'd spent with Henry and his family, the uneasiness about what was ahead but mostly, the certainty that whatever was ahead would be better than what I'd left behind. Then I finally opened up and told her everything that had happened over lunch.

'Relieved. Better. Free. Like I need to take this chance now to find what I want. So I can be happy,' I said as the scorching afternoon sunshine poured through the car window, heating up my bare arm.

'I'm proud of you,' she said simply.

'That means a lot,' I replied, giving her a grateful smile. 'You know what I think I'll do?' I said. 'Could you drop me off to at the florist's? We need more flowers for the watering cans I bought. I can walk back afterwards; it'll do me good.'

'Okay, good idea. I need to carry on with my pumpkin planting. You'll have dinner with us though, yeah?'

'Definitely.'

Willow dropped me off in the High Street. The flowers in the hanging baskets were vibrant and the bunting swayed in the gentle breeze. Kids passed me eating ice creams on the way home from school. The café door was wide open and there was a queue inside, people buying iced coffees and milkshakes and picking up sweet treats for the evening. Female Pat waved from behind the counter when I glanced inside. A couple of people I passed by said, 'Good afternoon.' It was all unusual after spending so long in the city. I found myself walking with a spring in my step as I headed for the flower shop.

Mary was outside, refreshing the flowers in the pink bike – adding in pink peonies that were in full, beautiful bloom. She turned when I approached, her face breaking into a smile. 'Hello, Daisy. You know, before I got married, my husband hated pink but then when we bought our first home together, every week, he would buy me a bunch of pink flowers. When peonies were in season, they were my favourite. Even when I opened this shop and was surrounded by flowers, he carried on the tradition. I still miss him after ten years but these help.'

'I never buy flowers,' I admitted as I touched one of the petals, so delicate in my hand, the scent of the shop washing all over me like the best perfume. 'I should, though. Maybe I'll get myself some peonies for my room at the farm. And we need some more faux flowers, please, for some watering cans I bought.'

It was silly to think of flowers as something negative just because of what happened to my parents. My mum adored them. They brought her joy. And she named me after one. I shouldn't turn away from things that could make me happy. I thought about Bronte's garden and how she was surprised I didn't have one of my own. Suddenly, it became a dream to have one.

'Come on in.' Mary jolted me out of my thoughts.

I followed her into the shop.

While I was picking out flowers to buy for the farm, three sets of customers came in: a family and then a man looking for an anniversary bunch and a woman wanting birthday flowers for her mum. Mary looked harassed at the influx of customers so I went over to the man who seemed lost.

'Can I help?' I asked him.

'I have no idea what my girlfriend will like. We've been together a year,' he said, his eyes wide.

'Has she ever mentioned a flower she likes or liked a bunch you've bought before?'

He shook his head.

'How about her favourite colour?'

'Oh, she likes yellow,' he said, perking up a bit.

'Well then, let's avoid the typical red roses and go with something she likes.' I helped him create a beautiful bunch of yellow flowers and then, while I waited for Mary to finish up with the other customers, I picked out the faux flowers I wanted. I also gathered a bunch of peonies for myself and once the shop was empty, placed it all on the counter so I could pay.

'I don't know how to thank you,' Mary said gratefully. 'The shop gets so busy sometimes, I can't keep up. I shouldn't complain about doing good business but since my part-time girl left for university, I haven't found anyone to help out. Sometimes, I worry about the future of the shop... but you don't want to hear me going on. Okay, let's put the faux flowers through the till but the peonies are on me to say thank you.'

I protested but she wouldn't change her mind. She also gave me a wicker basket to carry it all in. 'I enjoyed it,' I told her as I hooked the basket on my arm. 'I've had a pretty crazy morning, and helping you really helped calm me down.'

'I'm glad. It's been lovely having you here,' Mary said, giving me a fond smile. 'Come by anytime.'

Smiling, I said I'd see her soon and headed out to start the walk back to the farm. Her words rang in my ears. I already wanted to go back to the comforting shop. It was burrowing itself into my soul.

It was a slightly uphill walk so I went slowly with the big basket, the sun draping itself around my shoulders like a heated blanket. The walk was scenic and quiet and as I made my way back, I thought about how flowers could mean so much to people. They were there when you had something you wanted or needed to say to a loved one. They could brighten someone's day or show you care or remind you of someone. My mum had loved to fill our house with flowers that had the best scents so that every day, our home smelt amazing: lavender or lilac or gardenia or sweet peas, lilies and roses, and peonies too.

I lifted the basket so I could breathe in the peony scent and I smiled. I would ask Willow for a vase and keep these by my bed.

A car beeped and slowed down beside me, pulling in ahead. I recognised Blake's car and I walked over.

'Want a lift back?' he asked after he'd rolled down the window. 'You look full to the brim with flowers.'

'It's getting very hot walking up the hill, I have to admit, so thanks,' I said, climbing into the air-conditioned car, placing the basket on my lap. 'You're back earlier than I thought you would be.'

'You too.' He gave me a small smile. 'Are you okay?' Then his eyes fell on my hands wrapped around the basket. 'Your ring is gone.'

'Yeah. I've ended it for good with Henry.'

Blake stared at me. 'You have?' he asked slowly, like he couldn't be sure that's what I'd said.

I nodded. 'Yes. His parents showed up for lunch and his dad started talking about their plans for me if I came back with them. I knew that I could never be myself with Henry. That life isn't what I want. So, I said goodbye to them. I gave him back his ring. I—'

Blake leaned over and gave me a quick kiss on my mouth. 'Sorry,' he said hastily. 'I—'

I put the basket of flowers down by my feet, reached for the collar of his polo shirt and pulled him back across the gearstick towards me. I saw a flash of his dimples as our lips met again, our mouths crashing together this time with urgency and passion that I hadn't felt in years. I knew I shouldn't compare Blake to Henry, but I also couldn't ignore how many sparks I felt kissing Blake. Sparks that just hadn't been there with Henry. It made things all the scarier but all the more exciting too.

Blake tried to wrap his arms around me but his seatbelt pulled him back. He leaned back to look into my eyes. His were dark and sparkling just like I knew mine were. 'Kissing in a car really isn't easy,' Blake said with a wry chuckle.

I giggled. 'Yeah, let's head back to the farm. Maybe we can carry on the kiss there?' I asked with a shy smile.

'I bloody hope so, Daisy. I've thought about kissing you again ever since our first kiss.' He switched the engine back on and pulled out into the road. 'I can't help but feel really relieved that you've ended things with Henry. I hoped you would but I would have understood if you hadn't. I just wanted you to be happy.'

'Thanks, Blake. And I've thought about kissing you again too.' I picked the basket back up to hold it steady as we drove towards the farm. 'But what about you and Sarah, if it's okay to ask?'

'I want you to feel able to ask me anything,' he replied matter-of-factly. Those words made my heart swell. 'Sarah asked if I'd take her back but I said I don't think it can work after how betrayed I felt that she cheated on me. I also said I'm not sure we were ever really compatible. She asked me if I wouldn't try again because of you, because of us...' Blake glanced at me. 'And I said I feel like I can be myself with you.'

'Me too,' I replied with a smile.

'Sarah tried to persuade me to keep working on our dating app together. She told me to think about it overnight, then we can talk again. I reluctantly agreed to it. I keep thinking about all that money and time we've invested in the app... I just don't know what to do.'

'Would you be able to have just a professional relationship with her?' I asked him, relieved that he didn't want her back romantically. I understood that their business relationship was more complicated to end.

'That's what I need to figure out. And if not, what do we do about the app? I just don't know if I fundamentally like the idea that people can misrepresent themselves on there by using AI. I know she didn't like how I messaged her before we met but maybe that was a sign for us both that we weren't meant to be.'

We pulled into the farm then and were shocked to see an ambulance outside and Willow and Dylan by it, looking worried.

'Shit,' Blake said, hurriedly pulling into a space in the driveway. We hopped out of his car and rushed over to them.

'Willow, what's going on?' I called out as we approached.

Dylan had his arm around her and they turned to face us. Willow's face was white with shock. 'It's my dad,' she gasped out.

'Oh my God,' I said, fearing the worst.

Blake reached for my hand and I gripped his tightly.

'We found Adam lying on the kitchen floor and called an

ambulance. They've put him on a stretcher and...' Dylan stopped as one of the paramedics came out of the ambulance.

'Okay, your father is stable,' she said to Willow. 'He might have had a heart attack; they'll have to do more tests at the hospital. Do you want to come along with him?'

'Yes.' Willow clutched Dylan's arm. 'Will you come too? But what about Maple and the farm...'

'Don't worry,' I assured her. 'We'll look after everything.'

'Absolutely,' Blake added.

'Thank you,' Willow said, hurrying after the paramedic.

'I'll follow in my car,' Dylan said, rushing off towards it.

'Phone us when you know anything,' I called after Willow's retreating back. I saw her nod before she jumped into the ambulance. We stood back and watched as it left the farm with the sirens sounding, Dylan following in his car.

'I hope he'll be okay,' I said, leaning against Blake for support. 'We've lost so many people already. Willow can't go through what I went through.' My voice broke at the end. I couldn't bear to think of her losing both her parents as well. I felt panic edge in slowly like the way watercolour paint seeps across a blank page.

'From what I know of Adam, he's made of tough stuff. I think he'll be okay, Daisy,' Blake said, calm and stoic. 'Let's check on Maple and the ponies and do everything that we need to then I'll make us dinner. We'll keep busy until we hear from them, yeah?'

I looked at Blake and tried to focus on him, and what he was suggesting, rather than my fear. I nodded. 'Yes. I'll take these flowers out to the field too.'

He was right; making sure the farm was okay while they were all at the hospital was the best thing to do. I heard a bark through the closed farmhouse door – Maple must be freaking out. She needed me. My panic slid away. I hurried over to open it and I crouched down to pat her.

'Don't worry, girl. They'll be back soon,' I said, hoping with all my heart that's what would happen.

27

The afternoon was long while we waited for news. We tried to keep on top of everything that needed to be done on the farm. Then we headed into the shady, cool kitchen and Blake made us dinner. He admitted the only meal he was really good at was macaroni cheese and that was fine with me. I poured us both a glass of wine as he put the dish into the Aga to crisp up.

My phone, which I'd placed on the kitchen counter, rang out.

I grabbed it and answered the call from Dylan. 'Hi, is Uncle Adam okay?' I asked him breathlessly and hopefully.

'He's okay,' Dylan said without preamble. 'It wasn't a heart attack. He collapsed as his blood pressure spiked and he got really dizzy. They're putting him on medication and we're going to stay here overnight. But it wasn't a heart attack. They are trying to bring his blood pressure down, and are talking about changes he needs to make, but he will be able to come home tomorrow.'

I breathed out. 'Thank God.' I smiled at Blake, who was watching me with concern. 'Send him and Willow my love.' We said goodbye and I hung up, my chest sagging with relief.

'Will he be okay?'

'Yes,' I said, letting out a sob. I had feared the worst. But my uncle was going to make it. 'I've tried so hard not to get hurt again...' I started but I was unable to finish my sentence.

'Come here.' Blake held out his arms and I stepped into his embrace. 'It's okay. That was such a shock. Your uncle will be fine, right? What did Dylan say?'

I leaned against Blake's chest as I told him what Dylan had said on the phone. Blake stroked my hair while I talked, and it was so soothing. I looked up at him then. 'I stayed away from here for five years after my aunt, Willow's mum, passed away. I couldn't take losing someone else I loved. I really thought for a moment I was about to. But you know what?'

'What?' Blake asked me gently as he held me tight still.

'I realised I wouldn't have regretted coming back. If anything, I would have regretted it more if I hadn't seen Adam again and spent this time with him. I'm glad I'm here.'

'Your family are glad you're here. I'm glad you're here.'

'It really helped having you by my side today,' I admitted. Blake had helped me not panic by offering a practical plan. By doing what was needed, I kept myself in the present moment and didn't freak out over worst-case scenarios like I so often did.

Blake's face lit up, rewarding me with his full smile. 'I feel the same way. We hardly know each other but why do you feel so good in my arms?'

His words flooded me with warmth. 'I was so scared to let down my walls for years, but with you, I'm not so scared any more.'

'I don't want you to ever be scared again.' Blake leaned down and brushed his lips against mine, sending warmth trickling down my spine. 'I don't want to stop kissing you but dinner is ready,' he said with a smile.

Maple barked behind us like she recognised the word 'dinner' and wanted hers. I wouldn't put it past the clever dog either. We both laughed and reluctantly parted.

While Blake got our dinner ready, I fed Maple then we sat down together. Candlelight flickered between us and we smiled across the table at one another.

'Shall we toast to your uncle?' Blake asked after pouring us both a glass of wine. We had bowls full of comforting macaroni cheese in front of us.

'To Adam,' I agreed and we clinked glasses. I took a long gulp then Blake urged me to try the pasta. I took a big bite, suddenly starving. 'Oh wow,' I murmured. 'This is just what I needed.'

'Me too,' Blake said, catching my eye. I felt my cheeks blush a little under his piercing gaze. He flashed those dimples at me again and I wondered if he knew how they made him look as delicious as this pasta he'd made me. 'Are you blushing, Daisy?' he teased me.

'No!' I cried then I laughed. 'Maybe a little bit. Sometimes, it feels like you're guessing my thoughts.'

Blake chuckled. 'You do that to me too. It feels like I've known you for so much longer than I have. It's kind of crazy how Sarah jumped to the conclusion we were together...'

'Maybe she saw something before we even did.'

'I told you – when I saw you in your wedding dress, I wondered if I was having a premonition.' Blake winked then reached across to touch my hand. I moved it so he could take hold of it properly. 'It's never felt fake between us, even if our exes weren't sure what to believe.'

'Henry admitted he saw something and that's why he acted so adamant that we weren't together. Maybe he was trying to convince himself, and me. But you're right; I'm not sure it was ever a lie. We connected so quickly. I've opened up more to you already than I ever did with Henry. And when you kissed me, my world turned upside down.'

Blake nodded. 'I know exactly what you mean.'

We finished up our food and cleared up together as I told Blake I'd asked my cousin if I could stay for the rest of the summer. 'I just feel like this is where I need to be right now,' I said.

'She will need your help if your uncle has to take things easier. There's only a week until the pick-your-own opens, and Willow and Dylan seem to have so much to deal with. I think you're doing the right thing, Daisy.'

'Only a week left of your stay, though,' I said lightly, but the thought of him leaving already felt sad.

'Let's not think about that right now.' Blake gestured to Maple, who was sitting by us, her tail wagging as she stared us down. 'Think this one is waiting for her w-a-l-k,' he said, spelling the word out.

I smiled. 'I think you're right.'

'Why don't we go together? We can bring the ponies in for the night too. And it's looking like we'll get another beautiful sunset.'

I eyed him. 'You're a romantic, Blake Daniels, aren't you?' I said teasingly.

He grinned. 'You seem to make me think about romantic things, Daisy Connor. I don't think I looked at the sunset once in the city but out here, it's too beautiful not to want to look at it.' He reached out and took my hand. 'Is it too corny to say I feel the same about you?'

'Yes, definitely too cheesy. But I liked it anyway.' I kissed his cheek. 'Let's go outside. I know what you mean about being here; I want to be outside more than I ever usually do. Maybe it's a sign I don't really want to go back to living in a city now.'

We left the farmhouse, Maple running off in front of us, the light golden and hazy outside as the sun began to set.

'Being back at my family home has made me realise just how much I'd missed living in the countryside.' Blake looked out at the scenery around us. 'It's one of the reasons I'm reluctant to agree to carry on working with Sarah. We'd have to be in the city.'

'What would you do though if you let go of the app?'

'That's the million-dollar question.' Blake reached out for my hand and our fingers entwined as we walked out towards the crop fields. 'How about you?'

'Come back and ask at the end of the summer.' We looked at one another. After I'd said those playful words, I realised that Blake wouldn't be here then. Would we still talk? It seemed impossible that he could leave and that we wouldn't see each other any more. It felt almost as if fate had brought us both to the farm together this summer.

The pony enclosure came into sight then, the sun dipping behind the ponies. Maple barked as soon as she caught sight of Jasmine and Blossom.

'Still suspicious of them?' I asked the dog with a laugh. We followed her, and the ponies moved towards the fence when they saw us coming. I glanced at Blake as Maple barked again at the ponies. 'Hope she doesn't know something we don't. Stay, girl,' I said, gesturing for her to sit beside me while Blake went over to open up the gate to let the ponies out.

He clucked for the ponies and led them through the gate and I joined them, whistling for Maple. The ponies had got so used to this walk now that they followed us without us needing to use a lead. Maple ran off too towards the barn, also having memorised the evening walk now the ponies were on the farm. Animals were pretty remarkable.

Once we had put the ponies into the barn for the night, we walked the long way back to the farmhouse so that Maple could stretch her legs more. The sun had fully set then, the sky turning indigo blue. The stars had woken up and were twinkling down on us.

We reached the farmhouse door then and Blake turned to me. 'Shall we look at the stars again?'

28

Blake laid out the blanket on a patch of grass behind the farmhouse overlooking the crop fields. I had put Maple in her bed and followed him out here, the peace and quiet settling over me, calming after such a full-on day.

We got down onto the blanket and looked up at the sky.

'It would be a shame to miss the opening of the pick-your-own season,' Blake suddenly said, turning to look at me. 'After I'm helping to get the farm ready.'

I met his eyes and smiled, my heart lifting at the thought of him staying just a bit longer. 'It would,' I agreed.

'Are you really okay after saying goodbye to Henry?' he asked softly.

'Yes,' I replied to Blake's question without hesitation. 'I never loved him. And I'm relieved that I've closed that chapter. I've been scared of being alone for a long time but I know now that's better than feeling lonely in my relationship. I thought I'd found a family but I hadn't. I didn't belong with them.'

'I'm so happy to hear you say that,' Blake said. He leaned forward, gently kissing my lips. When he slightly pulled back, his eyes were dark and smouldering. I realised just how close we were. Out here all alone on the farm. The only things that could see us were the stars.

I smiled and he found my lips again. He let go of my hand and wrapped his arms around my waist, pulling me into his chest and I wrapped mine around his neck, eagerly kissing him back. From the first moment our lips touched, I'd wanted to kiss him more but there was the block of Henry and of Sarah between us. Now, we kissed freely and with abandon. I wasn't sure I had ever enjoyed kissing a man so much before. Blake was a mixture of gentle and passionate and our bodies curved against each other like they had always meant to be together.

Blake's hands moved into my hair then as our kiss turned electric. He pulled back, his eyes searching mine. 'I don't think I've ever wanted a woman as much as I want you.' Then he shook his head. 'I'm never this honest, this open...'

'Nor am I,' I whispered. I didn't want to hold back with Blake like I had with men so many times.

'You're gorgeous, inside and out,' Blake said then.

Those words lit a fire within me. I climbed up onto him, my legs draping either side of his waist. Blake sucked in a gasped breath as he looked up at me. I reached for my dress and pulled it off, leaving myself just in my underwear. 'I want you too.' His honesty was arousing and gave me the confidence to be honest right back.

Blake stared at me like he couldn't believe his luck. 'I wasn't expecting that,' he said with a gruff chuckle. He reached up, resting his hands on my waist, warm and strong. 'You're full of surprises, Daisy.'

'I told you, I'm feeling more like myself than I have felt in a long time.' I was once playful and passionate and right now, I wanted to be both with Blake. 'It's a warm night; maybe you should join me by taking some clothes off?'

Blake grinned, flashing his dimples. 'My turn to surprise you.' He suddenly rolled me over onto my back, making me squeal. Then he sat up and pulled his polo shirt off, revealing that toned, sun-kissed chest again. This time, I didn't want to hide that I was looking at it. I wanted him to see that I was. His eyes darkened further at my heated gaze. He leaned back down and kissed me hard.

This time, we went straight into a hungry, desperate kiss, his hands in my hair, mine clutching his bare back. Blake lifted off me a little bit and slid a hand from my hair down my cheek then he cupped my chin, raising it gently so I looked into his eyes. 'Can I touch you, gorgeous?' he whispered huskily, sending a delicious shiver down my spine.

I nodded desperately and was rewarded with another sexy smile. He touched my lips with his fingertips then carried on sliding them down my neck. He leaned down and kissed me under my hair, making me shiver again.

'Hmm, do you like that?'

'Yes,' I gasped.

Blake kissed me again. Then he trailed his fingertips down to my collarbone and across my chest before he gently brushed the tops of my breasts peeking out of my bra. He moved across and did the same the other side, leaving goosebumps on my skin.

My breathing had become shallow now. But it wasn't from panic. I felt his touch everywhere. And I wanted more.

'Can I take your bra off?' he whispered.

'Yes,' I breathed out as he reached behind me and undid the clasp. I lifted up from the blanket as he pulled my bra off and tossed it on the grass. Then he carried on gently touching me with his fingertips, teasing my nipples. I writhed beneath him, arching my back, wanting him to be less gentle.

'Are you feeling impatient?' Blake asked with a raised eyebrow.

'I want more,' I confessed breathlessly.

'I need to take my time, Daisy. I plan on making this last as long as possible.' He moved his fingertips across my breasts again, smiling at the little gasps I made. He leaned down and kissed me softly in between them, then on both breasts around my nipples, making me arch my back. Until finally, he put his mouth over a nipple and drew it inside, sucking on it gently. His eyes stayed locked on mine as he sucked harder and I let out a little moan. He moved to the other side and closed his eyes, cupping my breast with his hand as he sucked on the other nipple, hardening it instantly. When he lifted off me, I knew my eyes were as dark as his were.

He carried on with his touch, moving across my stomach and then down towards my underwear. 'How do you feel about getting naked?' Blake whispered as his fingers moved underneath the elastic.

'Yes,' was all I could gasp out. He grinned, definitely enjoying making me squirm. I exhaled shakily as he slipped his fingertips under my underwear and gently pulled my knickers down my thighs and legs, before tossing them aside. Then he let himself look at me, his eyes taking in my body from head to toe. I watched his gaze, feeling heated as he drank me in greedily as if I was the best thing he had ever looked at.

'God, Daisy, do you have any idea how sexy you are? So unbelievably hot. I can't take my eyes off of you,' he said gruffly but with such passion, I had to believe that was what he really did think of me.

'Blake, you're driving me crazy,' I admitted, my body tingling with wanting him to touch me more. I squirmed on the blanket again, wishing he would speed up just a little bit.

He stroked down my leg, lingering on my inner thigh as I trembled again. He stroked down one leg and then the other. 'So soft,' he whispered before he moved one hand back up my leg, moving so slowly, I was practically panting with want when he reached my inner thigh again. 'Do you want me touch you, Daisy?'

'Please,' I almost begged him now. Blake's touch was exactly what I both wanted and needed.

'Good girl,' Blake said, placing one hand on my stomach and then with the other, he gently stroked me, watching my reaction as he hovered above me on the blanket. I gasped when he found the exact spot where I ached for his touch. He was soft and gentle to start and then he applied more pressure.

I let out a moan, biting my lip self-consciously.

'Don't ever stop yourself from enjoying this,' Blake said.

I let go of my lip and our eyes locked.

'Hmm,' he encouraged me. 'Is this okay?'

I nodded but when he raised an eyebrow, I knew he wanted more. Needed more. 'Yes, just like that,' I whispered as he touched me. My right hand clutched the blanket as he hit the right spot over and over again, causing heat to pool in the pit of my stomach as I moaned my appreciation.

'Are you close?' he asked me then. I could only nod. He bent his head down and I gasped when his mouth found me. His tongue took over from his fingertips as they slid inside me instead.

'Oh my God,' I breathed as I reached out and ran my hand through his hair between my legs. 'Blake,' I cried, feeling free to enjoy this as much as possible. I basked in his attention. Pleasure rolled over me and pulled me under like the best possible wave.

My muscles tightened everywhere while I lost all control. 'I'm going to...' and then I cried out as I hit my peak, letting out a loud moan that echoed around the dark, still farm. Collapsing back on the blanket, my body throbbed with aftershocks of delight.

Blake leaned down to kiss me gently on the lips, stroking back my hair that had gone wild from my wriggling under him. 'Was that okay, gorgeous?' he asked.

I stared at him in wonder. 'Okay? Jesus, Blake, I don't think I've ever come like that,' I choked out breathlessly, still a bit dazed by how he had treated my body. I tried to think about a night like that with Henry, searching for a memory just as electric as that had just been with Henry but I came up blank. We'd never had that kind of passion. He'd never been as tender or as focused as Blake had been on me, like we were the only two people in the world. Just us.

I'd never been as focused before either. My mind had always wandered. I had still worried, still been anxious, not fully relaxed. I hadn't been swept up or carried away, but Blake had taken me completely out of myself in the best possible way.

I leaned in and gave him a long and lingering kiss. When I leaned back, he was the one who was breathless. I smiled. 'Can I touch you now?' I asked, raising an eyebrow playfully.

'I might die if you don't,' he replied huskily.

I reached for the buttons of his shorts, feeling how turned on he was by what had just happened, which made me feel eager to make him feel as good as he'd made me feel. Blake pulled me to him and we kissed again, our tongues crashing together as the passion just kept on burning. I reached down to stroke him through his boxers, making him gasp this time. 'Should we...?' I trailed off, unsure what he wanted.

'We have plenty of time,' Blake replied. 'I don't have a

condom out here and right now, I don't want you to stop for me to go and get one.'

I pulled his boxers down and added them to the pile of my underwear.

My body buzzed at him saying we had plenty of time. That this wasn't a one-moment thing. That he wanted more like I did. I touched him and thought about how good it would feel for him to be inside me. Then I slid down in between his legs, making his breath hitch in anticipation. I smiled as Blake moaned out my name as my mouth took over from my hand and I realised I'd never enjoyed doing this as much as I was right now.

29

I opened one eye and blinked as the early-dawn light streamed down on me. I groaned. My whole body felt stiff. I opened my other eye.

'Oh,' I said as I looked at Blake's face next to me, his eyes still closed, his chest rising and falling with his even breaths. I squinted and realised we were still outside on the blanket. No wonder my body ached. We must have fallen asleep after we'd finished kissing and touching. We'd slept on the grass with just a blanket. Blake's arm was draped across me and it felt strong and safe. But this definitely wasn't at all comfortable.

'Blake?' I reached out to touch his arm. 'The sun is rising,' I said softly, wondering when Willow and Dylan might come back to the farm and thinking about all the things we'd have to do before they did. All the morning chores. Plus we'd both need hot showers after sleeping outside. And I needed coffee if I was going to be capable of doing any of those things. 'We need to get up.'

Blake shifted beside me and groaned. He opened his eyes. 'You're still here with me,' he mumbled, half-asleep.

'Yeah, we fell asleep out here.' I watched as his eyes drifted shut again. 'No, Blake, we need to wake up,' I said, louder this time, and I nudged him again.

He responded by pulling me towards him and pressing his lips against mine. I couldn't help but melt into him and I kissed him back, my lips tingling from all the kisses last night. 'Hmm, good morning,' he said when he opened his eyes and took me in properly. 'It's nice to wake up with you.'

'You too, although I'm kind of concerned how our backs and necks are going to feel when we get up off the ground.'

'Oh, shit.' Blake looked around. 'We fell asleep out here.'

'Yeah, I seem to remember us getting dressed and you pulling us back down for more kisses...'

He grinned. 'The kisses were too good to stop.'

'Yeah, they were,' I agreed.

'Last night was special, Daisy,' he said then, wrapping his arms around me. 'For me, anyway...' he added uncertainly.

'Me too,' I assured him.

He smiled happily. 'I guess we'd better get up,' he said, stretching out his arms with a groan.

'Let's try.' I eased myself out from under him and sat up, my body not enjoying the movement at all. I rolled my shoulders and rubbed the back of my neck. 'We're too old to sleep out like this.' I giggled, thinking about summers here as a child and how I wouldn't have thought twice about lying out on the grass. Now, my grown-up body definitely preferred a comfortable bed.

Blake stood up and held out a hand, helping me to get to my feet too. Then he held out his arms and I stepped into his embrace. He held me tightly against him and we stood there for a moment hugging. I hadn't had a lot of affection recently and I wondered if Blake was the same as we leaned against each other, neither wanting to break the cuddle.

Until I heard a dog barking in the distance.

'Maple is up,' I said. 'We better go and feed her and start the morning chores,' I added with a sigh.

Blake let go of me but he dropped me a kiss on my lips. 'You're right. I need coffee first.'

'You read my mind.'

We grinned at each other and set off for the farmhouse, holding hands like it was something we had always done.

The sun rose behind us as we walked, promising another lovely day. Right now, before the farm would be full of visitors next week, it belonged just to us and it would keep our secret that we'd spent the night together. I knew I'd never forget that night with Blake. It had shown me that you had to grab moments in life that made you feel alive. Even if you were scared of what might happen next. You would end up regretting it otherwise.

I had shied away from moments like that for a long time. Too scared of loss and pain and sadness. Of feeling grief again. Of losing people I loved again. But I knew I had missed out on so much by doing that. So, as we walked back into the farmhouse, I promised myself that it was something I wouldn't do any more.

* * *

When Willow, Dylan and Uncle Adam returned, it was past lunchtime. I ran over to the driveway when I heard Dylan's car coming up the gravel. I'd been feeding the chickens and collecting eggs while Blake finished the second coat of white paint on the pony enclosure he had built with Dylan.

'I'm so glad you're all back,' I called out warmly as they climbed out of the car. I looked anxiously at my uncle. He looked tired and pale but he smiled back at me and looked at the farm-house behind me with relief.

'I'm so happy to be home,' he said.

'Let's get you up to your room and you can have a nap—' Willow began, the anxiety clear on her face and in her voice.

'Love, I'll go into the kitchen. I've only just left my hospital bed,' he said gently but firmly.

'And you say I'm stubborn,' Willow told him with a roll of her eyes.

'You both are,' Dylan butted in. 'Why don't you both get comfy in the kitchen and I'll make us all tea and we can have some cake?' He gestured around. 'The farm was in great hands so you can both rest for the day. No arguments. It was a long night,' he said, so firmly that neither of them protested. He nodded. 'Good. Let's go. Ah, here's Blake, so we can all sit down together.'

I turned around to watch him walking over, pulling a T-shirt back on after working shirtless and I got a lovely flashback of his arms around me last night. I blushed but luckily, the three of them were already heading for the farmhouse and couldn't see my shy smile as Blake approached. 'We're all having tea and cake, no arguments, apparently,' I said when we fell into step with one another.

'The pony enclosure is all done. They are ready to spend their days in the strawberry fields. It's looking really good out there.'

'Not long to go now,' I agreed. I had put the faux flowers in the watering cans. All we needed now were the picnic benches and the Portaloos to arrive, then set up the till table where people would weigh and pay for their picked fruit and veg, and for the Birchbrook Café van to pitch up, ready for visitors.

Willow was almost done planting her pumpkins and then she could focus on the pick-your-own season.

We paused at the door to the farmhouse. I heard Maple greeting her family with boundless enthusiasm, Willow laughing at her dog and Dylan telling Adam to sit down. I felt a warmth travel up my body. I hadn't heard family noises like this in a long time. I thought about Henry's house. It had often been so quiet, I was able to hear my heart beating. I looked at Blake, wanting to tell him all of this, but his phone rang before I could.

'It's Sarah,' he said, staring at it.

'Go ahead,' I said, although I really didn't want her interrupting our nice day. But he had his own closure to deal with as I had with Henry. I knew I needed to be patient because he had been so with me. I'd been wearing another man's engagement ring the whole time we'd known each other, after all.

'You're going back to the city?' Blake asked, his eyes catching mine. There was a pause as my heart lifted. 'What do you mean – a surprise? Why can't you tell me... Sarah, we need to talk... wait...' Blake sighed heavily as he listened to her. 'Fine, okay. I'll see you soon.' He hung up with a frown. 'Sarah is going back to the city. Says she is working on something to do with our app and won't tell me as she wants it to be a surprise if it all comes together. Said she'd call me soon. I guess at least she'll be away from Birchbrook for a while.'

I could tell he wasn't sure if her surprise would be good or not. I touched his hand. 'Maybe it will help you both decide what to do about working together,' I suggested. I knew it was foolish of me to hope that it was something that would let Blake walk away because Sarah had made it clear she didn't want that. And I needed to keep reminding myself that Blake lived in the city. He had talked about enjoying being back near home but that didn't mean he was going to let go of the life he had been making for the past year.

Blake nodded. 'I hope so, yeah. Either way, we'll need to talk when she gets back and make some decisions.'

I was dying to know what decisions he was considering but I wasn't sure I should ask. Things felt so new between us. I was glad Sarah wasn't coming here today, though.

'That sounds like a good plan. Maybe we can talk after dinner about last night?' There had been so much to do today, we hadn't had a chance to be alone really and we wouldn't now until everyone separated for bed.

'I'd like that. Do you want to come to the cottage when you can? I have some wine. We can talk then. And maybe...' He dropped a quick kiss on my cheek. 'I can kiss you properly,' he added in a whisper.

I chuckled, happy that he wanted to kiss me again. I wanted to kiss him again too. 'I might let you,' I replied coyly as we walked inside and through into the kitchen, holding hands until we reached the doorway then we let go before Willow or Dylan or Uncle Adam clocked us. We needed to talk before we let them see we'd grown even closer while they were away. But I longed to talk to Willow about how good it had been to kiss Blake. To really kiss him finally. I wondered if she had felt the same after she had kissed Dylan.

We sat down at the table opposite one another and Blake dropped me a wink, making me think he was thinking along the same lines as me.

'How are you all doing?' Blake asked the others as Dylan brought over a tray with mugs of tea and Willow carried over the lemon drizzle Uncle Adam had made a couple of days ago. 'We were worried about you.'

Blake using the 'we' made me smile although I tried to hide it because I knew Willow didn't miss a trick.

'Thank you. It was scary, I'll admit. But these two looked after me as usual,' Adam said, giving his daughter and her boyfriend a fond look. 'And I'll be right as rain.'

'You need to take things easier,' Willow reminded him. She looked weary from the night. 'They said you'll need to cut down on what you do on the farm...' she trailed off.

'I already have,' Adam reminded her. 'I've signed this place over to you, and let Dylan take on much more but I can't just put my feet up all the time...'

'But Dad—' Willow said before my uncle cut her off.

'I'm not going anywhere yet,' he interrupted, reaching across the table to give her hand a squeeze.

'Promise?' Willow asked lightly but I saw a flash of younger Willow across her face. The Willow who, like me, had lost her mother. I could imagine how scared she was of losing my uncle too.

'I'm like this farmhouse: built to last,' he replied with a cheeky grin as we all knew the house needed lots of repairs that Willow and Dylan were getting round to as and when they had the time and money.

'It does make you think, doesn't it?' Dylan said then. 'About how life can just throw surprises your way. Sometimes, they are good ones...' He reached for Willow's hand and squeezed it. I felt myself glance at Blake, who did the same to me. 'But they can also be ones that you never want to happen. All we can do is try to make the most of life while we can and be around the people we love as much as we can.'

Willow looked at him. 'Are you thinking about your family?'

'I guess you going to see yours,' Dylan said to Blake, 'did make me think about how long it's been since I've seen Nate and my father. Nate is my older brother,' he added so I knew who he was talking about. 'Neither of them understood me coming to live here and I just gave up trying. Maybe I should try again, though.'

'I was nervous to go home because I felt like a failure,' Blake said. 'But then I realised, it's home for a reason, you know? They are there for me whatever path I take, and I want to be there for them too.'

'No one fails in life,' Adam said. 'We are all just trying our best with what we've got and we all make mistakes. I know all your families just want to see you happy. It's all I've ever wanted for Willow. And they are proud of you. How could they not be?'

I swallowed a lump in my throat. We all came from families broken in some way – by death or by someone leaving – and yet here we all were around this table together doing our best to live our lives despite our losses. 'This summer is teaching me to not let life pass you by – if there's something you want to do or someone you want to tell something to, you need to just do it. Even if it's scary. I know my parents...' I took a moment to get the rest of my words out. Blake shifted in his chair and I just knew he was itching to comfort me. Even though he couldn't, it helped anyway that he was there and he was on my side. As they all were around this table. 'They would have hated to see me stay somewhere that I didn't want to be. And my mum. She wouldn't want me not to do something because it reminded me of her; she would encourage me to follow my heart.' I thought of how happy working with flowers these past couple of weeks had been making me. I knew I couldn't ignore that feeling. Nor did I want to. The thought of going back to an office job again made me sad.

'Your mother was a wonderful woman, just like my wife,' Uncle Adam said. 'Two women both taken from us far too soon. And my brother too. They would all be unable to believe the wonderful women their daughters have grown into.' He wiped a tear from his cheek and by this time, we were all feeling pretty choked up too. 'They would also laugh at us for all being so soppy right now,' he added then, making us all laugh. 'I just want to say, whatever happens in your lives, you can always come back here, okay? Can't they, Willow?'

She smiled. 'I'd kill them if they didn't,' she said, making us laugh even more.

We all tucked in to the tea and cake then, and I could tell we all felt a little bit better. I didn't know what it was about Birch Tree Farm but it seemed to be healing us all piece by piece.

30

I was able to catch Willow alone after dinner. I saw her walking Maple out on the Strawberry Fields Trail and I caught up with them before I planned to go and see Blake.

'I wanted to walk the trail,' Willow said, smiling when I fell into step with them. 'We open on Monday, which is crazy. I feel like we've been on this huge journey since last September. The farm looks so different but also, I *feel* so different. I thought I'd have to let go of this place and now I just want to make it as special as it used to be when my mum was still alive. I can't though, can I?' she asked, looking across at me.

Maple sniffed the sunflowers ahead of us, reaching up to catch the last rays of sun for the day. It was still warm – Willow was in denim shorts and a T-shirt, and I had on a linen shirt with my shorts, both of us in comfy trainers. Her hair was in its usual messy bun whereas I'd kept mine down but had on my straw hat to keep the sun off me.

'No, you can't, but you can make it your own,' I said. 'As soon as I came back here, I felt the same feeling that I felt years ago. It's so peaceful and homely. And your mum made it like that and now you have too. The farm will never be exactly like it was because she's not here but it can be just as special. And it is.'

'Thanks, Daisy. I'm really worried about Dad. The doctor said he really should retire completely. But I know he thinks we need him still. And I worry he's right.' Willow sighed. 'Will I really be able to keep the farm going long-term? Can I do it alone?'

'Well, you're not alone; you have Dylan, and I'll stay for the rest of the summer.'

'Dad's partner, Taylor said she'd come by more often to make sure he's taking care of himself so I can focus on the pick-your-own opening, but there feels like so much to juggle.'

'Maybe you could think about bringing someone on full-time, to pick up some of the slack.'

Willow eyed me. 'But that would take the farm out of the family! I don't know. I need to make the pick-your-own season the best this year then think about what to do. Will you help me make sure Dad takes it easy for the rest of the summer? We can't lose him.'

'Of course. And we won't, don't worry,' I told her firmly. I wasn't going to let her turn into me, worrying about losing people instead of living.

'It's not just Dad. I've been thinking about Dylan saying he misses his family. What would I do if he decides living here isn't working for him? If he goes to see them, they might persuade him to leave me.'

I shook my head. 'You two are rock solid. He chose to stay on the farm with you because he sees his future by your side. And you could always go with him.'

She grimaced. 'It didn't go well the first time I met Dylan's brother.'

'You can win anyone over, I think. You've got this place back

on track. You put your mind to things and look what happens...'
I gestured around. 'The pumpkin patch went so well; there's no
reason why this summer season won't be just as popular, or even
more so.'

'Unless it was a fluke.'

I nudged her. 'You're the optimistic one of the two of us;
what's going on?'

That made her laugh a bit. 'I know, I'm sorry. But sometimes,
that's been a fault of mine so I'm trying to be a bit more realistic.
And it's been a crazy twenty-four hours. Dylan thinks the farm is
solid profit-wise for five years based on our projections but
sometimes, his talk of numbers goes a bit over my head. I guess I
try to have on my business head but I end up feeling more than
thinking.'

'I don't think there's anything wrong with that,' I replied as
we strolled past the fruit and vegetables that were flourishing
day by day. The sprinklers and irrigation systems were on and
the air was cool and damp after the earlier summer warmth.
Everything felt like it was refreshing itself ready for a new day. I
wanted to do the same. 'You were always a dreamer. I was too but
I let it go. And it didn't make me happy, Willow. I want to get that
back. Feeling what is right for me, not talking myself into things
that seem sensible or make sense on paper but don't bring me
joy. I've spent so long doing what I thought I should do.' I
gestured with my arms. 'Look around. You're doing exactly what
you want to do. Never be worried or sorry about that. Yes, Dylan
may need to rein you in a bit,' I grinned at her and she rolled her
eyes, 'but he knows how special your dreams are, and wants to
be part of it all, and help you make those dreams come true.
That's the kind of partner we all want and deserve in life.'

We strolled on towards the strawberries in a thoughtful
silence. Jasmine and Blossom were grazing in their new enclo-

sure and they came over to the gate when they saw us, eager as usual for a treat. Willow bent down and picked two strawberries. She handed me one then ate one herself before picking two more and going over to give them to the ponies. The fruit was ripe now and sweet and juicy like the strawberries always were here. Tasting them sent me right back to when I was a child sneaking strawberries when my aunt and uncle weren't looking, running around the farm with Willow in the sunshine, watching my mum picking flowers to put in a vase on the kitchen table. Memories that would always be there. I looked around. I was starting to believe more in signs than ever this summer. It felt like the farm was giving me them every day; all I needed to do was listen, and follow where they were trying to lead me. That was the part that required a whole lot of courage, though.

'And what about you?' Willow asked me then. 'What happened while you and Blake were all alone here?'

'Well...' I trailed off with a coy smile.

'Daisy! OMG, tell me everything right now!'

'Okay, well, we kissed and a whole lot more,' I confessed as I joined her by the gate to reach out and stroke the ponies as they enjoyed their strawberry treat. 'And it was pretty amazing.'

'Wow. I knew there was nothing fake about your dating!' she declared.

I rolled my eyes. 'That was partly your fault.'

'Oops.' She shrugged. 'It all worked out, though, right? You've let Henry go for good, and now you can have a fresh start here in Birchbrook with Blake.'

'Well, don't get ahead of yourself; he won't be here for much longer.'

'You don't know that. Look at Dylan.'

I shook my head. 'It's all too crazy, though, isn't it? We've known each other less than two weeks, and we both were in long-term, serious relationships. I almost got married! We shouldn't even be thinking about each other. There is so much else I should be thinking about. What I'm going to do about work, where I'll live, what I want after summer ends... It's a lot.'

'We Connor women know how to overthink, that's for sure. But, like you said, we also are big dreamers. You'll work out what you want to do. You just need to let yourself dream again.'

We watched the ponies jostling each other for our attention and Maple came and sat by us, giving them a smug look when Willow reached down to pat her. Above us, the sky turned hazy, clouds drifting across it.

I tried to clear my mind and instead of letting myself freak out about the next few weeks and what came after them, I focused on what I wanted right here, right now in this moment.

And there was one clear answer.

* * *

Blake's cottage was cool and quiet when I walked in. With the other cottages being renovated first, it still had its quaint old charm that I remembered from years ago. Blake let me in and poured us two glasses of chilled rosé wine in the small but functional kitchen. He wore a plain T-shirt with jeans this evening and his arms were tanned from the day outside. 'Dylan wants to create small patio gardens out the back for each of the cottages,' Blake said. 'But right now, we have two options: drink these out the front – but the others might see us – or stay inside.'

'Let's stay inside.' Willow didn't know I'd come here after I said goodbye to her and Maple. I knew she was excited about the potential of me and Blake but I didn't want to get ahead of myself just yet. We went into the living-room part of the open-plan downstairs where there was a comfy but slightly threadbare sofa that we sank into. The late sunlight streamed in through the large window that offered a view of the birch trees and the farmhouse. I removed my straw hat and fluffed up my hair.

I took a sip of wine. 'That's refreshing after a long day. I'm still a bit achy from last night.'

Blake grinned. 'Yeah, me too, and tired, but it was all worth it. I had a great time with you.'

'Me too.' I found myself hesitating for what to say next. 'I guess though it's super complicated between us.'

'Hmm, true.' He leaned back against the sofa, our thighs almost touching. I longed to curl up against him but that felt like couple behaviour, which was far too soon for us. 'It has taken me by surprise. But a good surprise.'

'Not when you saw my wedding dress,' I couldn't help but joke.

'That was definitely a shock after all that had happened with me and Sarah. But I told you, I thought you were beautiful that day. I had an irrational thought that I wanted you to be mine.' He looked sheepish. 'Too much, too soon?'

'Probably, yeah, if we're being sensible about all of this. But it's hard to be sensible when I think back to last night...' I admitted. 'We've both been through a lot, though.'

He nodded. 'I don't want you to hurt you. That's the last thing I ever want to do.' He leaned in and gave me one of those soft kisses that were capable of melting me right on the spot. He tucked my hair behind one ear and smiled. 'Maybe one day, you could be mine?' he whispered then, looking deep into my eyes as if he was searching for something.

Perhaps we both were.

My heart sped up at his closeness, his touch, his words... I wanted them all. 'We have a lot of things to sort out first,' I said, trying desperately to be cautious because I didn't want to get hurt but I also wanted to climb into his arms and lose myself in them. 'But maybe one day, I could be,' I admitted, finally saying the words out loud that I'd honestly felt since our first kiss. Maybe even before. Because when Blake treated me so rudely when we'd first met in my wedding dress, I was pissed and hurt and disappointed. I knew now it was because he had attracted me from the off.

'Can I kiss you again, gorgeous?' Blake asked. It was sweet that he checked with me. Did he not realise how badly I wanted to be in his arms again?

'Blake, surely you know the answer is yes?' I put my glass down on the coffee table in front of us and he did the same. Then I reached for his T-shirt and pulled him towards me, catching sight of those dimples before our lips found each other again. We scooted closer and Blake pulled me into his chest, his hand on the back of my head as I clutched his shirt, longing for us to be closer.

I leaned against him. 'I like your chest,' I found myself saying after we broke apart and Blake kissed my neck in that sweet spot that made me sigh with enjoyment. I moved my hands from holding his shirt to run over his chest. 'So strong. Can I?' I moved my fingertips to the bottom and slipped them under.

'Surely you know the answer is yes?' Blake repeated my question, making me giggle. I lifted his shirt off him and was rewarded with his bare chest. He pulled me back to meet his lips, his tongue massaging mine as he murmured contently. He reached for the buttons of my linen shirt, undoing them and then peeling it off me, laying it on top of his on the floor. 'Come here.' He moved me so I sat astride his lap, bringing back memories of yesterday on the blanket outside. 'Do you have any idea how sexy you are?' he purred into my ear. Then he kissed the spot just underneath it as his hands slid up my back, holding me close to him.

I loved how complimentary he was. It made me feel like I didn't need to be anyone else but myself with him. Something that was incredibly intoxicating after years of feeling like I needed to perform a version of myself. 'You're so handsome,' I replied, trying not to blush but accept his words. I wasn't sure a man had ever called me sexy before, though. I leaned in and kissed him again.

Our kisses were becoming almost frantic as we gripped each other. His slight stubble brushed against my chin as we kissed passionately but I didn't care if it chafed. I just wanted to be closer to him. To become tangled up together. Our skin grew hot and sticky in the warm night.

'Can I take all your clothes off?' Blake asked urgently, the fire in his eyes reflecting my own back at me.

'Only if you take yours off too,' I replied, my voice husky with lust. I jumped off him and he chuckled at how fast I pulled my shorts down. But he got up too and we watched each other as we peeled all our clothes off.

Blake was as aroused as I was. He stepped forward and bent down to kiss my breasts as his hand gently parted my legs to stroke me. I gripped his shoulder with one hand and brought my other hand down to touch him. We both let out a moan when we started touching one another. It hadn't been long at all since we had touched but we were clearly desperate for more.

'I want you so much,' Blake said when he lifted off my nipple to kiss me again.

'Me too,' I gasped against his mouth as his touch was driving me crazy. 'Please, Blake,' I found myself begging.

'You want more, Daisy?' he asked gruffly. 'I want you to tell me what you want.'

I definitely blushed then. 'I can't...' I whispered, leaning against him for support as his touches were sending off shots of pleasure through my body. He felt so hard under my hand that I knew he wanted this as much as I did.

'Gorgeous, tell me...' he repeated gently, before giving me an encouraging kiss.

I'd never been particularly chatty in bed before but Blake had me more engaged than I ever had been so maybe I could be. When he teased a nipple with his tongue before sliding it into his mouth and sucking on it, all embarrassment faded because I wanted him, wanted this, so much. 'I want you inside me,' I gasped out as my body trembled beneath his tongue.

Blake lifted off me and smiled. 'Good girl. I want to be inside you so much too. Stay here.' He let go of me and ducked out of the room before returning with a condom. He sat down on the sofa as he slid it on, his hooded eyes on me the whole time as my knees trembled in front of him. 'Do you want to sit on me?' he asked when he was ready.

I nodded eagerly and went over to sit astride him. He found my lips, kissing me hard as he slid inside me. We moaned against each other's mouths as I sat on Blake, him filling me up in the best way.

'Wow.' He leaned back to look at me as I moved on top of him. 'You're a dream, Daisy,' he said as his hands found my breasts, massaging them as we both gasped with pleasure.

Blake felt so good inside me. I was kind of shocked at how we fitted together. How easy and comfortable it felt. And how passionate too. Sparks flew between us as we held each other, kissed and touched, and rocked together on the sofa. I moaned his name as my skin glowed with heat, both from being with Blake and the warm evening. He pulled me down and I leaned over him to kiss, still moving on top of him as he gripped my waist, moving with me. He lifted his hips and we both groaned as he moved in deeper. 'Blake, it's too good...' I gasped before I cried out with abandon, a burst of pleasure like fireworks reverberating through my body.

'Daisy,' Blake said, gripping me tightly to him as he moved under me, gasping and grunting as he reached his own peak.

Satisfied and exhausted, my body went limp on top of him. He moved out of me and laid me down beside him on the sofa, holding me to his chest as he sorted himself out. My pulse thrummed, matching his fast heartbeat against my ear as I leaned on his chest, his skin as slick as my own.

When he wrapped his arms around me, I moved even closer, nestling into him.

And when Blake kissed my forehead, I felt like I was finally me again.

31

Blake walked me back to the farmhouse as midnight approached.

'Are you sure you don't want to stay the night?' he had asked as we pulled our clothes back on, giving each other shy smiles each time our eyes connected.

'I don't want Willow to know about last night just yet,' I said. 'We don't know what this is...' I trailed off. I really didn't want to have the *what are we*? conversation yet. I was on a giddy high from being in Blake's arms but he had only planned to stay in Birchbrook for two more days. Plus, he was yet to work anything out with Sarah. I knew it was unlikely this could be anything more than a summer romance but maybe that was enough. I felt more alive than I had in a very long time. Blake had helped that happen.

And I was grateful as hell for it.

So, we had strolled back to the farmhouse hand in hand, the farm still and quiet in the darkness, a bright moon high on the horizon.

'I don't know how I'm supposed to sleep,' Blake said softly as he squeezed my hand. 'What if I'm thinking about you all night?'

I smiled. 'What if I'm thinking about *you* all night?'

He tugged on my hand and stopped, bringing me around to face him. He leaned down and gave me a kiss. 'That's why we should stay together and both not sleep.' He dropped me a wink, making me giggle.

'What's got into you?' I asked as Blake took hold of my other hand and stepped closer to me. I looked up at him, his handsome face silhouetted by the moon, his eyes bright and shining from the silvery glow but, I hoped, it was also from being with me.

'You,' he replied simply.

This time, I kissed him. How could Sarah have thought he wasn't good at speaking to women? He had no trouble with me. That one word melted me again. 'What's going to happen?' I blurted out before I could stop myself. I had wanted to go to bed without being needy but when Blake looked at me like that, I wanted to know if he was wondering about what we would do once he left.

Blake let go of one of my hands and reached out to stroke my hair. 'I don't know yet, gorgeous. But we will work it out, won't we?'

I nodded. 'I hope so.' I didn't want to lose the high of the night and feel sad so I kissed him again. 'Let's try to sleep. It's going to be a busy day getting everything ready for the opening, isn't it?'

'We work well together, don't we?'

I smiled. 'I think so.'

Blake leaned in and gave me a tight hug. 'Sweet dreams,' he whispered.

We held on for a full minute, clinging tightly to one another, unspoken wishes between us. Maybe we would speak them out loud soon.

'Goodnight,' I said reluctantly, letting him go finally. I walked to the door and pushed it open, giving him one last look over my shoulder, wishing I had just stayed with him, Willow or no Willow. Blake lifted a hand to wave and then his figure faded into the darkness. With a soft sigh, I went inside, closed the door and headed up to my bedroom.

I slipped into my pyjamas and opened the window slightly as the night was humid and sticky, and I lay down on the bed, unsure if I would be able to sleep but weirdly, my eyes closed and I drifted off calmly.

* * *

The following morning, there was no time to replay my evening with Blake.

Willow and Taylor were talking to my uncle when I came down after my shower, dressed for the day and in need of coffee. I walked into the kitchen and saw the three of them at the table. I was about to say good morning when I realised the atmosphere was tense but it was too late to retreat.

'You have to do what the doctor said,' Willow was saying crossly to Adam. 'And let me worry about being ready for the opening.'

'You need me to help; we don't have our summer staff,' my uncle replied stubbornly.

'We have Daisy!' Willow said, pointing to me.

'Should I...?' I offered to go away again.

'Help us talk some sense into him,' Willow said to me so I sat down and poured strong coffee into a cup. 'He wants to run the pony rides, but it will be too much for him. Dylan will have to do it.'

'He's renovating the cottages! You can't pull out after paying deposits for the work,' Adam pointed out. 'And Blake will be leaving soon so he can't help any more.'

'I'm here, though,' I said. 'I can do whatever is needed.'

'Can I say something?' Taylor said gently as Willow and Adam fell into an annoyed silence, glaring at one another. She was an attractive lady, smartly dressed, and I'd only heard good things from people about Birchbrook's mayor. 'I don't want to talk out of turn,' she continued. It must have been hard for her with the shadow of Willow's mum around the place. 'Perhaps Adam can help with something that would still fit with what the doctor told us? I know at the pumpkin patch, you helped customers when they came to pay but there won't be heavy pumpkins this time; you could man the till and be there for visitors when they have finished at the trail. A sitting-down job that is needed and will keep you busy.'

'I do like dealing with everyone,' Adam said, 'but I did more with the pumpkin patch than that.'

'That was a few months ago and you've just had a health scare, plus now I'm running the farm,' Willow pointed out. She smiled at Taylor. 'I think that's a good idea. Dad, you can rest until we open, then run the till table. One of us can give you a couple of breaks each day. I'll figure the rest out.'

'There might be some local teenagers who fancy a summer job,' Taylor suggested then. 'Weekends for now, then when the schools break up, they could help every day?'

Willow's eyes lit up. 'Great idea. I bet Sabrina knows who I can ask at her school. That could be really useful. See, Dad? We'll be fine!'

Adam sighed. 'Okay, okay, I can see I don't really have a choice, do I?'

'Why don't we find a nice pub for lunch? Let the others get the farm ready for the opening,' Taylor continued to Adam.

Willow sighed with relief. I felt it too. We didn't want my uncle doing anything that would make his health deteriorate any further.

Once Taylor and my uncle had left the table, Willow turned to me. 'There is so much to do; Dad was right about that. I'm almost done with the pumpkin field. Then I need to talk to Blake about the ponies so we can decide what to do with them. Dylan is busy all day with the cottages so can you please take over to make sure the finale to the Strawberry Fields Trail is all ready?'

'Definitely,' I said. 'It'll be fine,' I promised, although I'd never helped run the pick-your-own season before. But I was determined to repay my family's help this summer by doing all I could to make it a success. I headed straight out to the fields as the picnic benches Willow hired arrived in a van and I helped them be placed close to my flower arch.

Then, I put a watering can with flowers onto the centre of each one, a sudden brainwave that looked perfect if I did say so myself. The Portaloos came later in the day too so they were set up behind the driveway close to where visitors would be parking.

Finally, the Birchwood Café van arrived on site. Paul, the son of the owners – the two Pats – got out of the cream and green van and marched over to me.

'Willow said you're in charge,' he said gruffly, without preamble. 'Where shall I park the van then?'

Willow said the van had been really helpful in drawing customers to the first ever pumpkin patch, as the café was so popular, so she had let them have the pitch for free. But it had been so profitable, female Pat had offered to pay a fee for the summer: another reason why Willow was so anxious to make the Strawberry Fields Trail a hit.

'I'd say over here,' Paul said, pointing to the middle of the picnic benches.

'But then the van will be in people's photos if they sit on the bench with the flower arch,' I said, shaking my head. 'How about here, off to the side? It'll be easily spotted and then there's lots of space for people having picnics. I don't want the van spoiling the view.'

'Hmm. We'll see if that works okay. If not, I'll tell Willow we will need to move it,' he replied shortly.

'Fine. Have you decided on the menu?' I matched his brisk tone.

He ticked the items on his fingers. 'Coffee, tea, iced version too, obviously, seasonal sweet treats like Eton mess and lemon tart, and ice creams plus a selection of sandwiches too.'

'What about a picnic box? With one of each in? I think people would love that,' I suggested, picturing people eating that on the benches.

'I'll think about it,' he replied, shoving his hands into his jeans pockets. 'See you on opening day at midday then.'

'Wait,' I said hastily to stop him walking off. 'Will you have a bin for rubbish? We definitely don't want any litter left around the benches. That would spoil the vibe I'm creating here.'

Paul raised an eyebrow. 'You're just like your cousin.' He strode off back to his van.

'Is that a yes?' I called to his retreating back.

He nodded once.

I turned to Dylan, who was having a break from the cottages and had come over to secure one of Sabrina's *Strawberry Fields Trail* wooden signs as it looked a bit wobbly. Apparently, in autumn, they'd had issues with a storm and didn't want to take any chances. 'Is he always like that?'

Dylan grinned. 'Yes. He seems to hate Birchbrook and all of us who live in town but he never leaves so we all think it's just an act.'

I remained unconvinced but if Paul did as I asked then I'd ignore his grumpy attitude.

* * *

'What will people use to carry the fruit and veg they've picked?' I asked Willow when we were all having a quick break for iced coffees that Dylan had made us. He was pretty good at making coffees and although Blake had wanted one from the Birchbrook Café, he admitted this one came in as a close second. Willow had informed him there was too much to do for him to leave the farm just for coffee and the look on her face had made him quickly agree and drink what Dylan had made without comment. I had to smile at how my cousin was able to get people to do things for her. Her enthusiasm was contagious. Every time Dylan looked at her, I could tell how much he admired her and was proud she was his. That was something I longed for one day.

'People either bring their own things or use paper bags we leave out.'

I wrinkled my nose. 'That's not a great aesthetic.'

'You're right. What can we do?' She looked immediately panicked. 'We didn't have this issue with the pumpkin patch; people just carried them or we used wheelbarrows to get the pumpkins to their cars. I didn't think about anything for summer. Will this put people off?'

'No, but if you're trying to get people to share the farm on social media and spread the word then something cute to carry the fruit and veg in would be an extra bonus, wouldn't it? I wonder if we could get some cheap baskets or punnets from somewhere? Or make something?' I mused, pulling out my phone. 'I'll do some research. Oh, you know who might be able to help? Mary. Her wholesaler might sell something.'

'Go and ask her,' Willow instantly urged me.

'Hey, I was told we couldn't leave the farm!' Blake complained, earning himself a glare from Willow.

'This is *for* the farm,' she told him shortly.

I held back a grin but when Willow walked off with Dylan, I let Blake see it. 'You're in trouble,' I teased him.

'Your cousin is intimidating,' he said with a smile. 'No wonder Dylan gave up on his plan to buy the farm and ended up helping her save it instead.'

'She knows what she wants, for sure. I wish I did.'

'You'll figure it out,' he replied confidently. 'I better go and get the ponies ready; Willow wants us practice-walking the ponies around the enclosure. Her friend Sabrina is bringing a couple of kids from her school to see if the ponies do okay. I don't want to be told off for slacking.' He strode off and I giggled. Willow did run a tight ship here.

I wanted to feel as passionate about something as she did about the farm. Willow was inspiring me. The farm was too. I looked around at what I'd helped create. I was sure visitors would love coming here over the summer. I couldn't wait to see. As I left the field, I couldn't help but hope Blake might do what he'd mentioned during our star-gazing and stick around to see them arrive too.

I headed off into town in Willow's car and parked outside the florist's. The pretty, pink exterior and colourful blooms put an instant smile on my face.

I jumped out of the car and went inside, the doorbell

jangling as I entered. The sun streamed in through the window, pooling on the pink and white flowers by the till table where Mary was tying up a bouquet of roses.

'Mary, can I pick your brains, please?'

'Of course, dear. But while you do that, do you have any time to help me? Or are you in a rush to get back to the farm?' Mary asked, looking a bit frantic.

'Don't worry, we can help each other, and I've finished all I needed to today. Willow wanted me to come here.'

'Thank goodness! I've had an order for twenty bouquets of roses for a proposal and he wants them in an hour,' she said, her eyes wide. 'I rushed to the wholesaler and found the flowers I needed, but I've only made two so far. But with two of us, hopefully we could do it.'

'Of course I'll help.' I hurried behind the counter and looked at the buckets of roses, the pink paper and ribbon, and gathered up what I needed to make up a bouquet. I stood next to Mary and we both set to work making them up. Her customer had asked for pink roses mixed with baby's breath and greenery, all done up in pink.

'He's going to fill up the house he's rented for the weekend with the roses and he's also bought pink balloons so when she arrives and walks in, it will be a big surprise. It's so sweet but very last minute. He said he kept chickening out of proposing, although he's had the ring for ages. She told him her parents got engaged in Birchbrook decades ago so that gave him the idea to do it while they're on holiday here. It's all very lovely and I couldn't say no; I'm a hopeless romantic at heart,' Mary said with a shake of her head. 'But I forgot how much time bouquets take to make and I must admit, I'm slower now than I used to be. Sometimes, I forget that too. And without any part-time help... I was just about to phone him and say he needs to find another florist, although I would have felt terrible letting him down. You walking in was like a little miracle.' She beamed across at me and I felt a bit emotional at how grateful and happy she was to have me here helping.

'I remember watching my mum making up bouquets of roses. She helped with a proposal once too. It made her so happy to be part of something so special. She wanted the flowers to be perfect.' I looked down at the roses I was tying together. I understood why she'd been so excited now. 'We'll make these perfect too.'

As we busied ourselves in making up the bouquets, laying them on the counter as we did them one by one, Mary turned to me. 'So, what help did you need from me?' she asked.

'We were thinking we'd like to find some baskets or punnets or something cute that people coming to the farm could use for the fruit and veg they pick up. They haven't really offered anything before but Willow is trying to encourage more visitors this year and maybe this is an extra bonus that people might like. Obviously, we wouldn't want to spend too much. We'd get them to leave them once they've paid for everything so they can be re-used through the day but we'd need a fair few for busy days to make sure we don't run out.'

'Hmm. I have an old friend outside of town who's a grocer and they have punnets from the wholesaler I go to, so we could have a look together and you can see if they would work?' She looked excited. 'I can take you tomorrow before I open up the shop? You know what would be lovely: if you could label them with the farm name somehow...'

'Ooh, that sounds great. Maybe we can wrap a tag around them? Nothing plastic though; I know Willow wouldn't like that. She likes things to be sustainable as far as possible.'

'You could engrave a small piece of wood and tie that on them,' Mary said as she tied up another bouquet.

I looked across at her. 'That is brilliant! Hang on...' I took a minute to fire off a message to Willow. 'I know someone who could look into that.' I was sure Dylan would find somewhere online we could use easily. He was brilliant at research and sourcing suppliers. I also told Willow I'd be going with Mary to the wholesaler in the morning. It felt like everything was all coming together now.

We worked on and managed to finish the bouquets with twenty minutes to spare.

'I wish I could stay and meet him,' I said, 'but I better get back to the farm in case Willow has found something I need to help her with. I can't thank you enough for your good ideas.'

'It's me who should be thanking you, Daisy. I was in a right pickle until you walked in!'

I chuckled at the expression. 'I'm happy I could help.' I looked at the pretty bouquets. They looked perfect; I was sure the customer would be happy and surely, he would get a yes from his girlfriend once she saw them. Seeing the flowers made me think about Henry's proposal. There'd been no such thought or romance involved. We'd worked late at the office together one night and he'd received a message from his mother telling him that his grandmother was coming to stay for the weekend.

'I'm going to ask her for her diamond ring,' he'd said. 'She always said she wanted me to propose with it and it will look perfect on your finger. That's what we both want, isn't it?'

I'd said yes and the ball had got rolling on planning our doomed wedding. I had only cared about my future feeling safe at the time, but now I knew deep down in my heart, I wanted a romantic proposal, if I ever got another one. Someone who told me they wanted to love me forever. Someone I wasn't scared to love back the same way. Someone who knocked down my walls and made it impossible for me not give them my heart.

As I headed for the door, Mary called my name.

'You have a real knack for this, Daisy. And you seem to enjoy it. And the work you're doing at the farm. I know it can't be easy to be here knowing your mother used to help out too but I want you to know, you're great at it.'

My chest swelled with a thousand emotions. I looked around the flower shop. Yes, it was hard. Yes, it was painful. But Mary was right – I was having fun working with flowers here.

I felt a jolt of realisation then. I'd envied Willow being so passionate about the farm, but now I felt that same spark working with flowers. I was passionate about them. Just like my mother was.

'Mary – if I can make sure I do everything Willow needs at the farm, maybe I could help you more this summer? What do you think?' I asked, my heart speeding up instantly as I waited for her answer. I had to remind myself to breathe.

She broke into a slow, wide smile. 'I was hoping you were going to suggest just that.'

32

I didn't get a chance to be alone again with Blake until just before dinner time. Willow told me to ask him to come in to eat as he was still out with the ponies in the strawberry fields, so I headed out there. It had been a busy day and I was tired and hungry. But I walked with a lightness to my step. I had a plan for the rest of the summer that I couldn't wait to tell everyone about. Just two weeks ago, I'd felt as lost as I ever had been but slowly and surely, I was finding out who I wanted to be. Who I probably always had been. I didn't want to hide from living any more.

And Blake was part of that. I wanted to tell him how I felt.

I smiled when I saw him in the enclosure. The ponies were groomed to perfection and he was giving them a strawberry treat, patting and talking to them. His love for animals was something I really liked about him; it was so endearing.

'How are they doing?' I called as I walked through the open gate.

'They've been really good today,' he said. 'I mean, they're still mischievous and want a treat in exchange for doing pretty much anything, but they seem to be enjoying living here.'

'I know the feeling.' I reached out to pat Jasmine while I smiled at Blake. 'We haven't had much time together today. I have lots to tell you.'

'Oh, yeah?' His smile showed me his dimples again as he let go of Jasmine and turned to me. 'Do you want to come to the cottage again this evening?'

I nodded happily. 'Willow wants you to come in for dinner so let's go back and then we can—'

I was interrupted by Blake's phone ringing, making us jump. The ponies both snorted at the noise. He pulled his phone out of the back pocket of his shorts and frowned. 'It's Sarah. It might be about the app...'

'You should answer her,' I said, although I didn't really want him to but I knew they still had a lot to sort out. 'Shall I...?' I gestured out of the enclosure but he shook his head.

'Stay. We can walk back together afterwards.' Blake answered her call. 'Hi, Sarah.'

I was pleased that there didn't seem to be a particular fondness in his tone. It was still weird, though – listening to him to talk to the woman he had been about to ask to marry him.

'What? Wait... why?' he asked, listening intently. His eyes widened. 'Really?... but we don't know what we want to do. Yeah, I know we have worked hard. I suppose so...' Blake looked at me as he listened to whatever Sarah was telling him. He frowned. 'It does sound promising, you're right. Okay, okay.' He paced off into the pony enclosure a little bit. I watched him, wondering why my smile had faded. I was getting a bad feeling about this.

He listened to Sarah some more. She appeared to be making a long speech. And, suddenly, he was nodding along.

'Yeah, you're right.' He stopped pacing and looked at me again. 'Okay, I will... I said I will,' he said. 'I know. Don't worry.

I'll call you when I'm on my way.' As he hung up, my heart sank down to my stomach.

Blake put his phone away, took a beat then came back to me and the ponies. 'So, Sarah had a meeting in the city with a big tech company that's interested in investing in our app. Not only that, but they want to bring it under their company umbrella, which would be a huge deal for the business.' He ran a hand through his hair. 'They want to meet me and pitch their plans and make an offer so I need to go to the city.' He paused. 'And... I have to go now.'

'Now?' I knew originally the plan had always been for him to leave at the end of the weekend but he'd mentioned staying to see the farm open up for the pick-your-own season. 'I thought you were going to stick around, though?' I realised I'd been harbouring a hope that he might stay longer, not for the farm, but for me.

'This could make us a lot of money. Not only that, but they would take over the creating of the app, we'd have access to resources we could never dream of on our own, we'd get to work with the best in the business and the app would launch with a huge platform behind it. It could be huge. Sarah said the app could be worth millions in two years.' Blake let off a puff of air. 'I can't really take it all in, but I can't say no, can I?'

I looked at him, wondering if two weeks was long enough to know someone. I was realising it wasn't at all.

'I thought you didn't want to do the app any more? That you didn't like what it stood for? That you'd had enough of the city, and maybe you were thinking of coming... going... home?' I asked, confused how one call from Sarah was suddenly taking Blake back to the city, back to working with her and back to a life that he'd suggested he hadn't been enjoying at all.

Blake sighed. 'I don't know what to do. I can't let Sarah lose such a big opportunity. Whatever happened between us, we both put time, money and effort into the app. This could be huge for her. For us.'

'There's still an us?' I could feel myself getting angry and upset. And he appeared confused as to why I wasn't agreeing this was a good idea. 'I thought she was your ex? I said goodbye to Henry and last night, we slept together but now you're going back to Sarah?' I tried to stay calm but it was proving too difficult. I had taken a chance on Blake and I was rapidly feeling like he hadn't done the same thing. I turned around and walked out of the pony enclosure.

'Daisy, wait, it's not like that,' Blake cried, hurrying after me. 'I'm not saying I'm going back to her as a romantic partner but I have to go to this meeting. I've put money into this app. I've worked for a year on it; I can't just walk away from all of that,' he said, pausing to shut the gate then striding after me. He touched my arm. 'Stop a minute, please?'

I paused but I couldn't look at him. 'I thought maybe we were starting something,' I said quietly. I was hurt. And confused.

'We knew this was complicated.' Blake reached for me but I stepped backwards. 'These two weeks have changed so much; I don't know what happens next. But I've said I'll go and have this meeting. I need to do this. I'm sorry if that upsets you. It's the last thing I want. But we didn't know we were going to meet each other here. I was supposed to be leaving after this weekend. You've had closure with Henry. Will you give me time to have the same with Sarah?'

I met his gaze then. 'What do you want, Blake?'

He'd asked me the same thing. He'd helped me decide what I wanted. But it looked like I hadn't done the same for him after all.

Blake stared at me for a moment. 'I don't know,' he finally admitted.

And there it was. He wasn't ready to say goodbye to Sarah completely. Or decide whether he wanted to stop working with her or leave the city.

'One thing that I've realised after all that time with Henry is I don't want to be in another relationship that neither of us are fully in, with all our hearts. That's what I deserve.'

I turned and walked on, even though he called me again, I didn't stop for a second time. Blake had decided to go and I had to let him. Like Henry should have done when I left. Running or chasing after him would do no good. He had to make his own mind up and follow what was in his heart; I couldn't do it for him. Just like Henry hadn't been able to do it for me in the end.

When I reached the farmhouse, I walked into the kitchen.

'Where's Blake?' Willow asked, looking up from where she was laying the table for dinner.

'He's going back to the city,' I told her.

'What? Now?' She looked at Dylan. 'Did you know about this?'

He shook his head in surprise.

'Sarah called. She needs him to have a meeting with a company about their app. It sounds like a big opportunity for them.' I sat down at the table and avoided my cousin's concerned look.

'I thought he wasn't getting back with Sarah,' Willow said. 'He clearly wasn't happy with her. And that app sounds completely dishonest to me. I wouldn't want to date someone who used technology to write me messages. I'd want someone genuine.'

'I'm surprised Blake wants to carry on with it,' Dylan agreed with her. 'I'll go and talk to him.'

He walked out and Willow came to sit beside me. 'Shit, Daisy, I can't believe it. I thought you two were becoming a thing.'

'I did too,' I confessed, 'but I was clearly kidding myself. Maybe it was crazy to think we could be anything real after how things started. Fake dating to one side... we both were in serious relationships with other people this year. We've only known each other for two weeks. It's best he goes.' I looked away from her piercing gaze because although in my head, my words were sensible and made a whole lot of sense, in my heart, I knew there had been something special between us. A connection that you couldn't explain or... fake.

That's why it hurt that Blake was walking away from it.

'Anyway, I came here to decide what I want to do with my future,' I said, forcing that hurt away because I had made such progress since being here and I didn't want to go backwards; I wanted to keep moving forward. I didn't want to stop taking chances. Yes, there would always be pain if you really lived. But there was also a whole host of positive things too: joy, friendship, family, love, laughter, hope and happiness. I had been living a half-life with Henry. Even if I had to be alone, I wasn't going to do that again. I had to live my life to the full while I could.

'I'm hoping this is okay...' I told Willow the idea I'd had to help Mary out in the flower shop. 'I was thinking just twice a week – one weekday afternoon and a few hours on a Saturday when she's really struggling. But only if you think I can do the work you need me to do around it. I know how stressed you've been and I promised to help you this summer but being in that flower shop, it just felt... right.' I found myself smiling just thinking about it.

'Anything that puts that happy expression on your face gets my approval! Everything is almost ready to go now. We have to do something about the ponies...' She frowned for a moment.

'But other than that, you've done such a great job with the strawberry fields. I've asked Sabrina to let me know some teenagers that could do some weekend work for us. We'll all pitch in. As long as Dad keeps to his word and just mans the tills, we can make it work, I'm sure. It's only twice a week for a few hours.' She smiled. 'Daisy, I am really excited for you!'

'Thank you. For everything.' We gave each other a quick hug.

'You'll be amazing at this,' Willow said when we drew back.

I smiled through the sadness of Blake leaving because this was something I really wanted to try. 'I've shied away from finding something I love because of...' I took a deep breath. '... losing my parents but I know they would want me to do something I am passionate about.'

'I'm so proud!' Willow said. 'Maybe we'll even get to keep you for more than the whole summer,' she added, winking at me when she leaned back.

I let out a laugh. 'We'll see.'

Dylan came back in then. 'Blake's packing right now. He said he'll come over when he's ready to say goodbye. He says he has to see the app through. But I didn't think his heart was in it.'

I had hoped I was in his heart but clearly, I was mistaken. I picked at my food, not really tasting anything. It would be so strange to be here without Blake. From turning up in my wedding dress to now, feeling so far away from that woman, he had been by my side and I had been by his. Blake helped me to see that I'd been hiding for years and that it was okay to be me and to follow my heart. That's what I would go on to do without him, and I really hoped he'd do it without me too.

33

After dinner, Blake came into the farmhouse. I had no idea what he was thinking.

His eyes found me instantly. 'I'm all packed and ready to go.' He turned from me to Willow and Dylan. 'But I had to come to say thank you for having me these two weeks. You've treated me like part of the family. When I needed it the most.'

'I can't believe you're leaving us with the ponies,' Willow said, attempting a joke when everyone looked sombre. She coughed when no one laughed. 'Good luck, Blake,' she added more seriously.

Blake looked at me again. 'I'll see you then, Daisy,' he said finally, his voice quiet. I felt all eyes on us.

'I hope it goes well,' I said, forcing out a small smile. I did mean it. I wanted him to be happy. I just wasn't sure he could be if we went back to his old life.

'Yeah, me too, mate,' Dylan added, getting up to shake his hand. 'Let me help you with your things.'

'I'll come out too. Come on, Maple,' Willow said, whistling for her dog.

'I'm going to go for a walk,' I said. I didn't want to watch Blake leaving. Following them outside, I watched Dylan and Blake go into the cottage to collect his things. Willow and Maple stood by his car.

'Will you be okay?' Willow asked me then.

'Yes.' And I knew I would be. I would just carry around a pinch of regret for the rest of the summer. 'I don't want to watch him go, though,' I added. 'I'll put the ponies in the barn for the night; I need to do something.'

I set off and Maple followed me as if she knew I needed her more than the others. I had to pass by the cottages and as I did so, Blake came out with one of his suitcases. Our eyes met but I carried on walking. I wanted to look forward now.

But it wasn't easy when Blake had been such a big part of my new chapter here.

After a moment, I glanced back to see Blake open his boot and put in his case, Dylan joining him with his other bag. Willow was saying something to them. I hoped she wasn't berating Blake for leaving but if she was, I did like that she wanted to stick up for me. I let out a sigh and headed for the strawberry fields to find the ponies. Maple ran on ahead, enjoying the run after her dinner.

It was crazy to think what a big impact Blake had had on my life. Maybe I could learn to be grateful for that, instead of sad that he wasn't choosing me.

Maple started barking then.

'What's up, girl?' I called as I saw the pony enclosure in front of us.

Maple growled, which was unlike her. She turned to look at me and barked again.

'What's going on?' I sped up, confused what was up with her.

Then as I approached, I realised what had got her all upset: the pony enclosure was empty.

'What the fuck?' I said, breaking into a jog then. I reached Maple and gave her a quick pat as I stared at the wide-open gate. 'How...?' I thought back to being in there earlier with Blake. Sarah had called and we had had a heated discussion about it before I walked out, Blake hurrying after me. 'Oh, shit, Maple, he must have forgotten to lock the gate up after him,' I said, looking around for the ponies. I walked around the enclosure. 'Maple, can you see them?' She ran ahead of me towards the strawberries and let out a loud bark.

I took off after her and once my eyes caught up, I swore again under my breath.

Blossom and Jasmine were right in the middle of the strawberries, eating the ripe fruit and trampling on the plants as they did so.

I froze. For a second, I wasn't sure what to do. That familiar sinking feeling of panic settled in my stomach like a dead weight. I held my chest where my heart was speeding up and my breathing become shallow. I didn't know what to do. I was afraid of panicking and that made me panic more.

'No,' I said firmly to myself. I looked at things I could see. The ponies potentially ruining the pick-your-own area. Ruining our work. Maple distressed as she knew they were doing something bad. I lifted my face. The sun had just started drifting towards the horizon, casting a dewy glow over the scene, which was at odds with the chaos. It almost looked dreamlike. But I wasn't in a dream. I was here. This was happening.

I breathed in and out slowly. I focused. I wasn't going to panic. I needed to help fix this.

Snapping back to myself, I yanked my phone out my pocket

and called Willow. 'I need you in the strawberry fields now!' I cried when she answered, then I hung up and pocketed it again.

'You two are bad ponies,' I said as I reached them. Maple joined me, barking as if she knew they'd been naughty too. Blossom took one look at us and started off at a trot towards the sunflowers. 'No!' I called, running after her as Jasmine continued gorging on strawberries without a care in the world. Maple ran to her and tried to herd her away, but Jasmine ignored the dog completely.

'Blossom, stop,' I called as she trampled on the sunflowers.

I heard Willow calling my name and I turned and waved her over, as well as Dylan and Blake, who were jogging behind.

I didn't wait for them. I headed for the barn to find the ponies' harnesses and leads as they clearly weren't going to come of their own accord. They wanted treats, and strawberries were their favourite. Now they had found the supply, they were going to need to be led out.

Blake found me in the barn grabbing what we needed. 'Why are the ponies out?'

I spun around. 'You didn't lock their gate earlier! Too distracted after Sarah called.' I knew I was being unfair – obviously, he hadn't done it on purpose and I could have reminded him at the time – but it was an easy thing to have a go at him about, instead of the fact he was running out on me when we'd only just got started.

'Shit, I didn't realise. Here...' He tried to take their leads from me.

'I'll do it,' I snapped, walking past him and out of the barn.

'But I'm good with them,' he protested, following me.

'You're leaving. We have to be able to look after them without you,' I said as I hurried back to the sunflowers and strawberries. 'I got their leads!' I called to Willow, who was trying to coax

Blossom out of the sunflowers while Dylan and Maple were with Jasmine, trying to both herd her out and tempt her with an outstretched strawberry, but she just carried on eating.

'I can't believe this is happening so close to opening! Are we cursed?' Willow asked, putting her hands on her hips.

'I'm so sorry I didn't lock their enclosure properly,' Blake said as he walked past me and called to Blossom. I sighed and threw one set of harnesses and leads to Willow. 'You get Jasmine; we've got Blossom,' I said. She hurried off and I followed Blake.

'God, she's ruining the flowers.' I saw flattened and broken sunflowers as she carried on walking right down the middle of them. 'Come on, Blossom,' I encouraged her, stepping carefully around the remaining flowers to reach her. Blake beat me, though and was talking to her, reaching out to stroke her so she finally stopped moving, and snorted as she stood still, her tail flicking like she was the one annoyed. I supposed she didn't like being caught out.

'Come on then.' I hooked the harness over Blossom as Blake held her steady, reassuring her and being so sweet and gentle, my heart squeezed. I tried to ignore it and focused on securing the harness and lead on her. And then with a cluck of my tongue, I gave it a little tug. Blossom stood firm, eyeing me like I was a pain in her butt. The feeling was mutual right now. 'Party's over, girl,' I said, clucking my tongue again.

'Come on, Blossom,' Blake encouraged, giving the lead an extra tug and finally, Blossom took a step forward. I gave her another tug and with Blake encouraging her on, she finally started to follow me and I was able to lead her away from the sunflowers and onto the trail. 'Wait here.' Blake rushed off to help the others while I stood with Blossom, annoyed at his instruction but knowing it was unlikely I'd get her into the barn without him.

Now I was alone, I thought about how I'd frozen back there and almost given in to panic.

But I had got through it. I hadn't run away but I had tried to fix the problem. I hadn't lost my breath or got anxious. I'd pushed through and helped work things out. So, I was proud of myself.

I thought about all the time over the past five years I had panicked. The times I had backed out of things or lied to Henry, saying I was ill, or stayed quiet and not told him or his parents how I'd really felt until it was too late.

It had been like that on my wedding day. I had been so scared of speaking up and having to change my life, I'd left it until the last minute to do so. But now, I could see I was capable of doing that. I was changing my life.

Tonight, I hadn't kept quiet and pretended to be happy about Blake and Sarah. I'd told him I didn't understand why he wanted to go back to the city. I hadn't hidden my disappointment.

And now, with the ponies, I had stepped up too.

'Blossom, maybe I really will be okay,' I murmured. She nudged my shoulder in response. I rolled my eyes but I stroked her and she nuzzled me as if we hadn't just had a huge disagreement.

Maybe I didn't have to be as afraid any more.

It might have been a strange moment to have an epiphany but somehow, this had all helped me to realise that I could, and would, handle whatever came my way in life.

34

Looking over, I saw Blake had helped Dylan and Willow to put the harness and lead onto Jasmine. He was now coaxing her away from her strawberry feast. Maple hurried towards me, letting out a frustrated-sounding bark. She hadn't trusted the ponies from the start and now was being proved right.

'Now I know why those farmers down the pub sold me these two so cheaply,' Willow said, coming over to join me and Blossom on the trail. 'They aren't just cheeky and mischievous; they are menaces!' She threw her arms out. 'Look at the mess they've made.' She looked at Dylan. 'This is the pumpkin-patch disaster all over again!'

'We were fine then, and we'll be fine now,' he assured her, putting a hand on her shoulder for comfort. She gave him a small smile, unspoken words passing between them.

'Let's get the ponies into the barn,' I said. 'Then we can see what we're dealing with. Plus, Blake needs to get off, don't you?'

I saw him hesitate. He turned to Willow and Dylan. 'I feel so bad about not locking their enclosure properly...'

'It's okay, mate,' Dylan said as Willow tutted. 'You should head off, it's fine.'

'But—'

'Help Daisy put the ponies into the barn then we'll sort things out. You get going.' Willow looked away from him and I could tell she was as disappointed in him as I was.

'Come on,' I said to Blossom, clucking, and this time, she followed me willingly like she knew I wasn't going to take any more bad behaviour from her. I led her to the barn, Blake following with Jasmine. We put them inside for the night and I double-checked they were secure. 'Well, have a safe journey,' I said as we walked back out.

'Daisy, I really am sorry about tonight. About everything,' Blake said urgently, before I could head off.

I looked back at him. His eyes were wide with regret. 'I'm sorry too. I don't know what else you want me to say, though. You're leaving, Blake. I just hope you do what you *really* want to do.' There didn't seem any point in talking any more. I didn't agree with his decision to go but I knew he felt he had to. I had left something just two weeks ago and I needed to rebuild my life now. Blake was returning to what he had left. I would let him rebuild his life there. 'Goodbye, Blake.' I walked off then and didn't look back.

When I returned to the fields, Uncle Adam had joined Dylan and Willow and Maple as they surveyed the damage the ponies had done.

'I never want to say, "I told you so" but...' Adam was saying, looking around with a frown.

'I thought they would be cute,' Willow said. 'This isn't cute!'

'How bad is it?' I asked when I reached them.

'At least they kept to this area,' Dylan pointed out. The strawberry plants in the patch we found the ponies in had either all been eaten or trampled on. 'We can just clear it and maybe we can create something for people to look at or take a photo with so it doesn't look too bare.'

'We've lost money, though,' Willow said with a sigh. She wandered over to the sunflowers, and we followed. 'This is bad.' Blossom had trampled a whole row of sunflowers horizontally so it wouldn't be easy to just clear away the broken flowers. 'There's not enough time to plant or grow anything else here. And the sunflowers are the first thing people see! It's not going to be a good start to the trail, is it?'

'Maybe we can hide the damage with some sort of prop like the bench with the flower arch,' I mused aloud.

'Do we have time to sort all this out before we open, though?' Willow said anxiously.

'We need to start by clearing up the mess then see what we can do to hide the bare patches from visitors. And yes, we will have lost some money but if we can make the Strawberry Fields Trail a must-do activity this summer, hopefully, we will recoup as much as possible. I mean, you could always sell the ponies on too?' Dylan added the last part gently. Willow glared at him.

'Maybe we should just all go to bed,' Adam broke in hastily before Willow could respond to Dylan. 'Things always look brighter in the morning. And we've come back from worst disasters, haven't we? We can all have a think overnight and crack on first thing.'

Dylan and Adam started to walk back to the farmhouse. Willow turned to me. 'Do you think we should give up on the ponies?' She looked close to tears and after all she'd done for me, I hated to see it.

'Maybe we can find someone to help us...' We trailed after the other two. I didn't know who would be able to handle them as well as Blake had, though. Then I had a brainwave. 'I have someone I can ask! I need to go to the wholesaler with Mary to look at punnets for people to put the fruit and veg in that they pick. And then after I've helped her a bit in the shop, let me go and see if I can get us a hand with the ponies. If you guys will be okay making a start on the clear-up without me?'

'If you can come up with a solution to those ponies, you can take as long as you need!' Willow cried, shooting me a grateful look. 'I'll call the teenagers that are going to help on weekends to see if they can come over and lend a hand.'

Dylan looked back. 'Don't worry. Together, we'll sort it out ready to open up next week, right, guys?'

We all murmured our agreement but I wasn't sure if our hearts were really in it.

We sloped back to the farmhouse as the sun faded away.

As we passed the cottages, I looked at the one Blake had stayed in, now empty. It would be strange to be on the farm without him after he'd been such a big part of my stay here so far. But I had no choice; I would take the next steps towards my future on my own.

I knew I wasn't the only one glad to go inside and to bed so I could put this day behind me.

* * *

The next day was my first proper rainy one this summer. I listened to the soft pitter-patter dancing on the roof above my bed as I lay on my back looking up at the ceiling. I'd always enjoyed summer rain. I jumped up and pulled back the curtains, flinging open a window, breathing in the fresh scent and watching as droplets slid down the window in a lazy pattern. The rain washed over the farm like it was clearing a new path for us.

I remembered then a framed print my mum had had hanging in the hallway of my childhood home: a vase of flowers in front of a window showing a rainy day outside with the slogan *no rain, no flowers* at the bottom. If that wasn't a slogan for how things were on the farm right now, I didn't know what would be.

Snapping myself to attention, I left the window to get ready to meet Mary. It was going to be a long day, which I was ready to embrace; we were going to the wholesaler and then I'd lend her a hand at the flower shop before trying to find us some help with the naughty ponies. It would be good to be busy so I wouldn't have to think about saying goodbye to Blake. I hurried into the bathroom, had a shower and got dressed in record time before I went downstairs to find Willow was also up early.

'I couldn't sleep thinking about everything that happened and what we need to do today,' she explained as I poured myself a mug of coffee. She'd made a large pot and also had a rack of toast out with the butter dish and homemade jam plus a bowl of fruit.

'I know what you mean; I was pretty restless too. I know I can help with the ponies and I'll find us some punnets for the pick-your-own. I'll come back as early as possible to help with the clear-up operation.'

She smiled. 'I'm so glad you're here. I had this idea at about 2 a.m. Look...' She showed me a picture on her phone of a wooden swing with sunflowers behind it. 'I saw this on my friend Amy's Instagram. She posted about our pumpkin patch last year and that really helped bring us more visitors. I thought we could put a swing in the area Blossom trampled so people will think there is a deliberate cleared patch in the sunflowers, and it also turns it into a photo opportunity. What do you think?'

I smiled. 'That will look so cute, and will definitely look like there is meant to be a gap in the sunflowers. I could find some faux ones to drape around it today?'

'That's a great idea. That will look perfect.'

'Um... can you build a swing then?' I knew my cousin was handy around the farm but I had no idea if she could do something like that.

'Hopefully, but I'll go and see Dave in the DIY shop and pick his brains. I'll offer him a beer or two if he can lend a hand. He'll have the wood and rope we need for it. Dylan is grabbing the wheelbarrows from the barn for the clear-up. Sabrina said she'd come over as early as she can to help me and Dylan clear things up too and I'll call the weekend help in a bit as I don't want Dad doing too much physical work. I think me and Taylor did get through to him but he has the Connor stubbornness.'

'We all do,' I replied with a grin. I took a gulp of coffee. 'How about using the tractor you said is broken in the barn? You could also put it out in the strawberry field in the bare patch. People could use that in photos. It would look like we'd cleared it deliberately then.'

'Brilliant idea.' Willow let out a puff of air. 'We might actually be able to salvage it all ready for opening on Wednesday then. Dylan is going to start taking photos for our social media accounts and publicise the opening in town later so hopefully, if we can make it look as perfect as possible over the weekend, we will be all set. Honestly, there is always a last-minute drama around here!'

'It will all look great, I'm sure of it. And if I can get us help with the ponies, maybe you'll forgive them.' We looked at each other. That was going to be a tall order, that was for sure.

Willow took a bite of a slice of toast. 'Before you head off, how are you feeling about Blake?'

'I know that I should be fine. I knew him like two weeks! But we had so much in common and we had this connection; it felt a little bit like fate that we arrived here together – is that crazy?'

'No. I felt like that with Dylan. That he'd always meant to turn up at Birch Tree Farm. I mean, I hated him at first! I thought he was going to take the farm away from me, that we'd have to sell to him, but he ended up helping me save it. I think he knew before me that there was something between us. Sometimes, people just come into your life and change it for good. I thought it seemed like that was happening between you two too. I'm sorry he's gone, Daisy.'

'Me too.' I forced a smile. 'Maybe that was all we were meant to be. He helped me so much. There was a reason we met here, I think. I know what I want now. It's a shame I didn't inspire the same change in him. He's gone back to his life like we didn't happen, but I just hope he'll be happy, you know?'

'You're sweet. I'd be furious with him,' she said with a grimace.

'He never promised me anything. I am upset, sure. I let go of Henry and my old life but he didn't want to do the same. Or wasn't ready. Or just didn't feel the same about me.' I shook off the pang in my chest that accompanied that thought. 'I'm going to be fine. I'm here to change my life and I'm planning on doing just that.'

'You'll do it, I know you will. And I'm right by your side to help in any way I can.'

I smiled at her. 'I never thought I'd want to work with flowers like my mum did; I thought it would be too hard. But I know now that I need to do things that bring me joy, even if there are no guarantees they will work out. That is so much better than doing something I don't like just because it's easy.'

'Preaching to the choir here,' Willow said with a grin. 'You're so good at it. The arch you've made us is so pretty. And I bet you'll love working with Mary too.' She pushed the rack of toast towards me. 'Fuel up; you're going to need it. We both will.'

'Yes, boss,' I replied, butterflies swirling in my stomach at what might be ahead. It was unknown but exciting too. I glanced out of the window at the birch trees as the gentle rain fell on their branches, their green leaves bouncing back to life as they drank it in, and I realised my summer here was doing the exact same thing to me.

35

It was almost an hour's drive to the wholesaler. I wasn't used to so much driving and being this far away out in the countryside after living in the city where I could walk or take a short taxi ride everywhere I needed to go. I didn't mind, though when I had pretty scenery to enjoy. And Mary was good company too. She had so many stories about her life, and the town and her flower shop, but also, she wasn't scared to talk about my mum.

'She was the one who came up with the idea of the pink bike,' Mary told me as we drove past wildflower fields on either side of the car. It was still drizzling outside so the grey clouds subdued the colours a little bit but Mary had cracked open the car windows and I could smell the flowers as we passed by. 'I wanted something outside that would catch people's eyes and she spotted the bike at a shop that used to be on the High Street which sold all kinds of old things. It was a shame we lost that shop; I love second-hand hunting. Anyway, your mum spotted it in there and spent two weeks fixing it up. She suggested adding flowers to it. Now, I can't imagine the bike not being outside.'

I smiled. 'She loved second-hand shopping too and upcycling old things,' I remembered aloud. 'Our house was full of odd bits of furniture. Nothing really matched.' I thought about how Henry's house was styled to perfection; they'd used an interior designer and it was all cream and beige and white and so polished, I'd been nervous to drink or eat anything that might stain. 'There's a great shop you should visit nearby, actually.'

I told Mary about Bill's antiques shop. I wanted to go back and look at everything he had one day. But I didn't know if it would be too strange without Blake. Mary immediately said she'd have a look in there as soon as she could.

We reached the wholesaler and I was amazed at just how many things they stocked in there. Mary bought some of their fresh flowers, straight from the market, for her shop and some more faux ones as I had cleared out a lot of her stock. I found some wicker punnets that visitors to the farm could use and I also picked up some faux sunflowers and greenery to drape over the swing Willow was going to build. Dylan had looked into engraving a small piece of wood to tie around the punnets with the farm name on so I brought some string to attach them when they arrived.

We carried everything back to the car and then returned to the flower shop where I would help out for the busy Saturday-morning rush. Mary opened the door and put the fresh flowers into buckets of water, moving the bike out the front. I smiled to see my mum's idea still in action.

I was moving in her footsteps helping out in the shop. It felt good to be close to her again. She had loved flowers and that love had been passed down to me, even if I had tried to ignore it for a long time.

I also enjoyed working with people. That had been my favourite part of my office job. I liked greeting Mary's customers and finding out what they were looking for, and helping them pick the perfect flowers for their occasion. Or helping people who came in to treat themselves to a bunch to bring them joy. It was such a simple thing in life but it did brighten up people's days.

When we neared lunch, things quietened down a bit and I showed Mary a picture of the flower arch back at the farm now it was all finished.

'It's beautiful, Daisy. You have a real eye for flower displays. Honestly,' she said, matter-of-fact as always. I beamed at her praise because I knew she was always honest.

'I really enjoyed making it. Creating it, and working with you, is making me wonder if I can work with flowers in the future. And being on the farm this summer is making me unsure about going back to living in the city. I know I can't stay with Willow forever, though.'

'You'll figure out what you want to do. This is what you're meant to be doing,' Mary said before she left me to greet a customer.

Her words stayed with me for a long time.

* * *

After I left Mary, I walked back to the farm to check on things there. Willow was making a start on the swing and the place was bustling as everyone tried to fix what the ponies had messed up. Uncle Adam was being scolded for doing too much, but I could see how determined he was to help out. Willow was back from town, having brought Dave from the DIY shop with her, and Paul from the café was also there helping make the swing. Despite his grumpy attitude, he did seem willing to pitch in when needed, I had to give him that.

Dylan and Sabrina were clearing the ruined strawberries

and sunflowers while Sabrina's husband, along with their toddler, put the ponies back in their enclosure, adding an extra lock to make sure they wouldn't get out again. Willow's teen weekend helpers were clearing away the trampled sunflowers into wheelbarrows. And female Pat from the café had also turned up with drinks and snacks for everyone, which went down a storm.

I watched them all for a moment. The community spirit in Birchbrook was unlike anything I had seen, at least for a very long time. It was heart-warming to watch. I felt bad for not pitching in but Willow needed help with the ponies and that required me to head out of town.

Driving there, nerves settled in. I could have called but I knew this would be better in person, plus I wanted to go back to make sure my first trip there hadn't been a dream. It had happened.

Blake had happened.

When I arrived back in his hometown, I couldn't push him out of my mind any more. I thought about how we had come here together. His first trip back for a year. And he had chosen to return with me by his side.

Now, here without him, I pictured how nervous but happy he had been to see his family. How he had said he wanted to kiss me again but I wasn't available. I looked down at my wedding finger. There was no longer a diamond ring on it. I was free. But that hadn't been enough for Blake to stay. In the end, it was him who hadn't been free. I wouldn't regret breaking away from my old life, though. Because I hadn't done it for him. I'd done it for myself. For the woman who had looked in that mirror on her wedding day and hadn't recognised herself in the reflection.

Now when I glanced in the rear-view mirror, I liked who I saw looking back at me.

But there would always be a small part of me that wished Blake had broken away from his life with Sarah in the city.

I drove into his family's riding school and home. Here, there was no rain but a grey, cool day. I got out of the car I'd borrowed from Willow and walked towards the front door, but when I saw a figure out in the field heading into the riding school, I changed direction. I passed by the horses in the field. Blake's horse was munching on grass and I wondered if he would come back to see her again. He had looked so happy to be reunited with Midnight. It was a shame that he had stopped riding.

Heading for the barn, I spotted Bronte carrying a saddle back inside, hanging it up on a rack in there. She wore a riding outfit, her hair in a plait down her back, and she was humming softly to herself.

'Hi, there,' I said, as I hovered in the doorway.

She turned in surprise and when she saw me, her eyes widened further. 'Daisy! Back so soon? Is Blake with you?' she asked as she came over, looking over my shoulder for her brother.

'No, actually, he's gone back. Home. To the city,' I said, as she surprised me with a welcome hug.

'Back to the city?' She pulled back and searched my eyes. 'Without you?'

I nodded, shifting my feet at her piercing gaze. It was like she understood everything I was thinking and feeling. Maybe she did. 'He's gone for a meeting with Sarah about their app. A company wants to buy it, I think, or help them make it... It goes over my head a little bit, to be honest.'

'I can't believe Blake even knows what it's all about,' she replied. 'I thought we might see him again before he went back.'

'He left earlier than planned for the meeting,' I said. I could see the hurt in her eyes that he hadn't said goodbye. 'It was pretty sudden,' I added to try to soften the blow. 'I came to ask for your help with something at the farm, though, if you don't mind?' I suddenly wondered if this had been a bad idea. I stepped back. 'Oh, is that too weird? I know we don't know each other; maybe I should—'

'Daisy,' Bronte interrupted my babbling. 'Of course it's fine. Come on, let's have a drink and you can tell me why you're here.' She beckoned me to follow so I did and we strolled over to the house where she made us both a coffee and brought out a strawberry cheesecake too.

Once again, I felt at home as we sat at the kitchen table, the weather not nice enough to sit in the garden this time. I told Bronte what had happened at the farm with the ponies. 'So, we're trying to fix the mess they made but now we're all worried about how to handle them. Obviously, Blake has gone, so...' I cleared my throat. 'We don't have anyone who knows anything about ponies. Willow is upset because she had her heart set on offering pony rides to kids. I thought of you immediately, as you're so experienced and have your riding school; I wondered if there's something we could arrange together. That would benefit both businesses, maybe?'

Bronte smiled. 'We can definitely do that. I think my dad told you that the shop hasn't been doing great lately and our riding school has also been tough so I really appreciate you thinking of us,' she said. 'We really could have done with Blake around to help out. It's a lot for the three of us managing two businesses and having two kids plus animals to look after. I really thought Blake might come back; isn't that crazy?' She looked sheepish.

'It's not crazy,' I assured her. 'I thought coming here had made him realise he wasn't happy in the city, and he seemed to enjoy being on the farm...' I trailed off, not wanting to add *with me*. But I thought it. I thought he had been happy with me. That night we slept outside together, and in his cottage, we had felt so close. Now, I had no idea where he was or what he was doing. Was he thinking about me at all? Did he think about his family and his home? I looked around, amazed if he didn't miss it. I missed my childhood home so much sometimes. *I* could never go back to mine. It didn't belong to me any more. But all this was still here for him. At that thought, I felt a bit pissed off all over again. 'You know what? If he wants to live a life he doesn't enjoy and shut himself off then it's up to him. I can't see him enjoying that AI app or working with Sarah or marrying her and living in the city for the rest of his life but I don't know him well. Maybe I was mistaken all along. Maybe I just wanted to see what I wanted to see, I don't know.'

'No,' Bronte said firmly. 'He lit up here with you. You're only the second woman he's ever brought home. And the difference to that visit with Sarah was so marked. I saw the way he looked at you...'

'It's okay,' I told her. 'I'm not broken-hearted or anything. I just thought maybe we were starting something, that was all. And I did think he was happy to be back here. But, look, let's make sure us meeting wasn't for nothing. Why don't you come to the farm and meet Willow and see how you two could work together? I mean, if you want to deal with two mischievous Shetland ponies, that is.'

We both laughed at that. Bronte nodded. 'I live with two men and two kids; I can handle two ponies,' she said with a wink.

We finished our coffee and a slice of cheesecake then Bronte followed me out to my car. She needed to collect her kids from a party but said she could come to the farm tomorrow morning to talk to Willow. As I was leaving, she mentioned that Bill would love to see me so I decided to stop in at his antiques shop on my way home. I was intrigued to look around again anyway.

'Daisy, it's lovely to see you again,' he said when I walked into the shop. Like the first time I'd come in, there were no customers. I thought about Birchbrook's busy High Street and I felt sad for Bill. As Bronte had, he too looked behind me for Blake and I had to tell him he'd gone home. 'That's a shame but I'm not surprised. I think maybe Bronte got her hopes up that he might stick around this summer.' He sighed. 'She'll be upset with him.'

'I wish he had stayed too,' I admitted as I looked around the shop. 'You have some beautiful things in here. I'll tell everyone in Birchbrook they need to pay you a visit.'

'That's kind of you. I think it might be time to face facts that things aren't really working here, though. And we don't have the money to fix it.'

I felt another wave of anger towards Blake. His family were struggling and he was about to make money with this app and didn't seem to care about them back here. 'I'm sorry, Bill. Oh...' My attention was caught by a cuckoo clock propped up on a table. It was a pretty baby blue. 'Does this work?'

'Sure does.' Bill came over and moved the clock on so it struck the hour and a cuckoo slid out to announce it. It was painted white, matching the flowers on top.

'My mum had a cuckoo clock in her flower shop. This one reminds me of it. It's so pretty.' I stared at it, picturing it on the wall in the shop. 'I'll take it,' I said, knowing I couldn't leave without it. 'I keep saying I don't believe in signs but I don't know, this summer, I keep seeing so many that remind me of my mum and her shop, of flowers and new beginnings, like my name...' I realised I was half-speaking to myself but Bill was nodding along anyway.

'I once woke up and my ex-wife wasn't next to me in bed. I went downstairs and saw she was out in the garden looking up at the stars in the sky. I think I knew in that moment, she was going to leave. She was searching for something that she just couldn't find here with us.'

'How can you leave your children?' I wondered aloud as Bill carried the clock to the till and went behind the counter to start wrapping it for me. My gaze travelled to the other parts of the shop I hadn't looked at yet. The whole place was full of treasures. There surely were people who would want to come and unearth them.

'I think she found family life just too hard,' Bill replied. 'I think her going left my kids with two very different feelings. Bronte had always been keen to have a family of her own. And to settle down here. But Blake was different; he was always looking up at the stars like his mother had done.'

I thought back to the moment when I'd been star-gazing with Blake. 'I think maybe he thinks he should dream big, and that has taken him away from here. But all dreams are big. All dreams are important. We all want different things in life, and that's okay. There are people who explore the world and people who stay at home. It doesn't mean that one is happier than the other, does it?' I wondered if Blake thought his mum had felt happier by leaving. I wondered if the opposite might actually be true. 'And sometimes, people are scared to be happy.'

She might have run because she had too much here, she was too happy, she had too much to lose. I understood that feeling. I had spent half my life worried about losing things that made me happy, or worried about losing people I loved, so I hadn't let myself have either.

'You're wise beyond your years,' Bill said as he put the bubble-wrapped clock into a tote bag with the shop name written on it. 'You know what it's like to be scared of being happy, but don't let that stop you. You have too much to offer the world.

And your parents wouldn't want you to be scared of anything. They would want you to be fearless, and happy too.'

My eyes welled up. 'Thank you.' I pulled out my credit card but he shook his head.

'No charge today, Daisy. You brought back Blake to us, and that meant everything.'

I protested but he wouldn't budge so I left the shop promising I would come back again over the summer, hoping that he wouldn't let the shop go before then.

My anger at Blake rose up again then as I replayed the conversation I'd had with his dad and sister. They needed him, but he'd gone back to Sarah like they didn't matter. Didn't he realise how lucky he was to have them? So when I got back into Willow's car, after placing my new clock carefully on the seat beside me, I pulled out my phone and wrote a text message to Blake.

> I've just come from visiting your family. Your dad is suffering. Your sister was upset you left without telling them. She hoped you would come home. They both did. They need you, Blake. I know we don't know each other well but I saw your face when you came back here. You've missed it here, and them. Whatever is going on in the city, and with Sarah, don't forget about your home here. They need you and you need them.

> I would give anything to be able to go home. I wish I could turn back the clock and see my parents again. Don't wake up one day and regret not being there for them. You'll never forgive yourself. Your mum walked away. Don't do the same thing.

You worry about failing. But the only way you will fail is if you live a life that doesn't make you happy. Are you happy? I don't know. I hope you are but something tells me you're not.

People walk away, people dream big, people do all kinds of things but they also regret them. Maybe your mum regrets leaving you all. She will probably never admit it. But you're a better person than that. You can admit if you're wrong and you are capable of following your heart. Just like you told me I was. You encouraged me to live the life I wanted, to let myself really live again – why don't you take your own advice?

I wish you well whichever path you choose to take.

Just make sure it's your choice.

Before I could chicken out, I sent the long and impassioned message. It was the first text I'd sent him. We'd been together almost every day so we hadn't needed to message each other. But now he was far away.

I had no idea how he would take it but I felt so much better for sharing my thoughts. I hated to think he might have regrets like mine one day.

Driving back to the farm, I let Blake go.

The next few days were hectic to say the least. We worked hard to repair the damage done by the ponies. Willow made her swing and I draped it with faux sunflowers and greenery so it looked like it had always been in the middle of the sunflowers. I knew people would love it. The farm tractor was placed in the bare patch of the strawberry fields, again covering up the mess there. Now there was a lot for visitors to see and do, which could only be a good thing. We set up the till table so people could weigh what they bought and pay for produce, and we had a stack of punnets with the tags that had *Birch Tree Farm Strawberry Fields Trail* carved into them.

When Bronte came to the farm to talk to Willow, we both greeted her and took her over to the pony enclosure to meet Jasmine and Blossom. Seeing Bronte again did put Blake back into my mind. I'd checked and my message had been flagged as having been read but there had been no reply or other contact from him. Even though I had no idea what he thought about what I'd said, I was glad I'd got it off my chest.

Bronte followed Willow through the gate and walked up to the ponies to give them a treat. I leaned on the fence to watch.

'You two are very naughty, I hear, but very cute,' she said as she greeted each one and smiled as they nudged her for attention.

'I got them at a discount price, which should have been a red flag in hindsight,' Willow said ruefully. 'They have great personalities and we all love them but I'm nervous now for them to be around visitors. What if they play up when a kid is riding one? Plus, no one really wants to take responsibility for them now that your brother has gone.' She glanced at me then back to Bronte. 'I really don't know what to do.'

'We had a couple of ponies at our riding school for a bit – we were looking after them for a friend – so I'm confident they'll be fine with a firm hand. But let's see, shall we?'

Willow came to join me at the fence and we watched as Bronte put the harness and lead on them, before putting them through their paces, walking then trotting them around the enclosure. She'd stop and start, changing direction, talking to them the whole time. Bronte was clearly experienced and took no nonsense, which the ponies seemed to quickly sense and their behaviour was markedly different to how they'd played around with us.

'They definitely think I'm a soft touch,' Willow said, shaking her head.

I chuckled. 'Me too. They only ever really listened to Blake, let's face it. And now Bronte.'

Once Bronte was done, she unhooked their leads and gave them both a treat then came over to us. 'They haven't had great training. I would want to spend some more time with them before you open but I think they'll be fine. I'd recommend only offering rides for a short time each day to start with, just for an hour or so, then we can build up to more if they do well. I don't know if Daisy said but the riding school could do with some more riders. If you let us publicise the riding school, I could come for an hour each day for a reduced rate.'

'I'm happy to help you guys out; you'd be doing us a huge favour,' Willow said, relief written all over her face. 'We can see how it goes and extend the rides if they are as popular as I hope they will be.' She flung out her hand and Bronte shook it, both women smiling at one another.

'Thanks for thinking of me, Daisy,' Bronte added, turning to me.

'Sure. Like Willow says, it's nice to help each other out.'

Dylan called Willow then as a couple of teenagers had come to discuss working at the farm so I walked Bronte back to her car.

'I heard from Blake,' she said suddenly.

I tried not to react but my heart did a little skip. 'Oh, yeah?'

She glanced across at me with a raised eyebrow, as if she knew I was trying to be nonchalant, but it wasn't fooling her. 'He phoned to apologise for rushing back to the city without coming to say goodbye. Said he had important meetings to go to but he'd be in touch soon with some exciting news.' She shrugged. 'I have no idea what that means but he seemed happy so that's all we can ask for, I guess. I just wish he wasn't so far away again.'

I nodded, wishing that too. 'How's your dad doing?'

'Still thinking about selling the shop.' Bronte sighed as we paused by her car. 'I keep trying to come up with something that might help but I'm at a loss. At least now, we can focus on the riding school and hopefully, being here this summer will help.' She looked around. 'It's a lovely farm, and the trail looks so fun. I'll definitely bring my husband and kids for the day. I'd love you to meet them.'

'I'd love to meet them too.'

'And your flowers are so pretty. Maybe you'll have a garden of your own one day soon.'

I smiled. 'I'd like that. I'm definitely enjoying working with flowers this summer.' I told her about how I'd been helping out at the florist in town as well as working with Willow on the trail. 'I think being in your father's shop helped too. He had a cuckoo clock that reminded me of the one my mum had in her flower shop. It made me realise that I had seen flowers as a symbol of what I'd lost. But they're also a symbol of what I *had*. People I loved and who loved me. That shouldn't be something that I see as a bad thing.'

'Never!' Bronte cried. 'I always wanted a family of my own but I remember the night before my wedding having a sudden freak-out. What if I was like my mum? What if I couldn't be a wife and mother, after all? What if I wanted to run one day like she had? I went outside into the garden and Blake found me and he told me that love is a choice you make. And if this was my choice then I would just have to keep choosing it over and over, and reminding myself of that moment I made the choice, and then I wouldn't want to go anywhere. He said maybe Mum made the wrong choice once and then tried to stick with it but it didn't work. So, he asked me if I was making the right choice.'

'And do you think you made the right choice?' I asked.

'I do. And I make that choice over and over again. So, if you make the decision to see flowers as a symbol of love then you keep choosing that and you'll be fine. I guess what I'm saying is, life and love, it's all about perspective. You've had huge loss but you don't want fear of losing it to stop you from choosing love. It's all we have really, isn't it?'

Her words pierced through the final layer I had grown over the years, and which I had been shedding the last couple of weeks. I exhaled steadily. 'Yes,' I replied, unable to say any more as I felt quite choked up.

She nodded like she understood. 'Right, see you tomorrow afternoon.'

I watched her get into her car and drive off with a beep of the horn.

After the car had disappeared down the driveway, I stood there for a moment thinking about what she'd said Blake had told her the night before her wedding. I wished he'd been there to talk to me the night before mine. But what he'd said was exactly what I'd realised on my wedding day. I'd been making the wrong choice because I didn't love Henry. I never had. And I thought that was a good thing because I wouldn't fear losing him. But now, I wanted to love someone and to have them love me. And yes, I would fear losing them and yes, it would hurt if I did lose them, but loss was part of love. I didn't want to hide from it ever again.

And that wasn't just romantic love.

It was also the love of my family and friends. I had hidden from that too. And love of work. I had thought I wasn't passionate about anything like Willow was about this farm. But I was passionate about flowers. I'd just been hiding from it. I was finally putting that right.

I strolled back to the strawberry fields.

'I can't believe we open tomorrow,' Willow said when I walked over to where she was checking on the courgettes. 'Dylan said tickets are selling fast, although we're also allowing people to come by on the day if we have spare slots. He's taking some more photos around the farm to put up on the website and our social media.'

'What do you want me to do tomorrow?'

'Can you help Dad man the till table? I don't want him overdoing things and I need to be out and about, making sure every-thing is okay and helping visitors around the trail. Dylan will be out there with me and the local help we've got coming as well.'

I nodded. 'I can do that. I like greeting people and it will be fun to tell them all about the trail. I can help with whatever you need. I'm going to work with Mary twice a week; the rest of the time I'm all yours.'

She beamed. 'Perfect. And Bronte will be here in the after-noon for the ponies. Paul will come with the café van to offer lunch. Hopefully, in the summer holidays, things will be even busier and at the weekends, but I still think we'll get a fair few people through the gate tomorrow.' Her eyes sparkled. 'I love it when the farm comes to life.'

We stood and looked around the currently empty farm as the late-afternoon sun shone down on us. It was all peaceful but soon, it wouldn't be. I was excited to see it full of families. It reminded me of my own childhood. I hoped they would keep hold of these memories for life.

'I'm looking forward to it.' I wrapped an arm around my cousin. 'You know what? I think the farm has brought me back to life.'

'I think you might have done that all by yourself,' she replied.

37

Later that day, my things arrived from Henry's mum. Everything I'd had at their house, which wasn't much, was all neatly folded into two suitcases delivered by a van and carried up to my room at the farm.

I opened them up and looked at the things which I really hadn't missed. I pulled my clothes out of the suitcase and knew I'd end up donating most of them. They just didn't feel like part of my new life. There was make-up and toiletries and my Kindle, which I was grateful to get back. And then tucked under a pair of pyjamas was the framed photo that I had missed the most.

I put the picture on my bedside table and looked at it. It was a photo of me with my parents one summer when we stayed at Birch Tree Farm. We were in front of the farmhouse, all smiling, their hands on my shoulder. I swallowed hard. I hadn't had this on display at Henry's house. I'd kept it in a drawer. I found it upsetting to look at.

But now, I wanted it on my bedside table. It seemed right to have it out here. The memories of summers spent on the farm with them were impossible to escape. And finally, I didn't want to do that. I liked thinking back to being here with my parents. And helping out in the flower shop where my mum had also gained experience.

The rest of the summer was ahead of me and I had no idea what I would do at the end of it but for now, I knew I was right where I was supposed to be.

* * *

The following day, late morning, Willow opened up the front gate. The Strawberry Fields Trail was ready for visitors.

Nervous energy blew through the farm on the gentle summer breeze. The birch trees swayed like they had when I'd arrived a couple of weeks ago, ready to greet guests. I really hoped the season would be successful for Willow. She deserved it to be.

I started the day at the till table with my uncle, helping him to get everything ready there. As soon as Willow unlocked the gate, a couple drove in and came over to us before they started to walk the trail.

'We loved the pumpkin patch in autumn so we had to come back in summer,' the woman told me as I handed her a punnet for their fruit and veg. 'And it's a beautiful day too.'

'Enjoy yourselves,' I told them as they headed for the trail. I watched as they walked towards the sunflowers. Our first day open had dawned bright and warm, thankfully, and tickets were selling steadily, Dylan had said over breakfast.

Uncle Adam sat at a chair behind the table ready with the punnets to give people, scales to weigh what they picked and the card machine to take payments. The table was right by where people would park so he would be greeting everyone who came

to the farm. He was perfect for the job. I stacked the punnets by
the table as Willow came back from the gate.

'Amy and some of her friends are coming around
lunchtime,' she told us. 'She's an influencer and she takes really
great pictures of pretty spots and fun things to do. She really
helped us last year with Pumpkin Hollow and when I told her
about the swing, she wanted to come to see it.' We watched as
another car drove in. 'Ooh, another visitor already, great. I'm
going to check on the chickens, make sure there won't be any
more animal escapes. Come on, Maple. Dad, you're doing
okay?'

'I'm fine!' he told her, shaking her head. Once she had left, he
turned to me. 'You raise your child then suddenly, you get to an
age when they try to raise you.'

I smiled. 'It's lovely how you both take care of each other.'

The Birchbrook Café van pulled into the farm then.

'Right, I better go and check Paul parks in the right place and
everything is okay at the finale. Message me if you need me.' I
heard him tut so I headed off quickly.

Paul had, thankfully, parked where we had discussed and as
he got everything ready to open for lunchtime, I put out the two
bins he had brought along and then I checked my flower arch
looked okay. And made sure the baskets with flowers either side
of the white iron bench looked good. I also straightened a couple
of the watering cans with flowers on the picnic benches. The day
was warming up already and I was thankful I'd worn shorts with
a linen shirt and my straw hat. It was perfect picking weather
and I hoped that meant lots of Birchbrook locals would stop by
the farm.

Willow seemed in good spirits as she called over to say a
couple more cars had driven onto the farm and then she and
Maple went over to put the sign about pony rides by Blossom

and Jasmine's enclosure. Bronte would be over in the afternoon to run those.

Walking down the strawberry fields, I scanned to make sure everything was looking good for visitors. The strawberries had burst into full life now, perfectly ripe for picking. They were juicy and sweet and I tried not to eat Willow's profits as I walked along the path, the plants surrounding me in neat rows. I saw a figure heading my way then and I shielded my eyes from the sun to see who it was.

When I realised I recognised the person, I stopped right in the middle of the strawberries, unsure what to do. I had no time to gather my thoughts before he was in front of me.

'Daisy,' Blake greeted me in a soft tone.

Confused, I lifted my eyes and met his. 'Blake?' It came out as a question as I was so stunned to see him back here. I had told myself he wasn't coming back. Why was he standing in front of me now?

He smiled and flashed those cute dimples at me. Damn it. He wore city shorts with a polo shirt and had faint stubble on his chin. He looked relaxed, which was annoying when I could hear my heart thumping. 'I couldn't miss opening day. It all looks great.' He scanned the strawberry fields. 'Thank God you managed to clear the mess the ponies made. I texted Dylan and he kept me updated. I love the new swing and tractor. But the highlight is still your flower arch,' he added, looking back at me.

He had texted Dylan, not me. Was he going to mention my message to him, or just pretend it hadn't happened?

I raised an eyebrow. 'I thought you were gone for good,' I replied, unsure how he could be acting as if this was a perfectly normal development. He'd been away for a week with no contact. Half the time I'd known him, which seemed crazy when he felt so familiar to me. 'Why aren't you in the city with Sarah?'

I tried to ask without any bitterness but I wasn't sure if I fully managed it.

'I have a lot to catch you up on, but I was thinking maybe I could do that at the same time I talk to my dad and sister. Do you think Willow could spare you for a couple of hours at some point today and we could go home together?'

Home together.

Why did those two words give me a jolt in the pit of my stomach?

'You want me to come with you? Is Sarah not here?' I was so confused.

'I'll explain everything later, I promise. Will you come, Daisy? Please?' he pleaded. He looked so hopeful, I wasn't sure how to say no but I didn't understand why I'd be involved in anything to do with him any more.

'I guess, if you need me to. I could come on my lunch break. I need to be back this afternoon to see Bronte.'

'Bronte?' It was his turn to look surprised.

'Your sister is going to be running the pony rides every afternoon. We had to think of something once you'd left, and it will help out the riding school too. A win-win situation,' I explained.

Blake watched me for a moment. 'You came up with the idea?'

'Yeah.' I shrugged. 'I thought Bronte was the perfect person to help with Blossom and Jasmine.'

'That's such a great idea. I should have thought of it...' He trailed off. 'I better go and say hi to Dylan. Thanks for agreeing to come with me, Daisy. Find me when you're ready to go.' He started to walk away as suddenly as he had appeared but he paused. 'It's good to see you again.'

Then he strode off, leaving me staring after him, wondering what was going on in his head.

38

'Did I just see Blake?!' Willow rushed over to me. 'What's he doing back?'

I filled her in on our brief interaction. 'God knows what it's all about.'

'Well, I'm glad he came to his senses and is back in Birch-brook. This is turning out to be a great first day!' She winked as she went over to speak to a couple picking strawberries, offering to take a photo of them. I rolled my eyes. She was confident this was a good sign but I wasn't sure. I wasn't able to brood for the next hour though as Adam asked me to help him at the till table. We had an influx of people wanting to pick over lunch as they knew Paul's café van was on site so there was a rush of checking tickets, taking payments and handing out punnets.

Dylan then came to relieve me from my post, and also hand me and Adam a sandwich and orange juice each. When I was ready, I found Blake greeting the ponies.

'Let's go,' was all he said so we strolled over to his car and set off.

I eyed him as we drove out of the farm, wanting to see if our week apart had changed anything. He hummed as he drove, as if he didn't have a care in the world. It was pretty annoying.

'The farm looks great,' Blake said when he caught me glancing across at him. 'I'm so glad the ponies didn't ruin things. I've been so annoyed at myself for leaving the gate unlocked. Things were so chaotic that day. I wish I'd done a lot of things differently.'

'Is this why we're doing this?' I asked curiously, wondering exactly which things he would have changed. It was all so cryptic.

Blake nodded. 'I want to put right what I can. Will you trust me, Daisy? I'll explain everything when we get there, okay?'

I sighed but I leaned back in the seat and decided not to ask anything more. He clearly wanted me to find out along with his dad and sister. It was frustrating to have to wait. I wasn't sure why I was even involved but a small part of me did wonder whether my message to him might have sparked something, and that's why he wanted me here too. I hoped he was doing something that would make him happy. I was sure it wouldn't include me, and I told myself not to have any hopes related to that. But my heart wouldn't listen; it had been beating faster ever since Blake came back to the farm.

The now-familiar sight of Blake's hometown came into view and we drove through the High Street, passing by his dad's antiques shop, before heading out to his family home. Blake said he'd messaged ahead so his father and Bronte were expecting us. When he pulled into the driveway, the two of them came outside and I could tell they were just as confused as I was. Blake jumped out and hugged them both and I did the same, then we walked out into the garden and sat at the patio table with a pitcher of iced lemonade.

I glanced around, breathing in the scent of the lovely flowers

Bronte had planted. It helped calm me down a little bit. When my gaze met Blake's, I couldn't wait any longer. 'Are you going to tell us what's going on?'

'Yeah, please, this is all very mysterious,' Bronte agreed. She spoke lightly but I noticed that her knuckles were white as she gripped her glass of lemonade. She was nervous like me, definitely.

'First of all, I'm sorry I took off in such a hurry without saying goodbye or anything,' Blake started, a little bit falteringly like he was also nervous. He cleared his throat. 'I felt I owed it to Sarah to go back to the city and have some meetings about our app. Plus, I couldn't just forget about all the work and money we'd put it into it over the past year, you know?'

'We understood, son,' Bill said kindly. 'You didn't need to come all this way to tell us you are moving back there.'

'Why would you...' Bronte began indignantly but a sharp look from her dad made her stop. 'I just don't understand,' she mumbled, shifting in her chair.

'I'm not moving back there,' Blake said quickly. He glanced at me again but I tried not to react. I took a deep swig of lemonade. 'That's why I wanted to talk to you guys. We met with a large tech company interested in our dating app. Listening to them talk about the use of AI and how they would like to develop it made me nervous, though. I told them about the concerns I had with it, much to Sarah's annoyance,' Blake said, his voice becoming more confident as he spoke. 'The company ended up actually agreeing with me. They suggested turning our AI idea into a dating coach app. Instead of using it to meet people, you would use it to help you with the dating process on apps or in person so it will be like having your own personal dating coach. The aim would be to make people more confident and to help them choose the right way to meet new people. That made me feel better about the use of AI. What do you think?' He looked at me again.

I was surprised he was asking for my opinion. I felt better that he had changed the concept of the app. 'It did feel weird to think people would be chatting to someone who was using words dictated by AI. You want to know if you have a connection with someone, not that they're telling you what you want to hear. But I found using apps a nightmare so having something that might help you could be good. I kind of wish we could move away from technology altogether in the meeting process, though,' I said. 'I'd much rather meet someone organically, offline.' I tried not to meet Blake's eyes after I said that.

'I'm so glad I met my husband at school,' Bronte agreed. 'So, you're going to help develop this dating coach app?' she asked Blake.

'No. I've sold my share in the app. They've paid me off basically to play no further part in the company. I wanted to have a clean break from it, and from Sarah.'

There was a short silence after Blake said this. No one seemed to know what to say or do.

Even though I wished it hadn't, my heart had leapt at his words. I took a long a sip of my drink in case I smiled too widely or something.

'Sarah told me I was a fool – if the app becomes huge, I'll lose out on millions – but they paid me enough to walk away. I don't want to be part of her life any more or to live in the city. The app was never something I was passionate about. I just fell into it.' He leaned forward. 'It's not the life I want.'

I read between the lines – Sarah wasn't who he wanted either. I tried not to feel any sort of hope but it was hard – Blake was single again and didn't want to move back to the city.

'So, what do you want?' Bronte asked him, thankfully, so I didn't have to.

'I want to put the money they've given me into the family businesses and help you both with them. I want to come home. For a bit anyway. I might want my own place one day soon...' He grinned. 'But I know the businesses aren't doing as well as they could, even though you tried to hide it from me, and I want to help.'

I let myself smile then. I was so happy to hear he wanted to help his family. I wondered if I'd played any part in him coming to this decision or not.

Bronte looked at her dad in shock then back at her brother. 'But I thought you didn't want to work in the family businesses any more? I mean, you left us.' Her voice broke a little at the end of her sentence, although she tried to hide it, showing just how hard she had taken Blake leaving last year.

'I'm sorry I did that,' Blake said quietly. 'Sarah got into my head about it all. Making me feel like I wasn't good enough for staying in my hometown and working with family. She kept saying I should want bigger and better things, that I would regret it one day. And I guess...' He visibly swallowed hard. 'I thought about Mum.' He glanced at his dad apologetically.

'What did you think?' Bill asked him.

'Well, that maybe I would end up feeling like she had done and that I should try to broaden my horizons as maybe I'd be happier if I did, like she was. But Daisy said something that made me think. I have no idea if Mum was any happier when she left us, or if she is happy now.' He paused and glanced at me. I knew then my message to him had struck a chord. I was relieved, and happy to hear that.

He was going to help his family. I could see they were thrilled. Now I knew what he had wanted to tell them, I couldn't help but wonder why Blake had wanted me here too. Was it just because of my message? He knew I'd be happy he was going to help his family but was there also a possibility that he might want me to be part of his new future?

'I've realised that I loved living here,' Blake continued. 'I love the antiques shop and our horses. I missed it all after I left. Especially you guys. I know I will regret not coming back much more than regretting coming home.' He paused and turned to his dad and sister. 'I mean, that is if you'll have me back?'

'Of course,' Bill said. 'But are you sure about putting your money into the businesses? I was thinking maybe I should sell the shop as it's struggling so much. Maybe there isn't a way to save it.'

I couldn't stay quiet any longer. 'You can save it,' I said. 'Willow's farm was struggling and she's turned it around so much. And I love your shop! I know people who will love it too. You just need to spread the word and... Sorry, I'm getting carried away,' I said, my cheeks turning pink at my burst of passion.

'No, it's nice to hear someone who loves the shop like I do,' Bill said. 'I was beginning to think I was the only one.'

'I agree with Daisy.' Blake threw me a warm smile. 'We can save it, Dad. And I want to invest in our businesses. It's not only about *my* future but *our* future.' He looked at Bronte. 'What do you think though, little sister?'

'You told me once that love is a choice. And you have to keep on choosing it. Is this really a life that you can love like we love it?'

'I never stopped loving it,' Blake replied.

'Then let's do it.' She grinned. 'You could buy me a present with the app money too, if you like.' She nudged him and they giggled like they were kids again.

Their family moment made me miss mine. I was happy for

them, though. I just wished I knew if Blake wanted to include me because I'd encouraged him to help his family or if he thought there was any chance for us.

'There is so much to plan but I know you need to get back to the farm soon, Daisy,' Blake cut through my thoughts. 'And you're coming too, Bronte, in a bit?'

His sister nodded.

'Okay, well, I'll drive Daisy back then maybe we can chat about things later? I could come and stay tonight here if that's okay?'

They both assured him that was more than okay.

We left then, with the assurances that they'd talk about things in more detail later, saying we'd see Bronte at the farm soon.

I followed Blake out of the house and back into his car, curiosity burning in me and hope that I was trying to keep under control while it desperately tried to burst out of my chest. I waited until we had set off towards the farm together.

'Why did you want me to be there for that?' I asked him.

'Surely you know?' he replied, arching an eyebrow.

We glanced at one another and I wondered if Blake felt as aware as I did of how close we were. My body turned towards his like it couldn't help it. But I shook my head. I needed him to explain so I didn't get carried away, and hurt again.

'Because of what you said in your message. But also the look on your face when I said I was leaving... You were so disappointed in me, and I've been thinking about it ever since. I went back to the city and Sarah just assumed we were back together and I felt like I was being swept up in it all again. I couldn't stop thinking about you and I wanted to leave immediately. I had to sort things out, though and think about what I wanted. But when you sent me that message, I knew you were right. About it all. It's taken a week to sort it all out but I know I've done the right thing.'

Exhaling, my head swam with all what he was telling me. My hope kept on blooming. 'I've been worrying that my message was too much. But I came to talk to Bronte about helping with the ponies and saw your dad in the shop, and I did feel a bit disappointed with you. That you could leave all this...' I gestured outside of the car. 'I would give anything to have all you have,' I added quietly.

'I know.' Blake reached over and touched my hand briefly before letting go. My skin warmed instantly at the contact. 'I thought about that. I realised I was making a huge mistake. I belong here. I know that now. God, this sure has been a crazy summer so far. I started it ready to propose to Sarah and now I've left her for good.'

'You have?' My pulse spiked at those words; I couldn't stop it.

'I realised that being with someone who makes me feel bad about my life isn't what I want. I want someone to support my dreams, to dream *with* me, not to tell me what I should want. That's why you've changed things so much, Daisy. You keep asking me what it is *I* want out of life.'

'You asked me that too,' I reminded him. Henry and his family hadn't cared what I wanted from life either. 'You made me think about what I want too. This summer has turned everything around for me.'

Blake glanced at my lips then quickly lifted his gaze back to my eyes. But I saw it. Was he thinking about our kisses and touches too? I bit my lip to stop it from tingling in anticipation. 'I felt so shit about how we left things,' he said then. 'Can you forgive me for leaving like I did? I just needed to sort my head out. So much had happened in such a short space of time. I didn't want to hurt you. I'd never want to do that. But when you sent me your message, I realised I had hurt you by leaving.'

'I guess I did think what had happened between us kind of meant nothing to you,' I said softly.

'What?' Blake cried, looking over at me. 'Are you serious?'

I nodded. 'Yes,' I whispered, remembering how shocked I'd been that he could just go back to the city when meeting him had shaken up my whole world.

'God, Daisy. Hang on...'

He surprised me then by pulling the car over to the side of the road.

39

'Daisy, let's talk outside for a minute, please?' Blake jumped out of his car and curiously, I followed him. He came around to my side and I leaned against the passenger door as he stood in front of me. The road was quiet and the sun beat down on us from high in the sky.

Behind Blake was a field of delicate wildflowers, but all I saw was him. We were just as delicate, I realised.

'What we had, what happened between us, meant so much to me, it forced me to re-evaluate everything,' Blake started urgently, gazing deep into my eyes. 'I told you, I started this summer thinking that my life was in the city with Sarah, that I was going to propose to her and work with her even though there was always this doubt in my mind. I kept trying to ignore it. Telling myself I was living the life that I had wanted, that I had chosen, too scared, I think, to admit I'd made a mistake.' He shook his head. 'When she cheated on me, I immediately ran. I didn't want to fix it. I was bitter and angry and hurt, yes. But also, I felt relieved. And then I ran right into you wearing a wedding dress!'

I snorted. 'Yeah, not the kind of meet-cute you find in a romance book, was it?'

'Wasn't it?' Blake stepped closer. 'The thing is, ever since that moment, things started to clear for me. I started to realise what I wanted. And that was because of you. You pushed me to see, to face the truth, to look into my heart and to follow it. I can't believe we pretended we were dating. I've never done anything like that before! But it didn't feel weird to me, did it to you?'

'No,' I admitted, softly. 'It felt strangely... right.'

He reached out and tucked a strand of my hair that was blowing in the breeze behind my ear and then touched the daisy hair clip holding that side back. 'It felt right to me too. And lying with you and looking up at the stars, I felt peace for the first time in a year. With you, I never struggled for things to say. I never felt awkward or shy or embarrassed about who I was. I could just be myself. And that is fucking rare, Daisy. I never felt that way with Sarah. Did you with Henry?'

'Never,' I replied instantly, losing myself in his eyes. When he smiled at my response, showing his dimples, I itched to reach out and touch them. 'I didn't ever open up to him. I was never honest with him or myself. But with you, it came so easily. I didn't feel like I needed to keep my walls up or to protect my heart. We had a connection that I never had with Henry. Or anyone before,' I admitted. 'But we don't know each other well and we've both come out of these big relationships and are making all these changes to our lives... maybe you were right to walk away.'

'I didn't walk away from you... from this... from us, I swear.' Blake stepped closer so there was only an inch of space between us now. 'I had to sort everything out. Like you were doing. You inspired me. I know that we don't know each other well but we know enough, don't we? You've seen me warts and all. You've met my family, seen where I come from. You've called me out on my bullshit.' He grinned and leaned in, speaking in a low voice. 'You've come on top of me.'

'Blake,' I said, startled, blushing and giggling. But his words brought back our two nights together. I met his twinkling eyes and grabbed his shirt, pulling him closer so our lips met. They melted together as we frantically made up for our week apart by kissing each other hard. Blake leaned in, hooking an arm around my waist, curving around me as I leaned against the car. I moved my arms around his shoulder. When he let go of my lips to kiss down my neck, I murmured out a breathless, 'Yes'. A car drove past us, and Blake lifted himself off me to look into my eyes while we both tried to get our breath back.

'I've wanted to kiss you from the moment I saw you again,' he said, his hazel eyes darkening as he drank the sight of me greedily. 'Even if it hasn't been long, I still missed you, Daisy.'

I nodded. 'I missed you too.'

'How about we get to know each other properly then? This summer? While you're in Birchbrook, and I'm at home. We'll only be forty-five minutes apart. While we work on changing our lives, can't we also work on seeing where this might lead?' He reached out to touch my lips and I curved them into a smile.

'Yes, please,' I whispered. A calm settled over me then. I had been restless this week, wondering where he was and what he was doing, missing him but thinking there was no chance of seeing him again. But he was back. He was here all summer, and wanted to spend some of it with me. 'I want that too.' As Blake leaned in to kiss me so softly on the lips, my body sighed into his. He wrapped his arms tightly around me and I leaned against his chest. I didn't have to let him go like I thought I would have to.

'We have all summer,' he whispered back.

That sounded good to me.

40

The second week of the Strawberry Fields Trail went as smoothly as it possibly could. Word started to spread about the things Willow had added to the farm this year and people spent longer on their visits now, enjoying the photo opportunities, walking through all the fruit, veg and sunflowers, and pausing for refreshments at the café van. Bronte's pony rides also went down a storm. They loved children and as long as they got a treat at the end, they were happy to walk around their enclosure each afternoon. Bronte had a board up, showing details about her riding school and displaying a discount to anyone who came for a lesson.

The farm was working well. Willow had me helping her with whatever she needed, and Dylan was able to be around quite a bit now that the builders had started the renovation work on the cottages as he just needed to supervise them. Taylor had come by on Wednesday when I worked in the flower shop to lend a hand so my uncle could stay at the till table and not do anything physical. This weekend, the local teenagers would be working too. Once the schools broke up for the summer, they could help out every day so I was hopeful Willow wouldn't get too stressed with me gone twice a week, and my uncle could take things easier.

Friday arrived and I was looking forward to having a restful evening after a hard week's work. As dinner time approached, Blake drove over to eat with me. I suggested we have a picnic out in the strawberry fields. We'd both worked on the area but hadn't had a chance to enjoy it so it seemed perfect. Blake said it was a great idea and told me he'd bring everything we needed.

When I walked out of the farmhouse, I smiled to see him pulling out a large picnic hamper from his car.

'It's good to see you.' Blake leaned in to kiss me softly on the lips. 'I feel like we haven't had much time together this week.'

'Looking forward to fixing that tonight,' I replied, smiling because I too had felt like I wanted to see him more. I slipped my hand in his and we walked down the Strawberry Fields Trail together, the sun growing hazy around us. We both wore shorts, T-shirts and trainers. I had no make-up on and my hair was loose. Blake was as simply dressed and as sun-kissed as me. I felt calmer around him. It was nice.

'How was today?' Blake asked as we walked down the trail together. The farm was closed now and the others were all inside the farmhouse so it was peaceful out here. We passed by all the fruit and veg, the sunflowers and the strawberries, the ponies grazing in their enclosure, the chickens winding down for the day, and strolled over to the picnic area.

'We had our busiest day yet as it was Friday and some people don't work or finish early. Once school finished for the week, we had a few families stop by. But the weekend is when we'll see the biggest influx.'

'Dylan told me that tickets were already over half-booked for the summer and you've had a few walk-ins each day. He's hopeful that in the summer holidays, visitors could double,' Blake said.

'I'm relieved that things are starting out so well after all our hard work,' I replied. 'Willow deserves it to be a big success.'

'It will be, I'm sure.'

We reached the finale to the trail then and sat on the bench closest to my flower arch. Blake opened up the hamper, pulling everything out.

'I confess my sister had a hand in helping me put this together,' he said as I marvelled at everything he placed on the table. 'But I made sure that we had this.' He pulled out a chilled bottle of rosé wine and two glasses, and he poured us both one. He sat down next to me on the bench, our thighs touching. 'Cheers, Daisy.' We clinked glasses, smiling, and both took a sip. 'Okay, pile your plate up. Then I need to know how Wednesday went in the flower shop. I know you gave me a brief lowdown on the phone but I haven't seen you to hear all about it.'

We hadn't been fully alone since we'd kissed by the wild-flower field; things had been so full-on for us both. It was nice that he wanted to know how I'd enjoyed working with Mary so I chatted as I filled my plate with salad, chicken wings, crusty bread and quiche. There were strawberries and whipped cream for dessert and a tub of chocolate brownies that I couldn't wait to try too.

'I loved it. Even more than working out here, which has been really fun. I love advising people which flowers will work for them. Helping them find what they are looking for. And Mary is so nice.' I could feel myself smiling with happiness. 'She found this the other day.' I pulled the photo out of my pocket to show him. Mary had taken a picture of my mum next to the pink bike outside the shop. Mum was beaming with pride, her hands resting on her large belly, where I was waiting inside, ready to see the world for myself.

'She was pregnant with me here. Helping Mary out one summer. It was her idea to have the bike outside with flowers in it.'

'Your hair is just like hers,' Blake said. 'And you have the same smile. I think she would be so happy that you're working with Mary too.' He picked up my hand and kissed the back of it.

I smiled happily at him. 'I think so too. I didn't realise when I cut my hair, how similar it was to Mum's back then. I think it just fits this summer and all the changes I'm making. So, how are things going at home?'

'Well, I've been thinking about the money I'll be getting for the app and how best we can spend it in the right way to improve both businesses. The riding school needs work in terms of the indoor and outdoor arenas and the stables, plus my sister could do with another horse or pony for real beginners. Then the antiques shop needs customers through the door – we need to work on visibility and advertising and spreading the word. I think the shop itself could be spruced up too and the stock needs looking at. It's hard to see the wood for the trees in there.'

'I think that all sounds great. I love the clock I bought from your dad. It's in my room here, and one day, I'd love it to be on the wall somewhere of my own.'

'I wish my dad had reached out to me after I left. He said he didn't want me to feel obligated to come home. My sister thought I was like our mum. There was so much we weren't saying to one another. I'm glad we're getting back to where we were. I do like working with them. And being back home. I missed it. And my horse.'

'I've never been on a horse,' I confessed then.

'I'd be happy to teach you to ride if you ever wanted to.'

I nodded eagerly. 'I'd love that.'

We finished eating our picnic, catching each other up on everything that had been going on. Then we poured out a second glass of wine, which we enjoyed with the strawberries and cream.

Contented, we lapsed into silence as we gazed out at the farm. The sky started to shift into hazy pink and orange patterns, the sun lowering towards the horizon. I looked at the beginning of the sunset, thinking how, for the past five years in the city, I hadn't noticed the sunset much at all. Now, I loved to drink it in, enjoying the beauty around me.

'I really like living back in the countryside,' I mused aloud. 'This place feels more like home than anywhere I've lived since childhood.'

'Good. I want you to have somewhere you feel like you belong. You deserve that.' Blake wrapped an arm around me and I scooted closer to him on the bench. 'I'd love it if one day, you felt like you belonged with me,' he added in a softer tone.

'You would want that?' I asked him, smiling at the thought.

'I wasn't sure about trusting someone so soon after what happened with Sarah,' Blake said. 'But you are nothing like her. I just would want to make sure you really are happy with me?'

I understood why he was asking me that. I had spent years with someone that I didn't have deep feelings for. 'I would only be with you if that was the case.'

'And you forgive me for leaving you for a week?'

'We both had things to sort out,' I told him.

'I want us to work out,' Blake said then.

'Oh, yeah?' I leaned in to kiss him. 'You going to make a wish on the stars?' I teased, thinking back to our night looking up at them together.

'What makes you think I didn't that first night we laid on the grass together?' His hazel eyes sparkled as we looked at one another.

'You can't have wanted that so early on,' I said, shaking my head, but I couldn't help swooning a little bit inside at the idea he might have done.

'I told you, I wanted you as soon as I saw you in that white dress. What if it gave me ideas?' He winked and I giggled. I knew he was joking around but I knew if I wore a wedding dress again, I'd want to be 100 per cent certain. And if it was Blake waiting for me at the altar, I had a funny feeling that I would be.

I leaned in again and this time, we shared a kiss that deepened, our tongues caressing each other's as we held on to one another tightly. I let out a small moan and Blake pulled away to drop kisses behind my ear, on my neck and moving my T-shirt to kiss my collarbone. He pulled away suddenly.

'Daisy, I need you closer.' Blake got up and lifted me so I was sitting on the end of the table. I wrapped my legs around his waist as he leaned down to kiss me again, tilting my chin up towards him. He glanced at the farmhouse before looking at me with a pained expression. 'I want to take your top off but we're not alone out here like we were before.'

'Yeah, they might walk Maple soon and put the ponies away,' I said breathlessly as Blake leaned down to trail kisses along my jawline. I groaned as he moved down my neck again, making me shiver. 'Let's go to my room,' I suggested. He was causing goosebumps to appear on my skin. I wanted him to take my top off too but I didn't want Willow or, God forbid, my uncle to stumble on us out here. 'Let's sneak in so we don't get stuck talking to anyone,' I added, pulling Blake up from my neck so I could kiss his lips again. I let out a giggle. 'Is that bad?'

'It's naughty, gorgeous,' Blake murmured, his eyes twinkling. He gave me a quick kiss and grinned. 'And I love it, let's go.'

Laughing, we quickly packed up the picnic and, hand in hand, hurried into the farmhouse as quietly as we could. I could hear everyone still in the kitchen from dinner and before they left to do the final farm chores of the day, we went softly upstairs and into my room, closing the door with relief when no one appeared to have spotted us.

Blake put the basket down and then he wrapped me into his embrace again. 'I have always been nervous around women,' he confessed in a hushed tone in between kissing me. 'I never knew what to say, or my mind would overthink while I was doing this...' He slipped his hand under my T-shirt and raised an eyebrow. I nodded quickly and he lifted my top off of me. 'But with you... it's different.'

I smiled as I reached for his T-shirt. I took it off, my eyes drifting to his toned, tanned chest. 'I used to be nervous too,' I agreed. 'You know sometimes, I can get anxious or panic or freak out... but with you, it's easy. And fun.'

'I'm glad,' he said as he reached for the button of my shorts. He leaned in to kiss me, his tongue massaging mine with such passion, I gasped. He undid my shorts and broke away from me to slip them down my legs. He looked at me in my underwear with darkening eyes. 'You are a dream. I never thought I could feel like this with a woman. Like I could tell her anything.'

'I feel the same,' I assured him as I reached for his shorts and undid them, keeping my eyes on his as I pulled them down his muscular legs.

Blake wrapped his arms around my waist and picked me up, making me gasp again as I hooked my legs around him. He carried me to the bed and put me down gently, leaning over me as I laid back. 'Our first time in a bedroom – we are getting more restrained,' he teased as he ran his hands over my body.

'That sounds far too wholesome,' I complained with a sigh.

'You're right, we definitely can't have that.' He reached around me and undid my bra, slipping it off, and began to caress my breasts. Then he leaned down to kiss them, his hand sliding down my stomach to my knickers, stroking me there, making me gasp with want. 'I never want to be restrained with you,' he said as he slipped his hand inside my underwear, causing my back to arch. He drew a nipple into his mouth, sucking it hard as his fingers stroked me and I clutched the duvet of the bed as I tingled with desire. 'God, I want you so much,' he said as I moaned under his touch.

'I want you too,' I gasped. 'Blake, please.'

'You want me inside you?' he asked, slipping his fingers inside me as I writhed underneath him. 'Do you, gorgeous?'

'Yes,' I gasped. 'Please.'

'Hmm, tell me again,' he grunted.

'I want you inside me.'

Blake pulled his hand out and yanked my underwear down my legs. I lifted my bum so he could remove them then he stood up, pulling down his boxers, keeping his eyes on me as he gave himself a stroke. I bit my lip when I saw how eager he was for me.

He reached for his wallet and pulled out a condom, sliding it on before he came back to the bed and stroked back my hair, looking into my eyes like he was searching for my soul. 'This is so different,' he whispered. He parted my legs and I propped them up. He reached down between them and stroked me again.

'It is,' I agreed, practically purring at his touch.

Blake leaned down, covering my lips with his as he let go of me and slid inside me instead. He kissed me deeply as he held me tightly against him. I wrapped my arms around him and gripped his strong back as we moved together. When he pulled back from kissing me, he looked into my eyes again and I let out a gasp at the passion in them as well as the pleasure I was feeling all over.

'I need you on top again.' Blake rolled us over. When I sat astride him on the bed, we both moaned. 'I love looking at you,' he gasped as he reached up to caress my breasts. He lifted himself off the bed to draw a nipple into his mouth as I moved on top of him. Then he pulled me down so we could kiss. I leaned over him, gasping as he lifted his hips off the bed and pumped into me harder. We kissed with abandon, our tongues dancing in each other's mouths as I rocked on top of Blake.

He pulled away to gasp. 'That feels so good, Daisy. Doesn't it?'

I looked at him and pushed his hair off of his face. 'So good,' I moaned.

'Are you going to come again for me?'

'Hmm,' I murmured as pleasure shot through me from tip to toe. Blake gripped my waist as I leaned back and he moved me faster on top of him, meeting me thrust for thrust. We kept our eyes on each other as we moved, both gasping and moaning now, completely lost in each other. I'd never been lost in someone else before. 'God,' I cried then as my body pulsed and throbbed and Blake sent me completely over the edge. I think I said his name as I leaned down, clutching him as I rode waves of pleasure.

'Good girl,' he gasped as his fingertips threaded through my hair. He gave it a tug so I lifted up off him. He pressed his lips to mine, giving me hard kiss as his body shuddered beneath me. He cried my name into my mouth as he came too and we both slowed to a stop, holding each other tightly as we trembled, our skin sticking together, our hearts both racing.

I rolled off him, slowly getting my breath back. Blake tossed his condom into the bin before opening his arms to me, where I curled up against his chest, nuzzling into his nook, as if I had always meant to snuggle right there.

'That was the best yet,' he murmured into my hair. 'It will keep getting better, I just know it.'

'God,' I said, 'we won't want to do anything else.'

He chuckled and kissed the top of my head. 'Works for me, baby.'

I smiled at the term of endearment. 'We have all summer,' I replied softly.

'We're going to have a hell of a lot longer than that,' he promised.

41

'Daisy!'

I groaned as something woke me up and I snuggled in closer to Blake to try to escape it. I hoped I was dreaming. Blake pulled me tighter, asleep beside me. He felt so warm and strong. I kept my eyes shut and willed sleep to come back to me.

'Daisy!' Someone banged hard on the door. I groaned again. Maybe this wasn't a dream after all.

Then the door opened with a thud against the frame.

'Huh?' I opened my eyes and saw Willow standing by the bed, hands on her hips. 'What's up?' I mumbled, as Blake jolted awake beside me.

'Please get up, you two; we have visitors. They have turned up with an entourage and I don't know what to do. Are they here for you?' Willow was speaking in a rush, confusing me. She walked over to my window and yanked the curtains open, flooding my bedroom with light.

'The hell, Willow?' I said, clutching the duvet so my nakedness was hidden from her.

'Get up, I need you to help me with this! I'll go out and see what's going on but only because I love you guys,' she replied before turning and marching out of the door, closing it behind her. 'But get up now!' she added as she left.

'What was that all about?' Blake asked.

'I better look and see what's going on,' I said with a sigh, wondering what had my cousin so het up. She was ruining my morning afterglow.

'Wait.' Blake leaned down to give me a kiss and a dreamy smile. 'Morning, gorgeous.'

I smiled back. 'Morning, handsome.' I gave him another quick kiss. 'Hopefully, she's being all dramatic for no reason.' I climbed reluctantly out of the cosy bed, away from Blake's arms, and stepped over to the window. I peered carefully outside, shielding my naked body from anyone looking up.

'Nice view,' Blake commented behind me.

I chuckled but then my eyes widened. 'Oh, shit,' I said as I noticed the cars parked in the driveway and the group of people talking down there, two of whom I unfortunately knew very well. I could also see a photographer and some more family members, and Dylan and my uncle were there too.

Then my eyes fell on Willow and who she was talking to. She was shaking her head, arms gesturing, but I knew the look on that man's face: he was determined to succeed at whatever he was trying to do. My heart sank. This felt... bad.

'You won't believe this.' I turned to face Blake, who was now sat up in bed, his delicious chest on display, but I couldn't enjoy my view like he had been enjoying mine. 'Sarah and Henry are here.'

'Are you joking?'

'Nope, come and see.'

Blake jumped out of bed and came over to the window, putting a hand on the small of my back as he leaned out to look. He swore under his breath. 'That's Sarah's parents,' he said, frowning.

'That's Henry's dad and he looks like he's giving Willow a tough time.' I watched as he shoved a brown envelope at her. 'What's he giving her?'

Willow looked shocked as she took hold of the envelope. Then the group started walking past her. She was shouting after them but they ignored her and headed for the Strawberry Fields Trail.

I frowned at Blake. 'What's going on?'

Blake sighed. 'We better go and found out, I guess.'

We dressed as fast as we could in yesterday's clothes, running combs through our hair and splashing water on our faces, quickly brushing our teeth. Somewhat presentable, we hurried down and out of the farmhouse, walking the trail, looking for where everyone was. Blake didn't take hold of my hand and I was unsure whether to take his or not. We hadn't had a second to talk about our night together.

I was stunned as to why either of our exes were back on the farm, let alone here together. Along with their parents. And a photographer. I really hoped whatever was going on wouldn't derail what was blossoming between me and Blake.

We approached the strawberry fields to find everyone had assembled close to my flower arch. Sarah appeared to be directing people to stand in various spots near to it. She wore a stunning white dress with pretty, light-blue flowers, heels, and her hair and make-up were flawless. I looked around for Henry. He was with his parents and was wearing a crisp, white shirt and navy trousers. A photographer was setting up near to the arch.

'There you are.' Willow hurried over to us. 'Henry's father is so rude! He just kept demanding I let them go over to the flower arch. I kept saying I didn't want them on the farm, that I needed to speak to you two. Then he said he'd give me all this cash...' She showed me the envelope stuffed full of money. 'He shoved it at me then they all just walked out here. What should I do?' She looked at me worriedly.

Before I could answer, Henry strode over, full of confidence, with a dazzling smile on his face as though he was thrilled to see me. 'Daisy. I'm glad you're still here. I wasn't sure if you would be.'

I frowned, finding that hard to believe. 'What's going on, Henry?' I asked, really hoping he wasn't here to try to get me back again.

'And why did your father shove money at me and then act like he owns the place?!' Willow cried, exasperated.

'He just wanted to thank you for letting us do this,' Henry replied smoothly.

'I didn't let him!' Willow cried, throwing her arms up in the air.

I knew how she felt. Henry's dad steamrolled over people. 'Henry, what are you all doing here?' I asked him sharply, my patience evaporating.

Henry ignored my question and glanced at Blake, who was standing a couple of feet from me, keeping a careful distance, as if he didn't want anyone to know we'd spent the night with each other, and he shrugged. 'I know you lied that you two didn't know each other,' he said, turning to me. 'You're here together still. You must think I'm an idiot.'

'We've been through this...' I began, wishing we'd never fake dated. Henry would never accept that I didn't want to be with him, Blake or no Blake, now.

'It's fine,' he said to me. 'I don't care any more. You can do whatever you want. Sarah and I have moved on. We spent a fair bit of time together while we were here and when I got back to the city, I asked her out for a drink. We were going to console each other about what happened but to be honest, we both found we didn't need consoling.' He shrugged, still smiling his charming smile, as if he wasn't dropping a dig at both me and Blake. 'We actually fell hopelessly in love.'

My mouth dropped open. I glanced over at Blake, who was looking away at Sarah. She was fluffing her hair up as the photographer took some snaps of her in front of my flower arch. 'You and Sarah?' I checked as Willow snorted under her breath beside me.

I felt relieved Henry wasn't here to win me back but I had no idea how to feel about him being with Sarah now. That was a plot twist I hadn't bargained for.

'Yes. Sarah and I are more real than you and me ever were.' He turned to Blake. 'And far more real than you two ever were, *mate*,' Henry said, his voice dripping with sarcasm on the word.

Blake finally turned from Sarah to look at Henry. I was getting worried as to why he wasn't looking at me or standing beside me. How did he feel about our exes being together? 'I'm not, and never have been, your mate.'

'They're ready,' Henry's mum called out then. She was all smiles and she gave me a little wave, but before I had time to wave back – not that I was going to – she'd turned around like I'd already been forgotten.

'Ready for what? We don't want you here!' Willow cried, shaking her head.

'You owe us,' Henry said coldly. 'All of you. You were cheating on us the whole time, I bet. And you were all in cahoots,' he added, glaring at Willow. 'My father has given you plenty of money. We won't be here long. We don't want to be around any of you longer than we have to but this is important to us. This is where we met; it's special.'

'We weren't cheating on you!' I cried. 'I never met Blake before I came here the day of our wedding!'

'You two deserve each other,' Henry said, ignoring me, and hurried over to Sarah.

'What can we do?' Willow asked us. 'Can we call the police? Or you and Dylan could kick them out?' she demanded of Blake. 'I'm not an advocate for violence usually but...'

'I understand your feeling, believe me,' I told her.

'It's too late to do any of that,' Blake said then, pointing. Willow and I turned around to see Henry joining Sarah at the flower arch. They faced one another.

The photographer crouched down by them and told them he was ready.

We all stared as Henry got down on one knee and pulled out a small jewellery box. Sarah gasped and put her hands over her mouth, looking shocked, although from the fact that their parents and a photographer were here, she can't have been surprised at all.

'Are they actually...?' Willow whispered beside me.

I nodded because it looked like they were. I glanced at Blake, who was shaking his head at the spectacle. I turned back to Henry and watched as he pulled out a diamond ring and asked Sarah to marry him.

She gasped out, 'Yes, yes, yes!' and he slid the ring on her finger before jumping up and kissing her. Then he picked her up, twirling her while pictures were furiously snapped.

'The audacity to do this here,' Willow said, shaking her head.

'I assume they are trying to prove that they are over us.' I was kind of amused now. Did Henry think I cared about this show he was putting on for me? 'It feels fake, don't you think?' I turned to

Blake but he had stridden off. My stomach sunk. Was he upset about this? I hurried after him to find out.

'Don't leave me with them!' Willow cried after us. She swore under her breath. I felt bad for the invasion of her farm but I was worried about what was going through Blake's mind.

Blake finally stopped by the chicken pen and leaned on the fence.

'Why did you walk off?' I asked. 'And you didn't seem to want to be near me back there...'

'I wasn't sure you wanted them to know about us,' he replied.

'I can't believe they're together,' I said, trying to decipher his mood. 'I can't believe they're *engaged*.'

'It's crazy. They only just met.'

'Do you think they're trying to get revenge on us? They think we care that they're together? They want to show us they're fine without us?'

He shrugged. 'I don't care about them. I care about us. How do you feel seeing Henry and knowing he's moved on already?'

'I can't believe they're actually in love, but they can do whatever they want. I don't care about Henry or Sarah any more, but I care about us.' I cared more about Blake than I thought I ever could about someone again.

'Really?' Blake turned to me hopefully. 'What if we're rushing into things just as much as they are?'

'You think we are?' I asked worriedly.

'All I know is, I almost proposed to Sarah and you were about to get married to Henry. Watching them just now made me worry... we're not each other's rebound, are we?'

That question made me hesitate. He was right that things between us had been quick, just like Sarah and Henry. But I had let Blake into my heart in a way I'd never done with Henry. And my feelings for Blake were real. Last night had been perfect.

I shook my head. 'No. People saw our connection so much, they thought we were seeing each other when we'd only just met! Henry still thinks we've known each other years. We have something special. We felt it all along, didn't we?'

'Yeah, but I know you stayed with Henry for a long time because you didn't want to be alone. I don't want you to be with me unless you're 100 per cent sure. I want you to be happy with me.'

'You left me. You went back to the city. I thought I was alone. And that was fine with me. I'd rather be alone than be with someone I don't love. I didn't love Henry. I have no idea if what he and Sarah have is real, and honestly, I couldn't care less. They really wanted us to watch them get engaged; that's why they turned up here. To show they don't care about us. Although it kind of shows to me that they do. It hasn't worked. If they are happy, good luck to them. Henry is my past. Not my future. I am hoping *you* might be my future.' I wanted to be honest with Blake; I'd had enough games this summer to last me a lifetime.

'I want to be your future. But we started out as a fake rela-tionship. Sarah betrayed me, hurt me; I can't go through that again,' Blake said. 'Seeing her with Henry... it seems just as fake as we started. How can we be sure what *we* have is real?'

I knew he was scared. Our connection scared me too. But it was also everything I had ever wanted.

'We just have to trust what we have is real. Can you trust that my feelings for you are real?'

'Can you trust me?' he countered.

We stared at one another.

I heard voices and turned to see everyone trooping back past us, all smiles.

'Thank you for letting us do that here,' Sarah said loudly to

Willow even though they hadn't given her a choice in the matter. 'That flower arch is such a good backdrop for proposals.'

Despite the situation, her words echoed through my mind. The arch *had* made an excellent backdrop for their proposal. I wondered if other couples might want something like that too.

Blake and I started to follow the group back towards the farmhouse but once again, he walked a few feet away from me, making no move to take my hand or anything. It made me nervous. Why did he suddenly seem unsure about us?

Sarah waved her left hand, her ring sparkling in the sunshine. It was bigger than Henry's grandmother's ring. I wondered if that was on purpose. 'I'm sorry, guys, but I found my soulmate.' She gave Blake a sneering smile as Henry came over and slung an arm around her. 'You can't fight true love, can you?'

Blake didn't respond. I stared at the gap between us. I felt panic rise up again but I tried hard to stay calm. Deciding I needed to get away from our exes, and worrying about what Blake was thinking and feeling, I broke away from the group.

'Good luck to you both,' I said before I turned around and walked back to the farmhouse.

Blake followed me, calling out my name. 'Daisy, what's wrong?'

Spinning around to face him, I took a deep breath. 'Has them being here changed things between us? I thought last night was the best night of my life.' My voice wobbled and I tried not to let any tears fall.

Blake grabbed my hand. 'God, Daisy, it was for me too.' He pulled me into his chest, wrapping his arms around me. I leaned against his chest, taking solace in his strong embrace. 'I loved last night and waking up beside you. I want to do that every night if I can,' he said, holding me tightly against him. 'They haven't changed anything for me. It's none of their business that we're together. I don't want them having any bearing on us at all. I just wanted them to leave as quickly as possible. And leave for good this time, hopefully. I wanted to wait so we could talk alone about us.' Blake leaned back and looked down at me.

I gazed up into his eyes. 'I thought you might have changed your mind.' I hesitated then asked the question on my mind. 'Have you?'

42

'Definitely not,' Blake said firmly. 'We haven't had the most conventional of beginnings. But I wouldn't change a thing. Do you trust me? That I won't leave? That my feelings are genuine? That we are real? Can you be happy with me too?'

Relief washed over me and I nodded firmly. 'I trust you. And I am already happy. We've been real all along.'

He grinned, showing off his dimples. 'So, it's not quite as grand a question as we just witnessed, but will you be my girl-friend, Daisy Connor?' Blake reached out to touch my cheek.

'Yes. But what do we do after summer ends?'

'We'll figure it out; I just know that I want to be with you.'

'Me too.' I leaned in and we shared a long, lingering kiss. 'I've actually had an idea about the future. Will you drop me into town on your way back home so I can speak to Mary? And I'll explain what I'm thinking on the way.'

'What are you planning, gorgeous?'

'A way for me to stay in Birchbrook beyond this summer.'

Blake's eyes lit up. 'You want to stay around here? That makes me even happier.'

'I was meant to come here,' I replied simply. Somehow, when I left my wedding, I knew I needed to find my cousin and now I had found myself too.

'I was meant to come home,' Blake agreed.

Henry and Sarah probably hoped that their engagement might stop whatever was happening with me and Blake, but it had instead made us realise this was special. And something we both wanted to continue for a long time.

As we walked back inside the farmhouse together, arm in arm, I could hear the sound of cars leaving the drive, indicating that Henry, Sarah and their families were leaving. But I didn't turn around to watch them go. Their future was nothing to do with me.

Mine was right beside me.

* * *

I found Mary in the flower shop, the door propped open as it had turned into such a lovely day. She was behind the counter working on a bouquet.

'Hello,' I said warmly, 'do you have a few minutes to talk?'

Mary smiled. 'Of course. This is a nice surprise; I didn't think I'd see you until your shift later. Everything okay?'

I went over and leaned against the counter. 'I couldn't wait to talk to you. I have a business proposition for you.'

'I'm all ears.'

'I'm really enjoying working here and I've been thinking about what might happen at the end of summer. I am happy helping my cousin out on the farm but it isn't really what I want to end up doing. I've rediscovered my love for flowers and I think I'd be happy to work with them.' I told Mary about seeing a proposal of marriage in front of my flower arch, although I left out the fact it was my ex-boyfriend. I'd fill her in on the gory details later. 'It made me think there must be lots of people looking for a flower display like it. For engagements or weddings or birthdays, all kinds of events. Some people have balloon displays but I could offer flowers arches. And I know you said you're often asked for displays for events but you lack the time and the help so I wondered if we could work together? I could carry on helping out in the shop when you need me and I could take the lead for doing flowers for events with you helping me? I have some money I could invest. We could offer flower arches and decorations and bouquets... What do you think?' I bit my lip, nervous she might think I was nuts to consider such a thing.

Mary stared at me for a moment then tipped her head back and let out a laugh. 'I was hoping you would suggest something like that, Daisy. I love us working together and I think we could build a great business together. I have no children and have found it hard to find anyone as passionate as I am about my shop but I can tell you are, and will continue to be. And I might only have a few years until I retire so knowing this place would be in good hands...'

'Oh.' I felt a lump rise up in my throat. 'Okay, I have to hug you.' I bolted around the counter and we shared a tight hug. Mary let out a sob and my own eyes welled up.

'Your mum would be so happy,' Mary said into my ear.

I nodded, unable to speak for emotion. I just knew she was right. I had found Mary like my mum had. Maybe she had brought us together somehow.

After I had spoken to Mary, I walked back to the farm and into the house. Willow and my uncle were in the kitchen preparing lunch. I told them what Mary and I had discussed.

'So, I was kind of hoping that there might be room for me to stay here beyond the summer?' I asked hopefully.

'Of course,' my uncle cried. Then he looked at his daughter. 'Sorry, love, it's not my decision. It's a habit; it's your farm now.'

'Don't be silly, Dad,' Willow said. 'It's yours too. And of course, Daisy, we'd love to have you here for as long as you want to stay. And we'll rope you in to help out whenever you have a spare minute.' She winked and I laughed.

'Deal,' I said.

'What about Blake? Will he be around too?' Willow asked eagerly.

'I'm always in the way when you are having girl talk,' Adam said with a chuckle.

'I don't mind at all,' I said, and I nodded happily. 'Blake is staying to help his family out so he won't be far away. It's actually down to Henry and Sarah. They gave me an idea for a business and made me and Blake realise for sure we want to be together. They wouldn't want to know that, I bet.'

'I have no idea if their love is real but this farm is magic when it comes to making people fall in love,' Willow said, smiling as Dylan came inside with Maple. She lit up instantly and for what might be the first time since I'd arrived, I was no longer envious to see it. I knew what it was like now to know you've found someone that you connect with.

'We were rattling around here on our own for so long,' Adam said. 'I'm glad we're not any more.'

'Maybe Taylor will move in too,' Willow teased.

'I'm too old for all that,' he replied, but he blushed in a really adorable way.

We all sat down at the table for lunch and caught Dylan up with the news.

'Someone just contacted me on social media to ask if we'd be opening for sunset visitors,' Dylan said once we'd finished eating.

'That's a great idea,' Willow said, her eyes lighting up instantly. 'Think of the photos you could take at sunset.'

'You could serve alcoholic drinks; maybe the landlord of the pub would do it,' I suggested. 'I bet you'd get even more proposals,' I added jokingly.

'We need to look into this,' Willow said to Dylan.

'You're taking on so much, love,' her dad said.

'We can handle it,' she replied. 'Where is anywhere more beautiful than our farm at sunset?'

I thought back to when Blake and I had watched the sunset together and I had to agree with my cousin. 'People will love it.' I hid my blush behind my glass as I thought about what had happened with us out there after sunset. I took a sip of home-made orange juice and listened to my family discussing how sunset nights could work.

It was crazy how long I'd kept away from them, and from letting myself love for fear I would lose people again. I'd missed out on a lot, for a long time, but I was determined that that stopped from here on out. I was going to stay with my family, build a business with Mary and fall in love with Blake. Although if I was honest, I was head over heels already.

As if he could feel me thinking about him, Blake sent me a message then. I picked up my phone to read it.

> I can't wait to spend the rest of the summer with you. And every summer if you let me.

My smile matched the lightness in my heart. Those words were everything to me. I had clung to Henry for safety and security, thinking that not opening my heart to him would give me both, but it just made me unhappy. Now I had someone I wanted to open my heart to, and who was offering his in return. Yes, losing people I loved would always be something that I feared but I didn't want that to stop me loving. Love was safety and security. And I never wanted to be without it again.

Me too.

I replied to Blake, thinking that the summer stretched out before us like a soft picnic blanket, promising more kisses as sweet as the strawberries here. And just like a sunset, it would be a chance to let go of what had come before and enjoy a brand-new day, and new beginnings, together.

EPILOGUE
THE FOLLOWING SUMMER

I stood in front of the mirror and looked at my reflection. My shoulder-length hair was clipped back on one side with a new daisy clip that sparkled and had a delicate pearl on it. My make-up was light and in my ears were a simple pair of pearl studs. My eyes travelled down my body. I wore an ivory dress with a pretty lace bodice then the skirt swirled out to my mid-calf in a floaty fabric. On my feet were simple ivory ballet pumps.

'Here.' Behind me, Mary held out a bouquet she had made. She wore a smart, blue skirt suit and a proud smile on her face. I had wanted a cream and lemon colour scheme and the delicate, fragrant flowers looked beautiful tied into a posy. 'You look beautiful.'

'Perfect,' Uncle Adam added. He wore a suit and had welled up twice already. Mary pinned flowers into his buttonhole to match mine.

'Everything is ready,' Willow said, walking into the room. Her simple, long lemon dress looked lovely on her, and she held a smaller version of my bouquet. Next to her, Bronte was dressed the same. My two bridesmaids.

I smiled. I felt completely relaxed and confident today. I had chosen everything along with my husband-to-be and I had zero doubts that I was making the right decision.

A year had changed so much.

This summer, I was about to step into the future that had been waiting for me all along.

'I'm ready,' I said. I thought I would need to take a deep, calming breath but my heart beat at a steady pace. I was excited. The butterflies in my stomach weren't from nerves. I was surrounded by the people I loved most in the world, and was about to tie myself to my favourite person of them all.

We all walked out of what had been my bedroom, when I'd stayed on Birch Tree Farm last summer. Willow had welcomed me back when I told her what I wanted for my wedding. She had obtained a licence so I could get married on the farm and held off opening this year's pick-your-own season until after this weekend for me. I now lived halfway between Birchbrook and my groom's hometown so I still saw everyone on the farm a lot. We had a cottage with a garden that I loved to tend, that was alive with flowers and trees, and one day, it would be the perfect family home for us.

It had all started out here in Willow's strawberry field, and it seemed fitting for it to come full circle today. We left the farmhouse and walked up the Strawberry Fields Trail, passing the sunflowers and fruit and veg, to end up in the strawberry finale where a flower arch stood waiting for me. I'd spent hours on it, creating the perfect display with beautiful lemon and cream flowers – real this time – and greenery. My arches were the most popular part of my now joint floral business with Mary. We ran her flower shop together and also provided flowers for local events. On the wall on the shop, we'd put the cuckoo clock I'd bought from Bill's antiques shop and every time it chimed, I thought about my mother.

I knew I had to make a flower arch for my own wedding. In front of the arch were two rows of pretty white seats and the aisle was lined with pots bursting with flowers that Mary had arranged. To one side, a man sat with an acoustic guitar, ready to play The Beatles 'Strawberry Fields Forever' to accompany my walk.

Above the proceedings, a warm sun shone down from a clear blue sky. And in the distance, I could see Blossom and Jasmine pausing in their grazing to look over at me. Beside the front-row seats was Maple, eyeing the ponies to make sure they were on their best behaviour today.

As I walked, holding Uncle Adam's arm, Bronte and Willow following behind me, I looked ahead as my groom turned around. His hazel eyes sparkled as he flashed those two cute dimples when he saw me. He looked as calm as I felt, thank God. He wore a navy suit, his buttonhole matching Adam's, his hair styled to perfection with that line of stubble that I liked on him. Beside him stood Dylan and Bill.

I walked towards Blake with a lightness in my step and a smile on my face that matched his. When I reached him, Uncle Adam gave me a kiss and shook Blake's hand, and then he sat down. Willow and Bronte stood behind me as I took hold of Blake's hand and he squeezed it.

'Gorgeous,' he said softly. 'I love you more than I ever thought was possible.'

I forced myself not to well up but that man's words would always make my heart swell. 'You're my future,' I replied simply.

As the celebrant welcomed everyone to our wedding, a pool of sunlight shone down on my flower arch. I now firmly believed in signs. I thought that the people who were no longer with us might be looking down on us and giving their blessing to finding happiness and love after loss. I hoped my parents were with me in some form today.

I would miss them forever but I knew they would both be happy at me carving out a life that I loved for myself. A life I was going to live with Blake right by my side. A life that was meant to be – that I was sure of.

* * *

MORE FROM VICTORIA WALTERS

Another book from Victoria Walters, *Hope and Hot Chocolate on Mistletoe Lane*, is available to order now here:

https://mybook.to/HopeHotChocBackAd

ACKNOWLEDGEMENTS

A huge thank you to the amazing team I have behind me and my books. Hannah Ferguson, my fabulous agent, for always being there to listen and advise, and for all your encouragement and hard work on my behalf!

Thank you so much, Hanna Murrell, for taking my books around the word; and to Caroline Hardman, Jo Swainson and Lucy Malone at Hardman and Swainson for all your support.

Emily Yau, my amazing editor, for your hard work, support and encouragement on this book! Your insights were invaluable, and I can't thank you enough for helping me make this book what it is now.

Huge appreciation to the whole team at Boldwood Books working so hard behind the scenes on my books. As always, Niamh Wallace for being so enthusiastic about my books as I am and supporting them so well. Special thanks to Wendy Neale, Megan Townsend, Isabelle Flynn too.

Thank you to my copy editor Emily Reader and my proof-reader Anna Paterson for all your hard work on this book. And Alexandra Allen for creating such gorgeous covers for my books – I love the Birch Tree Farm covers so much!

So much love to everyone who has taken Birch Tree Farm into their hearts. The love I saw for *Love and Lattes at Pumpkin Hollow* was some of the most enthusiastic of my writing career so far, which was so lovely to see. I appreciate your social media posts, messages and reviews so much. I really hope you enjoy this book as much as the last one!

Thank you so much to my author friends for your support – Kiley Dunbar, Anna Bell, George Lester and Mary Jayne Baker. Lots of love to all my family and friends, for being the best support system.

PLAYLIST FOR PICNICS AND
PROMISES AT STRAWBERRY FIELDS

Girl on the Run – ILUKA
Lemonade – Maren Morris
Henry, come on – Lana Del Ray
Flower Child – Kacey Musgraves
Spring Into Summer – Lizzy McAlpine
Strawberry Wine – Noah Kahan
Under The Aurora – Counting Crows
Fall in Love & Find Out – Maddie & Tae
Dandelions – Aly & AJ
Summer Song – Remy Bond
Kiss Me – Sixpence None The Richer
Purple Irises – Gwen Stefani, Blake Shelton
Us. – Gracie Abrams, Taylor Swift
Summer Girl – Haim
Something in the Orange – Zach Bryan
Cicada Choir – Dylan Gossett
Wildest Dreams – Taylor Swift
Wildflowers – Sarah Darling

Because, of course – Maren Morris
I Want To With You – LeAnn Rimes
Strawberry Fields Forever – The Beatles

ABOUT THE AUTHOR

Victoria Walters is the author of both cosy crime and romantic novels, including the bestselling Glendale Hall series. She has been chosen for WHSmith Fresh Talent, shortlisted for two RNA novels and was picked as an Amazon Rising Star.

Download your exclusive bonus content from Victoria Walters here:

Visit Victoria's website: www.victoria-writes.com

Follow Victoria on social media:

instagram.com/vickyjwalters

facebook.com/VictoriaWaltersAuthor

x.com/Vicky_Walters

bookbub.com/authors/victoria-walters

youtube.com/@vickyjwalters

threads.com/vickyjwalters

ALSO BY VICTORIA WALTERS

The Love Interest

The Plot Twist

The Paris Chapter

Long Story Short

Birch Tree Farm Series

Love and Lattes at Pumpkin Hollow

Picnics and Promises at Strawberry Fields

Hope and Hot Chocolate on Mistletoe Lane

Boldwood

EVER AFTER

XOXO

JOIN BOLDWOOD'S
ROMANCE
COMMUNITY
FOR SWEET AND
SPICY BOOK RECS
WITH ALL YOUR
FAVOURITE
TROPES!

SIGN UP TO OUR
NEWSLETTER

HTTPS://BIT.LY/BOLDWOODEVERAFTER

Boldwood

Boldwood Books is an award-winning fiction publishing company seeking out the best stories from around the world.

Find out more at www.boldwoodbooks.com

Join our reader community for brilliant books, competitions and offers!

Follow us
@BoldwoodBooks
@TheBoldBookClub

Sign up to our weekly deals newsletter

https://bit.ly/BoldwoodBNewsletter